HALLEY'S COMET

Hannes Barnard

CATALYST PRESS
Anthony, Texas

For further information, write Catalyst Press at
info@catalystpress.org

In North America, this book is distributed by
Consortium Book Sales & Distribution, a division of Ingram.
Phone: 612/746-2600
cbsdinfo@ingramcontent.com
www.cbsd.com

Originally published in Afrikaans by Lapa Uitgewers,
in South Africa in 2019.
FIRST EDITION
10 9 8 7 6 5 4 3 2 1

Library of Congress Control Number: 2021940057

Cover design by Karen Vermeulen, Cape Town, South Africa

To Yolandi.

My first reader

and partner

in all things.

To the reader:

"We learn nothing from presenting
a sanitized, scrubbed version
of history for posterity."
—Bettina Wyngaard.

This book does not shy away from
sensitive and complex issues that
people of color, women, and children
faced in the past and still face
in society today.

INTRODUCTION

Apartheid is an Afrikaans word meaning separate-ness, or apartness. Segregation laws emerged while South Africa was under British colonial rule early in the 20th century, but, in 1948, this term, Apartheid, was used to describe a new formalized method of governance. The theoretical idea behind it was the separate development of the different cultural groups in South Africa, with the ideal to preserve cultural identity—especially that of white South Africans. This system of governance was based on racial classification and in practice meant formalized (legal) racial discrimination. It was a way for the minority white government to divide and diminish the power of the majority of South Africans.

South Africans were (and still are) classified into the following four groups: White (European descent), Black (African descent), Coloured (mixed-race people whose descendants are a combination of Malay or Indian, black, white, and/or Khoisan), and Indian (Indian descent). The few references in this book to "coloured," refer to the racial classification of South Africa.

In 1950 the Group Areas Act was passed enforcing the segregation of the different race groups to specific areas within the urban areas. Towns and urban areas all had separate areas for the different race groups, to fulfill the ideals of separate development: AKA forcing race groups to be apart. Mostly, white areas were located near the town/city centers and were the best developed and maintained. The other racial groups were often allocated areas far away from the urban centers with poor infrastructure and substandard living conditions, often without access to the most basic amenities. There are numerous references to white, Indian, and black areas in this book. These refer to the separate designated areas as imposed by the Group Areas Act.

It is also worth noting that for most of the Apartheid era, interracial marriage and sexual relations were illegal.

This chapter in South Africa's history was a violent one with many casualties in the bloody struggle between the oppressive government and the well-organized militant liberation movement.

Apartheid officially ended in 1990 when the discriminatory laws were abolished, and South Africa's first democratic election was held in 1994 when Nelson Mandela became president.

TABLE OF CONTENTS

PART ONE

PROLOGUE

It was almost too dark to see. His feet danced blindly over the hard ground. He peered over his shoulder but couldn't see the man anymore. Then a shot rang out. Somewhere behind him. Closer. Each shot was closer, and his pursuer's bestial laugh louder.

His lungs were on fire, tears impeded his vision, but somehow his legs kept driving him forward. What was he thinking? What? Playing hero, or whatever that was? All for nothing.

No one was supposed to die before their sixteenth birthday.

Another shot. A bright yellow spark spat against a rock less than two meters from him.

Run, Pete. Run.

THE DAY AFTER

Pete de Lange stared out of the bus window. The early morning sun slowly raised its head, illuminating the world in golden pastels. Farms lay stretched out in a pale-yellow mist to the horizon, watched over by the silhouettes of black wattle—and eucalyptus trees. Strewn puddles of crimson mud formed a glistening mosaic to remind farmers of the harshness of nature. Everyone waited in hopeful angst for the first rain, but all they got was the fist of the unrelenting sun. Last night in a thunderous explosion the rain finally quenched the land, but it was too late.

This new year whispered promises of hardship to Northern Natal.

"Are you going to play senior rugby this year?" Michael asked, the second smartest and second smallest guy in Standard Nine. He had short dirty blond hair, so perfectly combed that the rows his comb left were still visible. Without any conscious thought, Pete shifted his gaze from the outside world to the guy next to him. It was difficult to look at Michael without recalling Joe Bester tackling him with such force that his broken rib pierced his lung. It was more than seven years ago now, but he could still hear the wheezing sounds escaping Michael's gaping mouth. And all because his dad wanted to toughen him up. He wondered whether Michael was grateful for Joe Bester's tackle, that it saved him from a lifetime of rugby.

Pete just nodded. He tried to force a smile but couldn't tell if it worked. He knew Michael was just trying to make conversation, but the last thing he could bear right now was idle chat.

Did it happen? Did yesterday really happen?!

"What's today's date?" Pete asked, taken aback by his question.

Michael laughed softly, shyly, almost imperceptible against the cacophonous background noise of teenage voices on the bus.

"Hello? It's Wednesday 15 January 1986. The second day of the new school year." Michael shook his head. "Did you bump your head or something?"

"Just checking if you're awake," Pete said in a deeper than usual tone. This time certain his smile happened, albeit slightly abashed.

Pete turned to the window again, not looking at the world beyond, but the shallow reflection of himself in the dirty glass. His eyes looked tired, their usual green replaced by a vague gray, framed by blackish half-moons. His lips were dry and when he opened his mouth it felt as if they would split open and bleed. He looked like a child, he thought. He had shaved a week ago, but the lines his Wilkinson Sword had drawn were still there. The fluff apparently dead under his skin, just like this year's corn crops. He gazed up at his large forehead to where the zit with nine lives had finally packed its bags and left. But before he could stop himself, his eyes panned upwards. And there it was. That hair.

It happened. Yesterday happened.

It was supposed to be the perfect day. And it

was until good old Raj had butchered his hair. Pete tapped his fingers against the severed ends of where his painstakingly crafted fringe was still his pride less than a day ago. It had taken all summer holiday, six long and boring weeks, to look like Don Johnson.

It was a new year, his Standard Eight year, and he could almost be considered a senior. It was that difficult to define place on the seesaw between juniors and seniors—the middle child of high school. This was the year where high school careers were made because if you waited until Standard Nine it was too late; then your social status was elevated purely because of age. But if you could make a name in Standard Eight: That's when the hot girls noticed.

That was why he had forgone his divine right to claim the prime seat in the junior bus and ventured onto the senior bus, and why he was seated in this seat, next to a nerd.

But where he sat was inconsequential. He was one of only three Standard Eights on the senior bus. With him was Ivan, back for his third—and apparently final—attempt to pass Standard Eight, and Renate, who could sit anywhere she pleased because she was without question the most beautiful being in all of creation.

When Walter, the pesky Standard Nine with hair so orange that carrots envied him, shouted from the middle of the bus, "Hey, what are you doing in *this* bus, China?" a hot poker pierced his gut. He knew he was found out, but he had practiced that moment in front of the mirror a hundred times and answered with feigned confidence and without hesitation, "Ah no man, don't tell me this is the wrong bus. I'm sure my parole officer told me this was the bus taking everyone back to prison." Walter had no retort, some giggled, but most importantly: He was in.

Yesterday had started so well. There was even a split second when he could swear Renate smiled at him. At school, Don Johnson made an immediate impact. No longer the insecure Standard Seven with a permanent pimple on his forehead, no, this was a confident, zit-free, man-of-the-moment. That was of course until the hair inspection at the end of the assembly. The new headmaster glared at him as though he had the mark of the devil tattooed on his forehead. But *that* wasn't going to ruin his moment. He took his caning knowing that it was like a badge of honor, a rite of passage. The awe in the eyes of his classmates was something to behold and made all the pain worthwhile.

Now, with his hair destroyed, all the awe and respect would be gone before the first bell rang. But what did any of that matter now, after last night?

The bus crawled past the drive-in. He couldn't believe they were going to shut it down—he had dreamed of taking Renate there someday. But his thoughts would not let go, it kept taking him back to that moment yesterday, standing in front of the bathroom mirror, inspecting his newly destroyed hair.

"Come on, Pete, let me have a look," Deanne de Lange said from behind the bathroom door.

"I'm not eight anymore, Ma," Pete said as he opened the door.

Deanne struggled to conceal her grin and let out a muffled snort. "I see Raj used his blunt pair of scissors

6

again," she said as Pete tried to walk around her standing in the way. Her outstretched hand dangled in the air, trying to touch what was left of his hair. Pete had to duck low to escape her searching fingers.

"I told you I should have gone to the salon."

"Don't be cheeky. You know very well that there is a big difference between fifty cents and five rands. Besides, salons are for women."

"But look at this, it looks like a blind crab cut my hair."

"There's a lesson here, Pete. You were the one who insisted on keeping that fancy Hollywood hair even though you knew how strict the school rules were."

"But, Ma!"

The back of her right hand nestled in her hip. "Rules are either kept or broken."

Pete gave a long sigh. "Everyone said they might change the rules with the new headmaster coming in."

"Stop listening to *everyone*. Those rules have been in place since before the Second World War and they will stay like that long after your grandchildren have finished school."

"Whatever," Pete mumbled, striding toward the kitchen.

"What did you say?" Deanne asked.

"I said: I'm going for a run."

"Be home before dark!" she shouted as he flung open the kitchen's screen door. "And stay away from Uncle Gerrit's farm—remember what happened to Bennie's dog!"

"Okay, Ma-a."

Pete saw the reflection of his smile in the bus

window. He knew his mom saw right through him. She would have watched him closely as he pretended to run toward the primary school only to run in the opposite direction minutes later.

How he wished he hadn't gone for that run. Nothing, not even getting into the first rugby team or being good enough for Renate, was worth the price of that run.

Pete hated running: It was a futile exercise of forcing your body to overheat. To make it worse, the scenery along the way wasn't exactly awe-inspiring. Things like the swimming pool, the broken streetlamp, the rusty 1956 Studebaker abandoned in the empty field that burned down at least once every two months. The monotonous houses of New Extension which seemed to wait in a perpetual sigh along Faversham Road for something to happen, and the same people doing the same things every day of their lives in a carousel of aimlessness in this armpit of a town.

He ran along the edge of the small fishing dam with the best clay in the district, but his thoughts were wholly occupied by Renate. He could see her perfectly formed calves running in front of him. Her small, green running shorts a flame luring him in, and her long blond hair dancing about her shoulders, a playful promise. Then she turned. The sun glistening on her pure white skin. Her smile was diamonds framed by the most sumptuous red lips. Faster and faster his legs carried him forward, the fire inside him scorching. He pushed himself until he was sprinting flat-out, past the ruined remains of the old farmhouse and the tiny handwritten sign which read, *Private property—Keep out.* He tiptoed at speed across the cattle grid, leaped over the sagging fence and ran the final stretch toward the top of the hill to where the rocks rose like towers in the elongated shadows of the setting sun. There was only one turn left before he would reach the top, then he would turn around. First, he had to douse the Renate-fire.

At the top of the hill, Pete dropped to his haunches. He fought for air but felt good. The sun was perilously close to the horizon and he knew his dear mom would not be impressed if he got home after dark again. Her disappointment had to wait though, he wanted to take in this moment first. A sudden rumble drew his attention. A dark bank of cloud had appeared above Durnacol, the nearby mining village, and it seemed to be heading this way. *Probably more bark than bite,* he thought, *like all the other times.* He turned back toward the west. The big red ball had almost dipped half its body behind the vast majesty of the Drakensberg, surrounded by a few dotted clouds painted in pink and purple. *Who knows,* he thought, *perhaps Dannhauser wasn't that bad after all.*

A shrill whistle sliced through the dusk air. Pete turned toward the sound, deep in thought. From the other side of the hill a black guy, probably his age, was running toward him. His mind flashed back to the previous night's news bulletin about exiled black communist terrorists, plotting to slaughter all the whites. He strained his eyes trying to see if this guy was carrying a gun or a knife, but he saw nothing. He considered running but then it hit him: Black guys were faster than whites, everyone knew this, so it would be futile. All Pete could do was watch as this potential communist came closer and feel how his left leg started to shake. The black guy wore faded blue safari shorts which were too big for him, a torn T-shirt with the words *Durnacol's 25th Anniversary* written in faded red letters, and he was barefoot. Sweat formed a laager around his short black curls. He was the spitting image of the painting of Shaka Zulu in tribal dress and assegai in hand on the wall of Pete's Standard Three History class.

"This is private property. You are not allowed here." The words were like a bucket of cold water in Pete's face. His voice was deep, with a particularly heavy, strained accent.

Pete felt the anger ignite in him.

"You don't talk to me like that, kaffir!" And there for the first time, he heard how the k-word fell out of his mouth. His parents said it was a swear word. It grated his tongue, but in a way made him feel powerful *and* ashamed. Simultaneously.

"Is this your farm now all of a sudden? And my name is *'baas,'* you don't get to call me 'you,' hear me?" The words jumped out before he could even process them.

The black guy stopped a few meters from him. A frown cut his forehead in two, he sucked his fat bottom lip into his wide mouth and seemed to dig his teeth deep into it. His arms were tucked safely behind his broad-shouldered frame.

"This farm is the property of Mr. Gerrit Jacobs. He does not like trespassers, *baas*." He spoke laboriously as if someone had just heaped two large bags of corn on his shoulders.

A strange sensation bounced around inside Pete.

He wanted to smile. He had never spoken more than two words to a black guy his age and here in one quick swipe, he had rendered young Shaka harmless. How he wished Renate were here to see him in action.

The black guy peered over his shoulder twice.

"Serious, *baas* Gerrit will shoot, no jokes." He was staring straight down at the uneven road at his feet. His shoulders drooped somewhat and beads of sweat rolled down the sides of his face.

Pete looked at him. He appeared smaller than at first glance. "And what about you, hey? Are you supposed to be here? Maybe I should tell *baas* Gerrit that you're sneaking off to town?"

"Please, I was just running—" The sound of an approaching vehicle stalled his words. They gawked at one another in panic. Pete could almost feel Uncle Gerrit's bullet slicing through his flesh. His mom's warning spun around in his head. Why was he always so bloody stubborn?

A moment petrified in disbelief floated by. Then, as if a gear simultaneously started turning in their minds, both darted for the nearest rock, the black guy running around and Pete leaping over it. They flopped down with their backs to the rock. In all the haste, Pete accidentally brushed his arm against the black guy's arm, he pulled it away and without thinking wiped his arm on his shorts. Their breathing was fast and shallow, each trapped in their fears, both regretting that they had gone for a run.

The vehicle stopped close to the rock. Pete looked at the black guy next to him. He saw raw fear in his eyes—the darkest ones he had ever seen. There were tiny yellow lines in the whites of his eyes, and for a moment Pete wondered whether that would be the last thing he'd ever see.

A door opened. Music leaped into the dusky sky. Pete recognized the song in an instant, Duran Duran's *Wild Boys*. He was confused. Why would a fifty-year-old farmer listen to *Wild Boys*? The black guy must have had the same thought because without a word or gesture both of them turned as silently as they could. There were a few crevices in the rock and each chose a vantage point as far removed from the other as possible, but with the best possible view.

A young man in his early twenties stood next to the driver's side of his brand-new Toyota Hilux. He was singing along with gusto whilst pissing on an unsuspecting khaki-bush. Pete recognized him. He'd seen him at church, not every Sunday but often enough. He farmed somewhere near Uncle Ampie on the Normandien road. Rudie-somebody. But what was he doing there?

The passenger door swung open. Pete almost gasped aloud. A young Indian girl jumped out and started running straight toward their hideaway-rock. Her arms flapped like that of a trapped bird, her mouth was half open, her eyes puffy and damp.

Pete couldn't bear it, he had to look away. Without realizing it, his eyes were on the stranger next to him whose face mirrored the emotions coursing through him. Pete could feel the blood drain from his face with every step the girl took toward them.

A moment later Rudie realized what was going on and chased after her. Mere meters from their hiding place he kicked the girl's shin, she lost balance, flew through the air and tumbled to the ground in a dusty heap. Rudie swooped down on her and grinned. She sobbed and tried to wriggle free, but he had pinned her arms down with his knees and sat on her chest. He started laughing. A thunderous, fiendish laugh.

Pete couldn't look. What do you do? What do you do?

The girl did her best to twist herself out of his stranglehold but she couldn't move the six-foot-five Rudie.

"I like a curry with a bit of a kick," Rudie hissed. "Tonight's your lucky night; you're going to taste some proper *boerewors*."

With renewed determination, she writhed and kicked and managed to throw him off balance. But he recovered quickly and gave her three quick slaps in the face before he moved his hand down her leg and started lifting her dress.

The black guy gestured for Pete to do something. He felt his anger rise again.

The girl screamed.

"Scream as much as you want, bitch, no one will hear you. Scream your little heart out, get those vocal cords nice and loose, because you'll be screaming with pleasure very soon." Rudie leaned in again, this time pressing his left knee against her neck, his full weight behind it. In one swift move he reached under her dress—the rip of her panties echoed amongst the rocks.

Pete motioned with his head to the black guy, pleading with him to do something. But he just shook his head and pointed at his face, like *that* was supposed to be an answer.

When he looked again, Rudie was standing and

had planted his giant red leather boot in her neck. He slowly started undoing his belt, pulled down his zipper and let his shorts slide down his legs and drop onto the girl's face.

"Please, please don't. I won't tell anyone, please I beg you, sir, please, please," she cried out in the brief moment he lifted his boot from her neck.

A smile curled into his sparse yellow mustache. He shook his head very slowly, not breaking eye contact, and dug his hand deep into his gray Y-front underpants. She was screaming but no sounds came out and tears left muddied lines on her face.

"Stop!" Pete carefully opened his eyes and realized he was standing. He started blinking his eyes feverishly and he could swear he saw his heart beating against his shirt.

In the corner of his eye, he saw that the black guy was also standing. Pete had never fainted before, but he suspected he was about to; black dots appeared in his vision and he struggled to focus on this young giant glaring at him.

Rudie took a small step backward and pulled his hand out of his underpants.

"I see what's going on here." He wiggled his finger in the air. "Snuck away from home to come and roll around in a mud hut." He stepped closer. "Now listen to me, you *moffie*, faggot piece of shit. Be a good little Nancy and piss off home. And tell that pillow-biting turd next to you to fuck off. I'm busy with grown-up stuff." Rudie pointed his finger straight at Pete's right eye, making him feel as though it was thrust right into his skull.

Pete's lips moved but nothing came out.

"I'm only going to ask once," Rudie growled and gave a couple of steps forward.

"You can't," was all Pete could mutter.

"I can't what, faggot?" Rudie adjusted his kudu-skin hat and Pete could see his red-blond hair stuck to his forehead.

"It's...against the law." Pete tried to breathe but his throat had closed up completely.

"I'll give you a little lesson in *my* laws," Rudie shouted and stormed off to his truck.

Before his brain could process what was going on, Pete seized the moment with Rudie's back turned to him. He raced around their hideaway-rock, realized the black guy was with him, and helped the girl to her feet. Her arm felt thin and fragile. She had no chance in hell. They turned and ran as fast as their feet would carry them past their hiding place, past more rocks, straight toward the horizon where cerise and violet had morphed into dark gray.

The black guy took the lead. He seemed to know where he was going and at that point, Pete wasn't about to question his knowledge of the farm. The girl ran closely behind Pete and he could hear soft little yelps as she suppressed her tears.

"Run! Let's see how you outrun my bullets!"

Rudie's voice drowned out everything, even the sound of their feet hitting the dry ground. Then Pete heard a shot.

They clambered down a little ravine. The going was painfully slow and Pete could sense Rudie gaining on them with every step they took. Another shot reverberated in his ears, or perhaps he was replaying the first shot in his mind. The girl was not a natural runner and even less of a climber. Every time he had to stop to help her and urge her on, he gnashed his teeth a little harder. In contrast, the black guy danced down the ravine like a *klipspringer*. Pete always thought he was agile, but he couldn't keep up with the floating feet of the guy in front of him.

A bright yellow spark spat against a rock less than two meters from Pete. The sound followed a moment later. A chill, unlike he had ever experienced, scraped along the soft skin of his back like a frozen spike.

Rudie's laughter crashed like waves over the three of them. "That was close! Woohoo! The next one will leave brains on the ground, eh. And then I'm going to get me my curry!"

At the bottom of the ravine, twilight was starting to wane, making it hard for them to see where they were running. The black guy ran next to Pete and gestured that he should follow him. Pete reluctantly obliged, as a better alternative was hardly jumping out at him.

The girl fell and the two boys grabbed her in the run; she barely touched the ground. The black guy led them through thick reeds, birds chirping and fluttering angrily. On the other side was a muddy dam which was almost completely waterless. Without hesitation the black guy flung himself into the mud, smearing the thick black gunk all over him. After a moment's hesitation, the girl followed suit. Pete kept looking around him, but he couldn't see or hear Rudie anywhere. Then a loud bang silenced the birds. A deep thud echoed against the dam wall. Pete dived full-length into the mud, rolling around, smearing as much as he could over him. With lumps of sticky black muck smeared all over their bodies, the three crept into the supposed safety of the reeds. Twilight had almost completely stepped aside to make way for the night, with only the mountains in the distance harboring the last few dabs of daylight.

In the reeds, however, there was not even a hint of light.

"I've got all night! No worried mommy waiting for me at home." Rudie's voice was very close now.

"How original. I know you're in the mud, dip-shits! Do you think I've got arsehole written on my forehead?"

A long silence followed. Pete couldn't believe how loud his breathing was and how deadly quiet the others were.

"Last chance. Come out now, give me the bunny chow and you can go suckle on mommy's tits..."

Pete closed his eyes when a couple of shots splashed into the shallow puddle in the center of the dam. Then silence. Where was he?

Bang!

It was the loudest sound he had ever heard. The reed next to the girl exploded in a powdery mess. A muffled shriek escaped her pursed lips. She slapped her hand over her mouth, but it was too late, Rudie had heard.

"Ha! Gotcha!"

His oversized boots slowly, purposefully shuffled toward them through the reeds.

Pete opened his mouth, desperate for air to fill his lungs. He gawked at the unending darkness for answers, but only more questions came.

Something broke through the infinite darkness.

Two beams of light illuminated the horizon—his heart beat in his mouth. The beams moved quickly and grew bigger by the second. Uncle Gerrit? He must have heard the shots...

"Shit!" Rudie growled so close that Pete could hear his breathing. "Shit! You lucky piece of...aargh!"

The hate in Rudie's voice was like the claws of a beast digging into Pete's skull.

As the two headlights got closer, they could hear Rudie's footsteps moving away from them.

"I know who you are, Petrus!" The black guy jerked his head around, the whites of his eyes the only thing Pete could see in the faint light of the approaching vehicle.

"Or Pete, like you call yourself these days. Think you're super-cool, don't you? Pete de Lange, son of Rikus and Deanne." The black guy's eyes disappeared in the darkness. Pete tasted bile in his mouth.

"If you ever say anything about tonight, and I mean even in your bloody sleep, then I'll tell the whole freakin' world that you are a *moffie*. A faggot. You understand?! But not just a normal faggot, no, everyone will know *exactly* who you like to pull your pants down for. Your life will be over, dipshit! Oh, and Pete, I've seen how your mommy checks me out with those hungry eyes of hers, gagging for a taste of my *boerewors*. So if you, that pickaxe, *or* that curry munching slut do so much as think of tonight, I'll give your mom more than just a taste! That I promise you. You hear me, Pete-de-fucking-Lange?!"

Rudie's footsteps became fainter and fainter.

In the distance, they could hear the door of the Hilux slammed shut and then how it raced away without the lights on. A couple of minutes later Uncle Gerrit arrived. He got out of his car without killing the engine, inspected the tire tracks in the beams of his headlights, got back in and followed the tracks in the direction of town. Not very long after that he was back, turned off his headlights and switched off the engine. He started walking, his flashlight dancing about wildly in the darkness. Pete watched him closely as he climbed down the ravine and came toward them. His flashlight suddenly stopped, zoning in on something on the ground. He bent down and picked up a shell casing. Pete didn't dare to blink. Uncle Gerrit turned the shell casing around and around between his fingers and sniffed it. Pete wondered if he had forgotten how to breathe. Uncle Gerrit slipped the shell casing into his pocket and walked toward the dam. The beam from his flashlight broke through the reeds. The three lay still, frozen in their muddy fortress, hoping, praying, that he would just turn around and go, and that this damned night would end.

The earth's orbit came to a near standstill. In mud, time was like a scalpel slicing open your soul from side to side. Uncle Gerrit kept on walking up and down the dam wall. More than once he flashed straight at them, but thankfully he didn't spot them. After his fourth turn along the dam wall, he stopped dead in his tracks. For Pete, it felt like ice was being pumped through his veins. But then he turned around all of a sudden and walked back to his car.

For several minutes the three of them watched Uncle Gerrit's car until long after it had disappeared behind the hill. No one had dared to move or make a sound since the girl's near-fatal shriek.

A rumbling of thunder woke Pete from his daze. He drew a deep breath and slowly lifted himself out of the mud. The mud was reluctant to let him go, so much so that he nearly fell over when he finally managed to pull himself free. He scraped his fingers over his mud-covered arms; it was sticky like syrup and reeked of compost. The others followed his example and together they staggered through the reeds and out toward the ravine. The silence was unbearable. Pete's mind was spinning between thoughts of his dad's impending dismay, Rudie's fiendish laughter and the pleading eyes of this girl walking behind him. He wanted to say something, even if it was only to break this insufferable silence, but it was as if the mud had sucked his lips closed too.

The girl hesitated for a moment at the place where Rudie had pinned her down. Her silhouette was shaking. They pressed on, over the sagging fence, the cattle grid, and past the ruin of the old farmhouse when the black guy suddenly stopped. Pete and the girl stopped too, turning to him questioningly. It was he who broke the silence.

"I must go back. Eish, I'm in big trouble already."

"We have to get her home," Pete protested.

"People don't like blacks walking around town at night. I'm sorry...I—"

Before he could finish his sentence, the girl threw her arms around him and whispered a thank you. He stood frozen as if he had seen a ghost.

A sudden flash illuminated the world around them. Lightning pirouetted in the clouds and the veil of imminent rain galloped across the parched earth. Pete glanced at the other guy. In a bright, prolonged flash their eyes met for a moment, they nodded, and both turned away.

The heavens opened. In true Northern Natal style, the rain everyone was so desperate for, bucketed down in large lead-like drops. Heaven's silver bullets burned Pete's skin with each strike, taking with it lump by lump of the mud he was covered in. He loved it; the rain at its intense best was one of his favorite things—standing outside, experiencing every piercing drop. Tonight, however, the rain had an entirely different meaning, because with every stride he took, it washed away the tears which had appeared uninvited. Yes, with every step it washed away more and more of the stinking mud, and with every step, he felt as though he was getting further and further away from Rudie's laugh. But when he looked to his right, *she* was still there.

By the time the realization had dawned on him that she was still running next to him, the rain had cleansed her from nearly all the mud. In the thundering symphony of lightning, he could see how her long black hair had stuck to the sides of her face. He couldn't recall noticing her face up until that moment. She had high cheekbones, perfectly ovoid, her eyes were an incredible light brown, which appeared almost translucent in the radiance of the blazing sky. She also wasn't as skinny as he first imagined, she had the curves of a woman.

Pete looked away. How could he look at an Indian like that? She was an Indian. A blasted In-di-an.

He snuck a quick look at her again and noticed the cutest little dimples in her cheeks. Stop it now!

A car approached and they ducked for cover behind a jacaranda tree. He looked at her again, and then quickly away before she could notice. He took off his windbreaker—which he only wore to sweat more to lose weight quicker—and draped it over her head and shoulders. She accepted it bashfully. Her eyes gave away her knowing that she looked far too Indian to be out in the white area at night.

They ran past the swimming pool and the primary school, past the library to the corner near the police station. Here she stopped.

"I live down there," she said, pointing to a little side road and hastily took off Pete's windbreaker and handed it back.

"I'll walk you home," Pete said hesitantly.

"My dad will come out swinging an ax if he sees any boy near me." She smiled and her mouth curled effortlessly into her dimples.

Almost mechanically Pete stuck his hand out. She ignored it and hugged him. A soft hug, lingering for a fleeting moment.

"Thank you." Her whisper caressed his skin and tickled his ear.

Then she let him go, turned around and scurried down the street.

Pete gaped after her. His arms hung next to his body like two rugby socks. His mind was still, the rain was loud, and within seconds, she was gone.

DON'S GONE

"Ha-ha! Did mommy make a booboo with your hair?" Comment number nine. Pete's faint hope that he could keep his newly destroyed hair quiet was futile. It was just so utterly annoying that a prick like Devon van Zyl just couldn't let it go. Every time Pete was in the vicinity of girls, Devon would pop up like the rinderpest and start with all his "booboos." Who talks like that? Pete counted each and every one of Devon's remarks. He bit his tongue, took it on the chin, but promised himself that after comment number ten, Devon would be picking up his own rotten teeth off the floor. Besides, after yesterday, someone like Devon—a Matric boy who acted like he was in Standard Six, who couldn't even make the fourth rugby team's starting line-up, and with a nose so crooked it seemed desperate to escape his ugly mug—meant nothing to him.

In maths class Mr. Human told them stories about his upbringing in the Kalahari, but Pete barely heard a word. His hands frequently and involuntarily touched his hair, until he realized what he was doing. Then he would slowly pick up a pen and glance around to see if anyone had noticed. He kept staring out of the window—his gaze drawn to the bright light streaming in and making him wonder if he could ever face darkness again.

His friends' chatter was incessant, there was

23

constant noise around him. He yearned for a few seconds of complete silence. But as soon as he thought of silence, he could feel the darkness engulf him, and see the shock of light as the bullet ricocheted off that rock.

"Hey, check!" Barend whispered loudly. "Nine o'clock."

Pete was convinced that if Barend had a tail it would be wagging right now. His black curly mop bobbed in excitement and his round cheeks turned pink.

Pete forced his tired eyes to wander to the large oak tree. The leaves were a pale green and some of their corners were scorched brown. Under the tree was an old wooden bench, with large strips of dark green paint peeling off it. Three girls sat on the bench: all three were blondes, all three wore school skirts tantalizingly shorter than the rules permitted, all three were giggling as they paged through a pink-and-white polka dot-covered book.

"Check: her skirt is lifting a little. Come on, wind, come on." Barend squinted, leaning forward with his arms crossed over his tummy.

Pete studied the girls. The one getting Barend's juices flowing was Philippa Hughes. She was the school record holder in long jump and 100m hurdles, but hockey was her main passion. She had lean, muscular legs, and she was pretty, but more like a wax doll than an actual person. For Barend however, she was the face and body of all his night time—and daytime—fantasies.

Pete cast his eyes over the other two girls. Seated

in the middle was Andrea Weyers, the girlfriend of Gareth Joubert: first team rugby captain and supreme asshole. She knew she was beautiful and always strutted around as though the world should stop and bow at her feet. No one liked her, but there wasn't a boy in the school who wouldn't mind a couple of rounds with her—except Pete and Barend, of course. Pete's eyes settled at the third girl. Renate. Her tied-back ponytail revealed her perfect face and that shy smile.

Pete stared at her, not even caring if she noticed. Worrying thoughts had marched into his head again. He closed his eyes. Every time he breathed, he could feel the rough edge of that reed brushing against him. He could feel the powdery mist of the reed exploding in his face, and he could hear Rudie's large boots sloshing closer through the mud.

"Hey, hair-bear! Are you praying that your pretty hair will grow back?" It was Devon, and that was comment number ten.

The excited cries of "Fight! Fight! Fight!" rang out over the school playground. The bloodthirsty mob formed a ring spurring Pete on as he sat on Devon's chest and peppered him with his fists.

Left, right, left, right.

Rage became a roadmap of blood on Devon's face. He no longer fought back and just watched as tears and blood formed balls of mud on the ground.

"Stop!" Barend's desperate plea was swallowed up by the cheering horde.

Left, right, left, right.

Every time he reloaded, Rudie's laughter would echo, but every time a punch landed, the laughter

25

was muffled—slightly—and further away.

"Mrs. de Lange, I cannot begin to stress just how serious this matter is. By rights, Petrus should be expelled. He broke every conduct rule the school has." Headmaster Gray closed the book from which he was pretending to read. He had a pensive look about him. Pete snuck a quick peek at his mom. Her thin lips had virtually disappeared, her nostrils were flaring, and her eyes were covered with a film of tears. He suddenly bemoaned the fact that the office where his mom worked closed down a year ago. If it hadn't, then she wouldn't have been able to attend this meeting, and he wouldn't have seen that look in her eyes.

Mr. Gray eyeballed Pete. "You're an extremely lucky boy, Petrus." Mr. Gray took a moment to adjust his glasses.

"Devon is bruised and has a nasty swollen lip, but it could very easily have been a lot worse. Then, I'm afraid, this matter would have been out of my hands. It would have been up to the authorities to decide what action to take, but one thing I can promise you is that there would have been no way back to Dundee High. Or any other school in the district." Mr. Gray straightened his back in his oversized leather chair.

"It was only because of my experience in this kind of situation, from my time in Durban, that I was able to persuade Devon's mom not to press charges." Pete stared at his knees. Small stones and dirt stuck to them.

"Mr. Gray," Deanne inhaled through her nose as if hoping it would bring her courage. "Pete is a good boy. I don't think...he has never, ever, been in a fight."

26

She looked away and wiped her eyes, her voice trembled. "Please give him the hiding of his life. Six of the best or whatever you call it these days. Heaven knows, he deserves it."

Pete's eyes were fixed on his mom. He had never seen her look at him like that. The anger lashed from her eyes and small muscles under her brow contracted like it was in spasm. He felt incredibly small and powerless, like a toddler.

She looked at Mr. Gray again. "I will see to it that my husband does the same at home tonight because he needs a lesson he will never forget. But please, I beg you, he's a good boy." She stopped suddenly like her brain had switched off.

Mr. Gray glared at Pete. He scribbled down some notes, pushed his notepad aside and tilted his head slowly to a painting on the wall of two men wrestling.

"Besides apologizing, do you have anything to add, Petrus?" Mr. Gray asked after a while.

Pete sneaked a peek at his mom. His head was throbbing, and his teeth hurt from gnashing. Then he looked at the dark brown desk in front of him and at Mr. Gray, who like his mom, seemed to have grown significantly bigger than usual. His throat was dry as a desert and his left eye itched ceaselessly.

He rubbed his eye. "It won't happen again, sir."

"Correct." Mr. Gray stood up. His big belly brushed the table on the way up and a little bit of the hairy white skin from under his shirt peeked out.

"From now on I'm going to keep my eyes on you. You hear me?"

Pete nodded, his eyes only making it as far as the headmaster's red-and-black alumni tie.

27

"No stepping out of line." He pressed his fat hands down on the desk and glared at Pete.

"Yes, sir," Pete's mom said and got up.

She thanked Mr. Gray and walked out of the office with Pete. She glared at Pete, and even though she didn't utter a word, he knew that no hiding could ever be more painful than that moment trapped in his mom's disappointment.

"Petrus," Mr. Gray called from behind his desk, "let's make sure my words sink in."

Pete glanced back at his mom, but her head was turned away. In the office, Mr. Gray was busy flexing a long reddish-brown rod between his hands.

Time to pay.

THE RADIO

Venny Naidoo closed the small metal door behind him. The solitary light bulb dangling from a wooden beam bathed the windowless enclosure inside his garage in dim yellow light. Around him stacks of newspapers and notes filled the room—barely leaving enough space for the old wooden chair with its faded red-and-purple cushion and the beige plastic desk in the corner. A large radio, earphones and a microphone occupied most of the desk's surface. Three pens—blue, black and red—lay neatly placed next to the microphone, ready for action. A small fan, stuck in one position, flirted with a small stack of newspapers near the door.

Venny swirled the contents of his blue ceramic cup, took a deep breath and nodded in appreciation of its fine aroma. *Proper Indian tea,* he thought, *not the weak tasteless crap white people drink.* After a large slurp, he sat down and switched the radio on, looked at his watch and adjusted the frequency. He slipped the headphones over his ears, making his sparse black hair stand upright, adjusted the volume and flicked the switch on the microphone.

"Protea Eleven ready. Over." He pulled the microphone closer and cupped his hands around the headphones. After a few moments, he tried again.

"Protea Eleven ready. Over," he said a little louder and slower.

The crackly silence annoyed him. He slapped the microphone's switch and slurped his tea with one long sigh. He looked up at the wall in front of him. On it was a black-and-white photograph of a police officer beating a young Indian woman with a baton. A poster lay trampled at her feet. It read, "Freedom in our lifetime." Like every other time he looked at it he was held captive by this woman's eyes. He could see the anguish and pain in them, but more than anything else, the flickering of hope that was lost.

"Protea Eleven, this is Protea Ten. Continue," a voice broke the silence.

Venny fumbled with the microphone in an attempt to switch it back on and adjusted his headphones again. "Protea Ten, do you have any new commands?" he asked, his lips so close to the mouthpiece that it nearly touched.

He slid his hands deep into his pockets and tapped his right foot like a pot about to boil over.

"Not at this stage, Protea Eleven. Status quo, I repeat, status quo. Over."

Venny grabbed the microphone, peered over his shoulder and whispered: "Protea Ten, please make the others understand that I'm available, very willing, and absolutely ready. Just say the word, and I'll do it. Anything, anywhere. Over." He released the microphone and exhaled through his pouting mouth.

"Protea Eleven."

Silence.

He adjusted the volume dial, inspected the radio, tugged on the cable, but all remained quiet. He closed his eyes, nibbled on the inside of his lip and ran the back of his index finger over his neatly trimmed graying mustache.

"Your comments have been noted." Venny tilted his head to the right.

"Status quo is confirmed, Protea Eleven. Protea Ten out." He sat back in his uncomfortable chair, took the headphones off very slowly and stared at the radio. His eyes caught the newspaper clipping of the young woman being beaten by the police again, but his gaze shifted to the wall on his right, to a golden frame with a picture of his daughter in it. With pride, he beheld her near-transparent hazelnut eyes, her long black satin-like hair, and those little dimples which made his father-heart melt.

"No!" he said out loud, grabbed the nearest news-paper and flung it against the wall. "When will these dumb bastards learn that nothing will ever happen if we just sit around and wait?"

NOW WHAT?

"Let me tell you something, Pete, you can count your lucky stars that we live in a small town like Dannhauser," Rikus de Lange said, shook his head and took another sip of his ice-cold Lion Lager.

Pete looked at his dad—a dark cloud of worry enveloped him. Pete wondered how his dad managed to give the same cautionary speech every night when they watched the news. "We're so lucky we don't live near a city—here we're safe—the kaff...black people in the rural areas are still good old salt-of-the-earth people, not like that bunch of terrorists who burn and bomb everything in sight. The closest we ever get to that is a strike at the mine, which is bad enough but hardly ever escalates to much more than shouting and a few scuffles. And the reality is, even that is orchestrated by those Commies in the city. I can see it in the eyes of the miners when they strike here: It's not out of free will, it's intimidation, violence. All part of some plot concocted by a few bloodthirsty Bolsheviks somewhere in a Johannesburg basement. You're young, so you might not see it right now, but one day you will shake my hand and say, 'Thank you, Dad.'"

Pete braced himself for tonight's speech, but the advertisements were over, and his dad's attention returned to the news.

"Astronomers have confirmed that Halley's Comet will be visible in the South African sky between April and June this year. The best time to see the comet in all its glory will be when it passes closest to the earth, around the end of May. This heavenly spectacle has created great excitement and anticipation for star-gazers across the globe."

Pete watched as the news anchor's lips continued to move, but all he could think of was his grandad's recollection of the 1910 Halley's Comet. "The sky was ablaze as if the heavens were torn apart and the most amazing silver light was trying to break through." He had been waiting for 1986 ever since that moment when his grandad's eyes had lit up and his face seemed young again, two days before he died, lying in hospital with a million tubes stuck in his body.

"Pete, show me your homework please?" Deanne stood at the door of the TV room. She had her red-and-white apron on and was busy removing her bright yellow dishwashing gloves.

"It's all done. Don't worry, Ma," Pete said without taking his eyes off the television.

"Well if it's all done then you shouldn't have any problems showing it to me."

"I said it's done, Ma. Don't you trust me?" Pete turned to his mom.

"Trust? You're going to talk to me about trust?" Pete realized a moment too late that he should have just shown his mom his homework. He moved to speak, but it was too late. Her gloves were off.

"Let's consider the facts. To start, I asked nicely all summer holiday long for you to sort out the store-room, and until this day, the only change is that you have piled more of your old rubbish in there. Six long weeks and you couldn't even do that one small thing for me." Pete thought he spotted a gap and tried to say something, but his mom stopped him summarily, finger in the air.

"To crown it all, I expressly told you to be back from your run before dark. Now, I don't have proof, but I will bet this house that you disobeyed me and went running all over Uncle Gerrit's farm. Not only disobeying me but nonchalantly risking your own life in the process. But—" His mom wiped the corner of her mouth with her little finger.

"I can't prove it. What I do know, however, is that when you snuck back here it was pitch dark and pouring with rain. We were worried sick; we were just about to start calling around and Pa was even considered calling Uncle Gerrit. Can you imagine how embarrassing that would have been? And your clothes reeked; heaven knows where *that* stench came from. I want to laugh when I think about the pathetic excuses you came up with, or perhaps I should cry. You must think your old mom is over the hill, deaf, blind, and can't smell a rotten egg when it's shoved in her face."

"Ma, I—" Pete started.

"Have I finished?" Deanne threw her hands in the air. Rikus got up to turn the television down.

"And what in the name of all that's good do you call your antics yesterday? Teenage hormones? Since when do we beat people up? Are we any better than the riff-raff we see on television?" Deanne stepped into the room. Pete felt his ears glow and there was urgent itchiness in his right eye.

"So, when I ask you to show me your homework, I mean immediately! I don't want stories or to hear a word about doing it later." Her voice broke.

Rikus positioned his six-foot-one frame between Pete and the television. "Listen to your mom, Pete. No more television tonight, no sports news, nothing. And this weekend you will sort out the storeroom exactly like your mother told you. Or else!"

"Pete, Pete, Petie; you naughty naughty boy." Devon sat on Pete's chest. His swollen lip had grown black and covered half his face. Pete struggled for air. He wanted to move but couldn't. Devon smiled. His fat black lip arched wide across his face.

"Who do we have here?" Rudie appeared behind Devon. Pete couldn't see his face; it was above him somewhere, but the light was too bright to see properly.

"My little faggot-buddy." Rudie's laughter dropped from the sky like hail.

"I got you an early birthday present." Rudie forced Pete's face to the left. On the ground, the black guy lay motionless in a pool of deep red blood. Behind him, the Indian girl and Renate were tied to a telephone pole. Renate's face was detached and cold, her eyes dim. The Indian girl cried tears of mud that dripped in dark stains on her white shirt.

Rudie walked up to the Indian girl and started undoing his shorts. Pete wanted to scream, but nothing came out. He looked up and saw that the headmaster was sitting on his chest now. He turned his head back to Rudie, but he was gone, and so was the girl. The headmaster whispered in his ear, "You did this, it's all your fault."

"No, no!" Pete pinched his eyes shut. He felt something strange and opened his eyes. Now it was

Renate who was sitting on his chest. She was crying: "You will pay, Petrus, you will pay."

Darkness.

Pete raised his head off the pillow. He took small quick breaths through his nose and could feel his heart pound against his chest. He slowly moved his right hand to his thigh and pinched his skin until it hurt. It was a dream, but it didn't feel like one.

He sat up, dropped his head into his hands and rubbed the back of his neck. His left hand searched in the dark and finally, with a loud click, his bedside lamp's soft glow illuminated the room. His eyes scanned the room, searching for any sign of movement. The closet door was slightly ajar. The darkness inside it infinite.

He blinked again.

Nothing.

He grabbed one of his pillows and pulled it in close to him, curled into the corner with his back to the room. The light cast a soft gray shadow of him against the wall. He kept staring at the outline of what had become of him: He was so small, so faint.

FIFTH

"China, who is she?" Barend sat on the top row of the primary school's sports pavilion, sucking on a green Fizzer.

"What are you talking about?" Pete asked, sitting two rows down, reading the facts on the inside of a Chappie wrapper.

"You came fifth, China. Fifth! I've run and lost against you in the hundred meters since we were eight, but I have never seen you run like today. Never! Not even that time in Standard Four when we played open-the-gates just before the race and you twisted your ankle. That day you came in third, with one leg. So what the hell is going on, China?" Barend lowered the Fizzer and gave Pete a dispirited glance.

"That's why I'm asking: Who is she? Who is this mysterious girl making your legs malfunction?" Barend scratched his head. "Come to think of it, you've been all over the place since the start of the year." Pete felt a pinch in his heart. Did Barend suspect something?

"First, you drop me to go and sit on the senior bus," Barend continued full-steam ahead. "Then you nearly kill that asshole Devon, and today you run like a girl. You could have won that race with one leg tied behind your back. Now Brett thinks he is Carl Lewis, as if he wasn't a complete prick already, just imagine him now. He ran 11.3 seconds, Pete. *I* could have beaten him!" Barend's cheeks glowed in that familiar pink hue.

"Easy, tiger. Remember, when *you* run the hundred meters, they use a calendar to measure your time, not a stopwatch." Pete smiled and blew a large bubble with his chewing gum.

"Funny. But I'm not the fast one: you are. Now Brett is going to rip us all year long with his stupid rock-spider jokes."

Pete clicked his tongue. "We'll just double tackle him at the first rugby practice. That'll shut him up." Pete opened another Chappie wrapper, intent on avoiding any eye contact.

"Maybe, but still." Barend looked out over the patchy athletics track and rugby field. In the distance, two young boys were kicking a rugby ball about.

"Something's wrong." There was a seriousness in Barend's round face. His light-colored eyebrows stood to attention and the side of his mouth twitched. This was Pete's best friend and had been since the day Barend was introduced as the new kid in class when they were eight. Barend had his previous school's uniform on and looked like a stuffed sausage. His cheeks were pink, and his hair was shorter than that of most soldiers. Kids laughed at this fat kid with the silly red uniform, but Miss Thomas forced Pete, as the class captain, to make friends with him. And so he did, he couldn't help it. It was impossible not to like this freckled fat kid with the squeaky voice who ruined the punchline of every joke he ever told. He looked at how that little round boy had grown. The freckles were mostly gone, as was the baby fat. All that remained of that boy was his round face, pink cheeks, and the superpower to ruin jokes. Barend was the reason no one ever solved the mystery of who broke the magistrate's window, and the reason that no one dared bully him in Standard Six. This gentle giant was his safety net in times of need.

Barend's eyes refused to let go of him, waiting for an answer. A contorting, burning pain filled Pete's chest. He was lying to his best friend. Couldn't he just sit next to Barend and tell him every sickening detail of *that* night?

"It's Standard Eight, man," the words stumbled out of Pete's mouth. "This is the big one. Senior rugby, choosing school subjects, girls like Renate realizing they are no longer kids and that they can get anyone they want. I probably had too much time this summer to think about it. I wish we went away like you guys did." Pete stood up and arched his back into a stretch, without looking at Barend.

"Ha! Three weeks working like a slave for my Uncle Carel, then two weeks of non-stop rain in a caravan at Wagensdrift dam? Believe me, you had the better deal," Barend said, shaking his head and folding his arms over his knees.

He turned to Pete. "So, what's the plan for this year?" The burning pain in his chest relented slightly and Pete slipped his hands behind his head and stared up at the rusty corrugated roof.

"Last year we planned to play for the under 15A's and to get Renate and Philippa," Barend said and scratched his curly black mop again. "Hell, one out of two ain't bad. Just a shame it's the wrong one."

Pete smiled briefly but then burst out laughing. Barend followed with an uproarious, high-pitched giggle. They laughed until tears formed in their eyes;

this went on for several minutes. After their laughter subsided, Pete took the chewing gum out of his mouth, placed it in one of the Chappie wrappers and flicked it as far as he could over the back of the pavilion.

"This year we're going to play first-team rugby." Pete said, hands in pocket.

"In other words, we need to pray that a lot of guys get injured," Barend said, but Pete reprimanded him with a stern look.

"We *will* play first-team rugby, and before the winter holidays, Renate will be mine." Pete gazed at the blue of the sky getting lighter in preparation for the sunset.

"And...me and Philippa?" Barend asked softly.

"Dude, if we are going to make a name for ourselves this year, it all depends on us. Whatever you are planning to do with Philippa totally depends on you. Only you." Barend's always joyful face faded into glumness.

"Think about this, if we're in the first team, we can have any girl we want. Philippa will come to you; you can just sit back and watch her throw herself at you." A twinkle flickered in Barend's eyes.

"The key to it all is the first team. After that, everything will be easy." Pete listened to his own words as if someone else had spoken them. All he wanted to do was tell Barend. He knew he could trust him with his life. But why then did the words keep getting stuck in his throat?

THE ROOSTER
CROWED SUNDAY

The church bell knocked on parishioners' doors through the hazy morning fog. This prowling and suffocating mist always forebode a breathless, stifling day. The type that made chickens hide in the shade of shrubs, beaks wide open. The second bell was louder, urgent, to remind worshipers that they had thirty minutes left to polish their shoes, clip on their ties, adjust their hats and count out their offerings.

Pete was already dressed. Outside his door he could hear his mom bellowing desperate final instructions as his dad paced up and down the hallway, carrying out his mom's orders like a faithful servant when all he wanted to do was to just sit down and drink his morning coffee.

The long thin mirror with a single crack running from left to right, which his grandad had given to his mom as a wedding gift, reflected someone with pointy dark blonde hair, a nose that was just ever so slightly too big, and a light green safari suit. Pete ran his hands over the coarse material of the safari suit. It was supposed to be cooler than a normal suit, but Pete hated how the material always scratched him and made him itch, mostly at the most inopportune times, and he hated how he looked in it. Only old people wore them. His dad wore one. He looked like his freakin' dad!

But his mom said it was going to be a hot day and kindly left it for him on his bed with that I'm-not-asking-I'm-telling-look. Besides, he'd been treading very carefully around her since their altercation the other night. She had been very cold. He hoped a joke would melt the ice. "Van der Merwe was standing on his porch. Suddenly his phone rang, and he ran inside. Breathless, he answered the phone, 'Van der Merwe.' The person on the other side said, 'Gee, sorry, I think I've dialed the wrong number. Apologies for the inconvenience.' Van replied straight away, 'No trouble at all, I had to come in anyway, the phone was ringing.'" But it didn't help. She just walked away and said it was an old joke. Cold.

There were dark half-moons under Pete's eyes, and they were growing. As it turned out, sleep could be quite elusive when it wanted to be, quality sleep especially. The other thing is, it also felt as though you at least had a fighting chance of controlling your thoughts while you were awake, but even that didn't always work. Dreams had no rules; Rudie could waltz in and out as he pleased, torturing and tormenting everyone he held dear. With nothing to stop him.

Rudie.

It felt as though his brain was placed in a vice-grip and someone was tightening it slowly. Suddenly the whole idea of walking into that church made him feel physically sick. What if Rudie was in church? It was sheer luck that Rudie had not been to church since *that* night. But with every passing Sunday the inevitability of that filthy, trigger happy asshole showing up at church became more of a nauseating reality. What would he do if he saw him? Would he have the courage to confront him then?

Pete fell back on his bed and pulled a pillow over his face. What if Rudie started whispering in people's ears, planting seeds; what if he told everyone that he, was the world's biggest fag, and a kaffir-brother to boot?

Outside, an Indian mynah gave a distressed shriek. Pete sat up and rubbed his itchy eyes. Perhaps he should tell the Reverend everything, in confidence. The Reverend would know what to do, and he wouldn't go around telling people. But what then? It would always be his word against that monster's, and to the world, he was still a kid, and the monster a respected member of the community. Who would they believe? Who would the Reverend believe? And his parents?

"Five minutes." His dad's voice flicked his ear.

All he could see in his mind's eye was walking into the gloomy church, the sun's red fingers scraping against the stained-glass windows, the uncomfortable wooden pews, and the Reverend's insistence on using archaic words no one had heard this century. He could see the thinning carpet with its faded colors and frayed ends. The silent walk as Auntie Betty's old fingers fumbled over the church organ's keys. Some people would peek in your direction, others would stare, flashing their judgmental smiles as if they felt sorry for you. Everyone except the poor people, the lot from Genadendal. They were there every Sunday, sitting in the same spot in the corner of the church, with the same clothes they wore last year and the year before that. Their hair appeared dirty—not greasy, just dirty, like yellow mud was stuck to every strand and nothing would ever be able to wash it off. They

43

were all dark-skinned, charred by the sun as they toiled in vain to resuscitate their old 1970 Ranger station wagon, or chasing yard chickens for the pot. They looked different, and many people suggested they only came to church to steal from the offerings basket. Auntie Hendriena would say to Pete's mom, "Have you ever noticed that when they receive the basket, it always takes an age to reach the deacon?" The Reverend just smiled every time a new allegation was made, "Does the Bible not say we must look after the poor—and our neighbors?"

"We're leaving *now*!" Pete's dad said with the right amount of urgency to reassure his mom.

"Y-e-a-h...yes." Pete looked in the mirror, his shoulders sagged and he had to force himself to follow his parents down the street to the corner where the church tower rose higher than all else, and the weather vane sat quietly in wait.

Absentminded, he watched as cars pulled up and people ascended the steps to where the gaping black hole swallowed them one by one. His eyes searched for a certain Toyota Hilux, but he couldn't see it. That very familiar taste of sick filled his mouth. He hated church. Of course, he believed, and even though he secretly believed that something like evolution was possible, he similarly couldn't imagine a universe without God, where everything existed by accident, and everything came from nothing. No, he believed, but he didn't know how many more times he could listen to the Reverend reprimanding them for their sinful ways. Or for how much longer he could listen to Auntie Gertie—unaffectionately known as the cat choir—and her eternal search for those elusive high notes.

He involuntarily followed his parents up the steps and into the dark abyss. The sounds of Auntie Betty's slow murder of the church organ made him want to turn and run, but somehow his legs kept following his parents. His gaze was fixed on the faded carpet, but as they turned left, he saw those immaculately polished black shoes. His heart raced. Should he stop? Tell him everything? The shiny shoes called out to him: "Say it. Come on, just say it."

From that moment when he had walked back into his house, drenched, reeking of the mud, the thing he wanted to do above all else was to tell this man everything. This man with the shiny shoes. He dared not look up; Captain Burger might see it in his eyes. Pete thought of the twenty or thirty times he had started dialing the police number. The dozen times he had walked to the gate of the police station. He couldn't. He was a weakling, a coward. How could he not tell the police? This was a serious crime. But he couldn't, no matter how many times he chastised himself, screamed at himself, or cried.... He couldn't; fear won every time.

After an eternity they finally reached their pew, where they had always sat, four rows from the front on the left-hand side of the church, right next to where the deacons sat. His dad squeezed his mom's hand and joined the other deacons. His mom glanced at him briefly and then started to flick through her hymn book.

Pete's mind was still with Captain Burger. Would it really be so bad if everyone thought he was gay? Surely that would blow over as soon as the truth came out. He wondered whether a young black guy and an Indian girl would testify against a white farmer. Would they dare? Would anyone believe them? Indians are not particularly known for their trustworthiness, and the guy, well, he was black. So what was left? His word against Rudie's?

Auntie Bettie's unique interpretation of Beethoven's fifth was euthanized. When Pete lifted his head, he realized that all the men were standing. The Reverend had appeared out of nowhere and stood with outstretched arms on the pulpit. His mom's elbow jabbed him in the ribs. Pete carefully raised his body out of the pew, but the creaking old wood echoed like a tree falling in a forest.

The Reverend must have slept well because he was completely in his prayer zone. He prayed for every sick person by their full names, detailed their diseases and ailments, and of course, he bemoaned the plight of the farmers during the drought. He prayed with fervor for our leaders, from the mayor to the State President, and most in between. Pete's safari suit started to make his thighs itch, so he unlocked his hands from behind his back and slowly snuck a quick scratch. But the itchiness wouldn't relent. He scratched again, only this time he accidentally leaned into the pew and that familiar creaking sound almost drowned out the Reverend's words. Someone coughed behind him. His curiosity reflex made him tilt his head to the right, and peek through his eyelids. Pete thought he was going to throw up right there, mid-prayer. A wave of nausea pushed up from his tummy and waited in his mouth. The taste was that of sickly-sweet fermented nastiness. He tried to swallow but the taste remained. He peeked through his eyelids again—yup, he was going to puke.

Rudie stared right at him. His eyes were wide open and his crooked smile dug into that wispy yellow excuse of a mustache. His red-blond hair was licked down by an extra helping of Brylcreem and his broad shoulders bulged under his faded light-blue jacket. And those dead, gray eyes did not blink. They burned through Pete.

He was now certain he was going to puke. Little convulsions between his neck and his chin became so frequent that he could already see how he was going to lose his morning's Postoasties all over the Smiths in front of them.

"O Lord, in the epoch of your begotten Son, you quenched us with silver streams of living waters—" The Reverend was on a roll. Pete just wanted to sit down, hold his tummy and keep his eyes closed in the hope that when he opened them, Rudie would be gone. Forever.

Once more that pointy elbow found his ribs, only much gentler this time. He felt cold plastic knock against his hip. He glanced at his mom. She was holding out a small water bottle, like the one in his lunchbox. How did she know? Did she see something? The first sip was a small one, but then Pete drank greedily. The cool water broke through the plumes of nausea hovering in his mouth. The relief was instant. He didn't care what she knew or didn't know, she had saved his life.

The Reverend preached about Sodom and Gomorrah, their sinful ways, the lust, the evil homosexual urges of those deplorable people. Gays...

faggots: That's what people thought of them. Whether they were gay or not, evil or not, it didn't matter, it would be the end. The end of his life and everything he had.

Pete took another sip of his mom's water. He had the best part of three years left before he could leave this town and go to whichever university in South Africa was furthest away, or maybe even to Windhoek in South West Africa if that was possible. Three years was a long time to hide, to be shunned, without friends—surely not even Barend would be able to stand by him—without any way to escape. He pictured Captain Burger laughing in his face as he told him. He pictured Renate's disgust, Barend who couldn't look him in the eyes, his parents' eternal disappointment, and Rudie's yellow mustache, and mouth full of dirty teeth, whispering, "I warned you."

The church stood up to sing another hymn. Pete's mouth moved but no sound came out. The words in the hymn book swam in concentric circles and then fell off the page, one by one. The blank page stared back at him, his mom's sweet voice the only thing he could hear. A yearning filled him, for fresh air and wide-open spaces where he could run, and never stop.

After the blessing, everyone left the church. Rudie was nowhere to be seen. The adults congregated on the church hall's large veranda for tea and coffee as the children scurried away to Sunday School. Pete's Sunday School class was in the church hall, up the stairs in a small sun-baked classroom. He suddenly remembered that Uncle Willie had given them homework, an essay on sin or something. Excuses raced through his mind, but nothing useful. Perhaps he should just tell the truth? Now that would be novel. Uncle Willie wouldn't know what hit him. A fifteen-year-old boy telling him that he didn't do his homework because his mind was too messed up by a crime he had witnessed.

"Pete!" The devil's tail swirled in the air and lashed Pete on the chest. It was Rudie, all smiling and chatty, standing with his parents. His large right paw hovered in the air, waiting for Pete to succumb.

"My hand's not going to shake itself, or would you rather like a kiss?" The taste of bile was back.

His parents glared at him, embarrassed by their son's unwillingness to shake this nice man's hand. Pete succumbed. Rudie's hand was like sandpaper and he gripped Pete's hand with gusto. Instead of letting go, Rudie kept on squeezing and squeezing until the pain became unbearable. Pete wrestled his hand away, tried not to rub it, but failed.

"I thought you were some hotshot rugby player, but you can't even take a firm handshake like a man." Rudie laughed from his gut, a hollow, eerie sound, and Pete's parents tried to laugh along but weren't very convincing. Pete gestured toward the hall, words had stopped forming in his mouth.

"I'll see you soon, Pete. You take care of yourself now, okay?" Rudie's voice squashed Pete's intestines and a new taste filled his mouth—heavier, musty and urgent. Pete pushed his way through the tea drinkers until he reached the hall. His class was to the right, but he turned left and ran, up the stage and down the steps at the back, along a corridor to the third door on his left. He flung it open, then opened another door and slammed it shut behind him. He fell to his knees, lifted the toilet seat and waited. His body shook, tears welled up, and then the sluice opened.

KISMET

It was two weeks since that hour spent dry heaving over the church toilet. With the help of his brother's old punching bag, which he rescued from years of dust, his guilt was now almost at a manageable level. The running helped too, but the monotony of doing lap after lap around the primary school's athletics track made him feel as though the cage in his mind was getting smaller every day.

Kismet Supermarket on Dannhauser's Main Street was bustling. It was the day after payday at the Durnacol mine and everyone seemed to believe that all the money not spent immediately would be lost— although for a decent chunk of those working at the mine, most of their wages went straight to Palm Liquors, on the corner of Newcastle Road and Camp Street, not Kismet. Because, as Belchie's dad—a shift boss at Shaft no. 3—liked to say, "Bread makes you fat, but brandy makes you strong."

His mom's black perm floated in between the aisles while Pete meandered around the shop without looking at anything in particular. He would pick things up, and put them back, without registering what they were. Shopping was not his favorite pastime, but this was payday shopping, so he knew if he stayed close enough to his mom, he might be offered a sweet reward. Perhaps a Tempo and a can of Mello Yello. He could almost taste it.

"Have you seen her?" A voice snatched the Mello Yello from his mind. His heart was racing.

Pete turned his head but didn't want to look. Yet, there he was. Muscular and black. His fellow witness and burning ember in the pit of his stomach.

He stood two meters away from him and picked up a large bag of onions. At once Pete's thoughts became a vortex filled with memories of that night. He saw the girl's pleading eyes again, her tears, brushing this black guy's arm, the mud, the gunshots ...calling him the k-word. Pete swung his head from side to side like a tennis umpire, desperately trying to ascertain if anyone had seen the two of them talking—if his mom had seen.

Pete made a nasal grunt followed by a muffled "No," turned and walked away, not looking over his shoulder, in single-minded determination to find his mom and leave.

She was in the queue, with her trolley filled to the top, inspecting a Tempo bar deep in thought. Pete weaved his way through the barricade of trolleys and price checkers, but just as he was about to reach his mom, a bag of onions fell at his feet. The boy leaned in to pick it up and whispered in his achingly strong accent, "Meet me there at the place. We need to talk. Same time—any day." And just like that, he was gone. His mom turned to him and smiled, holding up the Tempo bar. Pete fought the series of small explosions in his head and fabricated a smile that hurt more than the six of the best Mr. Gray had given him.

WORDS

Four days had dragged by after the meeting in Kismet. It consumed Pete's thoughts, at school, at home, and especially alone at night, lying in his bed. What was so urgent? Why did that guy want to talk to him? He played out scenario after scenario—perhaps to pressure Pete into going to the police, or maybe he was after money for his silence. Perhaps he had told people, like Uncle Gerrit, and Uncle Gerrit...Pete forced himself to think of Renate in her short skirt, the wind teasingly playing with it...what if Uncle Gerrit told the police, what if the police confronted the black guy and this was a trap, what if Rudie found out?

"I'm going for a run, Mom." He couldn't decipher his mom's response, but by the time he reached the primary school's athletics track, he was already out of breath. He stopped and looked back at his house; all seemed quiet. The houses behind the single row of pine trees watching over the track had a serenity about them, just like this perfect little town where they lived. Everyone knew each other, everyone grew up together, and everyone knew everything. There were no secrets here. None. Behind this serene facade, what did they know? Did everyone know the truth and were pretending that nothing had happened? It was only an Indian girl after all, not one of "their own."

The horizon was locked away behind a thick gray cloud, the mountains completely hidden behind a shroud of rainless vapor. Pete imagined Uncle Gerrit as the black guy kneeled before him and told him every nauseating detail. He imagined him telling the others in town, perhaps at one of those strange Free Mason meetings where they slaughtered goats and other things—if one were to believe Barend's stories. They would huddle in a dark room illuminated by black candles and take some blood oath to keep it quiet, for the good of the town. Even Captain Burger nodding in agreement. Even the Reverend.

Pete started running, past the pavilion where he couldn't tell Barend the truth, the tennis court with the hole in the gate where kids slipped in to play without Mrs. Muller's permission, and the creaking old corrugated iron shack with its two personas: tuck shop for sporting events, but more regularly, a smoke den for teenage boys.

He didn't run the bend of the track, he ran straight on, across the netball court, to the edge of a steep grassy embankment. At the bottom of the embankment was a rusty razor-wire fence. Pete surveyed the fields beyond the fence for a moment. A few cows grazed to his left and to his right. In the distance, he could see the row of poplar trees he had in his mind. Behind those trees lay the fishing dam with the good clay. And not far from there was...

He had to lean back on his heels to avoid toppling over as he went down the embankment. It was steeper than he recalled from his days as an eight-year-old when they used to close their eyes and slide down it on a piece of cardboard. The damned fence caught his thumb, but with a little hopeful jump, he was over. His mom's words continued to haunt him, "Remember what happened to Bennie's dog." Bennie's dog was shot more or less where he was standing. Uncle Gerrit and his beloved rifles; everyone always had a story about them. Barend claimed he had a collection of over two hundred guns, ready for the terrorists. You would still need two hundred people to shoot them though, but that said, it's not the two hundred guns that bothered him, only the one aimed at *him*.

Running across the uneven fields was slow and uncomfortable, but it was the shortest route and he had to get there before his mind exploded. His eyes were on the mounds and holes in the ground, like dark snares under the cloudy sky, but every couple of breaths he would raise his head to scan his surroundings for a gun-wielding farmer.

The fishing dam came and went, as did the ruins of the old farmhouse, the *Keep Out* sign, the cattle grid and everything else that made him feel sick. When he reached the point where Rudie had stood with his hand shoved down his underpants a few weeks ago, his legs felt dead, lame. Pete shut his eyes. He desperately wanted any memory of that night to be erased—buried somewhere so deep that he would never find it again.

Their hideaway rock was in front of him, and he considered whether it would have been better never to have confronted Rudie. To have just closed his eyes and covered his ears and acted as if nothing had happened.

Had he not gone for a run that day he wouldn't feel like he was aging a hundred times faster than he should. But then that yellow mustached rubbish would have raped the Indian girl—or worse. Would the black guy have stood up then, on his own? Rudie would surely have killed him there and then, just like that, for fun. Because Rudie followed his own laws.

Footsteps. He swung around. It was the black guy. The original aura of mighty King Shaka gone; he jogged up the hill like a small kid who knew he was guilty and was running toward his punishment. He stopped near Pete. Neither of them braved eye contact. Their voices muted by this place that so cruelly introduced them to one another. The easterly breeze blew a waft of yellow dust up between them.

Words spun around in Pete's mind like a lost sock in a washing machine; just as he thought he had one in his grasp, it would dive back into the frothy water. The silence was intolerable, almost painful, but eventually, a single word wriggled free.

"Talk." Really? Of all the words he has been forced to learn, the hours of reading, studying, words from television, out of all of those, *that* was the one to surface?

The black guy seemed surprised and somewhat hurt. The single, poorly chosen word might as well have been a slap across his face. Pete cast out his net for more words, desperate.

"You wanted to talk to me?" To Pete's great relief more actual words made their way over his lips, and they looked like colorful cressets in the gray afternoon.

The tension in the boy's curved jaw eased, and his eyes opened wider.

"I, I just wanted to know if you've seen that girl, maybe—" His voice became mute as if he too was fighting for words.

"No." Was Pete's blunt response, but realized

immediately how cold his answer was, like his dad when Pete asked him a big favor. Come on, words.

"I don't know where she lives...I don't even know what her name is." Pete exhaled, words appeared to be tamer now, easier to catch.

"But that night...I thought you took her home? Was she okay? Did something happen?" Sweat appeared on his brow, murky beads against his dark skin.

"Nothing happened. She just said her dad would... you know, she said, I mean, asked, that I wouldn't take her to her front door. She was fine. Really. Fine."

"I saw her," the black guy said.

"Where?" Pete was surprised by his response, especially at how the thought of seeing her again made him feel.

"There in town. I helped my father deliver eggs to the butchery and I saw her. She walked across the street, but she didn't see me. She went into *Naidoo and Sons* but I didn't see her come out again."

"Do you think she works there?"

The boy shrugged his shoulders. "Maybe."

Pete saw the boy look over his shoulder as if expecting imminent peril. His face started to look strained again, jaw clenched and eyes small.

"Please, you have to go see her, please *baas*?" The words were like a punch in Pete's gut. Of course, he wanted to see her, but fear is a dark shadow. And why did the word *"baas"* suddenly sound so wrong?

"I can't, you know I can't. You heard that man. You'll have to go." Pete gave a snorting laugh. "Besides, imagine the uproar if a white boy spoke to an Indian girl, in *this* town?"

"Believe me, it will be easier for a black boy to kiss

a farmer on the lips than to speak to an Indian girl in public."

Pete believed the angst he saw in his eyes.

"Have you told anyone?" Pete couldn't hold it any longer.

"Told anyone? Are you crazy!" The boy grabbed his mouth. "I'm sorry, I'm sorry, *baas*."

Pete stood unmoved, wondering whether he was indeed crazy.

"No one will listen to a black boy from the farm. No one will listen, and no one will care. If it was a black man who assaulted a pretty white girl, then he would be in prison by now, maybe even executed."

Pete knew it was true. It would have made national news, the man would have been sent away for life if he was lucky. Did people really care less if it was not one of their own, someone who didn't look like them when they looked in the mirror, someone that didn't sound like them, walk like them, someone with a different...

"That man..." The boy interrupted Pete's thoughts. "He said your name is Petrus. Is that true?"

"What's it to you?"

"It's just funny."

"Funny?" Pete felt that original anger well up in him again, like on that day when he first met this boy. Was he making fun of his name? Who the hell did he think he was?

The boy must have seen the flash of anger on Pete's face because his smile disappeared instantly and he looked at Pete with apologetic sorry-I'm-alive eyes.

"I didn't mean...all I meant was...my name is also Petrus."

Great, now this boy thinks we're buddies. If Rudie

found out...

"I'm Pete, no one calls me Petrus." Except of course his mom when he upset her. "It's just some old family name. No one uses it."

"It's a good name, my father is also Petrus." The pride was obvious in the boy's eyes.

"Well, okay then, Petrus, I have to go." The sun was setting but that was not why Pete wanted to escape.

"Will you try to find her?" Petrus asked.

"I don't know. I'll see. I don't know." Pete turned. "I have to go now," he mumbled and started running.

"I come out here every day, just not every Friday and Saturday!" Petrus called out, but Pete didn't respond, he just flinched.

The road home took an eternity, no matter how hard he pushed himself. Seeing Petrus and being back there made him feel like he was walking back home with that girl in the pouring rain all over again. Her face was suddenly before him: her perfect dimples etched on her beautiful face and her long black hair sticking to her cheeks. He turned into Caister Street, ran hard up the hill, stamping his feet deep into the loose gravel of the dirt road, hoping with each stride that her face would be trampled from his memory.

LEGENDS

"Don't get me wrong, last year—as juniors—you played some good rugby, but..." Mr. Theunissen lifted his green-and-yellow John Deere cap and ran his hand over the fluffy remnants of his hair. A black whistle dangled around his neck and his school golf shirt was weathered and half a size too small. He stared into the distance, to where the first and second team boys were running the long way around Dundee High School's sports fields.

"I'm not going to beat around the bush or blow smoke up your arses. We have a settled team full of experienced players. I have good centers and wings in spades—and the same goes for props. I can't see how two...I think you will get better opportunities if you play for the third-or fourth team this year. Next year some of the established boys will have finished Matric, then we might take another look, see if you can cut it at this level. Go and speak to Mr. le Roux, he's expecting you, both of you."

Mr. Theunissen left his words behind, turned and walked to the orange cones stacked near the poles. Pete saw in Barend's face the same emotions he was feeling. Mr. le Roux had been hockey coach and was only coaching rugby this year because the new P.E. teacher was some former hotshot hockey player. Now Mr. le Roux was stuck coaching a sport he hated and didn't understand, with a group of boys as talentless as burned-out charcoal. Thirds and fourths were the wine-and-cheese teams for talentless, lazy and—or —crazy seniors whose only joy in life were brawls on the rugby field.

"If we play for those teams we're done." Barend's eyes begged Pete for some wisdom.

"I know." Pete turned toward the twenty or so unfit boys laying on their backs near the pavilion: the mighty thirds and fourths. Mr. le Roux sat on an old school chair writing down names.

"Here's what we're going to do," Pete said and Barend stepped closer, hopeful. "We'll play thirds."

"What? No hell, we'll be—" Barend appeared close to tears, but Pete continued.

"We'll play thirds for two games. And we'll play like demons. I will slice open defenses and you will destroy scrums. Then, after two games, we'll go back to Mr. Theunissen and say we deserve a shot. He'll say no, but then we'll threaten to stop playing rugby altogether."

"I'm no psychologist, but I don't think he is the type who likes to be threatened," Barend said.

"Well, tough. I'm not going to be stuck in thirds for the rest of the year. I don't know about you, but if I can't play firsts or at least seconds, then I might as well train hard on my own all year and make them all look like primary school kids next year." Barend took a moment to consider the plan, staring into the blue yonder.

"I'm in," he said suddenly. "Heaven knows, Philippa will never, ever look at anyone playing thirds. It'll be better not to play at all. We'll do weights and stuff, you know, bulk up good and proper."

"I tell you, dude, we'll show them. He who laughs last..." Pete said.

"Is the only survivor," Barend replied.

They giggled at their old joke for a few seconds and then headed toward Mr. le Roux.

A few boys sat up as they approached. "Well, look who we have here, boys! Junior superstars!" a boy with a belly that wobbled like jelly shouted. The other boys laughed.

"Kicked out of Mr. Theunissen's elite squad after two milliseconds. Must be some kinda record," another shouted and the laughter grew louder.

"Okay, okay, enough now," Mr. le Roux said.

"Positions," he asked.

"On their knees taking it like—"

"I said enough!" Mr. le Roux shouted at jelly-belly. He scratched in his ear with his pen and turned back to Pete and Barend. "Well, have you swallowed your tongues?" All the boys laughed.

Pete surveyed those around him; most of these guys were older than him. Quite a few were in Matric, but it was unlikely that the vast majority of those would ever receive a Matric certificate. Some were school legends, notorious for the things they did—although Pete was convinced that most of those stories were myths. Who, for instance, actually believed that Klayton had sex with Miss Schultz, the young German teacher, in the senior toilets? Who believed that Lawrence had caught a puffadder and released it into Headmaster Eyler's office? Although it would explain Mr. Eyler's sudden resignation from the school. And surely there was no chance that Clive blew up a toilet with kalium—was there? What was kalium anyway?

"Center, sir, and he's a prop," Pete said and pointed to Barend.

"Tighthead prop," Barend added.

"I'll show you a tight head, you stinking fat Dutchman," Clive, the kalium legend, shouted, with his greasy black hair, black eyes and the scar above his left eye, and pretended to pull down his pants.

Mostly the rivalry between the Afrikaans and English kids was lighthearted, just regular banter and the odd reference to the Anglo-Boer-war or something about the great British Empire or concentration camps. It rarely went any further than playing soccer against each other or tag rugby, the English kids calling the Afrikaans kids Dutchmen or rock spiders and the Afrikaans kids calling the English kids rednecks or salties. All fairly benign, all pretty friendly. But there were a few of the English guys who always took it too far, who never hid their disdain for anything remotely Afrikaans. Clive was one of the worst. Klayton and Lawrence not far behind.

"Welcome aboard," Mr. le Roux said, ignoring Clive. "We practice Tuesdays and Thursdays. And we need more players. We'll need at least forty players to fill two teams, plus reserves. Any suggestions?" Mr. le Roux spread his arms open to the boys.

"Well, sir, seeing that you just signed up two girls, perhaps we can ask the hockey and netball girls if they want to play for us," Lawrence (puffadder legend) called out.

Pete could feel the anger well up in him. He knew his ears went bright red. He wanted to punch a hole through Lawrence's hideous face, but Barend stretched his arm out as soon as he took his first step.

"Try it, bitch, I dare you, try it. I won't roll over and play dead like that fagface, Devon. Come on!" Lawrence mocked.

Pete sized him up. Lawrence was shorter than him and smaller, a stringy bag of sinews—with a fighter's reputation, *and* a winning reputation. Others stood up too: Clive, short and slight—no problem—and Klayton, taller and bigger than him. Three notorious legends against him. He took a deep breath.

"Okay, that's enough fun and games for today," Mr. le Roux said.

"Time for some fitness. Four laps of the fields then meet back here." He blew hard on his whistle.

Barend tugged at Pete's rugby jersey, and they started jogging.

"Relax, all you'll get from fighting those guys is a broken bottle in your neck," Barend said in a calm tone as soon as they reached a safe distance from the others.

"They think they're so bloody tough," was all Pete could get out. He ran out ahead of Barend, the warm air pressing against his face. He was trying to breathe evenly, to calm down.

The whistle rang out across the sports fields. He turned around and saw Barend struggling behind him. None of the other boys moved a muscle, still lazing around on the grass ignoring the cherry-faced Mr. le Roux.

By the time Pete and Barend finished their fourth lap, there were no boys left, just Mr. le Roux. He sat in the shade of the pavilion, gazing up at the deep blue sky.

"Training's over boys," he said. "Better move it

before the bus leaves you behind." He looked back up at the sky as if they ceased to exist. Pete turned to Barend and shook his head in disbelief.

The sports bus back to Dannhauser was filled with sweaty teenagers. It was quiet, and many sat with their knees lifted against the front backrests getting ready to sleep. Pete tried to sleep but couldn't get comfortable in his seat and shifted position several times, without success.

An hour later, the bus stopped in front of the petrol station. Sleepy kids trickled off the bus and Pete stared vacantly at the kids disappearing to different parts of town. The bus left for Durnacol to take the remaining kids on the bus home to their souless mining village five kilometers away.

"You coming?" Barend asked.

"Nah, I have to...Uhm...go to Kismet quickly," Pete replied.

"Cool, see you tomorrow," Barend mumbled and turned in the direction of his house as if programmed.

Pete tried to walk off the sleepiness, passing the pharmacy and Dr. Bayat's surgery. The bus station was packed with people waiting patiently for buses. For a fleeting moment he wondered where all these colorful people were going, but just as quickly his sleepiness took hold again and his thoughts disappeared into a thick fog.

Tip Top came and went as did the Eating House and Cassem's. He didn't notice anyone on the streets, like a blanket was pulled over his head. He had very limited thoughts, only vacantly mulling over his confrontation with Lawrence, Clive, and Klayton, until the letters rose up above him, big and blue, and the blanket was torn off him: *Naidoo and Sons*. His feet stopped. The letters swam around like sharks circling their prey. He was wide awake now.

He knew *Naidoo and Sons* well, mostly because it had the only pool table in town. He and Barend enjoyed playing there, even if it occasionally meant challenging a few Indian boys to gain rights to the table. He searched the outer reaches of his mind for any memory of the girl in the times he had been there, but there was nothing. Zilch. Was Petrus mistaken? He was only a farmboy, maybe...

His mind kept jumping and he was struggling to keep up. He realized that *Naidoo and Sons* consisted of two adjoining shops: one with the pool table and everything from fishing tackle to videos, and the other was more of a textile shop. Perhaps she worked there? That would be much better suited for a girl, rather than being surrounded by the constant stream of testosterone flowing around the pool table.

Pete jogged across the street. From up close the shop suddenly appeared colossal. All the moisture had evaporated from his mouth and his throat was tight. He peeked into the main shop, to where he could see the pool table. Two Indian boys were standing around drinking Fanta Grape, but she wasn't there.

He forced his legs to take him to the textile shop. Colorful materials adorned the windows, but it was dark inside. His head dropped, he sighed and looked at the dust-filled cracks in the concrete paving slabs at his feet.

A movement from inside the shop drew his attention. Was that her?

DONOR

Venny sat in his uncomfortable chair, tugging at the frayed ends of its small red-and-purple cushion. He tried flipping through one of his old folders with newspaper clippings of the Soweto uprising and Sharpville massacre. Then he put it aside and adjusted the volume on his radio again, to make sure the silence wasn't his fault. He kept flicking the microphone's switch on and off. To make matters worse, he'd already finished his cup of tea.

"Protea Eleven, this is Protea Ten. Confirm your password." Venny's whole body tensed up. He flicked the microphone's switch again, started speaking, but realized he'd switched it off.

He almost knocked the microphone over in trying to switch it on again. "Paulpietersburg. The password is Paulpietersburg."

The thing he hated most about these conversations was that Protea Ten could never just reply straight away. No, this piece of obtuse rubbish always had to wait for an age before he uttered another word.

"Password accepted," Protea Ten said just as Venny was about to start adjusting the radio again.

"Command is planning a series of initiatives."

"What kind of initiatives? Does this mean I can—"

"Protea Eleven, restrain yourself, no interruptions during a message."

Venny wanted to apologize but didn't want to

appear weak, so he pushed the microphone away.

"These initiatives will have a significant impact and will fast-track the way to our end goal. But as you know so well: the government has introduced increasing measures to thwart our plans. This is slowing down our efforts...and it's making everything more expensive."

Here we go again. He always volunteered to be part of the action, but all they ever wanted was money. Money, money, money. *Money for what?* he wanted to shout out.

"If you use your special talents to persuade like-minded individuals, true soldiers of our fight, *comrades*, like you, to come together and invest in the future, in freedom, then Protea Eleven, then..." Another one of Protea Ten's drawn-out silences. Then what? Venny wished he could reach out through the microphone and give him a slap around the ears. "Command is willing to consider you for the vacant Protea Eight position."

His mind raced. Yes, he was angry for always being considered a cash cow and boy; they had bled him dry, but word on the street was that Protea Eight was involved in something so big that he was now locked up on Robben Island. Imagine that. He was rubbing shoulders with the leaders of the movement. Venny's heart beat faster; the mere thought of getting so close to the epicenter of this cause he had devoted the past five years of his life to was almost too good to be true. He wondered if he truly had it in him.

"Protea Eleven, please confirm message received."

"Message received."

"Report back in one week. Protea Ten out."

"One week, yes, understood," Venny rattled off excitedly, but Protea Ten had already stopped the transmission.

He picked up the empty cup and tilted it so that the last remaining drop of sweet, cold tea trickled onto his tongue. The room felt smaller, and the stacks of documents seemed like chimneys billowing out thick airless smoke. He was Venny, the man with the quick wit, a man of influence, a man without fear. Why now, standing at the precipice of greatness, why now start to doubt, fear, tremble? He flapped his hands about but the trembling didn't relent.

"Pappa! Dinner's ready." The fluttering of his daughter's sweet voice was like a warm blanket being wrapped around him.

"I know you're busy, but Mamma started calling you Venkatapathi, so I think you're in trouble." She giggled.

How he loved that giggle. After his dad had drawn his last breath, the only thing that helped him through the second greatest loss of his life was that giggle. When his brother decided to take his share of the family money and seek a fortune in Chatsworth, leaving him to start from scratch, it was that giggle, again, that got him through. And, five years ago...

"I'll be right there." He rubbed his hands together and slapped himself on the cheeks. *Okay, Venny, toughen up, remember why you are doing this,* he reprimanded himself.

BOLLYWOOD

Thursday's so-called rugby practice was about as useful to their rugby education as a pickax was for changing a light bulb. Only he and Barend were doing laps of the sports fields, whilst the other boys, who had now grown to a group of thirty-five, sat around ignoring the increasing shrillness of Mr. le Roux's whistle. Later, with his rugby socks around his ankles, sports bag in one hand and schoolbag over his shoulder, Pete stood in front of *Naidoo and Sons* again. This time he saw an older Indian woman in the textile shop—probably her mom—selling a strip of green and silver paisley fabric to a smartly dressed woman. The darkness deeper inside the shop made it difficult to distinguish between what was textile and what was possibly her. Before he could even start considering how strange it must have seemed for a teenage boy in sweaty rugby gear to stare at sari's and rolls of fabric, his feet had taken him halfway home again.

He started going to bed later and later in the desperate hope that through pure exhaustion sleep would find him and carry him safely away from Rudie's incessant fiendish laughter into the open arms of the morning.

It didn't work.

He felt like a hamster, trapped in a wheel, because it was Sunday again and regardless of how much his intestines protested, his parents insisted he attend church. Each week the walk up the church steps had become increasingly terrifying. That gaping black chasm into which he was hoarded like a lamb to a slaughterhouse was now above all things, even sleep, the thing he feared most. The two people in the world he wanted to avoid at all costs lay in wait in that dark place. Captain Burger: his guilt that was slowly consuming his soul, like a waterfall of acid, spilling over everything he once believed in, everything he once thought, eating away, corroding his being. And Rudie: the devil.

Thankfully this Sunday the devil stayed away, and Pete sat in the Sunday School class nodding every time Uncle Willie looked in his direction, but it was only his body that was there. His mind scoured every shadow he saw through the *Naidoo and Sons* shop window, or at least, what he thought he saw.

So there he was again. It was a Monday afternoon, just past 3 o'clock. The bus came and went, as did Barend and all the others. The streets were quiet, and a warm breeze dragged its feet across the melting tarmac. The blue-and-white sign gaped down at him. He heard Petrus's words over and over again in his mind, "Please, you have to go see her, please *baas*?"

Before his mind had time to react, he stormed into the textile shop. It was cool inside and a strong smell of incense wafted through the dark shop. His eyes scanned through the jumble of color spun around him like a spider's web, but he couldn't see anyone. He turned quickly, grabbed the door handle, relieved to escape, but a voice from behind stopped him.

"Can I help you?" He turned around slowly and saw an Indian woman in a purple-and-orange sari, and a bright red dot on her forehead. Her hair was tied back in a plait, her glare accusatory, as if she could read his mind.

"Nah, I'm okay," he muttered, pulled the door open and escaped to the bright day and the warm breeze. She wasn't there, what more could he do? He tried his best, there was nothing more he could do. He couldn't go to her house, he didn't even know where she lived. Perhaps Petrus was wrong, perhaps she didn't even work here. Maybe she had left town. Yes, that would make sense, maybe she went to Durban, or even back to India. Yes, that would make a lot more sense.

He blinked, shook his head and looked up. Somewhere through the spewing geyser of his thoughts, something appeared in the periphery of his vision. All his focus turned to the larger of the two *Naidoo and Sons* shops. He heard a muffled shout, glass breaking. His thoughts jumped to *that* night, his mind's eye already picturing Rudie pinning the girl down on the pool table, her hair draped over her face and his tall frame casting the shadow of the devil over her. She just lay there, hopeless, waiting for him to destroy her.

The shop's door flung open. Two young Indian boys stormed out laughing impishly. Behind them, an Indian man appeared. His long fringe flopped up as he was running to reveal the true extent of his baldness. He was a little overweight and his trousers sat high up on his belly. He waved a finger in the air and shouted something in a language Pete didn't understand as he set off after the kids.

Pete stood there knowing that at some point in his life the memory of this middle-aged man chasing down two kids would make him laugh—now was not that time. He drew a deep breath, and again licked the corner of his dry mouth and walked to the shop door. The door was plastered with stickers of things for sale: Fish Licenses, Bicycle Licenses, Firecrackers, Fishing Tackle, Video Hire, Plumbing Accessories. The list was long, but without realizing it, his hand had pushed the door open and he was inside.

It was not as cool as the shop next door and there was no incense burning. It smelled of old cigarettes and Fanta Orange. To the left, on the pool table, a few balls were scattered on the faded green baize, in between two light brown pool cues. On the floor were a broken Fanta bottle and hundreds of tiny shards covered in bright orange liquid.

A door swung open somewhere beyond the broken bottle. First, he only heard footsteps, but then he saw a broom—in her hands. She didn't see him. Her eyes firmly fixed on the mess on the floor. Only with her second sweep did she look up. Her eyes were even lighter than he recalled, her hair tied back in a plait, with one long black strand swinging blissfully free from the others. She wore a blue apron over her school uniform: a plain white long-sleeve shirt, and a long gray skirt covering her ankles. She appeared different somehow, but maybe even more beautiful. A warm flush began to glow in his ears, and something squeezed hard at his gut.

"Have you told anyone?" Damn it, again. His mouth was a traitor. A rude traitor. And this after everything he wanted to say.

The girl came closer. She peered anxiously in the shop door's direction. Pete's tongue turned into the Namib desert.

"Shhh, please, quiet," she whispered. Her eyes were big, and her lips pouted in perfect symmetry.

"I mean...are you okay?" Pete was slightly happier with this follow-up effort.

She nodded but her gaze dropped to the floor.

"You can't be here, my dad..." she started softly, but her words were gobbled up by the silence.

"You didn't, I mean, you haven't?" Pete pictured his 1983 Junior Debate winner's medal in his parents' bedroom and wondered what had happened to that articulate boy.

Her gaze danced about feverishly.

"Of course not." She finally looked him straight in the eyes. He wanted to look away but couldn't.

"My family would kill me. Just the suggestion that I might have lost my—" Her hand shot over her mouth. "I will never tell anyone." Her head dropped.

"But you're okay?" Pete said. It felt as if his tongue was glued to the roof of his mouth.

She looked up, her eyes anchored in his, then a smile slowly curled into her dimples.

The door swung open and a stream of warm air surged into the shop. Pete grabbed the nearest video to him. When he looked up, he saw the girl dutifully sweeping up the mess under the pool table.

"Can I help?" her dad asked behind Pete, out of breath and confused. Pete saw the Bollywood video in his hand, his eyes stumbled over its strange title, *Dharm Aur Qanoon*.

He cleared his throat. "Firecrackers?" he asked

and slipped the video back into its slot.

The man led him to the counter with an enormous sign hanging above it which read: FIRECRACKERS. The man started taking out various rolls of crackers and tossed them in front of Pete. Pete didn't make eye contact and fought every urge he had to sneak a peek at the girl over his shoulder. He took a roll of red firecrackers, handed over twenty-five cents and escaped into the daylight. It was only when he reached the tranquility of the outside world that he realized that he had just wasted half his weekly pocket money on firecrackers, something he detested, but it was worth every cent.

The warm breeze had died down, and the afternoon sun lashed out at anyone breaking cover. Cool streams of sweat rolled down his back, and the school bag bounced uncomfortably against his hip. He tried to adjust the strap holding the bulging weight of his schoolbooks. His knees were weak as he walked, his thighs felt as though the muscles were simply going to peel off his bones, but there was a small smile hiding in the corner of his mouth. He didn't want his mind to wander. Every time his mind started drifting, he would focus on something on the pavement or in the shop windows with renewed interest.

Amidst this internal battle, a door suddenly flung open in front of him. It was Jeevan's Corner Shop, the cheapest place in town to buy Mello Yello. A young Indian woman stepped out of the hazy shop into the bright sunshine. Her long black hair glistened and danced in the breathless afternoon and her chocolate brown eyes smiled playfully at him. Her skin glowed like a light was burning inside her. Pete's tongue was as dry as a bone. Actually, every part of him felt dry. His eyes were bound to her as she glided across the street, her perfect hair frolicking in the warm air, and then she disappeared. He pressed his thumb hard on the little patch of skin between his eyes. His head felt heavy and his school bag was busy tearing his shoulder in two. First *her*, now this one. What was happening to him? It wasn't even natural, they were Indians.

The breeze started again just like a movie after an interval, and a plastic bag rolled by him, followed by a puff of dust. But Pete could not move, only his shadow shifted as the sun inched closer to the horizon.

THE TEAM

The night before, the easterly wind at its piercing best proclaimed that winter had plans. Cold, nasty ones. Even though it was only March this was a blunt forewarning to the people of Dannhauser. His mom said they might have snow in town again this year, which made Pete excited. He loved the snow. He loved how it covered the gray winter landscape in a blanket of perfect white, all the harshness transformed into a soft layer of magic. Now, however, he was standing with his hands on his hips, fighting to get his breath back. Mr. le Roux was telling the cheese-and-wine-team exactly how useless they were, not just regular useless, but bottom-feeding, runt-of-the-litter, rotten apple useless.

For once Pete agreed with him. This bunch of dim-wits gawking at Mr. le Roux with disdainful disinterest was lazy first and foremost, and secondly, and probably more alarmingly, without a shred of talent to back up their air of superiority. Worst of all was that he, dynamic up-and-coming center, was just as bad as the lot of them. He had stepped in their trap by listening to their relentless slating, training session after training session, and seeing how their laziness benefitted them. Now he too had become a very passive participant who subconsciously tried to fit into this group of misfits. In sharp contrast, his best friend for whom acceptance had always been just as important as sandwiches, shamed him by training like a man possessed, despite the torturous scorn from the others.

Pete wondered why he was so weak. Why he'd just given up? Could *that* night truly be the reason?

"Pete, a quick word." Mr. le Roux said. While the group was drudging away he walked back to Mr. le Roux. His coach still wore his Dundee High School hockey cap to every practice and spent most of the training sessions gazing longingly out toward the hockey fields.

"We've arranged warm-up matches against Mr. Theunissen's squads next Thursday. It'll give them a chance to prepare before their upcoming rugby tour." Pete wondered why Mr. le Roux had the look of someone about to break up with his girlfriend. The mere thought of going on a rugby tour sounded in-credible. He could see the tour bus cross the moun-tains, with him at the window, the first-team scarf wrapped around his neck, and perhaps, when the bus returned, he could remain behind, wherever that may be, anywhere but here.

Mr. le Roux fidgeted with his cap.

"I'm just going to say it. I know you have big rugby ambitions, but frankly, Pete, you've shown me bugger all: no guts, no drive. I'm going to start you on the fourth team. It's just a warmup game, but you need to pull up your socks and show me something before the league games start. Otherwise, you'll be in fourths all year. Am I making myself clear?" Pete's gaze was transfixed by the shadow cast over his coach's face. He could see himself walking away from the tour bus, down a long tree-lined street where he turned right and skyscrapers emerged out of the red dust like ant-hills. He kept walking, down a street with no one on it, opened the doors of one of the anthill skyscrapers, the cool rush of air conditioning flowing over him, and then he disappeared—forever.

"Pete, am I making myself clear?" Mr. le Roux seemed somewhat annoyed but also too bored with the conversation to commit to any emotion.

"Uh-huh. As clear as a mountain stream," Pete mumbled.

"You call me sir or Mr. le Roux, and you don't 'uh-huh' me." He was now fully committed to an emotion: He was livid. Pete smiled. Those words, or perhaps the tone in Mr. le Roux's voice, reminded him of that night, of Petrus, and how he had discovered a part of himself for the first time.

"If you laugh at me, you're out of fourths. Hell, you'll never play for any team in this school again!" Mr. le Roux's voice broke and he pulled his cap up so that it resembled a sinking ship on his head.

"I apologize, Mr. le Roux, sir." Pete's smile pounded against his mouth like a mosquito bite begging to be scratched. He had to bite hard on his bottom lip. Mr. le Roux waved him away and stormed off. Pete chuckled for a moment and thought about this man who had just lost his cool and thought about himself. He was Mr. le Roux. He must have looked like a total idiot, just short of loony, when he acted just like that two months ago. His smile faded and he stared at the grass. A sadness consumed him, out of nowhere; it had no face, no voice, but it was loud and urgent, and there was nowhere to run.

The sports bus's hooter yelped in the distance. He

dragged his sadness and sports bag up the embankment, through the bus door, past the impatient driver, past Barend, who would be playing without him for the third team next week, right to the back, alone on the broken bench. Just him and the churning sinkhole inside him.

FORGETTING

Venny's hand caressed the blue flowery patterns on the armrest of his oversized lounge chair. He loved the chair, even though it made his lower back ache, and its fabric was now so worn that the cushion underneath was showing. It was the first piece of furniture he ever bought, the place Sarita fell asleep in his arms for the first time, and the place he was sitting the last time he spoke to his dad. Sadness, anger, and nostalgia intertwined inside him. He missed his dad, his wisdom, his level-headedness, his smell. Or rather, his lack of smell. All around smells always dominated every room, every street, from freshly ground masala, to sweet, warm tea, and the floral song of his wife's perfume. But his dad's unique smell was nothing, even his clothes smelled of nothing. What he would give to smell nothing right now.

He lifted his hand from the armrest in the hope that these invading emotions would pull back into the chair. It didn't. He thought of Sarita lying in his arms, two days old, tiny, the smallest thing he had ever held. He held her close, his arms shielding her from the world. Against wind and rain, thieves and thugs, lies, boys...sorrow.

He could still recall her big baby eyes searching, seeing every inch of his soul—he had never felt so naked, so vulnerable, but so strong all at the same time. A strength he had never seen, a knowing that even if he was torn to pieces, those pieces would still protect her. When she finally drifted off to sleep, it was the closest thing he had ever seen to pure contentment.

He shook his head, stood up from the chair and gave it his best accusatory stare.

"Sarita!" he shouted.

Her hurried footsteps echoed through the house. Venny looked at the chandelier his mom gave them as a wedding present. Its size always surprised him, so too how intricate the crystal-like glasswork was, floating in the air like icicles. Twenty years later and he still despised it. He wondered if he could accidentally swing something through the air and smash it into millions of pieces. He smiled.

"You look happy, Pappa?" Sarita said, surprised. He just adored it when she spoke Hindi with her unique accent, even though he knew she preferred English.

"Come, my little river child, come sit." It was what he had called her from birth and even though he knew she was probably too old for that now, it just always reminded him of that moment in his arms, when she was two days old.

"Achala, where's my tea? The child is here, we're waiting!" He was annoyed, but then turned to Sarita and gave a cheeky smile.

"That stove needs replacing," Achala, his wife of twenty years, moaned. She stopped next to him and shoved a cup of tea into his hand, making a few drops spill onto the saucer.

All he could do was sigh and wonder why she had such a short fuse. She waddled to the chair opposite where Sarita was sitting. He studied her portly figure shrouded under a green-and-beige sari and thought of the girl he had met twenty years ago. She was fresh off the boat. After months of intense negotiations, his parents and hers agreed to this union. He remembered waiting outside in the vegetable patch where his new silk shirt started to stick to the perspiration on his chest. It wasn't a warm day, it was this time of year, late March. A cool breeze floated through the garden and cooled everything except him. He would meet her that day, one month before the wedding, as was arranged. They would have one hour together and then the next time they spoke would be as husband and wife.

Arranged marriages always struck him as a very strange way of doing things, particularly when he was a teenager, and never more so than after he met Ruhi.

His memories picked him up and whisked him away to the shade of a black wattle tree, with Dannhauser in the distance, the sticky feel of grass under him and Ruhi's silky, cool hand in his. Her eyes were almost blue, although most said it was gray. To him, it was the blue of the sky just as the sun was about to raise its head. Her hair teased her shoulders, fluttering like butterflies, and her mouth tasted like mango. Ripe, sweet, juicy.

But now as a father of a beautiful daughter, he knew the importance of finding the right husband for her. What would she know of love anyway? He and Ruhi were different. No, Sarita would have to wait until he found a man who could take care of her properly and deserved her. These things couldn't be left in the hands of a child; marriage was far too important to be spoiled by some fleeting whim or crush.

Sarita looked at him as if she was in trouble. Yes, he was hard on her, but a firm hand cultivated an adult of repute, integrity, and purity. He could never look at her for too long. As soon as that smile of hers curled into her dimples, he was just too weak to be firm. In those moments she was the two-day-old baby falling asleep in his arms, all over again.

Achala appeared to be bored, annoyed, angry, in fact, at all of them, or any of them, at any given time. He wondered where that shy twenty-one-year-old girl had disappeared to. She was so quiet, so soft-spoken, with the sweetest, most innocent—almost childlike—sense of humor. He liked her from the start, in fact, he still liked her, despite the changes—cosmetic and otherwise. But he often wondered if she knew, if her rage came from knowing that she could never be Ruhi.

"I see your father is daydreaming again. My child, we wanted to speak to you about something," Achala said, annoyed.

Venny sat down carefully in his chair, almost afraid to touch anything, balancing his cup of tea in his left hand.

"You are sixteen years old now. Your mother and I have spoken about our visits to Dādī. We know the last few have not been, well, particularly easy for you." Venny thought of his mother sitting upright under her bleached white bedsheet, her eyes like black holes, and the warm cup of tea she hurled at Sarita, shouting, "Run, child, run! The fire will burn you alive, the stones will break your back and flames will rain on you. Run!" And it wasn't even the first time.

Sarita tilted her head and leaned on her hand. She produced something resembling a smile, but Venny could feel her unease.

"We think it might be best, just for a short time, if you didn't go with us to see Dādī." Venny watched his daughter closely, his words seemed to lift some sort of yoke from her as her face lit up, and her smile was real, contained, but real nevertheless. He gave a sigh of relief: They were doing the right thing.

"This presents you with a wonderful opportunity to learn some responsibility. In the next five years, you will be married and starting a family of your own." His voice cracked slightly—she was just a little girl.

He cleared his throat. "So now is the time to become the woman you were born to be, one who will be diligent, hardworking, loyal, and above all a dedicated wife and mother."

"Very melodramatic, Venkatapathi," Achala said, rolling her eyes.

"Have I finished talking?" Being interrupted was high up on the list of things he hated the most. He glared at Achala. She used his full name, another thing he detested. Some ridiculous family name that was preordained by his mother, who was now crippled by Alzheimer's, or choosing to go crazy, as Achala called it. His tolerance of his wife had steadily decreased over the years, and now very few conversations ended without some hurtful remark. He missed that shy, soft-spoken girl in the gold-and-maroon sari he had met late March in 1966. The one who could barely look him in the eyes for more than a second without letting a smile reveal her thoughts. He struggled to recall the last time he had seen that smile.

"What I was trying to say, is that we want you to work in the shop on Sundays while we visit Dādī."

"But the shop is closed on Sundays." Sarita said.

"Not to do business. You will be cleaning, sorting out the shelves and promotional items, unpacking, taking stock...things like that," Venny explained.

"I already work there every day, and do all the—"

"Sarita, this is not open for discussion. Do you have any idea how much trust we are placing in you? We are leaving you on your own. And all we're asking in return is that you contribute. Help. Make the most of that time. And working in the shop, our family's liveli-hood, is making the most of that time. Understood?"

Sarita opened her mouth to say something, but quickly shut it, looked down and said, "Yes, Pappa."

Later while Achala and Sarita were cooking up a storm in the kitchen, Venny decided to slip out of the house. It was a free Sunday, one of the few where he didn't have to drive to Glencoe to listen to his mother asking them who they were and telling them how bad the food was. Today he was going to eat way too much and take a long nap, something he didn't do nearly enough. But first, he had to unpack the two boxes of videos that arrived the day before, to get ready for the new week.

He fumbled with his keys. "The bunch is too big now," he muttered. After he finally managed to get the right key, he pushed the door open and walked into the dark, deserted shop. It was his favorite time in the shop, no one else around, just him.

"Hey, you open?" The voice of a young man wafted in through the open door.

When he turned around, a tall, powerfully built man with a wide-brimmed leather hat and a sparse yellow mustache stared at him. The man looked at him as if he was in the way. He knew him.

"No, we're closed on Sundays. Sorry," Venny said.

"You look open to me. Get me ten rolls of firecrackers, those nice big ones, five medium sinkers and one of those videos you hide in the back."

"I'm really sorry, Mister Rudie, but we don't have a license to trade on Sundays. Now, please excuse me," Venny said and started thinking about which box to unpack first.

"Now listen here, you piece of shit, you're open when I tell you you're open. So move that fat curry arse of yours and go get the *baas* what he asked for." Rudie walked into the shop, almost knocking Venny down in the process, and started taking things off the shelves.

"Rudie, I—"

Rudie swung around, grabbed Venny by the collar and lifted him against the counter.

"I don't think you heard me. Go get my stuff, or I will throw you and your fat wife in the sea so that you can swim back to where you belong. Bloody curry muncher!" Rudie raised Venny off the ground with ease and threw him over the counter. He landed hard on his back, his arms outstretched. The room took a few seconds to stop spinning before he could see Rudy flicking items off the shelves and stuffing a whole Bar-One into his mouth.

"Okay, okay!" Venny said and tried to push himself off the floor.

Rudie grabbed a handful of Wonder Bars and

shoved them into his pockets, all the while looking straight at Venny. Smugness dancing in his dark eyes. Venny's hands were shaking and with a sharp pain in his lower back, he rifled through the drawer in front of him and slapped ten rolls of firecrackers on the counter. Then he walked to the back of the shop and came back with five medium sinkers and a video with a black and white paper cover with the words *Deep Throat 2* on it.

"Let me see," Venny scribbled on a small notepad. "Eight rands fifty."

Rudie took the items on the counter and sauntered to the door.

Venny walked after him. His eye caught a large hunting knife with a camouflage-colored handle in his shop window next to the door. He allowed his imagination to feel what it would be like to thrust the knife deeper and deeper into this arrogant, white asshole's back. Until he moaned like a little bitch.

"It's eight rands fifty!" Venny shouted but Rudie was already outside. Rudie turned with a big smile. His eyes like dark blue pits.

"Didn't you just say that you weren't allowed to trade on Sundays?" Rudie walked away, but paused in front of Achala's textile shop, snorting snot deep to the back of his nose, before spitting out the mucus ball against the window.

Venny stormed into the shop, snatching at the hunting knife in clumsy haste. He ran outside, but only came as far as the large ball of spit slowly creeping down the window in front of a bright orange gown. He rubbed his thumb over his mustache and aimed to throw the knife as far as he could but restrained himself. At the last second, he lowered his arm, walked back into the shop and locked the door behind him. He sat cross-legged on the floor, staring at the crumpled Bar-One wrapper next to him. He muttered, "Is this a life? Is this *my* life?"

THE TALK

The moment every teenager dreaded was knocking on Pete's door. Literally.

Over the last few weeks, he had noticed how his dad seemed to have cotton wool stuck under his tongue every time he saw Pete, and how he appeared to be petrified at the mere thought of spending more than ten seconds in Pete's presence. Later he would hear his mom scold his dad behind their bedroom door with a muted voice. It could only mean one thing, but life would have been so much better if this cup could have passed him by. Why couldn't they just let it go?

Surely the better solution would have been for his dad to stick a book in his hand and tell him he would be there if he had any questions. But that knock on his bedroom door sounded far too uncertain, far too faint and filled with trepidation, to be of a man who was about to deliver a book and flee. No, he was afraid his dad was here for *the talk*.

"Pete, can I come in?" His dad's usually powerful voice was meek and soft.

"Okay," Pete said, but in his mind, he was shouting, "No! Go away, give me a book if you must!"

His dad looked like an eight-year-old boy who had just been caught stealing pomegranates from his neighbor. The tall Rikus de Lange sat down on the edge of Pete's desk chair. He studied the posters on the wall above Pete's bed seemingly ignoring the fact that his son was sitting on the bed right in front of him.

"I, uhm, we..." He cleared his throat.

"Your mom and I wanted to...we thought it might be time for a little chat. You're just a kid. Aggh, I mean, you are not a kid anymore. You're practically sixteen, almost a man, eh?" His dad forced a smile and looked at Pete quizzically, almost imploringly, hoping that his comment would make Pete smile, but Pete couldn't react; his brain wasn't able to process humor right now.

"So, it's time we talked. Man to man. About, women. Girls. Not young ones, I mean, like, women-girls. You know, girls who are old enough...not that you are old enough...listen, these things should stay between a man and woman, a husband, and wife, in marriage. With true love." Pete cringed on his bed. His discomfort was almost excruciating, although there was a small part of him that enjoyed seeing his dad squirm like this. His dad was flushed, like the inside of a ruby grapefruit.

"When two people, a husband and wife, love each other, they...on their wedding night...to make babies...they. Look, what they do, is..." Pete couldn't take it anymore. Initially, he enjoyed watching his dad squirm, but as it went on, he realized he much preferred the man who made comments about the news, the man who taught him how to play rugby, and the man who fixed everything with duct tape. He didn't like or know who this stuttering mess of a man in front of him was and he was not ready to find out how his dad would explain the facts of life to him. The tiny part of him that was curious as to how his dad would go about it had suddenly vanished. He had enough rubbish on his mind; he didn't need this memory too.

"Dad," Pete interjected. His dad seemed grateful to be saved from his own words. "I know. They taught us about that at school. In biology."

"I was under the impression that they only taught that at Standard Nine level?" his dad said and exhaled slowly.

"They sort of taught us about reproduction and the discussion kind of went from there. Anyway, I know, so relax, Dad, I'm good." They hadn't talked about it in biology of course, but Pete had read *What Boys Want to Know* in Standard Four, and sex dominated most conversations at school. So he knew enough, but he wasn't going to bore his dad with the finer details of his sex education.

Rikus looked like a hatching chick who after much effort had finally broken out of its shell. Suddenly he sat upright, and his eyes were full of life.

"So, you know all of it? The whole thing?" Rikus must have realized he hadn't done a sterling job at hiding his relief and spoke with a deepened voice to allude to calmness and concern.

"Yup," Pete said, but quickly realized that he had to keep talking, otherwise his dad would pepper him with questions. Especially now that he seemed to be able to breathe again.

"So, Dad," Pete started and rummaged through his mind for anything that didn't include the wedding night. "In History, we started talking about the Group Areas Act." *Eureka! That's a good one,* Pete thought. "Do you think it should be changed? What I mean is, here in Dannhauser we have whites and Indians living on opposite sides of the same street, and on the other edge of the Indian area, the blacks live right next door to them, and we have no problems with crime..."

An image of Rudie with his hand stuck deep into his underpants popped into his head the instant he said the word "crime." He paused for a second, desperate for another image to exorcise the one of Rudie—he cast his eyes up to the wall and spotted the poster of Christie Brinkley in a red bikini. *That's the one,* he thought. *Thanks, Christie.*

"...or, you know, anything like that." It didn't look like his dad had noticed his moment of mental truancy, so he kept talking. "In Dundee, where the group areas are more defined, they have regular issues with crime." Unlike his biology story, they really did have a heated discussion about the Group Areas Act in History class, and for the first time, it was something he thought about. But today the Group Areas Act's job was merely to divert his dad's attention away from any sex-related topics, and for some reason, this was the first thing that jumped to mind, besides of course, what had happened *that* night. That was always at the forefront of his mind, every single minute of every day. But he would much rather listen to his dad's in-depth explanation of human reproduction—within a marriage, of course—than utter a single word about *that* night.

"I find it interesting that you talked about things like that in history," his dad started before he looked up at the ceiling for a moment. "The thing is, and I've said it many times, we here in Dannhauser live in a different world. Sheltered in a way. Places like Dundee and Newcastle are much bigger. Those towns were designed in such a way that it made it easy for each racial group to have their own very separate area. Our town is so small that I'm sure many visitors have mistaken the Indian area for the white area. It's even worse in Durnacol where the less affluent white people live right next to the township, there isn't even a fence."

A soft tap on the door interrupted his dad.

"Can I interest you guys in some ice-cold juice?" his mom whispered through the door.

"No thanks, love, we're a little busy right now," his dad said and winked at Pete.

"Oh, okay, no rush. I'll be in the kitchen." They listened to his mom's footsteps as they pattered along the long carpeted corridor toward the kitchen.

"You know your mom, she's very curious." Rikus's smile echoed that of a naughty teenager, but the distant glint in his eyes said something very different. Pete imagined it must be love or something.

"Where was I?" Even at the best of times his dad was prone to get sidetracked in the middle of a story.

"You said that Dannhauser was different from other places, we live in a cocoon of sorts."

"Ah yes. You know what? I believe in the Group Areas Act." His dad paused and rubbed his prominent, stubbly chin pensively.

"There are people, a lot actually, who hate anyone that isn't white. They stir and whisper about shadows, to make people scared, and to make people believe that those shadows will come out and bite you. That is not my kind of people. We don't *braai* together. The way I see it is there is enough space for all of us. Besides, imagine if all the blacks were chased into the sea like that Marais character advocated. What then?

Who would do all the work? Who would work in the mines or on the farms? And that is only two things. What about all the other work? Will Marais's cousins and buddies get their unsullied hands dirty? I doubt it. They've enjoyed the good life far too long. Sitting on their farms like kings, watching their people work, four, five maids cooking, cleaning, doing everything except wiping their buttered fat..." Rikus smiled at Pete.

"As you can hear, I'm not a fan of that bunch. You know what's funny? Marais wants to chase all the blacks into the sea, but Botha's people don't allow them on the beaches—so what do you do? How do you chase them into the sea if they're not allowed on the beaches?" Rikus chuckled heartily, so much so that Pete chuckled along, not because of the anecdote, but because his dad's eyes always disappeared into his face when he laughed, like something out of a Japanese cartoon.

"Anyway, those guys like the Group Areas Act, Homelands and all those things, because they abhor everything darker than a sheet of paper. But like I said, those guys aren't my pals, I don't have much time for them. I like the Group Areas Act because I like to think our cultures are completely different. Imagine for a moment that the blacks lived amongst us. They are very different, they have different ideas, beliefs, superstitions, and traditions. For instance, when they hold a funeral it can go on for a week. Cows are slaughtered, music is on full volume, everyone is there, and I mean *everyone*. Can you imagine if that happened next door?

"Or, when black boys reach a certain age, I think

95

it's around fourteen or so, they are sent into the bush for an initiation. They are circumcised with a sharpened stone and left to fend for themselves for a week in the bush. Can you imagine the outrage in our community if we started doing that?" Rikus's chest and shoulders started shaking with laughter.

"Most moms are so worried about their precious little babies, they don't even want them to play rugby. Imagine they were told their beautiful angels were to be chopped with a stone and then dropped in the bush!" Both bellowed with laughter, so much so that they didn't even hear Deanne's footsteps outside the door. Rikus's cheeks and ears were red as wine, and his eyes squinted with mischief. His laugh was like a diesel engine slowly gathering speed until it became unstoppable. Pete collapsed on his side, clutching his stomach—hurting from the laughter. The release of tension, in both of them, flowed freely through the room like a river in flood.

When the laughter started to subside, and Pete was able to sit up straight again, he noticed that his dad was looking at him as if he had just won a prize at the church bazaar. It had been a long time since they'd had a moment like this. His mom said he was acting like a typical teenager when he and his dad would throw word-filled grenades at one another, but he wasn't convinced. Perhaps it was that age-old thing, where you needed to stake your claim, to be your own man, or at least tried to figure out what "your own man" meant. That, together with that inevitable moment, when you see your dad struggling with something, cussing a screwdriver or the dog, and you realize: somewhere among the dark clouds of puberty you have become human, with human issues, and duct tape couldn't fix everything.

His dad leaned back in the chair, swung his right leg over his left and tucked his hands behind his head.

"What's the story with the rugby? Mom tells me you had a practice game playing for the fourth team? Wasn't the plan to play for the first team?" His dad was still smiling, but his voice let slip a hint of surprise.

"It was just practice," Pete said hastily. This was another conversation he had hoped to avoid. This was the man who taught him how to play, the man who was mildly obsessive and spent every Saturday afternoon watching rugby on TV—irrespective of who was playing, the man who came close to losing his voice every time he watched his son play.

"We played against the second team, and I sliced them open. You should have seen me, Dad." He hadn't. He had had a quiet game after Lawrence and Klayton (his own teammates) drove their elbows into his back at a ruck. It was an unsubtle warning not to stand out, so he didn't. Even if he wanted to, he was in too much pain. The only good thing was that his team was so pathetically poor that, by comparison, his efforts seemed almost passable. Almost.

"Maybe it's a blessing in disguise. This way you can stand out—the coach will notice you." His dad rubbed his chin again and inhaled audibly.

"I don't like that Mr. Theunissen. He prances around like he is God's gift to rugby. But I have to hand it to the bloke, he knows how to win. And you don't need to like him to learn from him."

Pete nodded, knowing that unless someone blew up the tour bus, he would have no chance of even being the waterboy for the first team this year.

"I've noticed you're jogging far less regularly in the afternoons. Don't give up, you were doing so well. It's tough to get into the first team, hell, neither of your brothers did. Mind you: Deon just wanted to play guitar all day long and Riku was so preoccupied with girls that he could barely remember his own name, nevermind how to catch a rugby ball. But you, Pete, you have more rugby in your blood than those two combined. You can go a long way; just don't lose focus. Hold on to your dreams, eh?"

"Yes, Dad." A silence filled the room. Pete could see his dad was searching for something to say and he couldn't even help, he was too busy hating himself for his diminishing rugby career.

"Right." That was Rikus de Lange's favorite saying. He always said "right" when he was ready to leave a conversation.

"I'm starving. I'm going to see if your mom remembered to get some food going." Rikus stood up and walked to the door, but as he opened the door halfway, he turned back to Pete.

He smiled, steeped in melancholy. "I never thought the Group Areas Act would make me laugh this much. Thanks!"

Pete smiled back. "It's high on the improbability scale."

Pete fell back on the bed after Rikus closed the door. He stared at the ceiling, at the cream-colored paint with dozens of tiny cracks in it. He replayed their conversation over and over in his mind and wondered how it was possible to miss someone who was still there. He also thought of his brothers, Deon and Riku, drinking from the fountain of student fun. And where was he? Stuck here, in Nowhereville, with a head so full of stuff that he didn't want in there, that everything became one thing, one big mushy mess.

He was angry. But what made him even angrier was that he didn't know where it came from. The fire raging inside him was all-consuming, but he couldn't see the flames.

"Dinner's on the table! Wash your hands!" Deanne de Lange's melodic voice sprinted from the kitchen, past the sitting room, glancing past Deon and Riku's empty rooms, all along the walls plastered with framed memories, through his door, to right inside his bloodred ears.

ONE SIX

Pete ran as fast as he could, but he was struggling. His lungs refused to give him air. It was his fault. But then again, you only turn sixteen once.

It was pretty good. He invited twenty or so people and twelve showed up, not bad considering four of them came all the way from Dundee. It was just a shame Renate couldn't come, well, he assumed she couldn't come or maybe she lost the invite—or maybe he wasn't playing for the first team and therefore an abject loser in her perfect blue eyes. No, she must have lost the invite, or there was a family emergency. Her mom always seemed to walk around with a bandage of sorts. Perhaps she had fallen again, and Renate had to help with the chores.

His lungs felt like they were being passed through a grater.

Everyone seemed to have a good time, except Barend who was unusually quiet. After the Dundee guys were picked up by their parents, three of the locals left too. He thought that the party was nearing its end, despite Belchie's proclamation beforehand that this would be the party of the decade. Belchie went to Sarel Cilliers—or Donkey Tech as the pupils from Dundee referred to it—the technical school in Glencoe, but the two of them and Barend had been friends since before they could spell the word "friends"—that said, he had serious doubts whether

Belchie could spell it now. For Belchie every molehill was a mountain. In his world everything was the biggest, fastest and coolest. Therefore Pete suspected his proclamation about the party was just another of his exaggerations.

After they had thanked his parents and promised not to be back too late, the party moved to Belchie's house, more specifically the small outbuilding his older brother called home. The same older brother who was in Johannesburg for two weeks. Belchie locked the door behind them and could barely contain his excitement. He unveiled a brown box with no writing on it. There were quizzical looks all round, and he lapped it up. The stage was his to surprise and shock. He slowly opened the box and revealed hundreds of cigarettes squeezed in like white-and-yellow sardines.

He didn't want to lose his crowd to the cache of smokes, so he waved everyone to the fridge in the corner. He held his hand on the fridge door to heighten anticipation, and then flung it open with a high pitched "Taadaa!"

The fridge was stacked full of Lion Lager bottles and there was one bottle of Russian Bear vodka in the freezer shelf. A few jaws dropped, and a collective nervous giggle filled the room.

Needless to say, the beer and vodka flowed, and a thick gray plume of smoke soon shrouded the room into murky darkness. With the music turned up and the laughter getting more and more rapturous, the five boys pretended to suddenly like beer and cigarettes.

Pete alternated between beer and vodka to neutralize the cigarette taste in his mouth. Nonetheless, he was on his seventh cigarette, and had even tried to inhale a few times. Barend appeared out of the cloud of music and smoke, his smile gone, and his shoulders slumped.

"What's up, man?" Pete asked.

"Listen, Pete, I..." Barend started.

"What's that?" Pete shouted over the music.

"Mr. Theunissen asked me to train with the first- and second teams after the holidays." Barend spoke quickly, avoiding eye contact.

Pete frowned. He wanted to say something but couldn't find the words. His best friend was standing in front of him, groveling, desperate to find the courage to get this weight off his chest.

"He said year after year props got injured on tour, so he'll need me...in case," Barend finally completed his unburdening.

An angry flash took hold of Pete through the beer and vodka. His ears were red already, but now he was boiling over. He took a quick sip of beer, looked at Barend, and looked away again.

"That's cool, man. Very cool. You'll have to fight off the chicks now, hey?" He slapped Barend on the shoulder and got up.

"Have we stopped drinking or what?" Pete shouted. This was greeted with a loud, approving chorus, except for Barend, who put his beer down and snuck out quietly.

Every shot of vodka and every Rothmans Kingsize chased vaporous waves through his mouth. He didn't want to be sick again and ran a little slower in the hope that the feeling would pass. Approximately thirteen hours ago, around two in the morning, he had stood outside Belchie's brother's smoke-filled flatlet and thrown up beer, vodka, dinner and cigarette fumes. His cheeks had been cold, his upper body shook, but he felt feverish, sweating, and tears jumped out of his eyes with every convulsive spew. He swore then, as he did now, that he would never drink again, and as certain as the sun rose in the morning he would never, ever smoke again.

He couldn't remember how he got home, or how he unlocked the house, brushed his teeth, or even how he got into bed. But what he did remember was that he was ripped from the serenity of dreamless sleep in a cacophonous and deafening rendition of "Happy Birthday," and thrust into the nauseating reality of his sins of the night before. His parents sang with gusto and held a large wrapped present between them. Their faces swirled in dull colors against the backdrop of the most blinding and painful light streaming in through the curtains. A cloud of smoke filled his whole vision, but he couldn't tell whether it was real or not. The sickening stench of stale cigarettes covered his pillow like a rug, so much so that he forced himself upright. The movement sent a rollercoaster around his stomach, and for a few moments, he was certain that he would cover his parents and his birthday present in whatever was left in his gut.

Thank goodness he kept it in.

Even through his haze, he could sense the air of disappointment behind the cheerful singing and broad smiles. They knew. How much didn't matter: They knew.

His hands were shaking like those of an old man

when he opened the present, and if he had to answer his mom's question, "Do you feel older?" his answer would most definitely have been, "Hell, yes!" His birthday present was a brand new Spalding tennis racket. If you used a hint of imagination it looked a little like Ivan Lendl's racket. The head was bigger than his old racket, and the grip was nice and solid. If he wasn't about to die, he would have been very excited.

Thankfully his good old dad stopped this little joyous get together. "Right," he said before he and his mom muttered a few more indecipherables and left his room. It was only then that he realized that his bladder felt like a cracked dam wall about to break. He forced his legs off the bed and felt another wave of nausea descend upon him. He got up, desperately searching for his bin, but decided instead to make a run for it. He did make the toilet—just. He threw up but struggled to contain his bladder while his upper body contorted, and splashes of urine darkened his shorts.

No, there's no chance in hell that he'd ever drink again.

His battered body was dragging him past the row of identically constructed houses of Dannhauser's New Extension. The sun was low and the air cool. The awfulness stuck around all day and even now in the late afternoon, it was still present. Mercifully the smoke-haze had evaporated by the time Sunday School finished. What didn't help was that he saw Rudie—for the first time in weeks. Thankfully only at a distance.

His mom cooked a feast and he tried his best to eat some of it, even though he just wanted to lay down and die. One way or another, he managed to survive the day and now he was trying to run off the last few remnants of the misery.

He thought about Barend, the best guy he knew, and how he treated him. He was so angry that his best friend was promoted to the second team that he hadn't even realized he'd left. What kind of friend was he?

And then there was Rudie, that satan drifting in and out of his life. Why couldn't he just have stayed away today? It was his birthday!

Guilt and anger raged in his beer-battered body as he ran next to the fishing pond. Barend and Rudie intertwined so much that at some point he saw just one face—Barend's, but with a yellow mustache, and *that* demonic laugh.

When he reached the top of the hill his legs were shaking and his lungs were fighting hard to catch up. The sun lingered above the mountain etched horizon like a blood-red cricket ball, staring at him, like it wanted to say something. He wanted to say something too, he wanted to say that he hated himself, he hated who he was. He wanted to tell the sun that there was no point to any of this, nothing whatsoever. He was an oxygen thief, for the past sixteen years. Would anyone even realize if he wasn't there anymore? A drop of water on the road, dried up by the first sun?

Pete closed his eyes. He let the cool dusty air fill his lungs and shut the world out. "Pete, I mean, *baas* Pete." Petrus interrupted his moment of self-loathing.

"Jeez, Petrus, you'll give me a heart attack!" Pete swallowed hard, and his eye started to itch. He couldn't believe Petrus ran up to him without him noticing.

"Sorry, sorry, *baas*." The black guy squirmed in front of him with twitchy toes and hands flapping at his sides.

"Call me Pete," Pete said, turning back toward the mountains, lifting his head and taking a deep breath.

Pete only caught a glimpse of Petrus's surprise. There was a long pause as Pete closed his eyes and let the soft fall air fill his recovering lungs. The silence lingered.

"Pete," Petrus said with uncertainty. "I was wondering...I haven't seen you for a long time, so I was wondering...if maybe you've seen her? The girl?"

Pete smiled. When Petrus said "girl" in his strong Zulu accent, it sounded like ghel.

"The *ghel*, I mean, girl?" Pete said.

"Yes, you know...*her*." This time Petrus's "her" sounded like hair. But Petrus's accent soon evaporated from his mind. Pete's thoughts had taken him to *her*, standing with the broom in her hand, one perfect strand of black hair stroking her flawless skin.

"Yup." He had tried everything to put her out of his mind, but at the same time, he suspected the only thing that might do that was one of Rudie's bullets.

"I went to *Naidoo and Sons*." Pete paused. He saw Petrus's eyes bulging, willing the information out of him. He realized that this was the first time he had spoken about his visit out loud, and to an actual person.

"She was there, working in her dad's shop."

"Was she okay? Did you speak?" Petrus was struggling with Pete's protracted answer.

"She was okay. We only spoke for a second, but I managed to ask her if she was okay. She looked—" Pete stopped just before the word "beautiful" leaped off his tongue.

"She looked?" Petrus asked.

"Uhm...she looked fine, healthy...she looked normal ...you know: okay," Pete said.

"Good." Petrus let out a relieved sigh. "I was worried, eish, I was *so* worried. It's all I've been thinking about."

Pete mulled over Petrus's words. His last couple of months had also been consumed by *her* and *that* night. There was a kindness to the breeze now, and he recognized it instantly; it was hearing the secrets locked in the dungeons of his heart aloud, and hearing it echo in someone else's voice.

"It's my birthday today," Pete said.

"Shoh! Happy birthday."

Pete didn't know why he had said it, perhaps it was the overwhelming relief of being able to loosen the iron grip of his painfully kept secrets.

"How old are you?" Petrus asked.

"Sixteen. Sixteen bloody years old."

"Me too!" Petrus cried out.

"It's a crazy age," Pete said. "We're old enough to join the army, you know—war, kill people, die for your country—but too young to drink, drive, and even to vote for that same country that will gladly offer you up as cannon fodder." A small grin curled in the corner of Pete's mouth.

They chortled for a few moments.

"Are you in Standard Eight?" Pete asked.

"Yes. You?" Petrus said.

"Yup."

A few moments elapsed as the conversation dried up and they stared at the sun seeking shelter behind the mountains before the night took over.

"Right." Pete couldn't believe he used his dad's term. "I need to go, my mom...you know how it is?"

"I know it well, same here," Petrus said. His gaze was fixed on the ground around his feet.

"If..." Petrus started, but stopped himself and fixed his gaze on the setting sun again. "If you see her, please...say...say...say, I said hello." Petrus looked like his eyes were trying to shoot down the words he had just spoken.

"Uhm, yeah, well...if I....Look, I don't go to town very often, but if I...I'll see," Pete said. He watched this black guy standing in front of him, his age, but so very different, pretending to be staring at the setting sun, but looking like his own skin made him crawl.

He peered in the direction of his home and forced his sore muscles into a trot. After a few meters, he stopped, turned back to Petrus.

"See you," he said and ran home in the hope, however strange it might be, that he would see Petrus again.

PART TWO

THE RUMOR

"See that guy?" Belchie asked. Pete's eyes immediately found the towering figure of the devil, shaking hands with a few of the church elders. He wondered why Belchie was pointing him out. Did Rudie say something? Did everyone know? Pete rubbed his itchy right eye.

"Rudie?" Barend said.

"Yes, Rudie. I heard he shot one of his boys and buried him somewhere on his farm." Belchie's protuberant eyes seemed to grow with each passing moment both in size and bulge and his eyebrows were raised high on his forehead. The breeze passing through the open window tugged at his thick bronze-colored hair.

"Aggh come on, there's always some story about that guy. No one believes it anymore." Barend shook his head and moved away from the window. Pete slipped away from the window too and sat down, relieved that this was not what he had feared.

"This is no story." Frown lines cut furrows across Belchie's forehead.

"I overheard some of the elders talk. That's why they're chatting to him now." Belchie looked out of the window as if that would somehow affirm his statement.

"No, China, this is just like the time when he returned from Angola and people said he won some sort of medal for bravery, supposedly because he single-handedly killed twenty terrorists with his bare hands. No one has ever seen that medal or read anything about it in the papers," Barend said.

"Well, I believe it. My brother was with him at school until Standard Eight and he said the guy is a psycho. He once caught a pigeon and ripped its head off in front of a few Standard Six girls, just for a laugh," Belchie said.

"Bullshit," Barend said.

"Okay, then tell me why he hardly ever comes to church, but today all the elders are talking to him? Hell, even the Reverend is with him now. Check for yourself." He motioned out of the window and Barend's curiosity got the better of him. Pete remained seated.

Belchie and Barend stared out of the window for quite some time, trying to read the body language of the elders, Reverend, and most importantly, Rudie.

Belchie tapped Barend on the shoulder, gestured they should sit down again. Barend followed his lead, but still had more than just a slight hint of skepticism about him for his classmate's story.

Belchie leaned forward, waving Barend and Pete closer, then peered over his shoulders as if someone might overhear. He sat on the edge of his seat, waited for Barend and Pete to do the same, their heads close to one another. Pete didn't know why he was doing this. All he wanted to do was sit in the corner and wish away time until he was alone again.

"The thing is," Belchie whispered, rolling his teeth over his bottom lip and taking a quick peek over his shoulder again. He suddenly squinted, a seriousness about him. He wiggled his finger at the other two.

"What I'm about to say stays between us, hey?" When he didn't get a response, he half-cleared his throat, looked toward the window and then back to the others. "I could go to prison because I know this," he said as if he was wholly convinced by his statement.

Barend threw his head back, made a loud puffing sound with his lips and shook his head.

"Genuine," Belchie whispered, but Barend had had enough. He was just about to get up with Pete grateful to follow suit when Belchie said, "Listen, listen. If I didn't hear this from a reliable source, I wouldn't believe it myself."

The look of unbelief remained on Barend's face, but he sat down again, though this time folding his arms across his chest and sitting back, not leaning forward. Pete looked around him, thinking of some way to escape this. What Belchie had heard he did not know, but he didn't like the sound of it. Just one ridiculous rumor could ruin him. His life over. For a fleeting moment he wondered if he should just walk out, go home, sleep until he was eighteen and he could leave home. But he didn't.

Belchie tilted his head sideways, pouted and whispered, "My brother told me." He started nodding, as if that would make his statement true. "My brother knows, he is well-connected. He hears all the stories when they drink at the Duchens over the weekends."

"I wouldn't believe a single thing that comes out of that place," Barend said. "That is the dodgiest bar in like, a thirty kilometer radius."

"That's where you're wrong," Belchie said with great conviction. "That is the place where the miners, the farmers and some of the people from Dannhauser go to drink. All the stories in one place."

Barend sighed, looking very disinterested in the conversation. "The farmers and the miners hate each other; they don't drink together."

"Why do you think there are fights there every weekend?" Belchie countered. "There are only two bars in the area, the Iscor Club in Durnacol—where only the people from the mine drink, you wouldn't find a farmer within a kilometer of that place—and Duchens. So where do you think the miners who don't want to drink with their foremen, shift-bosses and the engineers go to drink? Where do farmers and people from Dannhauser go?" Belchie flapped his hands open. "There is only one place: Duchens."

Barend looked disappointed at himself for being drawn into this conversation. He glanced at Pete but Pete was sitting hunched over, staring at the brown carpet. "Okay, okay, fine." Barend surrendered. "What is this big secret then?"

"Well, you are not going to believe this," Belchie said.

Barend grunted. "Just get on with it, for crying out loud man."

Belchie started to laugh but swallowed the laugh a moment later when he realized Barend wasn't joking. Belchie was whispering again, barely audible, hunching forward even more. "Rudie," Belchie thumbed toward the window, "likes to drink jungle juice, if you know what I mean?"

Barend looked fed-up with Belchie and his story. "What?" he asked.

"Jungle juice," Belchie said slightly louder.

"What the hell is that?" Barend sat with his back

arched peering down at Belchie.

"Jeez, you guys are so wet behind the ears, you need to get out more," Belchie said with a disgruntled shake of his head. "Jungle juice is a—" he peeked over his shoulder again, "when a white guy goes fishing in a black pond."

"Are you saying Rudie screws black chicks?"

"Uh-uh." Belchie nodded and tipped his tongue against his bottom lip.

"Utter nonsense!" exclaimed Barend.

"It's true," Belchie retorted, "it started when he was in the war in Angola. Apparently, a lot of guys did it but Rudie got a taste for it. Now he likes to dip his dipstick deep into the oil."

Barend made a vibrating sound with his lips and rolled his eyes.

Belchie wasn't finished. "From what I heard he has a thing for one of the maids on his farm. He goes to her khaya every time he has the urge. Let off some steam, you know."

"Have you been drinking?" Barend asked.

"Listen, listen," Belchie was desperate to keep Barend in the conversation, he could see he was really losing him now. "The guys at Duchens told my brother this maid who he was banging—"

"You mean raping," Pete said. It was an inner thought that somehow crossed his lips. He was just as shocked as Belchie and Barend by his utterance; he had been completely quiet up until that moment.

The word "rape" lingered in his thoughts. His mind took him back to that warm January evening when Sarita was assaulted–violated. Even though they had miraculously stopped Rudie from committing physical rape, by that point he had surely already scarred her for life. And what makes it worse is knowing that nothing in this world could bother Rudie less. Because to him, Sarita wasn't a human being. She was merely an object to quench his insatiable, deranged thirst. A wrapper to rip apart and cast aside once everything inside was devoured.

Belchie seemed to have lost the thread of his story, um-ing and ah-ing for a few seconds before his brain cast Pete's interjection aside. "Yeah, whatever. The point is, she is married, and her husband was so fed up that he told some of the other workers that he was going to"—Belchie made a whistling sound whilst dragging his finger across his throat—"make sure Rudie didn't touch his little woman again." Belchie threw his hands up in the air. "It looks like Rudie got to him first. That is the oke who apparently got smoked. Now Rudie can drink as much jungle juice as he wants without some tar-pole standing in his way."

Barend looked like he was about to say something but Belchie beat him to it. "My brother says Rudie has this old revolver, that his granddad gave him, and he like, sleeps with it, it's like his wife or something. I bet you that was the murder weapon. If I was the police, I would check that out.

Barend got up and walked to the window, studying the scene below, but not sticking his head out of the window.

"Well, there is a nervousness about Rudie, but that doesn't mean a thing. Maybe he's just embarrassed because the Reverend asked him why he wasn't in church anymore," Barend said.

"Think what you want, I only know what I heard," Belchie said.

Barend pursed the corner of his mouth and raised an eyebrow. "So, your theory is that the elders and the Reverend are helping him to cover up a murder, and what? Rape? Sex with a black?"

"Did I say that? Maybe they also heard the rumors and want to get to the matter of the truth."

"Truth of the matter," Barend corrected him like he had done so many times before. "And you said it, China, rumors, that's all it is! Freakin' rumors. It makes that head of yours overheat."

"Aren't you curious? What if it's the truth? What if this kinda thing happened all the time and he is like a serial killer or something with a massive graveyard on top of a mountain?"

"I think you might have watched one too many of those dodgy horror movies you like so much." Barend walked toward his chair.

"When he dumps you in a shallow grave, don't come crying to me." Belchie said, waving his finger in Barend's face.

"Check, Rudie's dad has joined them. Things are going to kick off now." Belchie almost hit his head against the windowpane as he tried to get a better view.

"Uncle Rutger?" Once again Barend's curiosity got the better of him and he joined Belchie at the window.

"Yes, check. I tell you what, not many people scare me, but that guy, Uncle Rutger, jeez, he'll make me leave brake marks all over my Superman underpants," Belchie said.

"He looks exactly like the devil from the children's

Bible, just bigger and balder," Barend chipped in.

"I heard he once slapped one of his boys so hard that his skull shattered. To this day it looks like his face is going to slide off his head."

"There you go again. Where do you get all this stuff? Is there some secret club you go to where people talk shit all night? S.T.B., the Shit Talkers Brigade?" Barend enjoyed his joke and turned to Pete for affirmation.

Pete sat quietly. He could see the two were talking, but their chatter was just a jumbled collection of sounds. Only when he heard the word "boy," would he feel a pinch in the back of his neck. He stared at a small crack in the corner of the stained-glass window. It was slowly growing, every week he could see the cracks reaching further into the window, like cancer where death was inching closer.

"What do you think about this rumor, China?" Barend asked Pete.

Time must have passed, Pete didn't know how long, his mind was still wholly occupied by the crack in the window.

"Did you step on your tongue or something?" Belchie added.

"Huh?" Pete said.

Barend turned to Belchie, head shaking. "Swallow your tongue! China, you must seriously sue your teachers. I don't know what they're teaching you at Donkey Tech." Then he shook off the thought and returned his attention to Pete. "The rumor about Rudie? Good morning!" Barend said, looked at Belchie and the pair of them shook their heads.

"I don't know anything about that guy." Pete felt an immediate stabbing pain in his heart; he lied to Barend again. To his face.

"In small towns, no one can keep secrets. If he did it, it's just a matter of time before everyone knows. Mark my words," Belchie said.

The other kids walked into the room followed by Uncle Willie. Everyone took their places and Belchie snuck one last peek out of the window. Uncle Willie opened with prayer but Pete's mind could only repeat Belchie's words over and over again: "Just a matter of time before everyone knows. Mark my words. Just a matter of time before everyone knows. Mark my words."

HOLIDAY

Pete drew a line in the coarse sand with his foot. He stood behind it, looked up at the white chalk line drawn horizontally across the red brick wall of their storeroom. He bounced the old battered tennis ball a couple of times, tossed it in the air, and whipped a serve just like Kevin Curran's. The new racket purred and sent waves of power through his arm. The ball crashed against the red bricks in a dusty puff a mere centimeter above the chalk line. Perfection.

The ball shot to the left where the apricot tree prevented Pete from sending the ball back with interest. He looked down at his racket in awe. Meanwhile, his black Labrador called Jimmy (named after Jimmy Connors, of course) chased after the ball. Pete couldn't believe how accurate this thing was. He felt immense, and for a second wished the whole bloody rugby season would just end so that he could rule the tennis courts of Northern Natal with this mighty new weapon.

Jimmy thought of his practice session as a game and made Pete run around after him before finally relinquishing the drool-covered ball from his impish mouth. Pete wiped the ball on the flaky yellow grass and stepped up to the line again. The ball hit the exact same spot as the previous serve. He looked around in the hope that someone might have seen this incredible moment of genius, but the only witness was Jimmy, wagging his tail, mischief in his eyes.

It was the first day of the Easter holidays and he had two weeks of utter boredom to look forward to. Barend and his family had left that morning to spend a couple of weeks in the Lowveld. Even Belchie wasn't there. His dad had decided to take his family on their first vacation in nearly three years, albeit two weeks of camping and fishing next to Chelmsford Dam, a whopping forty-five minute drive from their home, if you drove slowly. It was as if everyone knew that Dannhauser was going to be gobbled up by a giant sinkhole or something, but everyone conveniently forgot to inform the de Langes. No, as always, they stayed put, being treated to "the comforts of home," like his dad regularly reminded him. If only he could get a lift to Pretoria and hang out with his brothers. That would have been epic. He would have escaped this miserable place, away from his nightmares, and that ghastly laugh. There he could have checked out university girls, pretended to be a student, gone to bars, laughed, had fun...forgotten.

But no, his dad claimed his brothers were slacking already, failing subjects left, right and center. "Those two better pull up their socks or I'll have them back here shoveling coal by June."

First prize would definitely have been to experience the student scene and hang out with his brothers. But even a week's fishing at Chelmsford Dam sounded pretty good compared to being stuck in a place where every five minutes nothing happened. "Times are hard," his dad said. "We need to hold on to what we have, especially now that your mom isn't working anymore," he went on, "plus the economy is suffering, this is no time for fancy holidays." The economy was not the only thing that was suffering, Pete thought and whipped another serve against the wall, this time well below the white chalk line.

The faint outline of an ink stamp was still visible on his left hand. He inspected the black smudge: proof that he had paid his twenty cents entrance fee to the end of the term school dance. He tapped his racket against his calf and glanced up at the spattering of fleecy white clouds against the pale blue sky. All the effort of going and Renate didn't even show up.

It would have worked so well: Barend would have played cover by getting into rugby conversations with the Matric boys, leaving him to just casually swoop in, asking her for a dance—as if he couldn't care less—and then he would have held her close, so that he could feel her heart race against him. "I Want to Know What Love Is" would have played, the world around them would have faded to a gray mist and the strobe lights would have slowed down to the beat of the music. He would have made sure their gazes intertwined, taken her hand, and led her to the slow dancing area in the middle of the hall. He would have pulled her in close, feeling her sweet breath against his shoulder, and then just before the end of the song, their eyes would have met, and in one perfect moment, the world would have stopped, their lips would have locked and he would have felt her warm, searching tongue against his.

"Pete, have you tidied your room yet?" His mom's voice snatched his first kiss away from him before it had even begun.

"I'll do it later," he shouted back, pitying himself

that fate had turned so cruelly against him.

"I know your later, Pete. Do it now, then you can play to your heart's content afterward."

"Yes, Ma," he sighed. He patted Jimmy on the head and whispered, "Old boy, you have no idea how lucky you are," and ambled to his room. Clothes and books were strewn everywhere, but he knew exactly where everything was. He couldn't understand why he couldn't just keep it like that, it was a system that worked for him, and it was *his* room after all.

A couple of hours later he was happy with his room, his mom not so much. His dad was watching a replay of some old Currie Cup rugby final with his best friend, Uncle Ivor. They were shouting at the players as if it was a live game. His mom was busy taking more beer and snacks to the TV room.

"I'm just going for a walk. I'll be back now-now," Pete said as he walked past his mom just outside the kitchen.

"I'm not impressed with your tidying up effort," she said before taking the tray with drinks and snacks to the TV room.

That was her way of saying, "Fine, but don't get into trouble."

Pete unhooked the chain of their wide farm-style gate, hopped on, and rode it as it swung open. It was funny, he thought, that riding the gate was still just as much fun as when he was a six-year-old kid.

He walked in the middle of the gravel road. There was no traffic, no people, and even the dogs were quiet. It was Saturday afternoon which, besides Sundays, was the quietest time of the week in

Dannhauser. Later, when the sun would start thinking about setting, people would slowly spring to life again, fires would be lit and the intoxicating aroma of a multitude of *braais* would fill the air. But that was hours away; for the time being, the town was like a museum, except with nothing to see.

The church stood proud across the road from where he was walking, not far from their home, and he beheld the steps leading in from a safe distance. Tomorrow he would have to face those steps again, so too Captain Burger, and perhaps even Rudie. He shook his head and increased his pace, peeking over the fence of the crazy old lady with the seven black cats, giving the convent a wide berth, and on to the first stretch of tarred road: Church Street.

Past the library, he stared down the side street where the Indian girl had disappeared to *that* night. He paused. It occurred to him that he didn't even know her name. But perhaps it was better that way because once she had a name his thoughts might... He didn't understand his mind sometimes. It would drift, no—fly—without warning or any way of stopping it and take him places he didn't always want to be. Every night in his bed, as he waited for sleep to come, he would make up some story in his head and before he knew what had happened, his mind would have taken hold of that story and made it real. Well, *realish*.

He crossed the road just before the police station and admired the pretty red bricks of the clinic which had seen better days, and the big Indian family home on the corner with broken glass glued to the top of their wall. Something like that was quite uncommon in

Dannhauser, but they were the owners of Kismet, so he imagined they probably had a lot to lose.

Jeevan's Corner Shop was the first shop on your left if you approached the town center from the police station's side. It was closed. He looked down both ends of the long Main Street but couldn't see a single car. In the distance, a particularly large ginger cat chased a small black dog across the road. The dog yelped as the pair disappeared behind *Naidoo and Sons*.

There it was.

His eyes transfixed on the large sign that called out to him.

He surveyed the area, there was still not a soul to be seen. It was Saturday afternoon, all the shops were closed, and everyone was at home either sleeping or eating freshly made milk tart. The chances of seeing *her* were less than zero. "So, it's probably safe," he muttered to himself.

He walked across the road, picked up a loose stone and threw it as far as he could. The fleecy clouds from earlier had disappeared and the sky had turned into a deep blue. A few cans and wrappers lined the sidewalk, and a swarm of bees found a black dustbin irresistible. Pete steered well clear of it.

There it was again, rising from the shadows, towering over him, that very large and now very significant sign: *Naidoo and Sons*. He walked nonchalantly by, not even turning his head, but trying to squeeze every bit of information out of his peripheral vision. He didn't see a thing—not even the ginger cat.

He retraced his steps, walking backwards to have another look—still nothing. His eyes scanned both the *Naidoo and Sons* shops, just in case there was the slightest of movements, anything which might indicate that she was there.

"What the hell are you doing?" he said out loud. He shook his head and decided to go home.

"Who are you talking to?" a voice asked behind him. He recognized it straight away.

It was her.

As calmly as he could he peeked over his shoulder, and there it was: He wasn't imagining things. The Indian girl was standing behind him.

"O...just...I was...you know," he tried.

"You're not very good at putting sentences together." She smiled, her dimples turned effortlessly deeper into her cheeks and her eyes glistened in the bright afternoon sunshine.

Pete couldn't tell whether he was smiling or not, all he knew was that his ears and whole face were as red as the morning sun. Plus, his eye was itching like crazy.

"We're closed. All the shops are closed. What brings you out here?" she asked, still smiling. She tilted her head slightly to the right and Pete wondered if he had ever seen anything more beautiful.

"Yeah I know, I know. I was just a little bored at home, you know—" Why did he say "'you know" so much? Pete was getting annoyed with himself. He sounded like some brainless single-celled organism.

"I just had to get out of the house, go for a little walk, you know?" *Damn it, again!*

"Well, if you are so bored you should have said, you could have helped me with the rubbish." She raised the two empty green bins in her hands. He hadn't even noticed them until that moment. He wanted to say something smart, something that didn't contain "you know," but his brain had turned into that all familiar mush again.

She put the bins down. "Do you also have school holidays at the moment?" she asked, looking about her a little nervously.

"Yup, two weeks of fun." Did he really just say "two weeks of fun?" Really Pete? Come on, man!

"Same here. But not much fun for me, I'm afraid, I have to work," she said.

"In your dad's shop?" Of course in her dad's shop, where else? At the Wimpie in Newcastle? You bloody imbecile!

"Yes, in both shops. I'm supposed to work for my mom, but my dad always finds a way to get me to do his chores. What are you doing over the holidays?"

His life seemed so pathetic. He was going to sleep late, watch some television, practice rugby and tennis, annoy his mom.

"Mow the lawn, help out at church, study, rugby practice, that kind of thing, you know." There it was again, just when he thought it had left him alone, that damned "you know" popped out again.

"Oh cool. But I must say, I don't understand rugby. To me, it looks very...violent. I like cricket though."

"Yeah, rugby is...agh, it's not that bad, you kn..." He managed to stop himself just in time and cleared his throat. "I like cricket too. I used to be quite a good all-rounder actually." Ignoring the fact that in his last game, two years ago, he had managed to run himself out without facing a ball.

"Don't you play cricket anymore?"

"Uhm, no, well yes, I still play, but not this year. The school asked that I focus on tennis in the summer season, and we're not allowed to play both."

"Tennis looks like so much fun, you have to teach me sometime." Her last words seemed to steal her smile. There was a sadness about her, almost reproachful, which instantly made him feel like a jerk without any idea why.

"I can't...I have to go now," she said, grabbed the two bins and walked right past him without making eye contact.

"Hey," Pete called without realizing it.

She turned to face him, her expression like a warning of sorts.

"The black...the black guy, that was there with us that night...Uhm, I saw him. His name is Petrus, like mine, except everyone calls me Pete." His mouth was bone dry and his eye was itching terribly but he refused to scratch it. "He said if I ever randomly bumped into you, to say hello...he says hello."

Her eyes were fixed on a small patch of tall yellow grass swaying in the breeze next to her. Her full lips were now only thin lines, and her cheeks almost pale. She opened her mouth to say something, but stopped, looked down at the pavement and walked away. Two seconds later without turning to face him, she said, "I'm alone in the shop every Sunday afternoon between two and four." She started walking faster, her long black plait swinging from side to side across her back.

Pete's face turned to stone, his mind melted into a sloppy mess, and his heart hammered punches against his ribcage. He stood like that for a very long time. Cars started to go by as the town awoke for the evening braais, but he remained standing in that one spot, busy drowning in the sloppy mess.

EIGHT

"Protea Eleven, I can confirm that we have received the funds," Protea Ten said. Venny sat back against the hard backrest of his chair. A vein started throbbing on his forehead. *Of course you received it,* he thought. *All that bloody money! Do they have any idea how difficult it is to convince people to relinquish their hard-earned cash, damned whippersnapper!* He had to fork most of it out of his own pocket. Blood, sweat, and tears go into making that money and then poof—it's gone, gobbled up by this "cause" no one thought he was ready to be truly part of.

"Protea Eleven, this is goodbye from me. In the future Protea Seven will be your handler. He will initiate contact. Don't use this frequency again."

"Does that mean...?" Venny pulled the microphone closer.

"Affirmative. You are now Protea Eight. Protea Ten out."

Venny jumped up, wanted to shout, but stopped himself. He danced a little on the spot and punched his ragged old cushion several times. His eyes were drawn to the photograph of the young Indian woman being beaten by a policeman and said: "I'm in. The inner circle. Part of the action." He swung the cushion through the air and released a hushed yelp through clenched teeth. This was one of the best days of his life.

"Venkatapathi, if you want to go and see that crazy mother of yours, we better leave now," his wife shouted from behind the closed door.

He wanted to shout back at her, but nothing could douse the euphoria inside him—not even her nagging or her moaning about life and everything else. He would drive down to Glencoe, smile at his wife, and whisper the joyous news in his mother's ear. No one would be the wiser, but he simply had to tell someone: He was Protea Eight! He kissed his fingers and pressed them on the face of the woman in the newspaper clipping, turned all his equipment off and left his hideout.

He grabbed his car keys and whistled a song he couldn't quite remember, or perhaps he was just making it up. It didn't matter, life was good.

"You look happy, Pappa?" Sarita said.

"Just looking forward to seeing Dādī." He smiled at Sarita.

"Now listen, last week you didn't clean behind the counter." Venny's smile was instantly displaced by a solemn glare. "I don't want to walk in there tomorrow and see a single speck of dust, you hear me?"

"Yes, Pappa, I'm sorry, it won't happen again," Sarita said meekly, dropping her head.

"Correct, because if it does, you'll be seeing a lot of Dādī again."

"Yes, Pappa."

Venny scanned the large sitting room, then in the direction of the hallway.

"For goodness sake, Achala, where did you disappear to this time? Typical, you hurry me up and then you just vanish," he shouted.

"I waited for you for such a long time that Sarita has probably finished her school career by now." Achala waddled into the room, kissed Sarita on the cheek, gave Venny a venomous glance and walked out of the house.

Venny shook his head in disbelief, also kissed Sarita on the cheek, and said, "Behind the counter."

Pete looked at his G-Shock watch; it was 15:02. Light gray clouds filled the sky and there was a spiteful wintery bite in the air. Main Street was deserted, and *Closed* signs watched over the dusty street before Monday came around again.

Pete was standing on the steps outside the Eating House, hiding in the shadows. A fresh gust of angst blew right through him. He scoured the area, but all was quiet. He considered sitting down, but large patches of evaporated liquid of unknown origin discolored the concrete floor, and he didn't want to risk it. Besides, he was too nervous to sit. He glanced at his watch again, barely registering the time.

A whirlwind pushed past and sought him out in his hiding place. He pinched his eyes shut, but it was too late. Dust particles made it through his defenses and became lodged in his eyes. He started rubbing.

"Pete," a voice called from beyond the darkness of his burning closed eyelids.

When he peeked through his eyelid, he saw that familiar jaw, broad shoulders and bare feet.

"You're late," Pete said, still rubbing his eyes.

"Sorry, sorry. Eish, my parents waited a long time before they went to sleep." Petrus gestured with his hands exactly how long.

"Mine didn't look like they wanted to nap either. It's almost like they can sense stuff," Pete said, and Petrus nodded in agreement.

"She said she's alone between two and four, so we better hurry in case her dad or someone decides to stop by," Pete said.

"Are you sure I should go? Didn't she mean you should go alone?" Petrus asked.

"No, no, it's not like that. No, no, no. I didn't make this story up when I saw you at the rock three days ago, you know. So I'll say it again: She didn't say anything about being alone in the shop on Sundays until I mentioned your name."

"You sure?" Petrus asked.

"Yeah, man, come on, we're wasting time," Pete said and started walking.

"It's just...a black boy out in town on a Sunday... people will think I'm a *tsotsi*." Petrus walked a few meters behind Pete, constantly looking over his shoulder. When Pete looked back at him, he saw beads of sweat on Petrus's brow despite the chill in the air.

"Don't look so nervous. If you look around every two seconds, it draws attention. Walk in the shops' shadows as much as you can and relax—the town is dead."

Petrus walked to Pete's left, making sure he stayed out of sight, but he still looked around frequently and still looked like he was having trouble breathing, like a dying carp on a riverbank.

It wasn't long before they arrived at the patch of tall yellow grass where Pete had seen the Indian girl just over a week ago. His mind shot back to the feelings that had coursed through him then. The strange and unsettling feelings, for someone like him, that had kept him from going the previous Sunday.

"What's wrong?" Petrus asked.

"Nothing...nothing," was Pete's curt reply. He wasn't convinced that coming here was the greatest of plans anymore. Why had he come? Why not let it be? Clearly the girl was safe and unharmed. She was fine. So extremely fine. With her long, flowing black hair, and that smile...

What if she did mean he should come alone? What if it was *that* kind of invitation? But she was Indian. No, he was doing the right thing. Running to Uncle Gerrit's farm on Thursday and telling Petrus to come along was the right thing to do. They were all in this together. That was all this was, three people together in this, crazy, thing. Yes, that's all it was. And that was all she meant, probably.

"Pete?" Petrus said, struggling to hide his angst.

"Yeah, yeah. Uhm, it looks safe. Let's go." Pete hadn't even realized that he was standing still, as if the tall grass had hypnotized him, and started walking purposefully toward the *Closed* sign in the door of *Naidoo and Sons*. It was dark inside, and a very large part of him hoped that when he hadn't shown up the week before, after *the invitation*, she would have stopped waiting, stopped being alone in the shop on Sundays, perhaps taking a nap at home.

"Looks like she's not here." Petrus's eyes revealed the same fear that Pete felt.

"I guess...we should go?" Pete said, relieved. This was a stupid idea anyway.

There was a loud click behind them, followed by another one. Both boys looked at the sticker-covered shop door as if a lion were about to pounce. The door opened slowly, and the Indian girl's face appeared. She was smiling, but her eyes scanned the world behind them, in the direction of the street.

"Quick," she waved them in. They looked at one another, and then back toward the street before Pete slipped in first, followed closely by Petrus.

It was cold in the shop and the sweet scent of furniture polish filled the air. She locked the door behind them, and they followed her in silence past the pool table to a couple of tall shelves containing nuts, bolts, and fishing tackle. She smiled but seemed very nervous—fidgeting with her long purple pants first and then with her plait.

"I'm sorry about last week. I...uh...I couldn't make it," Pete said.

She didn't say anything, but something in her smile told him that she understood that it was fear that kept him away.

Her eyes went from Pete to the floor and around to Petrus, never really stopping for long. "Pete tells me your name is Petrus?" she said. Pete felt a fluttering in his stomach. She remembered his name! And it rolled so effortlessly off her tongue, with such relaxed familiarity, like...

Petrus made no attempt to look in her direction. Instead, his eyes were fixed on a shelf containing reels of fishing line. He nodded. "Petrus. Yes." He appeared to have a constriction of sorts in his throat, raised his fist to his mouth and coughed twice. He briefly glanced up at the girl. "I am so happy to see you." He spoke breathlessly, looked down at his feet, shook his head. "I was so worried."

"I'm fine." She smiled shyly and examined a tub with small fishhooks next to her without picking it up. "No need for concern." She said it automatically, without thought, like a response to a "how are you." Then she pursed her lips, forcing another smile, this time painful in appearance. "I mean, I appreciate your concern. Thanks." She struggled to keep the smile, it disappeared quicker than it had arrived. She fidgeted with the seams of her pants and then reached out to pick up the tub with fishhooks she had barely taken her eyes off.

Silence returned. The only sound was the tick-tocking of a wall clock somewhere in the shop. Even that seemed to whisper, too afraid to really break the silence. Pete knew he had to say something, take the lead, speak, chat, whatever—about anything—just so that they could get out of there and never return. But he had lost all ability to speak or make a sound. His eyes were somehow glued to the ceiling, his body utterly bereft of feeling. Motionless. A sudden and in-tense urge filled him to make up an excuse and leave. But he couldn't even blink, let alone move or speak, so he remained fixed in that one position, eyes on the ceiling.

It was the girl who disturbed this immense silence. "Uhm," she said, placing the tub of fishhooks back on the shelf. Whatever idea had formed brightened her face significantly, her eyes widened and the painful smile of earlier was replaced with a hope-ful one. It caught the attention of the boys, perhaps mostly because of the relief of being rescued from the treacly thick silence which was suffocating them. "Can I get you guys something to drink? It's a shop, so we have everything..."

The unexpected offer momentarily freed Pete's voice from the muteness which had befallen him. Almost without realizing it, he said, "A Coke would be great, thanks." He wanted to add something, but his voice had returned to its mute state.

He was thankful that Petrus was also able to break the shackles of silence. "Me too," he said hastily, before adding an uncertain, "please?"

The girl disappeared so quickly that for a fleeting moment Pete wondered if he had imagined her, the conversation, everything. But to his left Petrus, hands in pockets, was the reminder that it was not just his mind playing tricks on him. They remained standing there, not looking at each other, not looking at anything, really. Waiting in silence. Waiting for the girl, or rather, waiting for time to pass so that this meeting of awkwardness would end, and life could return to the way it was.

When she retuned, the boys accepted the ice-cold drinks with appreciative nods. Pete was thankful for the drink; it gave him something to do. Every time he felt the urge to say something or escape, he would bring the bottle to his lips and take a small sip. This happened every few seconds.

They were still standing among the shelves in the darkest part of the shop, hiding. From what, they did not know, possibly each other. The girl had picked up the same tub of fishhooks she had previously inspected and searched with her finger through the box. Then, as if addressing one of the fishhooks, she asked: "English or Afrikaans?" Her lips formed the same painful, shy, almost apologetic smile. She raised her head just long enough to meet Petrus's gaze before they both returned their attention to the objects they were pretending to look at. "I mean, which one do you prefer, Petrus? Feel comfortable with?"

"Eish, it doesn't matter too much," Petrus's voice sounded small, almost lost between the shelves, the constriction of earlier apparently still there, "but my Afrikaans is better." He turned his head to the side and took a quick sip of the Coke he was clutching in his right hand, like he was searching for courage in the sweet bubbles. "Sometimes the English—it turns square in my mouth," he said with slightly more power.

Pete cleared his throat. He was having trouble breathing, wondering if there was something strange in the air. Something both he and Petrus were infected with, causing their throats to contract, their lungs to stop working, and their hearts to race. Because he could see what he was feeling in Petrus's face, hear it in his voice

Then he dared turn toward the girl. Why he couldn't just have kept staring at the bottle in his hands, he did not know. It was as if he sensed that she was looking at him. In that moment he surrendered the ability to breathe, all air evaporated from his lungs, he almost gasped aloud. Even in the dim light of the shop, her hazelnut eyes still seemed to shine—and they were looking straight at him, trapping him.

He panicked. The first thought that crossed his mind was to put the bottle down and run out of the shop as quickly as he could. But he didn't. Instead, his mouth opened. "I just realized..." Pete started and scratched his eye, hoping he would be able to breathe again soon, "I don't even know what your name is?" He raised his hand and pointed his thumb toward Petrus. "We don't know what your name is."

She broke eye contact. Pete immediately drew a breath, letting the stale air fill his lungs. Glad he didn't pass out right there. "Sarita," she said in a soft, sweet tone.

Sarita. The word echoed in Pete's mind. Suddenly it was all he could hear. Her name escaping her soft lips. *Wow*, he thought. Could it be the most beautiful name he had ever heard? Sarita. It continued to bounce around his thoughts. What a name, he almost said out loud. It suited her perfectly.

"It's a really nice name," Petrus articulated Pete's thoughts and stopped the echo in his mind.

"Thanks," she whispered while turning her attention to the fishhooks again. "Another Coke?" she asked, which made both boys give the half full bottles in their hands a quizzical look.

Some minutes later Sarita had brought a next round of Cokes even though their first round was not finished. They stood around the pool table, not really knowing how and when they had moved from in between the shelves at the back to the center of the shop. Pete rolled the cue ball around in his hand and Petrus inspected the pool table's pockets.

Sarita took a step toward the opposite end of the pool table to where Pete was standing, Petrus to her right, and drew a deep breath. "Cokes okay? Cold enough?" she asked. The boys looked somewhat startled by the sound of her voice, taking a few seconds to register what she said before they both nodded in their different ways: Pete long, slow nods, and Petrus, short, fast nods.

Sarita bit her canine into her bottom lip, then let out a short, tense puff of air. Pete couldn't tell if it was a smile on her face or some kind of grimace. "This is awkward, isn't it?" she said. "Look at us, pretending like *this* is normal. And not pretending very well at that." She bit down on her bottom lip again. Pete wondered if she wished away her words.

For a moment Pete thought Petrus was going to say something. He had opened his mouth and straightened up somewhat, but no sooner had his mouth opened and it closed again.

"I imagined it would be weird, but—" She paused, appearing to consider her next words, but then she seemed to shrug it off—whatever inner debate she was having—almost smiling and no longer looking at the green baize of the pool table. "Not this weird!" The last words burst out of her mouth like a laugh, somewhat hysterical.

Pete was caught completely off guard by her sudden quip and laugh; he could not stop his guffaw. His outburst set Petrus off, and for a few unguarded moments the three of them laughed, until both Pete and Petrus tried to drown their hysteria in the bottles of Coke they were still clutching.

Sarita's shy smile returned. "I find hysterical laughter to be a great tension breaker." Petrus snorted, and Pete chuckled. Somehow, he felt slightly more at ease, but within the context of incredible unease.

"You're funny," Petrus said but then his face changed, like he was about to apologize.

The awkward silence that briefly subsided was

back again, like a self-closing door that just refused to stay open. The only thing occupying Pete's mind was an exit strategy. Surely he wasn't alone in thinking that whatever this was had gone on for too long. The momentary burst of laughter hardly broke the tension Sarita was talking about. Or was she being sarcastic? He pondered that thought for a moment. Would an Indian girl be sarcastic? Was sarcasm something that was used in all cultures?

It was Sarita again who ventured to unlock the silence. Pete wished he had spoken first. Excused himself. Said his goodbyes, but her melodic voice beat him to it, again. "I just had a crazy thought," she said. "Is this kind of gathering even legal? You know, with us being..." She tilted her head as a gesture. Perhaps for Pete or Petrus to complete her sentence?

"Different?" Petrus said, then his mouth continued to move as he fought for words, he was tugging at his ear. "Different races, together, like this?"

Sarita nodded.

"I seriously doubt it's legal," Pete said with so much conviction that he surprised himself.

"The irony is if we were caught, we wouldn't even be locked up together," Sarita said in a light-hearted tone. But the words "locked up" were all Pete really heard. What was he doing there? Had he truly lost it? Just because some black guy planted a seed in his head, just because his thoughts were so messed up that he somehow thought an Indian girl was...He couldn't even allow himself to think it. No. He had to leave. He had to leave straight away. Perhaps this was like a variation of that Stockholm syndrome they learned about in history. Only this must be Dannhauser syndrome. And he didn't want it—he had enough on his mind to last him a lifetime already.

"Listen, I, uh—" Pete mumbled, still uncertain of exactly what excuse he would use to get out.

His words dried up the moment he snuck a peek across the pool table. Sarita's hazelnut eyes on him, stifling all the other words he thought he might say. Rendering him paralyzed. She seemed to see that, or perhaps he just imagined it, but there was the slightest twitch on her face, like a smile, deepening the indentation of her dimples for one heartbeat.

She looked away, not at anything in particular, her face angled toward the door. The skin on her face tightened, her eyes barely open, her jaw muscles flexed.

"Why couldn't we have just been three rebel teenagers?" she said.

Petrus shot a confused glance at Pete. He could only answer with an equally confused shake of the head. Still Sarita looked away.

"Meeting up secretly for the pure thrill of it? Just because we knew it was illegal. Just because we were tired of society telling us what to do?"

Now she looked up. Her stare was somewhere between Pete and Petrus, her eyes glassy.

"But," she said and stopped. She frowned, cast her eyes downwards. "That is not why we are here. We are not rebels. We are not thrillseekers, law breakers, anything."

She threw her head back, eyes closed and let out a frustrated sigh.

"We are just—" she stopped again.

Petrus tugged on his ear. "Lucky?" he ventured.

Sarita let her head drop forward, her chin settling on her chest, she peered up at Petrus.

"To be alive," he added hastily. "We could have all died that night."

She considered his words for a few moments. "I don't feel lucky," she said. "When I struggle to fall asleep at night, knowing that as soon as I start dreaming that monster will be back, that doesn't feel lucky."

"I didn't mean it like that," Petrus tried.

Sarita waved his words away. "I'm sorry, Petrus, that came out wrong. It's just. It's so strange to have you guys here, you know?" It was obvious that she was trying to smile but couldn't. "Some part of my brain had hoped that I was just going crazy. That all of this...all of that night was just a story my mind made up." The tears in her eyes glistened under the dim neon light.

She threw her hands up. "But here you are." Her smile was achingly painful to look at, Pete stared down at the fading green baize of the pool table. "A reminder that I am not crazy. A reminder that it did happen. That night did happen." Her hand shot up to her face, the tears cascading over her skin.

"We'll go," Petrus said. He put down his Coke. "Sorry, we shouldn't have—"

"No!" she called out. "Please." Gesturing for him to stay. "Now at least I know I'm not crazy, hey?" She smiled through the tears, wiping them away as best she could.

"Did you know that I was on my way to a friend's house that day?" Sarita said, not expecting an answer. "I wanted to surprise her for her birthday. I even made Jalebi, her favorite." She saw the expression in

Pete and Petrus's faces and quickly added, "Indian sweets."

She tucked a loose dangling strand of hair behind her ear. "I didn't even have time to react. Before I knew it, I was in his car. He had a gun. I thought he was going to kill me but, in the car, just before we stopped, he told me exactly what he was going to do to me." Tears spurted out of her eyes, like a dam wall that just broke, it gushed out, all at once. "I begged and begged him to shoot me, break my neck—whatever. He laughed, kept laughing."

She buried her face in her hands. Her whole body shook. Petrus and Pete snuck a bewildered peek at one another, neither knowing if they should do or say something. Pete felt the blood drain from his face. His memories of that night, the demons in his mind, and Sarita's words all battled in his head for a place where all of it made sense. But nothing did.

Sarita took a deep staccato breath behind her cupped hands. Then she dropped her hands and raised her head. The enormity of her all-consuming pain needed no words. "You know what the weirdest thing is?" she said, her voice weak and trembling. "Some illogical, unreasonable, crazy part of my brain told me this was all in my head. Some hallucination or something. A thing my mind concocted. But—"

Her face contracted, she was trying to fight it, but losing the battle.

"Seeing you—" She couldn't look at them. Her head flopped down, tears plunged on the cold tiles at her feet. "It makes it real. It means I wasn't hallucinating. It means he did...That man did—" That was as far as her voice would go. Her hands covered her drenched face again, the shaking was violent, like a toy wound up too far, rocking to and fro until it knew nothing else.

Pete and Petrus looked at her, then at one another, eyes wide, damp.

A sudden realization dawned on Pete. The pain slowly seeping out of Sarita's face made his fears and anxieties seem completely trivial. To think that he was worried about being publicly shamed as a *kaffir-brother* or called gay.... Those things suddenly seemed unimportant and very egocentric. He couldn't believe that he was so preoccupied with his own fears that he didn't even consider that her trauma was ten, or even a hundred, times worse. Guilt weighed him down. Why hadn't he come sooner? And why was it that his curiosity and her bewitching eyes were the reasons he finally came here, rather than his concern for a girl who was viciously attacked by that yellow-mustached asshole? Was he any better? Was he any better than Rudie, if all he wanted was to satisfy his curiosity so that *he* could feel better? What about her?

What...about...her?

"We should have come sooner. I'm so sorry, Sarita. No one has the right to do what he did, no one should go through what you did. I'm so sorry I didn't...do more." The power in Pete's voice dwindled. He hated himself. He wanted to make things better for her, but he couldn't, he couldn't do a single thing, he couldn't undo anything. He wanted to scream. He wanted to bury his fists in Rudie's execrable face and keep punching until there was nothing left. No memory of the yellow mustache, no memory of that odious laugh, no memory of *that* night. Nothing.

"You did so much. Don't ever say you didn't do enough. You stopped him, risked your own lives. No, you guys are amazing. I'm sorry, look at me: I'm a mess. You come to see me, and I blubber like an old lady." She wiped the last few tears away with her thumbs and tried hard to smile.

"Oh dear!" she cried out.

"Who's there?" Petrus whispered and swung his head in the direction of the door.

"No, the clock." She pointed at a faded wall clock with a photograph of Charles and Diana on their wedding day.

"It's ten to four, my parents could arrive at any minute. They can never—" She spoke in haste and slapped her hands on her cheeks.

"We'll go," Petrus said and took a step toward the door.

"Yes, we're off. Thanks for the Coke," Pete aimed to say something else, but his legs had already taken him to the door.

She walked with them, peeked outside before she unlocked the door as quietly as she could.

"Thank you very much for the Coke," Petrus said, shaking his head. "I am sorry for your hurt."

"Yeah, I...aggh, people like that—" Pete struggled.

Sarita took them both by the arm and for a few moments locked their eyes in hers. "Please come again. I know it sounds crazy, and this was all a bit awkward and weird but please, I would love it if you came back."

Those were the last words spoken that afternoon. Pete and Petrus nodded deep in thought and walked side by side toward Main Street. Sarita remained standing in the open door until she saw Pete disappear to the left, and Petrus to the right. Then she locked the door and stepped back into the darkness.

CHRISTINA

Christina was fifty-three years old and had been working for the de Langes for nine years. Her duties included ironing, cleaning, washing up, chopping vegetables and doing the laundry. Before the de Langes, she was a maid for old Mr. Beukes on the Bitterberg farm. She worked there for over twenty years, but when the old man passed away, her services were no longer needed. Work was scarce. For months she tried to find something, but it seemed everyone had very settled, long term maids. She even asked at the mine whether there was anything she could do there, but 1976 wasn't a great year for job hunting.

One Saturday morning early in 1977 she walked the streets of Dannhauser once more, knocking on doors, calling from the front gates, asking for any work, even if it was one day per week. Her husband was hurt in a serious accident at the mine two years before and his sad little incapacity check barely paid for their children's school uniforms. He had also forged a strong bond with the bottle since his accident, which didn't help. She simply had to work. The few chickens she had left wouldn't last very long, and with the drought, her vegetables and corn died before they even broke ground.

A tennis ball flew through the air, like a large green apple. It bounced up in front of her and half in shock, she caught it. She studied the ball in her hand; the fluffy green wool was soft against her skin.

A poor attempt at a whistle caught her attention, followed by a child calling out, "Nice catch!"

The voice belonged to a little white boy with a wide forehead, a nose that was just a little too big for his face and sparkling green eyes. His dark blonde hair was very short, and his smile revealed two missing front teeth.

"That's my ball," he said and held out his small hand.

Christina handed it back to him slowly and whispered, "Sorry, *baas*."

"I have to play outside because Mom is angry with Dad because he chased our maid away. He said she was useless and Mom asked him whether his underwear would wash itself from now on. Mom sent me out because I thought it would be funny to see Dad wash his own underwear. It would be funny, eh?" The boy rambled on without taking a breath, but Christina couldn't help but wonder whether the green ball was a sign from God.

Perhaps it was because five minutes later an excited young boy told his parents that he had found a new maid. And nine years later it was as if she had always been there.

"Go ask Christina to iron that for you. If you insist on wearing that shirt to church tomorrow, it can't look like *that*." Deanne pointed at the creases in Pete's lime green shirt as if they were contagious.

Pete took his shirt and walked out the kitchen door, across the concrete slab, to the washing room, which was a standalone structure. The door was open and the ironing board stood next to the chest freezer. To the left were two deep washbasins, and next to it the washing machine.

Christina had the iron in her hand, working her way through some bedsheets. She wore a pale orange-and-white uniform that his mom had bought at Pep, and around her head, she had wrapped a dark green-and-yellow cloth. She always wrapped long, colorful sheets of cloth around her when she changed out of her uniform and she always wore a black shirt and a gray jersey, summer, and winter. Her face was round, warm, and compared to their previous maid at least, not particularly dark.

Pete liked her. He found her quiet sense of humor a real treat and sometimes just hung out with her whilst she ironed, just for fun. She was the one who made stews for them when their grandad passed away and even checked that all their homework was done. She covered for him when he broke the storeroom window with a cricket ball, and taught him funny, nonsensical Zulu phrases, like: "Do you sell two-legged cows?" and, "Thank you for spoiling my milk tart." She always thought he was funny when he came up with new phrases, and laughed every time, in her restrained, hand-in-front-of-mouth style.

"Christina, please iron this shirt for me?" Pete asked dangling it in front of her.

"Shoh-shoh." Her favorite expression.

"What did you do with this, *baas* Pete?" She shook her head.

"I was trying to buy a two-legged cow," he replied in his best Zulu. She burst out laughing, her hand over her mouth.

Pete stared out of the three small windows above the washing machine. The leaves on the trees lining their little street were changing very quickly into yellows and rusty browns.

"Why do you call me *baas*?" Pete asked as he turned back to face her. Christina stopped ironing and looked at him questioningly.

"I mean, my dad, he is your boss, so I understand it, but I don't pay you. Why call me '*baas*'? Why not just Pete?"

"Shoh-shoh. It's respect, *baas* Pete. I work for your family. Yes, *baas* Rikus pays me, but I work for all of you," she said.

"I think...I want you to just to call me Pete. The word '*baas*'...I'm not so sure about that word anymore," Pete said.

"*Aikona*, I cannot. It doesn't work like that. You are the *baas*, and I am the *ousie*."

"But what if I don't want to be called '*baas*' anymore?"

"*Baas* Pete," she said and clicked her tongue. "You cannot go changing things you cannot change."

Pete's eyes sought out the world beyond the windows again and followed a single yellow leaf as the breeze gently rocked it to the ground. The room was warm from steam spewing out of the iron. Christina worked her way around a beige bed sheet, pressing down hard, making the ironing board creak.

"Do you remember how you caught that ball the day we met?" Pete said with a bittersweet smile.

Christina continued ironing but nodded and flashed a shy smile.

"You should have become a cricketer. I tell you,

151

you've missed your calling," he teased.

She just shook her head and tried to suppress her smile. He stood there for a few moments watching how her hand steered the iron with great skill. Her smile slowly faded.

"Thanks for the shirt," he said. She looked up, ostensibly surprised that he was still there.

"When we're alone," he whispered, "please just call me Pete? Just once?" He turned and walked out. The air was unsettled, and the cold wind was tugging at his hair. All around him leaves and dry grass fluttered. The easterly wind never brought rain, yet it felt like a storm was brewing.

15:04

A gentle drizzle settled in over Main Street. The small drops barely touched the surface, and a thin layer of dust and fall leaves covered the pavement. Pete walked slowly, tilting his face skywards to feel the watery kisses on his skin. He walked with trepidation, wary of haste, not wanting to get there too early, but he didn't want to turn around either. If he stayed home he could have been paging through the latest *CAR Magazine* right now or listening to tapes, but instead, he was walking in the middle of Main Street— shrouded in this drizzly haze, seemingly without beginning or end, which had settled over this emptiness, this emptiness filled with secrets.

The only sound to be heard was his North Stars treading cautiously on the time battered paving slabs. In the distance an Indian mynah called out to a friend, but just as quickly the soft white blanket protecting this town drowned out its call. Just like it did everything else.

Pete stopped. He should have stayed at home. Around him dark shadows made the road appear void-like, as if he stood on the edge of a cliff and the wind begged him not to jump. But his North Stars had other ideas. His eyes followed one *Closed* sign after another, and with each step, the cliff came closer, and the drop seemed higher, until a strained accent called out from the darkness, "Pete...psst."

He was here again. It was Sunday afternoon, and he was standing outside the Eating House, hiding in the shadows with a black guy named Petrus. Couldn't he just step off the cliff and let the misty haze consume him?

"I thought you might not come," Petrus said.

Pete stared at Petrus's bare feet. Yellow lines of damp dust formed sagging socks around his ankles. His left leg was sprinkled with spots of white paint, and his hands were covered with scratch marks. It was not difficult to imagine what he had done during the time that Pete once half-heartedly started mowing the lawn, read the first twenty pages of *Animal Farm*, read the celebrity news in his mom's magazines several times, and listened to *Alphaville* and *Foreigner* so many times that both tapes got stuck. He had had to carefully remove the tapes, not to tear the delicate film, and wind the film back using a pencil.

"Are we not going?" Petrus was getting anxious.

"Yes, we're going," Pete said without intonation. He wiped the drizzle from his forehead and wondered why it felt like he was going to see her for the first time? Did everything change the week before? Was she right: Did their visit make it real? And by going back, did it mean that not one of them would ever escape this thing? *This* reality would become their reality, like a tape that was spinning, trying to play, but the film had fallen off, and now it was just spinning, eating the film—destroying it—until there was nothing left?

"Are we doing the right thing?" Petrus asked as they approached the *Naidoo and Sons* sign. Pete was taken aback. Could he read his mind? Did a witchdoctor give him some concoction which made him clairvoyant? The moment evaporated when Petrus started fidgeting with his black curls and then tugged his ear. He wasn't clairvoyant, Pete thought, he was just nervous, like him.

They walked up to the door and Pete tapped against the window with his fingernail that he really should have trimmed a couple of days ago. He looked at his watch; it had just hit 15:04.

"My mom always says a lady should never be kept waiting," Sarita said with a mischievous smile and handed them each an ice-cold bottle of Coke.

They both smiled uncomfortably and started drinking.

"So, back to school tomorrow?" she asked.

Without warning a burp was building up in Pete's throat. "Yup, back to the cage," Pete said with great effort.

"How about you, Petrus?"

"Yes, also tomorrow."

"Where is your school?"

"It's Jabulani Secondary School, on *baas* Lubbe's farm."

"How far is that from your home?"

"Eish, probably one hour." Petrus gestured with his hands that it was an approximation.

"Walking?" she asked.

"Walking, running. Both."

"You run two hours every day and then you go for a run in the afternoons as well?" Pete had to ask, it was just too preposterous to be true.

"Yes, I like it. It makes me fast."

"Dude, that's crazy." Pete shook his head, sipped his Coke, as his disbelief quickly turned into awe.

"And you, Pete? Are you in Dundee High?" Sarita asked.

"For my sins, yes. It also takes me an hour to get to school, but on a bus. If I had to run to school, I would have left school a long time ago. I probably would have dropped out in Standard Five and would be selling jaffles for a living now." Pete laughed, but it was funnier for him than the other two. He imagined humor probably didn't translate well, or perhaps they didn't know what jaffles were.

"Do you know jaffles?" Pete asked.

Neither did.

"It's very simple. You have these two round plates that you pinch together, almost like a hinged grid." Instead of the affirming nods he thought his story deserved, he was greeted by two vacant expressions.

"Anyway, it's basically like mince squashed in between two slices of bread, and you cook it over... agg, doesn't matter. One day when my business is up and running, I'll let you taste. So, where do you go to school Sarita?"

"In those ugly gray buildings at the end of Main Street, Dannhauser Secondary School," she said with a little sigh.

"Oh yeah, I know exactly where it is. I've heard that that school only goes up to Standard Eight, no Standard Nine or Matric. Is that true?" Pete asked.

"Yes, unfortunately. I'll have to go to a new school next year. There is a decent school in Ladysmith that my dad likes, or perhaps they'll send me to Durban. We'll see," she said.

"So, leaving Dannhauser?" Pete asked. Unexpected angst flowed through him like there was something very precious entwined within that moment, but something he couldn't place, and which felt like it was slipping through his fingers.

"Isn't there an Indian school in Dundee?" he asked before she could answer.

"There is, but we don't have any family there, so it will be Ladysmith or Durban. In both of those we have lots of family," she said and tucked the loose strand of hair behind her ear.

"Can't you take a bus?"

"There are no school buses for Indians. Apparently, public transport to Dundee is also very expensive."

"That sucks!" Pete realized he said that much louder than he should've. "I mean, that's bad, for you, and your parents, right?"

"I guess." She meandered away with her hands tucked behind her back and stared at some of the latest Bollywood videos.

"Maybe it's a good thing. We all want to leave Dannhauser eventually, don't we? I will just get my opportunity sooner," she said after a pause.

"My father says this town is the best place in the world. He says in cities you only find two things: hunger and trouble," Petrus said.

"So don't you want to leave?" she asked.

"Well, maybe one day to run the Comrades marathon." Petrus smiled shyly. "I don't know if there is anything out there for me."

Sarita turned away from the videos to face Petrus. "Aren't you curious?"

"Yes, but—" Petrus tugged his ear again. "Eish,

here I have a name, my father has a name, and my mother has a name. There in the city...I'll just be another black farm boy. I don't think—" Petrus stopped and took a short breath, the kind which doesn't even make it to your lungs.

"If you can get Matric, you'll do well out there," Pete said. "Not many blacks, uhm, black people, have Matric. You'll stand out. Our maid's son finished Matric last year and he got a job at the mine straight away. A good job."

"Eish, I don't know. I like the farm, and one day I'd love to have my own cattle, lots of them, but... sometimes I wonder what it would be like to live here in town, in a nice house, with a TV. Just for a little while." Petrus looked up at the ceiling and slipped his hands into his pockets.

"But it doesn't matter anyway. There's no place for us in town. My father says you shouldn't dream dreams that can hurt you." He jolted suddenly as if he had just been woken up. "Besides, I have to leave school after Standard Eight, to work on the farm full-time."

"Why can't you just finish Matric?" Pete asked.

"There is too much work on the farm. *Baas* Gerrit said he would pay for my books and uniform until Standard Eight, but then I have to work for him full-time. He said it's important to learn about reading and writing but the rest is just book stuff."

"He probably knows once you have Matric you could get work anywhere. I think he's blocking your progress because he is worried you might leave," Pete said, rather upset by the idea.

"*Aikona*, he's a good man, there's just a lot of work on the farm and my father also said that all this school business doesn't speak as loud as real work."

"What if you made him a deal?" Sarita interjected. Both guys turned to her in surprise.

"Deal?" Petrus dared ask.

"Yes, a deal. You could say to him, if he supports you through to Matric, then he will benefit because you will be able to take on bigger and more challenging roles to ease his workload. In return, you will pledge to work back the extra years he helped you. So, if you include Standard Eight, that means you will guarantee to work for him for at least three years after Matric."

Petrus pondered her words. He turned to Pete as if to ask for help, but Pete nodded in agreement.

"I don't know if *baas* Gerrit—" Petrus started.

"You will never know unless you ask. What have you got to lose?" Sarita said. Pete continued nodding to convince Petrus, all the while thinking that it was quite clear that Sarita was the daughter of a businessman.

"Eish, I'll try. He's a difficult man, but I really want Matric."

"You must. The worst thing that can happen is that you'll end up in the same position you are in now," she said. Petrus answered with a perturbed but agreeable moan, scratched his hair a little and focused all his attention on the last few drops of Coke in his bottle.

"Are you going to become a politician, Sarita?" Pete asked with a grin. He watched her face closely, how it lit up every time she thought of a new idea. There was a joy in her which was light-years away from the pain of the week before. But he knew it was still there, this was merely a temporary escape. What devils haunted her thoughts, he wondered, hidden behind the soft, impossibly smooth skin around her eyes? Did she cry softly into her pillow at night, hoping that no one would hear?

"Me?" She pointed to herself in shock.

"No, thank you. I don't like politics, or maybe I don't like politicians? Either way, no, definitely not. Heaven knows how they can sleep at night. To lie for a living takes a very special kind of messed-up human being...if you could call them that." She rolled her eyes at Pete as though he had gone mad and this was the most outrageous thing she had ever heard. Petrus laughed at her as she pulled all sorts of comical faces.

"So what *do* you want to be when you grow up?" Petrus asked. Pete was startled. He was so lost in her eyes that he completely forgot that Petrus was standing right next to him.

"I wish I knew," she said, followed by a nervous giggle. "When I was young, I dreamed of being anything from an astronaut to a nature conservationist." She turned her face and smiled slightly embarrassed.

"And now?" Pete asked.

She turned to face him and searched his eyes as if she were expecting to find the answers in there. Then she fidgeted with one of the buttons on her shirt. "I think it's our...duty to make the world a better place in some way. But what does that actually mean? Should I become a doctor, or a lawyer, or a teacher? I don't know anymore. And then I watch the news and I listen to my parents go on and on and it all starts to feel so incredibly..." She looked up, but not at them. "It feels so big, you know? They keep telling me that we can't fix it anymore. It's too broken. In pieces. Does it make sense?"

"But you don't feel the same way?" Pete said.

She drew a deep breath and held it for a few counts before she exhaled slowly. "I believe in hope." She smiled and shook her head. "I'm burdened with eternal optimism," she said and fluttered her eyelashes whilst raising her hands apologetically. This made the others laugh.

"One thing I do know, I don't want to be like my mom," she said.

"How come?" Pete asked.

"I just don't think...it doesn't look like she's happy. Like she's living inside a dark cloud or something. I sometimes wonder if she had dreams, you know, when she was young, to be something...else?"

"Like an astronaut?" Pete asked, and Petrus giggled.

"Maybe? I just wonder if she let go of her dreams, or if she still dreams? She never talks about things like that. She married young, then I came along, the rest..." She waved the words away as if they were inconsequential. "I'm babbling."

"Was it an arranged marriage?" Pete asked.

She nodded.

"I have to be honest, I don't get the whole arranged marriage thing," Pete said.

"You and me both. I swear I'll run away if my dad has to pick someone for me." The way she said it prompted a burst of laughter from the others.

"And children?" Petrus asked. "Do think you'd want to have children?"

"Probably? One day. I'm much too young to think about things like that. How about you?"

"Only if they are nothing like my little brother. Eish, he does whatever he wants. My parents do nothing.

My sisters say it's because he's the youngest, and all the youngest ones are always spoiled."

"Hey!" Pete cut him off. "I'm the youngest."

Petrus puckered his mouth and whispered, "Sorry," which made Sarita laugh.

When her laughter subsided, she said, "I must say, spoiled or not, I wouldn't have minded having a brother or sister."

"You haven't seen *my* brother," Petrus said big-eyed.

She glanced up at the wall clock, and her smile disappeared. Both boys knew what that meant.

Before Pete realized what had happened, she walked to well within his rather large personal space. It felt as though another person had climbed inside his skin, and he twitched and squirmed, trying hard not to show it. She smelled like furniture polish and a spring flower Pete couldn't place. From this close, he could see that the flawlessness of her complexion wasn't just in his mind. Her lips looked like the icing on his mom's coffee cake, and just as sweet, and were about to curl into her dimples.

"You guys are so cool. I cannot express how much I appreciate this." Her gaze dropped to the floor. Pete wondered if Indians could blush.

"We'll see you soon," Pete said, his voice croaky all of a sudden.

"Promise?" she asked, her eyes pleading.

"It's not easy, but—" Petrus started.

"—we'll make a plan," Pete completed his sentence.

"I can't next week, but really, any Sunday after that." She looked Petrus in the eyes for a long time, almost long enough to make Pete wonder if she had forgotten that he was there too. Her eyes finally broke away from Petrus, her head almost automatically dropping as if eye contact was somehow a heinous crime, before, just for a stolen moment, she quickly glimpsed up at Pete with a smile that he knew meant something, something important, but he couldn't decipher it. His stomach bounced up and down like a yo-yo.

Pete and Petrus walked back to Main Road. The drizzle of earlier was replaced by a light rain shower now, and the white clouds had turned to a dark gray.

"You running this week?" Petrus asked.

"I'll have to see. We have our first league game—rugby—this Saturday, so I suspect training might be brutal."

"Oh."

"Right, I suppose I'll see you when I see you? Good luck with Uncle Gerrit," Pete said and turned left. The breeze had picked up and the rain sprayed against his face. Over his shoulder he heard a soft "thanks" followed by the sound of bare feet running on damp concrete.

KICK-OFF

"Pete, hey, listen." Rikus rested his hands on Pete's shoulders and followed Pete's wandering eyes until he could no longer escape his dad's gaze. Pete suddenly wished his dad had just stayed at home today.

"Life isn't always fair." His dad spoke softly. "To tell the truth, it's more often unfair than fair." Pete looked at the checkred red-and-black rugby jersey he was wearing—a fourth team jersey.

"The coach hates me. He has made it his life's ambition to destroy my rugby career. He told me to my face that if Jannie van Niekerk hadn't hurt himself trying to sneak out of the hostel on Wednesday night, I would have spent my Saturday warming the reserve bench. A reserve! Not even good enough to start in a team where most guys can't even spell the word rugby," Pete said.

"Easy Pete. No one is out to get you. Your coach probably hasn't seen your true potential yet. You said he was a hockey coach?"

"Yup, and I wish I could shove a hockey stick up his—"

"Pete! Stop it now! No, no, no. You're a de Lange and we don't sit around feeling sorry for ourselves. That Jannie kid hurting himself has given you an opportunity, so you can either mope around wondering why the entire world has turned against you, or you can run onto that field like the champion you are and show that coach what you are made of. If you do that, and the coach still keeps you in the fourth team, I will personally go and kick his little hockey arse." Pete's dad looked to see if anyone had heard him.

"Don't tell your mom I said that. You know what she's like, but women don't understand. This is rugby." His dad winked, let go of him and gave him a firm punch on the shoulder.

"What do we always say?" his dad asked.

"Play with your head up," Pete said.

"And eyes open. Wide open."

"Yes, Dad."

Pete jogged to the large yellow patch of grass adjacent to the disused outside toilet, left of the pavilion. *Quite an apt meeting place,* he thought, as he trundled to a group of boys standing with their hands in their pockets, without a coach in sight.

In the first half, Pete didn't touch the ball once. It was either knocked on before it came to him or his teammates skipped passes over him, behind him or anywhere else outside his reach. There were a few snide remarks while they were sucking on orange quarters during the break, but the one that cut the deepest was a self-satisfying bark from Mr. le Roux. "This is not a train, de Lange, we don't carry passengers. We can't play fourteen against fifteen, so stop sleep-walking and help your teammates, or I will ask Klayton to ensure that you get substituted." Needless to say, Klayton loved the idea. His crooked mouth salivated with satisfaction. This was the green light he had been waiting for and Pete knew that whatever he was planning would be very primal, very brutal, and not something you could just walk off.

After ten minutes in the second half, he still hadn't received the ball, but his shoulders were aching from making tackle after tackle because of the incomprehensible lack of any rugby sense from his bungling teammates. Funny how Mr. le Roux ignored the fact that he was the only one who hadn't missed a tackle, the only one who had stopped certain tries. There could no longer be any doubt: Mr. le Roux had it in for him.

They were 0-12 behind the visiting team, Newcastle High School's mighty fourths, and Newcastle had just stolen another lineout. The ball was moving quickly through their hands, scrumhalf to fly-half, fly-half to inside center. They were whipping the passes and Pete's teammates were too slow to react. Gaps were starting to appear everywhere; it was just a matter of getting the ball to their wing and it was a certain try. Pete played outside center and his opposite number was a giant, all six-foot-eight of him. But he was slow and like his dad had taught him: the bigger they are the harder they fall. He had been tackling him around the ankles all day, and the sluggish giant had made no impact on the game. Now all he had to do was catch the ball and pass it to the wing, and the try was theirs. Pete's wing came to help defend the channel inside him because their fly-half was allergic to tackling, so Pete was the last line of defense.

The Newcastle inside center floated a beautiful pass straight into the giant's oversized hands. Pete raced up to put pressure on him, hoping he could catch him before he got his pass away. As the giant was about to catch the ball, he looked up at Pete racing toward him. Their eyes met for a split second, and then, in a moment of distraction, the perfect pass ricocheted off his right hand and hit his knee, his large hands flapped about clumsily but it was too late, the ball had spilled forward and bounced slowly to the right.

Pete's head was up, and his eyes wide open. A rush of adrenaline shot through his heart. He stretched out his left hand, and the leather of the ball sunk into his palm. He tucked the ball under his arm sprinting into the gap between the cussing giant and the wing who was too close to the sideline.

Pete lifted his knees high, running at full tilt, all his senses heightened. Thirty meters from the try line, no defenders near him, with only the fullback laying in wait near the line. The fullback stooped low, with his arms outstretched like he wanted to catch a runaway chicken, but Pete could see the uncertainty in his eyes. Pete knew what to do: He could step off either leg—that chicken-catcher had no chance.

"I'm open, I'm open," a desperate shout came from his left. It was Klayton struggling to keep up, lagging a good five meters behind him. Klayton was right, the try line was wide open in front of him, no defenders, a certain score. But then he recalled the countless balls Klayton had knocked on during the game, and in practice. No, this was Pete de Lange's moment, and no sadistic wash-out was going to take that from him, especially not after that knee in the back at the last ruck. His focus switched back to the fullback, and the barrage of expletives rolling off Klayton's tongue became a distant hum. The chicken-catcher was moving from left to right, dancing on his toes, trying to force Pete into giving his plan away, but Pete didn't swerve an inch, he kept running straight at him.

Just before impact, Pete shouted "Klayton!," and he could see the absolute shock on Klayton's face, so much so that he ran slower. The fullback glanced at Klayton, uncertain. He was now almost in the tackle zone. Pete pulled the ball back and swung his arms through the perfect pass, only to keep hold of the ball. The fullback followed his arms, lost balance and fell to his right. Pete didn't even have to side-step him, his path had been cleared, the perfect dummy. He ran in under the posts and dotted down. Dundee High 4, Newcastle High 12. An intoxicating rush pulsed through him.

Twenty minutes later large dark sweat patches discolored the referee's light brown jersey, and his bald head glistened in the sunshine. He took a deep breath and blew all the air he had left in his lungs into the whistle, before resting his hands on his thighs, panting.

It was the end of the match. Dundee 16, Newcastle 16.

There were a few half-hearted handshakes, and thirty tired boys, some with grazed knees, some with bloodied noses, ambled off the field. Their reward for putting their bodies on the line was small plastic cups filled with bright orange Oros, waiting for them on a steel table in front of the pavilion.

Pete didn't like Oros, but today it was like champagne. The morning sun was bright, and the sky deep blue. He took another sip. The sweet nectar tickled his throat, and he couldn't help but smile, because after his first try everything changed: He changed everything. He searched through the mixture of parents and children around him but couldn't spot his dad.

"Hey, shitface!" Klayton stormed him from behind, knocked what was left of the Oros out of his hand and grabbed him by the collar.

"Think you're some sort of hero? I was wide open! I swear, next game better watch yourself. If I get you in a loose scrum, I will make sure your rugby days are over."

"That won't be necessary, Klayton." Mr. le Roux stepped closer. Klayton gave Pete an almighty shove, making him stagger backward.

"Pete, I want you to soak in this moment." Mr. le Roux closed his eyes and breathed in through his nose. "The excitement in the air, parents, children, all here to enjoy one thing—team sports." He almost sang the words and waved his hands around like a hippie dancing to the beat of a bongo drum.

Then his face turned stark. He glared at Pete.

"Remember that term: team sport. Not mister, 'I want to do everything on my own because I think I'm better than everyone.' Well, I suppose in a dump like Dannhauser you might be considered some sort of a rugby star, and tonight mommy will give you sweeties and daddy will blow smoke up your ass. Everyone so bloody impressed with your four tries, and how you singlehandedly managed to snatch a draw from the claws of defeat. Now let me tell you something: If you hadn't played like a selfish git, we would have won. You, de Lange, cost us the game." He lowered the finger he was pointing in Pete's face and arched his back, looked around him, then said, "I want you to remember this moment because it will be the last time you play for one of my teams. Ever." Mr. le Roux glanced at Klayton, who gave him an approving grin before Mr. Le Roux walked off.

Klayton shoved Pete in the chest and leaned closer. "Perhaps I should punch your teeth out? Try whistling one of your stupid Dutchman songs then, hero boy." He laughed in Pete's face with his garlic breath, mocked a head-butt and walked off, still laughing.

His big day was over, and he would never play for Mr. le Roux again, but Pete's smile just wouldn't go away. Four tries in a match was a new school record, and all of them in the second half, and he hadn't missed a single tackle. To say the least, he was unstoppable. And even if he never played again, *this* game, the one where he destroyed a whole team on his own, would be the one kids remembered. And *that* thought would be gnawing at Mr. le Roux every time he saw him.

A familiar face appeared, hopping down the steps of the pavilion, with a Coke in his hand. His dad had an aura about him as though he had just won a car in a sweepstake.

"Pete, you bloody genius, come here." Pete tried to stop him but in one swift move, his dad pulled him in close, squeezing hard.

"My boy, now that was rugby! Head up the whole time. Jeez, I'm so chuffed!" His dad beamed and slapped the Coke into Pete's hand. His dad never bought him Coke, said it was bad for your teeth, and dentists cost a fortune.

"That second try...I was mesmerized. I thought I was watching Danie Gerber play. You weaved through them without anyone laying a hand on you. Jeez." His dad rubbed him on the head, threw his arm around his shoulders and started walking. Pete felt slightly embarrassed by the public show of affection, but feelings of pride, love, and vindication, soon extinguished the discomfort.

It was ironic that his mom did give him sweets after his day of greatness, just as Mr. le Roux had so spitefully predicted. They were covered in chocolate and delicious. By the time he had shoved the third sweet into his mouth, he realized that this was the best he had felt since the start of the year. Nothing, not even a flash in his mind of *that* night, could spoil his great mood. His adrenaline levels were so high that he just couldn't sit still. He grabbed his running shoes and was out the door before his mom could ask if he wouldn't rather rest his tired legs.

His feet pounded the gravel road rhythmically. In his mind, he saw the amazement in his opponents' eyes every time he had side-stepped, dummied, and raced away from them. Before he knew it, he was on Uncle Gerrit's farm, at the very spot which harbored the bitterest of memories. He wanted to bring his joy here, to bleed it into the hurt.

It was quiet. He scanned the area, but there was nothing. His eyes followed the long two-track road all the way to the farmstead. Petrus was nowhere to be seen. He was desperate to tell someone, someone who wasn't his parents. Barend wasn't an option because today was his second team debut, and Pete hadn't even stayed to watch it. In all the excitement they had just left. What kind of friend does that?

He looked in the direction of the farmstead again. The sun was low, but there was still no sign of Petrus. *It was strange,* he thought, *Petrus was always there.* He always went for a run at this time of the day.

For the first time since his try fest, he felt empty, like a cork had been pulled out and his life was slowly seeping out, leaving only a dry, hollow nothingness. The realization that he wouldn't even see Sarita the following day, hit him like a stinging pain in his side. The breeze played with his shirt, and the Drakensberg guarded the horizon like a dark, impenetrable wall. Dead, yellow grass stretched as far as he could see, and an intense longing consumed him. This was not what champions should feel like. And where was Petrus? Shouldn't he be *there*?

THE PACKAGE

"Protea Eight, a package will be delivered to you on Wednesday afternoon by a man who will introduce himself as Solomon. He will deliver it to your shop between two and four. Make sure you personally receive it. Do not open the package under any circumstances and ensure that it is stored safely. On Friday morning take the package and fifty rands to Newcastle. Go to the Stone Mills Bread Factory. Ask for Gys. Hand him the package and the fifty rands. In turn, he will give you two bags with fresh bread and rolls. Do not ask questions, do not linger, get out of there as quickly as possible. Message understood?" Protea Seven asked.

"Yes, yes, message understood. Loud and clear. Thank you," Venny said hastily, trying not to sound overexcited.

"Don't let us down. Protea Seven out."

Venny sat in his chair for a few moments just staring at the microphone. After all this time of being kept in the dark, he could finally see a slither of light. He was part of the action.

Outside the locked metal door of his operations room, he could hear his wife calling, but in there, nothing else mattered. He had a mission. He would deliver that package like a pro. What could it be? Surely a bomb? It had to be. Something big was going to happen in Newcastle, something profound, and he was the key to its success. Yes, he, Venny Naidoo of Dannhauser, master freedom fighter, hero of the cause. He desperately wanted to tell Sarita, tell her that her dad wasn't just some overweight shop-keeper in a small town, with a moaning wife, and love of Gunston plains. No, he was a man who leaped over the white fence of fear and faced his enemy head-on. If only he could tell her, she would no longer give him those disappointed looks. If only she knew he was doing all of this for her. It was all for her. Everything, always.

CRASH

Wednesday morning after assembly everyone dispersed to their classes. Klayton ran up to Pete and shoulder charged him off the footpath and mouthed something about rock spiders, followed by a cry of laughter from his friends.

Pete didn't react. He just stepped back on the footpath and continued walking. His mind was still caught up with the events of the day before. First Mr. le Roux told him not to go to rugby practice, and then to top it all he went for a run and Petrus wasn't there, again.

"Someone ought to hoist that guy up the flagpole by his balls," Barend said.

"Now that would be something to write home about," Pete said.

Barend let out a wheezy whistle and clicked his tongue. "Speaking of writing home about something. I haven't even told you about yesterday's practice. It was bonkers, China." Barend's eyes were as round as the full moon.

"Yeah?" Pete asked.

"We were doing laps and the first team had a contact session. Next thing we heard this sickening crash—bang—followed by some shouting. We ran back and all the first team guys were huddled in a circle. Coach was shouting at a few guys to get the first aid kit. We couldn't see what was going on at first, but it turned out Gareth and John-John both went for a loose ball and had a head-on-head collision. Some of the guys said John-John was lights-out for a few minutes."

"Bloody hell," Pete murmured.

"Yes, can you believe it? In one dopey moment, both first-team centers got themselves a date with the school nurse. Looks like they lost their heads." Barend laughed heartily at his joke, but Pete could only shake his head.

"Will they be able to play Saturday?" Pete asked after Barend's laughter subsided.

"Dunno. I think they went to the hospital last night to check for concussion."

"Wow," Pete muttered.

Pete's imagination ran rampant during his maths and geography classes. He imagined being called up to the first team, the tries he would score, the white first-team scarf draped around his neck. But by the time he walked into his Biology class, he reminded himself that he was not even playing for the fourth team anymore, thanks to Mr. le Roux's tantrum. But it would have been something amazing, he thought, as he watched Renate's blond hair, like a golden veil, floating past the classroom window. It could have given him a chance, however minuscule. A chance is a chance.

During breaktime, Pete and Barend sat on their favorite tree stump, as usual, immersed in their peanut butter and syrup sandwiches. They didn't really talk, except for the odd comment about how stupid maths was and discussing the practicalities of hoisting

Klayton up the flagpole by his balls. Around them some kids basked in the fall sun, others exchanged sandwiches from their lunchboxes, a few spent their pocket money in the tuck shop, and couples tried to sit close enough to one another so that the teachers and prefects couldn't see they were holding hands: strictly forbidden on school grounds, and anywhere else when in school uniform.

Mr. Theunessin appeared near the hall and was walking in their direction. They watched him as he snaked through the breaktime crowd, ignoring every single greeting that came his way. He headed straight for them. Pete turned to Barend, who just shrugged his shoulders and pursed his lips.

"Pete, Barend, good, you're both here," Mr. Theunissen said.

"Morning, sir" they said as one.

"Barend, Vleis has been struggling with his hamstring since Saturday. Yesterday he could hardly train. He needs a week or so to rest, to give his hammy time to recover. So, tomorrow, you are practicing with the first team. As long as you don't get up to something stupid and get yourself injured, you'll start on Saturday." Barend's face lit up—his cheeks like glowing pink tomatoes.

"I won't let you down, sir, I promise, I will—" Barend started.

"You'll only get one chance, so no, you won't let me down," Mr. Theunissen interjected.

"Pete, you probably heard about the unfortunate incident yesterday?" Mr. Theunissen continued without drawing breath. Pete wanted to answer, but the coach's eyes told him not to dare.

177

"It places me in a predicament. Saturday is derby day. We haven't lost to Sarel Cilliers in five years, and we are not about to break that run. They have some good players this year, some have played Craven Week, but we cannot, and will not lose to those bunch of spanner swingers." Mr. Theunissen spoke through clenched teeth and did not attempt eye contact.

"I'm going to have to do something I really didn't want to." He closed his eyes and tilted his head skywards.

"I'm pulling you in. Come to first team practice with Barend tomorrow. But you leave your cockiness at home, you hear me? By some miracle, I have to build a Rolls-Royce with tractor parts. Stupid kids. Concussion, pfff," he grumbled and walked off, not looking back, not greeting anyone until he turned toward the office block and disappeared out of sight.

Pete and Barend stared at one another, speechless. The bell rang, but they remained seated as if glued to their stump. It was only when a prefect whistled at them that they snapped out of their trance. They walked to Afrikaans class, wondering if they dared to believe that their time had finally come.

LITTLE BOXES

10:59, Saturday morning, "Eye of the Tiger" blasted from under the pavilion's corrugated roof. The crowd was split into two factions: one side dressed in blue, the other in red and black. Two small groups of pupils donning clown suits were going nuts in front of their respective factions: dancing, singing, shouting, urging their supporters to drown out the other group. The cacophonous chorus of these two rally cries slammed against the corrugated roof. The smell of pancakes and *boerewors* floated silently over the crowd, until that moment when the first boy in a blue and white striped jersey raced out of the tunnel in the middle of the pavilion, through a guard of honor of hockey girls drumming their sticks together. The crowd jumped to their feet and the blues cheered with all their might, as fourteen more boys in *their* colors sprinted onto the field.

An uneasy hush followed. A few boos rang out, then a joyous scream ended the anxious wait, as a tall boy with a flapping dark brown fringe emerged from the tunnel. His wine-red jersey and white shorts shimmered in the late morning sun, his shoulders pushed back, his head aloft. He ran through the guard of honor of hockey girls going crazy, screaming and jumping up and down. The red-and-black crowd raised the roof, the blues' boos and expletives drowned out by the Dundee High euphoria, the home team.

179

This was derby rugby. These were not their strongest opponents, but it was the one game in the year they had to win more than any other, book worms against spanner swingers, neighboring towns locked in an epic battle to win bragging rights for the year ahead.

In hockey, Dundee High won all their games and in netball, Sarel Cilliers won all theirs. So it all came down to rugby. In the junior rugby, Dundee had destroyed Sarel Cilliers, but in senior rugby, the tables were turned, Dundee's fourths were hammered by a record margin, and their thirds hadn't fared much better. Their seconds were expected to walk over their opponents but hadn't. In a match which had to be stopped twice for whole team brawls, Sarel Cilliers had scored a controversial try in injury time to snatch an unlikely victory. It meant it was all down to the first team to restore their time-honored superiority over their much-reviled neighbors. The first team with three debutants: both centers and a tighthead prop.

The noise above the tunnel made Pete feel ten-feet-tall and the sun winked at him as he ran out. A double row of the most beautiful and sought-after girls in short hockey skirts waved him in, although he doubted a single one of them had noticed him until that moment. The clanging of hockey sticks above his head and the distant roar of hundreds of teenagers was almost overwhelming, but his focus was on one thing only: not falling.

The third to last girl on the right looked straight at him. The intensity in her blue eyes hit him like a tsunami. It was Renate, and for the first time she saw him—really saw him.

The whistle blew, the crowd gave a deafening roar while parents barked incoherent final instructions from the touchline. Gareth Joubert's jersey fitted him perfectly like he was born for it. Pete had never felt like this before: he knew, come what may, they would not lose. Not today.

Sarel Cilliers had the ball and they played with an intensity and ferocity Pete had not experienced before. Their players seemed older somehow, or perhaps life had dished out a few harder blows. They were big, some with faces full of thick, dark stubble, making Pete feel a little self-conscious about his clean-shaven fluff.

His opposite number had the ball, he was taller than Pete, and very lean, with a square jaw and eyes ominously close to one another. He ran straight at Pete, his close-together eyes determined, and with the faintest of smiles forming in the corner of his small mouth. His strides were long and his two blue socks clung to his skinny calves. Pete focused on his two socks, hoping for a clue as to which way he wanted to step, but he just kept coming straight at him, his sole intent to steamroller Pete in a skinny-legged baptism of fire. He ran hard, ball tucked under his left arm and his right arm stretched out to wipe Pete out of the way. Pete raced forward to meet him, swooped low and drove his right shoulder into the blue socks. The contact was intense, and a stinging pain pinched his shoulder, but only for a moment, then it was gone. Old skinny-legs hit the turf with such force that the thump reverberated through the fall morning. The crowd gasped, and the ball flew from his grasp into the grateful hands of Dundee's fullback. An excited roar from the pavilion blew across the field. Pete jumped to his feet and two of his new teammates tapped him on his shoulder—he had arrived.

From that moment on, every attack from Sarel Cilliers was a little less convincing, and despite not playing well, Dundee was leading by nine points with five minutes to play. Pete tackled his heart out, stopped two certain tries, and made two crucial turn-overs. Yet he hardly touched the ball all game. All the moves were designed to use the core of the team, and the newbies were left to defend.

Against the run of play, Sarel Cilliers caught the Dundee lineout napping and a quick throw saw their hooker score in the corner. Their fly-half kicked a difficult conversion and Dundee's lead was cut to only three points with two minutes play remaining. Sarel Cilliers secured the kick-off and attacked with a vigor they hadn't displayed since before Pete's first tackle. It was fifteen boys throwing everything at it, running hard, whipping passes, hammering against the Dundee door, waiting for a gap to open. The Dundee fly-half tried to unsettle the Sarel Cilliers attack by rushing up in defense, but his opponent evaded him with ease and the gap they had been waiting for appeared. Pete's fellow newbie, the inside center, made a brave tackle, but there was a three-on-two overlap, with only Pete and his wing left to stop a match-winning try.

Pete watched the Sarel Cilliers player running with the ball closely. He could see he was waiting for the perfect moment to pass. Pete sensed an opportunity and moved slightly to his left, pushing his opponent further away from his teammates. The ball carrier's eyes widened. Then, realizing he had probably left it too late, let a looping floated pass go. It was high and heavy, and exactly what Pete had been waiting for. He stepped hard off his left foot, sprinted, never taking his eyes off the ball, jumped high, slapped the ball out of its trajectory, recovered, and plucked it centimeters from the ground. Defenders came at him from all directions, but his eyes were fixed on the corner flag. He ran with everything he had in him, forgetting all the sprinting lessons from their athletics coach, this was just raw, pure, running. The chalk waved him in. Five meters out, someone crashed into his side, but he somehow kept going. Three meters out, someone dived into his legs, he tripped, bounced hard on the bristly grass while another defender flew right over him. The line was right there, he reached for it, another hand appeared to his left, he reached and reached...

Rikus de Lange was a tall man but there, sitting behind the wheel of their VW Passat, he seemed eight-feet-tall. His chest was puffed out, and his smile so wide it seemed painted on. Pete sat next to him and let every drop of Coke roll over his tongue to allow the taste to linger. He was picking little bits of dirt out of the grazes on his legs. His dad didn't say much after the game, but he didn't need to, pride was like a dense fog around him. Pete replayed that moment over and over in his mind. The hand stretching to stop him, then the puff of chalk, the whistle—try time!

Every time he replayed that try in his head, his mind jumped forward to a few minutes later: The final whistle went, relieved and delirious supporters stormed the field, a barrage of taps on the back, and then the earth stopped turning, the sky burst into the illuminating glory of a thousand suns, and everyone disappeared, except for...Renate. Her smile walked closer, radiating the sweet nectar of honey, her long ponytail caressed her shoulder and she looked at him as if he was precious, worthy. Without warning or hesitation, her arms shot around his waist, and her head rested on his shoulder. She squeezed and lingered until his uncertain hands folded over her delicate back. It was a perfect moment, her breath warm against him, her whole body so close that he thought they were somehow now merged into one.

Dannhauser appeared on the horizon. The endless kaleidoscope of yellows and browns stretched out in all directions, melting into the sky's bright blue in a dusty haze. He had wanted to hold on to the moment for longer, to bask in the glory, not to be on his way to Newcastle for month-end shopping with his moment disappearing on the road at 100 km/h. But perhaps it was better this way, to leave before reality could clip your wings and everything was still perfect. Then those who remained would only remember that perfection.

They made a quick stop in Dannhauser to pick up his mom. She was dressed in a floral dress and a white cardigan and smelled like lavender. Dressed in her best for the big town. Pete barely had time to change out of his rugby clothes before his mom bundled him back in the car, eager to get to Newcastle before all the shops were empty. On the backseat, with his muscles cooling down and an aching stiffness creeping into his body, his mind could not escape, nor did it want to, that long, unending embrace. And that with the girl who had occupied his dreams and fantasies since that moment she stood in the January sun, just over two years ago, waiting for the bus. Her hair was neatly cut in a perfect short bob, her eyes like beacons for those searching for safe harbor. He knew then—particularly the lower half of his body—that she was the one. Two years is a long time to wait, watch as others with better credentials walk by her side; it's a long time to watch from the shadows and to yearn.

The road beyond Dannhauser was littered with hundreds of anthills. In the distance, the sun bounced off the mirror-like surface of Chelmsford Dam, much smaller than usual as the rain had only teased this year. It lay at the foot of the Drakensberg, which looked tired of wrapping its arms around their small province.

Every few seconds his mind would conjure up a different memory of *that* embrace. The feel of her delicate back under his hands, her soft bosom squeezed into his chest, the glow of her blonde hair as she tucked her face into the hollow of his shoulder, her smile which melted his heart, those perfect dimples that..."Wait a second!" he nearly said aloud. What were Sarita's dimples doing in his daydream? What was Sarita doing in his fantasies, period? She had no right to be there.

Did she?

Pete had to get away from his muddled thoughts as quickly as possible. He started asking his mom about the list of things she wanted to buy. He had no interest in it whatsoever, but his mind had turned on him, changing his sweet memories and fantasies into an unwanted battlefield.

To his relief, they reached the long swooping hill just outside Newcastle, with the town stretching out before them. It was their nearest large town with almost all the shops you would find in the city, everything from Pick 'n Pay, to OK, Clicks and even a Mike's Kitchen. Today though was a special day. After months of suggesting and asking, almost to the point of begging, Pete's dad finally agreed, or caved in, that the family could buy their very first microwave oven. More and more people now owned them, and it was fast becoming the must-have kitchen appliance for modern families. With its increased popularity the prices also started coming down and along with it, Rikus's resistance. And when Game in Newcastle advertised a one-week-only promotion of the Defy Deanne had her eye on, the writing was on the wall. So today wasn't about grocery shopping at Pick 'n Pay; it was about Game and getting that microwave, and for Rikus to score some indelible points.

The shopping complex around Game was bustling. It was the anchor store in a complex that contained a Clicks, CNA, pet shop, hairdresser, and the ever-alluring Milky Lane. Pete followed the same routine each time they went there. First, he would check Milky Lane for specials, then he would stroll around the pet shop to see what strange creatures they had. Once they had a small snake the size of a pen, the same bright blue as a bubblegum milkshake. He suddenly thought of Milky Lane again. The rest of his time was spent in Game's sports section, testing rackets, spinning soccer balls on his finger, trying out golf clubs until his mom had done all her shopping.

Today was different though. The sheer gravitas of buying such an expensive thing was enough to lure Pete away from his routine. Just before they reached Game's wide, inviting entrance he peeked over his shoulder at the daily specials sign at Milky Lane. It read: *Milkshakes less 50% for under 18s.* His mom saw it too, placed her hand gently on his back and whispered in his ear, "Let's get the microwave and then you can have a bubblegum milkshake—double thick." She smiled with an infectiousness that made it difficult not to smile back, her excitement palpable.

The day before Deanne walked into Game to finally become a microwave owner, Venny sat alone in his shop. It was half an hour before opening time, and all was quiet. Under the counter in the bottom shelf, the package was staring at him. It was neatly wrapped in plain brown paper with nothing written on it. It was the size of a shoebox, maybe slightly bigger. It required supernatural restraint not to carefully peel the adhesive tape back and sneak a peek at what was inside. It called out to him, but he covered his ears. The package was delivered the day before by a short, fat black guy called Solomon, who was blind in his left eye. Since then he had moved the package several times, and every time it became harder not to open it. Some of the ends of the adhesive tape had started curling up teasingly. He knew that even if he tore away all the packaging, he could just wrap it again without anyone being able to tell the difference—he had an abundance of brown paper in his shop. But he didn't and he wouldn't. He played by the rules. This was his first true test, his first true taste of the real thing, and nothing, not even the voice inside his head trying to convince him that no one would ever know, would stand in his way.

He wondered what time he should go. All Protea Seven had said was Friday morning, and Solomon wasn't a talker. He decided he would open the shop, tell his wife he had to pop out for some supplies, and race his Datsun Laurel to Newcastle and back in as close to an hour as he could. His wife would complain anyway, regardless of whether he was gone one minute or one day, so he wasn't too worried about her. The only thing he worried about was those damned traffic cops who loved to stop cars near the Chelmsford Dam junction, especially Indians. They loved nothing more than to stop a hardworking Indian businessman and throw allegations around that everything from his car to the clothes on his back was stolen. "Because all Indians are sly scheming bastards," Venny thought aloud. It was the motivation he needed. The picture was clear in his mind: He would take the package, place it in the trunk of his car and cover it with vegetables. If those pricks stopped him, he would use all his charm and humbly tell them that he merely had surplus stock and was taking it to a shop in Newcastle to be sold. He wouldn't show those opinionated, racist assholes a thing or two. It wouldn't even be hard. Those imbeciles had fewer brain cells than a wet rock.

As predicted, his wife moaned. "*Now* you tell me," her head shaking vehemently. "Right at the last minute. And where are you going that's so special that it cannot wait?" Her index finger shot up in the air, pointing right in Venny's face. "You can write it on that fat tummy of yours if you think I'm going to look after your shop. What about the loss of business? You pretend to be so clever, so let's hear it?" This carried on for a good few minutes while he just stared at her. Then he simply walked out of her shop without uttering another word, picked up the package and hid it under the vegetables in his trunk.

He loved his Datsun Laurel. He had bought it four years ago, second hand, from a cousin in Cato Manor. It had air conditioning and a tape player, not that he ever used either, because, as everyone knew, those things ate petrol. The car was gold and had soft fabric seats. It wasn't fast but the ride was smooth, and the automatic gearbox made any journey a joy. Achala hated it from the first moment, obviously, and Sarita always complained that it wobbled, which made her car sick. But to him, it was just perfect. He lit his Gunston and turned out of Dannhauser, driving faster than usual, but not too fast to attract attention.

The whole journey, lasting almost thirty minutes, was spent searching every hill, every shady tree, waiting for that moment when those damned traffic cops would leap out of the shadows and pull him over. It never happened, but by the time he turned left toward the entrance of Stone Mill Bakery he was drenched in sweat.

He pulled up in the empty visitors parking area, wiped his face with his handkerchief and slowly stepped out of his car. It was a cool, breezy morning, and the bite in the air felt icy against his sweaty skin.

From the trunk, he lifted the cabbage and cauliflower and took out the package. Holding it as if it were a loved one and this their final farewell. One last gust of curiosity blew through him; he swallowed and took a deep breath, placed the package in a plastic bag and covered it with cabbage.

"I'm here to see Gys, please?" he said to the morbidly obese man with white hair and a light blue golf shirt at reception. The man didn't respond. He slurped his Coke, made a sound that sounded like a bulldog when it got excited, and lifted the receiver as if it took enormous effort.

"Gys, there's some *coolie* here to see you," the man said, slurped his Coke again and stretched awkwardly forward to rummage through his drawers. He emerged with a large bag of Nik-Naks and started eating, open-mouthed, leaning back in his chair.

Venny watched this man devour the Nik-Naks with repugnance until another man appeared in the door. He was in his mid-forties, with an early onset beer belly and severely receded hairline graying on the sides. But the thing that really chafed him deep inside was that the bloody guy was white. A Whitey!

"I'm Gys," he said. Venny couldn't believe his eyes. A white guy who looked like a recruitment officer for the National Party was part of the Struggle, his Struggle. He didn't like it. He couldn't even begin to explain how much he didn't like it. It wasn't fair: Whites had everything their deceitful hearts desired and now they wanted to rip the one thing they didn't have away from the oppressed, the Struggle—their fight for freedom and justice. It wasn't right.

"Hey Hughie, someone opened a bag of cookies

in the canteen, if you're interested," Gys said to the large man at reception. With surprising speed, Hughie got up and waddled out of the room.

"Where is it?" Gys asked, as soon as Hughie disappeared behind the double swing doors. Venny's blood was boiling. He couldn't even look at Gys, this intruder polluting the sanctuary of his cause. He could spit fire.

"Listen, get over it," Gys said.

"Get over what?" Venny snapped.

"I'm white, deal with it. Where's the package?" Gys asked. Venny thought he was a master at hiding his emotions but imagined this man—this white man —fighting in a struggle alongside people of color, must have had his fair share of hateful stares.

"Here," Venny said and handed the plastic bag over. Those pale hands taking the bag from him burned his eyes. It just wasn't right.

Gys lifted the cabbage and inspected the package wrapped in brown paper. "Cabbage?" Gys asked, not expecting an answer.

"And this too." Venny slapped a fifty rand note in Gys's hand and peered over his shoulder.

Gys took the money and the package and disappeared through a side door off reception. After a few seconds, he returned with two large bags filled with loaves of bread and numerous bread rolls. He nodded to Venny as if to say it was time to go. Rage and questions seethed in Venny's mind. He wanted to know everything about the plan, the contents of the package, everything. But this was his first big break, and he would play his part. Without question.

Before Gys turned to go back to work, he simply

said, "Good work," without looking at Venny.

Venny trudged back to his Datsun, put the bread on the seat next to him, and closed his eyes trying to calm down. Then he started the car and drove back as quickly as he could. Only one thing playing on his mind—a bloody white guy?

Game was buzzing. It was packed with stressed-out moms, dads with distant and vacant stares and kids, mostly wearing dirty rugby, hockey and netball uniforms, pestering their moms for a sweet treat. Deanne was like a woman possessed. She marched in, grabbed a trolley and walked so quickly that Rikus and Pete had trouble keeping up. The appliance section was at the back lefthand corner of the shop. When they arrived, there was already a queue of women who all looked a little bit like Deanne. It was like some gathering of panicked, feigned smiles. Deanne tilted her head at Rikus with an undisguised accusatory glare and whispered in his ear that they might be too late already, but he just placed his hand on the small of her back and smiled reassuringly.

The shop assistant was a young man with thick glasses. He looked to be in a constant state of fluster, and Pete wondered whether he looked like that away from work too. The queue took forever, and Pete's initial curiosity was quickly starting to wane. There were still two ladies in front of his mom and at the speed old Nervewreck was helping them, Pete reckoned he had more than enough time to go to the pet shop and back.

"Just make it quick, I'm almost at the front," his mom said, now highly agitated and staring at her husband with a growing look of "I told you so."

Pete started walking toward the entrance. Outside, children were chasing each other in the paved courtyard onto which all the shops faced. He saw a few boys in Newcastle High first team rugby jerseys and reminded himself that he was now one of them, the elite group of high school boys who played first team rugby. The Newcastle guys were chatting to a few pretty girls in hockey skirts and his thoughts instantly raced to Renate, and *her* hockey skirt, so teasingly short, and her perfectly sculpted legs...

Without warning a bright silver light flared at the bottom of the courtyard, like a bolt of lightning. A loud thud followed, the earth shook under Pete's feet, and it sounded like a million little boxes came tumbling from the sky and smashed into the ground like hailstones.

Silence.

A woman screamed. Another one. Another one. People scattered in all directions like headless chickens. Parents caught their children in mid-stride and disappeared into shops. Within seconds the courtyard was empty. All that remained were a few cans of soft drink dropped in the chaos, and now leaking their contents over the paving.

Smoke slowly covered the gap where Pete had seen the bright light moments before. Through the haze, someone pulled him off his feet. It was his dad, Rikus. He somehow managed to throw his six-foot-tall son over his shoulder and ran.

Deanne was standing, with both hands over her

mouth, near the shop's music section. As soon as Rikus put Pete down, she pulled him close. Her whole body was trembling.

"What was that?" Pete asked, struggling to come to terms with his befuddled senses.

"A bomb, they say it's a bomb," his dad answered, slightly absent, his eyes trying to take in everything around them.

"Ladies and gentlemen, please form an orderly queue and evacuate the shop through our emergency exit to the left of the shop, next to the sports section. Please, no running, and keep your children with you at all times. We thank you for shopping with us today and apologize for any inconvenience caused," a female voice said over the store's public announcement system.

"Right, let's go," Rikus said straight away. He put a hand on both Deanne and Pete's backs and guided them toward the emergency exit. Deanne was sobbing softly, and Rikus looked as pale as a ghost, but there was a determination in his eyes that gave Pete a modicum of reassurance.

The emergency exit was a long corridor that led to a steel door on the side of the building. People pushed and shoved past them, running, some crying uncontrollably, some shouting, "Get out of the way!" Rikus gestured to everyone around them to calm down, but the urge to get out was too great for most.

With all the pushing and people cutting in they could hardly move in the corridor, despite the fading yelps of Game employees repeatedly urging everyone to exit in an orderly manner.

A single deafening bang echoed in the corridor.

Everyone froze.

Two, three, four more bangs followed.

Pete knew the sound, but this was even louder than Rudie's gun.

Rikus grabbed Deanne and Pete by the arms and pushed back against the wave of people to get back in the shop.

"Ambush! They were waiting for us," Rikus shouted and a bone-chilling scream echoed somewhere behind them. A mad rush from both directions clashed in the corridor: Everyone in the shop wanted to leave and everyone in the corridor wanted to get back in. Grown men pushed women and children in the face to get away. Fear had made them blind, fear had made them savages.

A flurry of shots followed.

This was a different type of gun—a machine gun. A kid next to Pete collapsed, calling out, wheezing. His dad scooped him up, but there was blood all over his back and legs, flowing like a tap had been opened. The few remaining shoppers who wanted to get out now realized the threat and turned. Some who tripped and fell were trampled as the horde forced their way back into the shop.

Another flurry of shots followed, and then shots which sounded different: clear, loud shots, that clapped one after the other. Everyone was back in the shop now, some spattered with blood, and the noise was frenetic and almost deafening. Pete thought he'd overheard someone say people had been killed, but with all the noise he couldn't be sure. One of the employees knelt next to the boy who was hit and opened her first aid kit. Rikus guided Deanne and Pete away and just said, "Let's give them some privacy."

Sirens grew louder and louder until it drowned out all other noise. Pete sat on a gym bench and stared at his dad who was holding his mom in his arms, slowly stroking her back. His mind was stuck at the sound he had heard only minutes before when he was standing in the shop entrance, and a million little boxes came crashing down, further and further. He pinched his eyes shut. Suddenly he was back in primary school, on stage, their Grade Two end of year play. Belchie was standing next to him. They both held a box above their heads, his was blue and Belchie's yellow. They were singing: "Little boxes made of ticky tacky...little boxes all the same..."

"Pappa, Pappa, you have to see this!" Sarita called out just as Venny opened the front door.

Venny threw his keys down and strode through the living room to their snug TV nook. Sarita and Achala sat next to one another in the corner. Sarita held a cushion close to her chest and Achala's left hand covered her mouth with tears rolling down her face.

"What is it? Is someone dead?" Venny asked out of breath. The TV was loud, and neither Sarita nor Achala broke eye contact with the TV.

"It's Newcastle, Pappa. There was a car bomb. And a shooting—" Sarita grabbed her mouth just like Achala, tears damming in her eyes.

Venny sat down and watched the images of a destroyed white Mercedes-Benz and puddles of blood on tiled floors.

"The families of the twelve deceased still have to be notified before names can be released. State President Botha released a short statement in which he said his thoughts and prayers were with the families of the victims in this dark time. He went on to say that terrorists will not win this war. They may be proud of the innocent blood they have spilled on the streets tonight, but they will not prevail. They will be destroyed, every single one of them."

"Serves them right. It's about time that the whites in Northern Natal were shown that they cannot just do whatever they want. This is a war for the soul of the people of color," Venny said.

"Venny!" Achala shouted, in shock.

"Pappa, six of the twelve who were killed were black, and two were Indian. This wasn't an attack on whites. This was just a brutal, cowardly attack on innocent people who were in the wrong place at the wrong time," Sarita said, sitting upright. Venny hated the loathing in her voice as if he were somehow crazy to think this was a good thing. Were they so blind that they could not see the bigger picture?

"I didn't know, okay? I just meant...Aggh, never mind," Venny mumbled and got up. He walked as quickly as he could to his operations room and shut the door behind him. He lit a Gunston and took out the half-jack of whiskey he hid at the bottom of one of the boxes. He took a couple of large swigs, sat on his chair and stared at the Indian woman being beaten by a policeman. He took a drag on the cigarette as if to finish it in one go, then watched as the white smoke slowly rolled out of his mouth. It was the right thing, he thought, it had to be done. Those others were just unfortunate, damned unfortunate, but they were now martyrs of the great struggle. Heroes whose blood would liberate them from the white rod.

A single tear slunk down his cheek. He wiped it away hurriedly and took another large gulp of whiskey.

THE PACT

Brushstrokes in every conceivable shade of blood colored the horizon. Pete sat on a rock, the very same rock he had hidden behind months before. He peered out at the angry horizon, shouting, screaming, crying, because blood was drying on the streets of Northern Natal.

Pete thought of the boy who had fallen next to him. He remembered the color of his blood so vividly, how life seeped out of him, without choice, without reason —just random pure ill-fated chance. He spotted the color of the boy's blood on the horizon, dark red like the wine his Uncle Kobus loved so much. He thought about the distance between him and the boy, it could not have been more than half a meter—half a meter away from being the one in a hospital fighting for his life.

The rock was warm after a day baking in the sun, and uncomfortable, but Pete didn't care. He pulled his knees up to his chest and stared at the angry twilight. Nothing mattered. Not rugby, not Renate. Right there, on the rock, nothing had a purpose, nothing made sense. Everything was just random bursts of futility —like the machine gun that had changed a region forever.

His dad said they must not give in to fear. That was what the terrorists wanted; once you showed fear, lived in fear, they won.

Well, they have won, Pete thought, *they have al-ready won.*

"Pete!" a voice called from the blazing horizon, there in the grip of the harsh rock and the foul taste of remembering.

"It's me, Petrus," the voice called again, but Pete sat unmoved, tucked in an upright fetal position.

"Hey, wena! You okay?" Petrus asked, now very close.

Pete realized this was not the whispering wind or the weeping mountains, this was a frowning Petrus.

"I saw a kid, probably seven-years-old, shot today. Right next to me." Pete's gaze did not leave the hori-zon for a second, no intonation in his voice.

"Eish, you joking? You don't joke about things like that," Petrus said and tugged his ear.

"I wish with all my heart it was a joke." He turned to Petrus. "You see the dark red just above the moun-tains?" He pointed to the west.

"Yes?"

"That was the color of his blood. It was everywhere …I don't know if they could stop it."

"Eish."

A moment slowly evaporated as Petrus and Pete looked at each other.

"Where was this? At that Newcastle bomb?" Petrus finally asked.

"Have you heard?"

"Yes, *baas* Gerrit told us. Eish, it's bad, very bad."

"We were there, in a shop. I was in such a good mood…Then millions of little boxes fell down."

"Eh?"

"That's what it sounded like to me. I was standing

200

at the entrance of the shop and I saw this bright flash, then the ground trembled, you know, like when they do the blasting in the mine?"

Petrus nodded.

"And then this crazy sound, like boxes falling from the sky, millions of them, tumbling down and crashing to the ground. It didn't sound like in the movies."

"Is that when you saw the kid?" Petrus asked.

"No, we were told to leave the shop through the fire escape, and then the terrorists started shooting at us. I didn't see them, I just heard the shots. This boy was standing right next to me. This far away." Pete measured the distance with his arm.

"Then he fell, and blood covered his back and legs. I don't even know where he was shot, but blood poured out of him like a fountain or something...I've never seen anything like that before. I never want to again."

Petrus covered his chin and mouth with his right hand and dropped his head. Pete was only now becoming aware of the stubby surface of the rock he sat on. Although it was very uncomfortable, he remained seated. Somehow, there, he felt removed from it all.

"Are you okay? And your family?" Petrus asked.

"I don't think so. Of course, we're thankful that none of us were hurt; we're very thankful and relieved, but I don't think we're okay. I don't know if we'll ever be okay again," Pete said.

"Tsotsis," Petrus said, shaking his head vehemently.

"Yes. Tsotsis. It was just a normal Saturday. People shopping, people selling. Normal people, like you and me. Now they're dead because some psychos thought killing innocent people was a worthy cause.

Aggh Petrus, what's the point? Is there even a point to all of this?"

"What? To life?" Petrus asked.

"Yes, of people going around doing things like this, is there any purpose to it? Aren't we just all doomed? No one won today. Everyone lost. They might call themselves freedom fighters, but today on a pavement in Newcastle white, black and Indian people sat next to each other crying. They cried together, Petrus, their hurt was the same. No freedom was won today, only hurt."

Petrus was still shaking his head. "Pete, I'm so sorry. It must...it must have been so bad."

"We're the lucky ones. We walked out of there with no bullet holes, no bloodied wounds, no wondering whether a loved one was dying or not. All we left with were the memories etched in our minds... we're the lucky ones."

"My mother said that these tsotsis, she says it's the Xhosa-Tsotsis, would kill their own babies," Petrus said without looking up.

"Your mom sounds like a wise woman," Pete said.

Petrus looked up, proud. "She is."

Pete rubbed his shins. There were still grazes on his knees from a rugby game that happened a lifetime ago.

"So, Petrus, what is your opinion about stuff like this? Is any cause big enough to warrant killing innocent people?"

"Some of the children at school they, they say it is our duty. Eish, I don't know if I should talk about these things."

"Please, I really want to know. And there's no one

around. I don't think I understand it. I know we have a minority government and blacks have homelands and some terrorists want to blow stuff up. But that's about it. I suppose I only see it from our perspective...you could probably call it a white perspective or something like that, I don't know?"

"These children say it's our country. We are Africans so it is our duty to fight for it. They say whites will kill us, so we have to kill them first. Before it's too late."

"Do you agree?" Pete asked.

"No, I mean yes. I agree that it is our country. I don't think it is right...the way we are treated." Petrus kicked at a stone lodged in the ground. "But, to kill? Aikona, to me that is even less right."

"It always felt like these things were so far away, like it only happened in the cities, you know? Now it's here in Northern Natal. This place is so boring who would want to attack us? But here we are, it happened." Pete jumped off the rock and stretched his legs. The sun was still red but disappearing quickly behind the Drakensberg.

"My dad's friend says civil war is inevitable. Can you imagine that? Fighting here, like it's the Anglo-Boer war or Angola or something? Who would we fight? I mean: our maid Christina is like part of our family... Would we suddenly fight her and her family? Would she show up one night wielding an AK and try to blow our brains out? And what about you and me? Sarita? Would we just kill each other? No man!" Pete leaned with his hands against the rock and gave a deep sigh.

"I will never fight you. I will never fight Sarita. I will never fight *baas* Gerrit. If *baas* Gerrit was attacked by my school friends, I would fight alongside *baas*

Gerrit. He is like your Christina, part of *my* family. You don't fight family, you fight beside them."

Pete walked right up to Petrus and immediately their eyes met. Tears were very close to the surface, they had been all afternoon. They spent a few moments locked in each other's gaze, searching for answers. Then Pete stuck out his hand. It hung in the air like a ship's mast after a storm, bruised and beaten.

"Let's make a pact. No matter what happens, ever, we won't fight against each other," Pete said.

Petrus peered at Pete's hand as if it was the first time he had ever seen one. He slowly stretched out his right hand and placed it in Pete's.

"If we fight, we fight together," Petrus said.

They shook hands but remained standing like that. Pete could feel the pain well up in his eyes, tears very close. It became too much to bear, he let go of Petrus's cold, coarse hand.

"I have to go. The sun is about to set and I don't want my mom to worry, not today," was Pete's excuse. Petrus nodded.

Pete turned and started running. Every step hurt and pain shot up through his feet right up to his neck.

"Pete!" Petrus shouted. Pete turned toward him mid-stride.

"Tomorrow, two-thirty? Eating House?" Petrus shouted.

Pete kept running but stuck his right thumb in the air to confirm the appointment. He didn't know why, but it made him feel slightly better.

PEELING PAINT

There were very few empty seats in the church. Usually, only a special event like a christening or confirmation, something with the promise of tables full of delicious treats afterward, would attract such numbers. But this was just a regular Sunday, except there was nothing regular about death. Pete and his mom sat in their usual spot and his dad with the deacons. When they walked into the church those immaculately polished shoes of Captain Burger winked at him, telling him that it was just a matter of time before he was arrested for obstruction of justice for not reporting Rudie. And of course, Rudie was there. All self-satisfied, grinning with yellow teeth under his equally yellow mustache. Rumor had it that there was some sort of an investigation into the allegations that he had killed one of his workers, but as far as Pete could gather, nothing had come of it. Pete never considered it possible, but he was looking even more smug than usual. As if untouchable. Even the most casual observer surely had to know that that man was the devil dressed in khaki. Yet, there he was, sitting like some lord amongst normal people, pretending like there was nothing wrong with rape and murder.

The church was cold and dark. Clouds gathered outside and the feeble lighting inside made it almost worse. The singing was dreary, old and young voices dropping off the melodies like coconuts in a storm.

Reverend stood on his pulpit for quite some time, observing his congregation in laden silence.

"Brothers and sisters. Today, I want us all to pray for those who were so prematurely, so savagely, taken from our midst on a day that will forever be shrouded in darkness. Pray for our sister congregation in Newcastle, who today mourn the death of two of their own...which makes it two of our own. Pray also for the thirty more people lying in hospital this morning, their flesh wounded, their spirits weak—pray for the strength of the Almighty to heal their wounds and resurrect their spirits.

"And pray for us. Pray without ceasing, pray like your lives depend on it, because, brothers and sisters, they do! The red tide of communism has splashed onto the shores of our beloved Northern Natal. Our haven here, at the foot of the mighty Drakensberg, far away from the heathenism destroying our country's cities—one at a time, has been stained...stained by blood. No longer will our prayers be for those being butchered in the cities and Angola, no, our prayers will be for our children to see the morning light.

"Be steadfast, brothers and sisters. Terrorists have no place in our community. If you know, suspect, or even wonder about someone, perhaps your garden-boy, or the milkman, anyone, alert the authorities. Captain Burger is sitting at the back. He wants nothing more than to safeguard our community. Speak to him, brothers and sisters. This is not a time to wonder, this is a time for prayer and vigilance. We must protect our own, our community of believers. Stand strong against the oncoming red tide. Our prayers will be our ships, and we will sail until the sun breaks through the all-consuming darkness.

"Let us bow our heads. There is now an opportunity for a few minutes of contemplation as we pray in silence." Silent prayer was not common in their church, half the men started getting up but then sat down again. The silent prayer lasted nearly five minutes. Five minutes filled with children trying to whisper— quickly shushed by their moms, a few coughs, one sneeze, and creaks from the tired old pews.

"Amen. Thank you, brothers and sisters. Now, let us turn our Bibles to Romans 1:18," Reverend finally broke the silence.

Pete leaned back against the wooden pew. It was not the first time he had heard Reverend talk about the red tide, but it was the first time he could recall the Reverend sounding so garbled. Pete thought of the red tide, and the people sitting and crying together on a sidewalk the day before, and wondered if it really was a tide, or whether it was just people who were already crazy and latched their craziness onto a cause.

The Reverend looked quite pale, and his normally faultless readings were replaced by an error-strewn, stuttering reading from Romans. Next to Pete, Deanne's eyes were puffed up, red, and damp. She clutched a rolled-up tissue in her left hand and discreetly tried to dab the dampness away. *It affected us all,* Pete thought, *just in different ways.*

The afternoon was every bit as bleak as the morning. Clouds in shades of gray filled the sky, comfortably holding back the sun and the heat. Lunch was a very quiet affair. Rikus focused every sinew on eating his chicken pie, mash, runner beans, and pumpkin. Deanne picked at the food on her plate and smiled vacantly the couple of times Pete looked in her direction. In unspoken haste, the three of them finished washing up and much earlier than usual his parents closed the door behind them for a nap. Pete could hear his mom sob behind the door, stepped outside, and sat on the mound of surplus river sand left over from their renovations two years ago. Jimmy was in a playful mood and tried everything to grab Pete's attention. Out of frustration at being ignored, Jimmy sprinted away and brought one of his tattered old tennis balls back. Pete smiled. Jimmy's face was pure anticipation, his eyes transfixed on the ball. Pete looped it high and far, toward the lemon tree. Jimmy skidded on the loose sand and chased after it like there was no tomorrow, leaping up, and plucking it out of the air. He tripped back like a show horse, tail wagging with delight.

After spending some time playing fetch with Jimmy, Pete checked the time and made his way out of the gate, to his dog's bitter disappointment. As usual, all the streets were quiet except for the odd unconvincing bark, and the sound of Pete's North Stars on dust and asphalt.

He arrived at the Eating House fifteen minutes earlier than planned, but Petrus was already there. As per usual he was barefoot, but for the first time since they met, he had pants on—proper pants covering his ankles. The combination of pants and a smart dress shirt made Petrus look older, distinguished.

"I almost didn't recognize you. Did you get married today or something?" Pete said.

"Eish, aikona—no, I just went to church, but shoes; I don't like them too much, so..." Petrus replied, visibly uneasy.

"You look smart," Pete said.

Petrus didn't respond, he only scratched his head and stared at his toes.

"Shall we go?" Pete asked. Petrus nodded, and they started walking.

"Are you okay?" Petrus asked.

Now it was Pete's turn to silently nod, pressing his lips together.

"My dear Petrus, look at you!" Sarita said and slapped her hands together. Petrus didn't know where to look. He flashed a distressed smile and then walked to the pool table, pulling and tugging at his shirt as if it suddenly made his skin crawl.

"If I had known, I would have worn my best sari," Sarita continued to tease. Petrus did not look up, his gaze fixed on the pool table.

Pete laughed. It was the first time he had laughed since the attack. It felt good. Sarita winked at Pete, mischief dancing in her eyes. She walked to Petrus and placed her hand on his back and whispered, "I'm just teasing, but you do look really handsome today." It looked like he wanted to say something, but nothing came out. All the while his eyes remained on the pool table.

Sarita walked away and returned a few moments later with two Cokes. Pete noticed for the first time that she never took a Coke for herself. He wondered why but didn't ask, because you don't look a gift Coke in the mouth.

Sarita's expression changed suddenly, now very serious. "How crazy was that terrorist attack in Newcastle?" Sarita said.

"He was there." Petrus broke his silence, pointing at Pete.

"Pete, really?" she asked and came closer.

"Yeah, we were in Game," Pete said.

Sarita walked up to him and placed her hands on his arms, her hazelnut eyes brimming with concern. "Are you okay, your family, are you all okay?"

"Yes, we're fine...no injuries or anything like that," Pete said and retreated from Sarita's grasp. The emotions churned inside him but he sure as hell wasn't going to cry in front of her. He turned to one of the racks where washers and screws were displayed in small brown containers.

"The bomb sounded like millions of boxes tumbling to the ground. There was this bright light—I thought it was lightning. Later we were in a tunnel, the fire escape, and they just started shooting at us, without warning. Luckily, we weren't near the front, but..." Pete took a handful of washers in his hand and started dropping them back into the bowl one by one. Sarita aimed to step closer again but restrained herself.

"There was this boy, I don't know, I guess around seven years old. He was right next to me, right there, within touching distance. He was hit. He fell and was bleeding as I've never seen anyone.... We heard on the radio that he died this morning. He was right there." Pete gestured with his arm exactly how close.

Sarita's self-restraint withered and she threw her arms around him. The side of her head lay gently against his chest. She pulled him in close. Pete's arms were outstretched, hovering in the air. He looked at this girl wrapped around him, with no idea what to do. Tears were so close now and he didn't know whether he could stop them anymore. He stood like that for a moment, hoping Sarita would just let go, but she didn't, and the tears won.

At first, the tears trickled, but before long they were rolling down his face. He wept quietly, and closed his arms around Sarita's slender body, resting his chin on her head. Her body felt warm against his and like a warm water bottle in the depths of winter, it soothed him. Her hair was soft and floral in scent. He gave in to the moment, into the grief he felt for an unknown boy, and the hurt and fear smoldering inside him.

Pete didn't know how long he stood like that in Sarita's arms, but by the time his tears finally subsided, Petrus's Coke was half empty. He cleared his throat and gently unlocked himself from Sarita's embrace.

"I'm sorry, I don't know what happened there," Pete said and tried to clear his throat.

"Someone must be chopping onions," Sarita said, with the same mischievous smile of earlier.

"Yes, it must be the onions," Petrus jumped in.

Pete laughed a little, his voice still coarse and heavy. He didn't quite know where to look, so he stared at the wall.

"Now both Pete and I have cried here, next week it's your turn," Sarita said to Petrus.

"Bring the onions," Petrus said smiling broadly.

"Well, I think we need to talk about other things... normal things. This attack has messed everyone up, my dad even said it's a good thing, that the government can't go on oppressing the masses. People of color must rise up. I couldn't believe he said that on the same day as innocent people died. Both my mom and I shouted at him, but I thought afterward that perhaps it was just his coping mechanism. I mean, there is no manual to teach you how to deal with things like that, and we all feel things differently. So—" Sarita wiped the loose strand of hair out of her face and tucked it into her plait.

"I want to hear about normal things." She paused to think for a moment. "Petrus, have you had that chat with your boss, Mr. Gerrit, about finishing Matric? Have you managed to make a deal?"

"Eish, it is difficult." Petrus tugged at his ear.

"So you haven't?" Sarita asked.

"Not yet," Petrus said and quickly brought the Coke to his lips.

"Don't leave it too late. My dad says it's just a matter of time before we have a black president, and I for one would definitely want him to have Matric." She smiled, her eyes twinkling.

Then she slapped her hand over her mouth. "Oops, will I go to prison for talking about a black president?" Her eyes were round and big, and her hand couldn't hide her smile.

Pete started laughing and Petrus joined in, but only a little.

"I will talk to him...I just need some courage," Petrus said.

"You have more than enough courage," Pete said and Sarita nodded in agreement.

"You guys make me blush," Petrus said, smiling, and looked away.

All three laughed, but each differently, burdened

by the thoughts weighing heavily on their minds.

"So then, Mr. Pete," Sarita said.

"Mr. Pete?" Pete said.

"I don't know why I said it, it felt appropriate," Sarita said and Petrus laughed. Pete just shook his head.

"I heard something in the shop yesterday. Two boys from your school came in here to play pool and they couldn't stop talking about how your first team destroyed the team from Glencoe. They said there was this new guy, a certain Pete, who was the star of the show. So is it a coincidence, or was that you?" Sarita tilted her head searching deep in Pete's eyes for an answer.

Pete looked to Petrus for some help, but Petrus flapped his hands open, asking the same question.

"There were a few injuries and coach let me play for the first team. I don't know about being a star, I just did my job. It's a team sport, you know?" Pete said, uncertain where to look or what to do.

"And so modest." Sarita turned to Petrus and pointed at Pete.

"It was a good game," Pete said, mostly to himself.

"Did you score any points?" Petrus asked.

"I scored a try," Pete said.

"How many points in a try?" Sarita asked.

"Four."

"Shoh, four points, that's good, eish!" Petrus looked impressed.

"I was a bit lucky; it was an intercept try," Pete said.

"Okay, I don't know what it means, but from the way those boys were talking it didn't sound like luck to me," Sarita said. Pete found a sudden and intense fascination with the screwdrivers in a box next to him. Was it weird that he found Sarita's accent so cute? Especially when she tried to speak Afrikaans. Both he and Petrus understood English perfectly fine, but she insisted on trying Afrikaans, even though she struggled with certain words. But heck, it was just so damned cute—her pronunciation, the way her mouth twisted and pouted to get the words out, it was so different, so beautiful.

"Do you have a girlfriend?" Petrus said.

Pete was so engulfed in his thoughts that he was completely taken aback by the question. "Uhh...no..."

"Aha! That sounds like a hidden yes." Sarita stood next to Petrus and folded her arms across her chest. "Come on, tell us? Out with it."

"I don't have a girlfriend," Pete said and raised his hands to plead his innocence.

"But there is someone? A possible Mrs. Pete?" Sarita asked.

"Aggh come on, guys, let's talk about other things, don't be like this." Pete struggled to hide his smile.

"Seriously, who would we tell?" Petrus said, pretending to look around the shop for other people.

Pete lifted one of the screwdrivers out of the box. It had a black and yellow handle, and he stared at it for quite some time.

"There is this girl," Pete said hesitantly.

"I knew it," Sarita said to Petrus.

"Her name is Renate, she lives here in Dannhauser, near the reservoir. They moved here two years ago. Anyway, I don't know...I sort of, right from the start... you know?"

"You like her," Petrus said.

"Yes. But she is really beautiful. I mean really, as in slap you with a wet towel on the forehead beautiful. I don't know whether it works the same way at your schools, but in our school, if you're beautiful you're automatically cool, and if you're cool then you are only supposed to date cool guys."

"But you're a cool guy?" Sarita said.

"Cool means you either have a dad with lots of money, or you play first-team rugby, but preferably both. Up until yesterday, I didn't fulfill either of the two criteria. Therefore, neither she nor any other pretty girl in school knew I existed. But yesterday she, Renate, hugged me after the game. She noticed me, after all this time."

"Wow, she really sounds like something special," Sarita said and pursed her lips.

"Oh yes, she is. She looks like Christie Brinkley. Do you know who that is?" Pete asked. Petrus and Sarita shook their heads in unison.

"She's a model, and American, and the most beautiful woman on earth."

Sarita smiled at Petrus, but her gaze was distant.

"So what's the plan? How are you going to conquer her heart?" Sarita asked walking toward the counter and started to wipe the surface with a piece of bright yellow cloth.

"I don't know. There's this dance in a few weeks... I guess I thought maybe I should—"

"Are you going to wait that long?" Sarita asked. "By the sounds of it, you need to strike fast. This girl won't hang around waiting to be asked to a dance."

"Do you think so?"

"Yes! You are this hero now, make the most of your fame."

"Come on, I'm not a hero or something."

"You're missing the point. It doesn't matter: she's impressed. And she's impressed right now, who knows what a few weeks would do to that feeling?"

"Mmm...any suggestions?" Pete asked, but both were struck with silence.

"Petrus, you strike me as a bit of a ladies' man, any advice?" Pete said.

"Eish, I'm not good with them. Girls are so tricky. My last girlfriend said I was afraid of everything. I explained that I'm just naturally cautious, but she didn't like it. Now she has this other boyfriend... Trouble follows that guy and he gets chased away from school a lot. One of my friends says girls like bad boys, so I don't know. Girls are too difficult for my brain to understand." Petrus shook his head.

"Yes, we are complicated. I am not even going to try and argue." Sarita put the cloth down. "And at our age, probably more so—according to my mom, anyway. We are turning into women, and it's strange, everything changes. Sometimes we can't even control our own reactions or emotions.

"But, it's not true that we only like bad boys. I know I don't, perhaps it's the idea of fearlessness that attracts girls to those guys. What I can tell you, is that most girls want a few very simple things—kindness, respect, a good listener, and someone who makes a fuss, who thinks you are the greatest thing in the world. I think the girls who fall for bad boys do so because they know that it will only be temporary. In a strange way, they are doing that to protect their hearts. If they truly fell in love they could really get hurt. And that won't happen if they're with a bad boy," she said.

"But why not give a nice guy a chance? We'll protect their hearts," Petrus said.

"They don't know that. And I won't pretend like it's easy, but you need to show them that you will look after their hearts."

"How?" Petrus asked.

"It's different for every girl. But small things like showing someone that you can keep a secret, for instance, or talking to people with respect, things like that go a long way," she said.

Petrus sighed. "Eish, girls..."

"Not all girls are like you, Sarita," Pete said.

"What do you mean?" she asked.

"You are so..." Pete stopped and scratched his chin.

"So?"

"You just look like you have things figured out. I don't know, perhaps you are just more mature than the girls I know."

"Believe me, I wish I had things figured out. I think as soon as you hit sixteen your mind makes a somersault."

"You're funny," Pete said, his eyes locked in hers. She smiled back and then dropped her head, playing with the strand of hair that was now dangling loose again.

"My advice, Pete, is to make it clear that she is the girl for you. Don't treat her and all the other girls the same, make sure she can tell that you treat her differently. And take her for a walk, or a cold drink, here, in Dannhauser, far away from the other kids at school. Perhaps when you get off the bus or something like that? You must make her feel special," Sarita said and tried to smile.

"I think I heard something," Petrus said, his eyes wide open.

"Shhh," Sarita said and slowly crept to the door. She peered through the gaps between stickers to the world outside.

"Quick, go. I can't see anything, but let's not take any chances," she said.

A car door slammed close by. All three froze. Petrus stared at Pete, pleading for a plan. Pete signaled they should keep going. Sarita unlocked the door as quietly as she could, but the clicking of the lock echoed like a rockfall through the shop. Pete stuck his head out first but couldn't see anything. He turned back to Sarita who was holding both her hands over her mouth and winked. She dropped her hands a little and the faintest of smiles started to form. Pete slipped out, stooping away from the store. Petrus was so close behind Pete that for a moment Pete thought he was going to hop on his back.

They heard a voice, that of a man, and then a woman's voice, so they ran. They sprinted around the corner and stood under the large *Naidoo and Sons* sign, out of breath, next to each other, backs against the wall. In the distance they heard, "Hi Pappa, hi Mamma, you're back early!"

They shared a glance and started laughing, trying to keep the sound down. They jogged down the middle of the street. The breeze was cool but refreshing. Pete felt a rush of energy course through him. He looked at

Petrus who was smiling, running as if the breeze was tickling him, pure enjoyment streaming out.

Pete stopped suddenly.

"Crap, I'm going the wrong way!" Pete rolled his eyes and pulled a funny face. Petrus laughed, a fun laugh, one Pete had not heard before. The kind of laugh you only shared when you're getting up to mischief with your best friend. Pete didn't know what to do with it. He panicked, gave a robotic wave and sprinted away from Petrus, running hard, hoping that each stride would take him back to when he was five years old when everything was fun, everything was easy and complicated was some big word only grown-ups used.

SOMETHING IN THE WAY

"Protea Eight, on behalf of Command, I would like to congratulate you on the successful completion of your mission," Protea Seven said.

Venny slurped his hot tea. His eyes stared vacantly at the microphone.

"It has not gone unnoticed," Protea Seven said.

Venny pulled the microphone toward him.

"There were six blacks and two Indians killed," Venny said. He held the microphone so tight that his knuckles turned pale.

"An unfortunate by-product of our work. No war is won without sacrifice. We have to move on, their names remembered as fallen comrades on this twisting, difficult mountain road to the summit."

Protea Seven drew a deep breath through his nose. "My comrade, the summit is in sight, but the final climb will be the most difficult. There is no path, only a sheer rock face. We have to climb with our bare hands and feet as the rock crumbles around us, but we will not look down. We will fix our eyes on the summit and we will rise, we will rise like an awakening giant, and we will conquer that summit. It will be ours, once and for all."

Venny tried to say something but Protea Seven was not to be stopped. "Comrades will fall, and a trail of blood will remind us of our humble, oppressed past. I wish it wasn't so, truly, but it is the only way.

Words bounce off pale white skin like rain, but bullets penetrate. The goal, this summit, is far greater than one life, or even a thousand lives. It is what will shape the lives of millions, now and until the end of days. Therefore, my dear Protea Eight, mourn our fallen comrades, mourn them well. But rise up to fulfill our destiny, for them, for their children, and *yours*."

Venny held the microphone close to his mouth but words did not come. His eyes flickered between the newspaper clipping of the woman being beaten and the photograph of Sarita. He thought of the two Indians who had died in Newcastle. He wondered if they were just like him, fathers, husbands. He wondered what would happen to his family if it was him that was the accidental martyr.

"Protea Eight?"

"I'm here." There was no power left in Venny's voice.

"Because you have proven your dedication to the cause, something is being planned, at a high level, something for your town."

"Here? This place is tiny."

"Yes, the awakening of fear begins when you have no refuge, no sanctuary. Can we count on you? Or should we go in search of a new hero?"

"No, no...I'm in. You can count on me, always—always. This cause is my calling."

"Excellent. We will be in contact soon. Protea Seven out."

Venny turned the microphone off and pushed it to the back of the table. He took a small sip of tea and inspected the cup. His mind ran in so many directions, he didn't know which thoughts he should let go and which ones he should grab hold of. His mind whisked him away to rows and rows of dead Indian men who all looked like him, lying on the road packed next to one another like sardines, covered in blood, with him towering above them with the brown package in his hand. Just as quickly his mind took him to a crowd of people hoisting him onto their shoulders, cheering, chanting his name as the Union Building burned in the background. And then it was gone, and Sarita stood in front of him, smiling, hugging him, and then out of nowhere slapping him in the face and weeping uncontrollably. He slowly opened his hands and blood dripped from them.

Venny jumped up. He glared at the chair as if it was trying to poison him, grabbed his cup, unlocked his metal door and stepped outside. It was a dark place, and for the first time, there was an unwelcome air to it. As if it was no longer his sanctuary.

DRESSED IN WHITE

It was Wednesday afternoon, a day without rugby practice. Pete gazed out of the bus window as the world crawled by. The mornings were quite cool now, so the winter uniform, including their blazers, came in handy. But in the afternoons, especially after the bus had been baking in the sun, the uniform was less comfortable. It was one of those days when Pete knew that taking off his blazer would bring instant relief, but he didn't do it. It was too much of an effort, and he was tired.

Next to him was Barend. He joined Pete on the senior bus for the first time that week, following his newfound first-team status. Michael, whose seat he was now occupying, moved to the back of the bus, to sit in the seat vacated by a kid whose parents just took him out of school one day, and the whole family vanished. He was a goth, and no one really knew him, but the disappearance was strange nonetheless.

Four rows behind Pete, Renate sat next to a Matric girl named Hermien. She was a weird kind of pretty, the kind that most guys found attractive but were too ashamed to admit. There always seemed to be an unkemptness about her, and she had big, wild eyes. Most boys were more than just a little afraid of her. Her dad lived on a smallholding and there were always rumors doing the rounds that he was smuggling diamonds. She also had an ever-expanding reputation for her exploits of the sexual kind, very little of which had ever been confirmed. According to those who said they knew, she had made a bet with someone to sleep with all the apprentices (or *appies* as most referred to them) at the mine, before she finished Matric, and if you believed the rumor mills, success was within reach.

With only a few kilometers left before Dannhauser, Barend leaned in close. He looked like a cat who stumbled upon a freight ship full of cream, his cheeks were beaming pink orbs. Pete was half dozing, his knees high up against the backrest in front of him, arms folded.

"China," Barend whispered and peeked over his shoulder to see if anyone could hear.

"I think Hermien is giving your girl all sorts of naughty tips. I think she might use them on you," Barend said. Pete elbowed Barend in the ribs. Barend burst out laughing.

"Seriously, I think you might be in for a thing. She will make a man out of you yet," he said with a teasing smile.

"Zip it, Sparky, I'm trying to sleep," Pete said, closing his eyes and resting his head against the window. Barend laughed and slid down in his seat raising his knees high against the seat in front.

The bus stopped in Dannhauser. A silent cloak of after school drowsiness covered all those who got off.

Barend and Pete ambled toward their respective homes. "I wonder what tips Hermien gave your girl?" Barend said.

Pete was about to punch Barend's shoulder when a

voice behind them asked, "Do you have a girlfriend?"

They slowly turned as one. It was Renate. She looked completely untouched by the day. Her eyes sparkled, her hair perfectly tied back with not a single strand out of place. Pete thought of the hug after the rugby, and something stirred deep inside him, burning like fire. He wanted to pull her in and kiss her until everything around them dissolved into a blank canvas.

"Uhm..." Pete said.

"I was just joking," Barend said in a squeaky voice, but then cleared his throat. "This guy is as free as the wind." Pete glared at him, Barend responded with a pawky smile.

"That's good news," Renate said. She smiled and slowly looked up at Pete, seemingly studying his whole face. It was too much to take, he had to swing his school bag around and clutch it in front of him.

Pete tried to force a cool and collected smile but could feel how every corner of his face was glowing. Barend was already completely pink.

She stepped closer.

"Uhm...uh...I'll see you later," the words fumbled out of Barend's mouth. He turned and started walking, but almost immediately looked over his shoulder.

She came another step closer. Pete's heart was in full gallop. He could smell her. Sweet as the Edgars perfume section. He tried to swallow, in vain.

"Do you know the pond beyond New Extension?"

"Uh-huh." His sounds were blunt and heavy. His eye itching like crazy.

"Buy me a cold drink and meet me there. Four o'clock." She tilted her head, and flapped her eyelashes. "Please?" she added in a toddler's voice.

"Okay," Pete said. He had nothing else. Words, thoughts, everything got stuck against his palate.

She didn't say another word, just gave a playful smile, stepped right up to him and kissed him on the cheek before he could even blink. Then she turned and walked away.

He wanted to call out after her—to make sure this was real. But the words got stickier, and his mind more of a mess.

Did this really just happen?

Lightheaded, he stumbled away. Blinded. His heart almost stopped when a fist came out of nowhere and punched his shoulder.

It was Barend. He grabbed Pete around the neck and wrestled him to the ground.

"You're in, China, you're in!" Barend shouted. He let go of Pete's neck and slapped him on the shoulder, grinning from ear to ear.

"You bloody sly bastard, you're in! She digs you. She digs you big time!"

"I'll see you later," Pete said to Barend when they got to Pete's house. Barend had deemed it necessary to impart wisdom all the way home.

Barend was the embodiment of what Pete was feeling inside, you could almost touch his excitement.

"Okay, but details, everything…we're best friends, I need details," Barend said. A knot had formed in the pit of Pete's stomach, but he smiled and strolled away as casually as he could, his legs were like jelly though and he struggled to walk.

Just before four o'clock, he took his place on a

rock overlooking the pond. He placed the can of Mello Yellow he had brought along for her next to him, his shaking hands struggling to hold it. And his sweaty palms were making it warm.

He was trying to think about what to say and do, but his brain wouldn't allow it—a blob of gray matter blocking all thoughts. His throat tightened.

It was a mistake. He was going to look like a bloody fool.

He got up, scanned the area and started pacing up and down next to the pond.

Quarter past four. No sign of her.

He felt woozy. His heart would surely give in, or he would just pass out or something.

Half-past four. Still nothing.

He sat down again. His feet sore from all the pacing. He held the back of his hand against the can of Mello Yellow. It was no longer cold.

He knew that everyone always said women took their time, but hell, a man's nerves could only take so much. Or was this a prank? A stupid prank and he fell for it? Hook, line, and sinker.

Damn it! He couldn't believe he was this gullible. He sat hunched, dropping his head in his hands. What an idiot.

"I hope you haven't fallen asleep?" a voice supplanted his self-loathing. He craned his neck.

A vision of loveliness, shining like the evening star called out to him. It was Renate. His eyes glazed over staring at the breeze playfully caressing her golden hair and teasingly lifting her short white dress. A heatwave besieged every part of him, his breathing shallow.

"Look at you! I wear a dress especially for you and you didn't even bring me flowers?" Renate teased.

"Warm Mello Yello?" Pete said and held the can out to her.

Renate started laughing. She grabbed the can from his hand, clutched it against her bosom and twirled like a ballerina whilst singing an exaggerated "Thank you." Her dress fluttered as she twirled revealing her panties for a fleeting moment. Perhaps he should go to a doctor: There were weird stabbing pains in his heart. But it appeared as though the doctor might have to wait because she hooked her arm into his as if it was the most natural thing on earth and started walking.

"Why have we never spoken?" she asked and leaned her head against his shoulder.

Because before last week I played fourth team rugby and my dad isn't rich? Pete thought.

"Ships in the night?" he said.

"Mmm...I always find that saying very sad, so I'm glad I found my ship." She didn't look at him, but her whole left side was now touching him. He tried to take long deep breaths to control his hormones which were begging to be let loose.

"So, you're a city girl?" Pete asked.

"Uh-huh, Fontainebleau in Johannesburg, born and bred."

"Fontainebleau sounds quite exotic."

She chortled. "Compared to this place, sure."

"What's it like, you know, to be here, in Nowhereville?"

"It's different, definitely different. Aggh, I don't know, it's kind of nice. People are really friendly, and my dad says there is no crime, so...I guess it's not so bad."

"Well I'm glad you're here," Pete said, staring into the distance and then quickly turning back to her. It beggars belief, he thought, he was walking arm-in-arm with Renate—in real life. This was not a dream, this was not a dream, he repeated over and over in his head.

"And I'm glad you're here," she said, then stopped, unhooked her arm and walked out in front of him. He knew this was probably some game and he had to react. Running after her and throwing her over his shoulder was probably not a good idea, although that was pretty much what his primal instinct urged him to do. *Think, Pete, think.*

He walked faster to catch up, laughed in his head about the thought of her dangling over his shoulder, and took her hand, slipping his fingers in-between hers. To his surprise, she let him and gave his hand a little squeeze. Now his hormones kicked and screamed to be let loose.

They walked slowly, in a tense silence but to Pete's despair all too soon her house was visible in the distance.

"Are you looking forward to Saturday's game?" she asked.

"Ladysmith? Yes. They have a good team this year, so it will be a tough one, especially as they'll have home-field advantage."

"If you play as you played on Saturday, they'll have no chance." Her voice was soft and husky and Pete's mind was shattered. They were getting closer and closer to her house, but he couldn't think, it was as if his body was attacking his mind. He stopped, she continued walking but he held her hand tight. He reeled her in, close to him. She smiled as she looked up at him, the blue of her eyes like a tropical sea. Movie scenes played through his mind searching for one that could work in this situation. Then she closed her eyes and leaned closer. He placed his index finger under her chin and pulled her lips into his.

Her lips were soft, sweet, and tasted like strawberries, her tongue searching for his as they stood under a leafless jacaranda tree. Her taste awoke something in him, something unstoppable, and the kissing became firmer, more intense, deeper. His hands slipped down to low on her back, and he pressed her body closer to his. She let her hands drop onto his hips and her fingers clawed into his skin.

"Okay...wow." She pushed him away, standing with her arms stretched out against his chest, out of breath.

"You okay?" he asked. Worried.

"Okay?" she laughed, trying to catch her breath. "I'm much more than okay."

She leaned in again but this time, just as his hands found her back again, she gave him a short soft kiss on the lips and then withdrew.

"I have to go." She smiled at him with droopy eyes, which made his brain explode. Her lips were dark red now.

"Save a seat for me on the Ladysmith trip," she said and blew a kiss at him, turned and walked away. Her swaying hips completely hypnotizing Pete. Even after she was out of sight, Pete remained frozen on the same spot. Eventually, his mind slowly started filtering back. His first kiss. His first kiss! "Woohoo!" he shouted and quickly looked to see if anyone had heard him. He set off, sprinting home, knowing that the only thing that could save him from a near-certain catastrophic mind and body explosion was a long, cold shower—ice cold.

THE TRIP

Away games in Ladysmith were the worst. There was nothing wrong with the town itself; it was large and had a few grand old buildings. Albeit that the place had seen better days and had a tired look to it. Just like the busloads of traveling rugby, hockey and netball players arriving after their painfully slow Saturday morning journeys. It was particularly bad for those living in Dannhauser. Long before the sun rose you had to get the school minibus, which then took you in completely the wrong direction, back to Dundee. Here all the teams boarded the school buses and set off on the red-eye trip to Ladysmith. From the pick-up in Dannhauser to the large field at the rear of the Ladysmith High School's main pavilion, it easily took two-and-a-half soul-destroying hours. It was the single biggest reason why Dundee didn't have a fantastic record against them; the kids were too tired to be motivated.

Today though, as the bus filled with senior rugby and hockey players made its way along the drawn-out hilly road to Ladysmith, Pete was loving every minute of it. On his shoulder, Renate was sleeping peaceful-ly. She made soft breathing sounds and her arm was anchored around his middle.

He gazed at the sun dangling low above the horizon, illuminating hundreds of acacia trees and rocky hills in its fiery glow. It struck him how incredibly inexplicable the human mind was. A week ago, he was a mess, almost killed, but now, with his arm around Renate, he felt as though life could not be any sweeter. Are our memories so weak that the simplest positive can blank out the most horrid memories? The image of that boy, the now-dead boy, who had been right next to him, was still very raw. He could see the blood pouring out of his young body, the fear, hate, and anguish in the father's eyes as he scooped up his son, knowing that as a father he should have protected him—but he couldn't. No one could have. Perhaps we paint over the dark torrents of hurt with a thin layer of caramel-ized sugar, to keep some sort of grip on our minds, to stop us from drowning in what lies beneath. If only caramel didn't fracture so easily and release that hidden dread to spoil the sickly-sweet coating.

The bus struggled up a long slow-turning hill. The driver, Mr. Watson, a retired former biology teacher, searched through the gears for more power from the aging beast, but all he managed was to agitate the sleepy teenagers. Renate's head slipped off Pete's shoulder and onto his chest. She woke briefly, her eyes fluttering rather than open, and she smiled at him, before nestling her head on his shoulder again. There it goes again, one quick smile and the feel of her small, delicate hand finding a new resting place around his middle, and the caramel hardened all over again. No darkness or grief, just rainbows, and butterflies. He couldn't help but to smile and shake his head, before staring out at the vastness of his home province, as it arced in understated, timeless elegance toward the motherly arms of the Drakensberg.

The Dundee buses arrived one after the other, and hundreds of sleepy, tired teenagers disembarked wearing their travel-disheveled school uniforms. The first games kicked-off at 8 o'clock. The poor under fourteens were first up, followed by the under fifteens. The A-teams played on the greenish field in front of the main pavilion, and all the lesser teams on patchy fields around the perimeter of the large sports grounds. Ten-thirty was the big one: the first team kick off.

Unsurprisingly, all the junior Dundee teams lost, as they did every time they traveled to Ladysmith. Most of them unable to lift the web of sleep spun around them.

The first rugby and hockey teams sat on a smaller pavilion adjacent to the main pavilion, looking cool in their school uniform and white scarves—the sole privilege of those who attained the glory of representing firsts.

It was a strange bunch. You had the perennial overachievers who couldn't remain seated for long, always looking for a teacher to impress. The rest mostly tried their best to look as disinterested in the day and life as they could. The girls pretended like the boys were beneath them and made suggestive comments when some of the older men walked by. Renate sat next to Pete, holding his hand, but her back was half turned away from him as she chatted to Philippa and her other friends. Barend sat next to Pete. They made the odd comment about the junior rugby games, but in general felt awkward, not knowing what to say or do, in this bizarre subculture seen as the pinnacle of high school life.

"China, you have to have a word," Barend whispered.

"I will, relax, man," Pete said. Barend looked at him with great skepticism. "I will, promise."

Later most of the group disappeared to the tuck shop and for the first time, Pete and Renate were alone again. It was difficult to talk to her without wanting to pull her in and kiss her.

"Your friend, Philippa," Pete started.

"My bestest friend in the whole world?" she teased.

"Yup, is she...sort of, seeing anyone?" Pete asked.

Renate opened her mouth wide and slapped him playfully on the shoulder.

"Are you looking to trade me in already?"

"No," he answered sheepishly, scratching his itching right eye. "It's not for me." The words came out milliseconds before it dawned on him than Renate was teasing.

"Who wants to know?" she asked, but he could tell she knew the answer.

"Barend. But please, he doesn't want the world to know."

"I thought I saw something in his eyes, the way he looked at her. It's cute," she said.

"So, is she?" he asked.

"What you really want to know is, does she like your friend?"

"Well...yeah. But if she doesn't please don't tell her about this conversation. Please?"

"Don't worry, P." She had started calling him "P" that morning. He didn't like it, but it was a small price to pay for being on the arm of your dreamgirl.

"I think she might have noticed him if you know

what I mean?" He didn't know what she meant but nodded as if he did.

"Tell him to get a window seat on the way back and I'll arrange the rest. But only if you guys win today. If you don't, well, then you two can sit together." She smiled, but he couldn't tell whether she was joking, so he just winked at her, and turned to watch the under fifteens who were losing badly.

The group of white scarves dispersed to change and start their warm-ups. Dundee's second team was busy destroying their opponents, which would be the first win of the day for the school.

Pete stood next to Barend as they were leaning forward to touch their toes, as part of the warm-up.

"I had a chat. Make sure you get to the bus early and get a window seat, Renate will arrange the rest."

Barend nearly tumbled forward. "Serious?"

"Yup, the only condition is that we have to win. So scrum the life out of Ladysmith and you get Philippa as the prize."

"If this is some joke then I'm going to kill you, sl-ow-l-y," Barend warned.

"Believe me, I wouldn't joke about something like this."

"Bloody hell, China, the first team jersey hey? It's like a magic wand. Without it, these girls look right through you as if you are nothing more than a fart in the air. But with it on, these same girls who are way out of our league are suddenly part of our league. Like magic." Barend shook his head, dumbfounded, and bent forward to try and touch his toes.

"Did Renate say anything about Philippa, does she

like me or something? Is she even interested?"

"She didn't say much, she just said she thinks Philippa has noticed you."

"What the hell does that mean?" Barend asked.

"Damned if I know. She said it like I was supposed to know, like some code word for something. But I think it's good, so..."

"Jeez, China, if I could get Philippa—me?" Barend stood upright and looked at the sky, his gaze far away. Pete knew this was not the strong, muscular sixteen-year-old Barend talking, but the fat kid with the pink cheeks whom everyone teased. Pete was worried about the bus ride back. He didn't quite know what Renate meant and if she was setting Barend up for some catastrophic embarrassment. Then he would have to consider the unthinkable. Belchie referred to it as "bros before hoes"—a by-product of watching too many American movies, and Barend was his best friend after all, and probably would be for life. He would have to dump Renate, choose Barend. The thought of Renate's soft lips interlocking with his overwhelmed all other thoughts, the softness of her body against his. *No, I must always choose Barend. That's what friends do,* he promised himself. And then he closed his eyes. *Please, dear Lord, I pray that Renate is not busy setting Barend up for the biggest fall of his life.*

"Amazing game, Pete! Great tries, Pete! You were awesome, China!" The chorus of hundreds of Dundee High School kids shouted out as Pete and the rest of the first team made their way to the bus. He didn't know how to react to his newfound fame, but Renate walked right next to him clutching his hand so tightly that it almost hurt. Her smile was broad, and her hair waved like a victory flag.

Pete's mind was far away from the game in which they had run riot against an unsuspecting Ladysmith. Even his two tries were far from his mind, all he could think of was Barend.

As he stepped into the bus, he saw Barend sitting alone in a window seat. Despite playing the game of his life and scoring his first ever try Barend looked lost, uneasy, as if he was sitting on an anthill. Pete wished there was something he could do. He couldn't shake the sickening feeling that Barend was being set up. He studied Renate's face, desperately trying to see if there was some hidden clue to decipher, some tell he could spot to stop the impending catastrophe, but she was chatting away to her friends in blissful ignorance of the anxiety of the guy whose hand she held. Pete and Renate slipped into seats three rows behind Barend. There was no sign of Philippa. Two first-team boys wanted to take the seat next to Barend, but he protected it with his life.

Then Philippa slowly made her way into the bus. Her lean muscular body was accentuated by a very tight-fitting hockey uniform, the skirt revealing just enough leg to make Barend, and many other boys, head for the cold showers. Her hair was darker than Renate's but still blonde: a deep golden blond. It seemed impossible that her doll-like features were real, and Pete wondered if her face would break like a porcelain cup if a hockey ball struck her. She smiled and took her time to speak to almost everyone, as she meandered down the aisle. As far as Pete could tell, she had not looked at Barend once, and could only imagine the things that must be running through his friend's mind. He desperately wanted to stop this car crash he was witnessing but didn't know how.

Philippa nonchalantly walked closer to Barend's row. She looked around the bus as if Barend didn't exist, and then her gaze fixed on Renate. Pete flung his head around to watch Renate, she was hiding a grin behind her hand. Pete felt sick. *If they do anything to Barend, so help me...*

In one swift floating move that almost made her skirt lift like Marilyn Monroe's, Philippa flopped down next to Barend. Pete could see the pinkness in his friend's cheeks glowing, but Philippa was smiling and chatting, and somehow, old Pinkerbelle managed to chat back.

He observed them intently for quite some time, hoping that this wasn't still part of a plot to humiliate his friend, but all seemed quiet, almost natural. The teacher supposedly chaperoning the bus fell asleep before the bus had even left Ladysmith and all the couples started snogging as if there was some big announcement which Pete missed somehow.

Renate reached out to Pete's chest, grabbing his jersey by balling her hand into a fist. She plucked him closer, almost so fast that there was a clash of noses. The kissing was amazing, her tongue continually chasing, and teasing his in an amazing game where all involved won.

They snogged for half an hour, during which time Pete thought his body would fail him several times.

Then Renate gave him a peck on the cheek and snuggled against his shoulder and fell asleep within seconds. But there wasn't much time for recovery, because three rows in front of him, he witnessed something special. His best friend was slowly leaning in, nervously, and then Philippa completed the rest of the journey: they kissed. His best friend's first kiss!

He watched how the uncertainty of years of self-loathing broke off his friend's brittle crust, fell to the ground, and how he was suddenly beaming with confidence. Now he was the one taking Philippa in his arms. She was no longer leading, he was her man, and she was weak in his arms. Pete wondered if the feeling of pride he felt was the same as what fathers felt.

A week after he had almost lost his life, life was perfect in every way. He couldn't quite believe it; it felt like a dream, but one he was directing, one in which he said what happened next. He couldn't imagine life getting any better than this. He recalled his conversation with Barend at the start of the year and realized that this *truly* was their year—the best year ever.

PART THREE

ALMOST

It was Sunday afternoon, twenty to three. Pete was stretched out on his back staring at the ceiling, Foreigner was playing on his tape player, "I've been waiting, for a girl like you." He could feel the silkiness of Renate's legs under his touch, as his hand dared to go a little higher, still safe, but higher. Something in his head started to pulse, tick-tick-tick. He and Barend had been talking about snogging girls since they were twelve, and here in less than a week, both of them had crossed that magnificent bridge. It was even better than he imagined. Fantasizing alone in your room has its moments, as nothing is off limits, but the feel of a girl, her smell, her breath against you, her tongue, her skin, it was just so much better than imagining Christie Brinkley inexplicably walking into your room, standing there in her red bikini with lustful, devouring eyes.

He looked at the Christie Brinkley poster on his wall. "Sorry, Christie," he whispered.

Just after lunch, he made his first phone call to Renate's house. He was petrified that her dad would answer, but to his relief it was her mom. She sounded nice, a little skeptical, but nice. And it was so cool to speak to Renate, to hear that sexy huskiness over the phone. It was an awkward chat though. He phoned without any idea of what to say to her, nor did he have anything to say. He had only called to remind her that he was still there, he was still her…boyfriend? He wondered what the protocol was. Should he ask her out, officially asking her to be his girlfriend, or was that uncool, should they just be *together*? It was tricky, no one had a rule book, and it changed constantly. He wanted to ask her out, to make it official, to bind her to him in a sense, but what if she thought he was some inexperienced dork?

His eyes scanned the room. On the furthest wall next to his closet was a photograph of him and Barend with the trophies they had won in Standard Five, at the end of their primary school careers. They were both so young then, Barend still had most of his baby fat. It made him think of the day before when Barend's life changed in the arms of Philippa. Part of him was happier about Barend's first kiss than his own, but that said, not a very big part. He started laughing out loud recalling Barend's moment by moment recollection of the kiss after Sunday School. He described the way Philippa tasted, felt and smelled in so much (unnecessary) detail, that he thought it was he who had snogged Philippa. He chuckled, thinking of Barend's expressive face as he talked about the best moment of his life. He had wanted to laugh then, but he couldn't bring himself to laugh in his best friend's face during his paean about the perfect angel he had found.

"I bet she doesn't even need to use the toilet," Pete remarked, for which he was rewarded with a punch on the shoulder.

"You don't talk about my girl like that," Barend said.

"So, it's official?" Pete asked.

"Well yeah, we kissed."

Pete still wasn't convinced that that was enough. It felt as though they needed something on paper, something more official and lasting than sealing it with a kiss, although it was much more fun that way.

The tape stopped. He sat up, took the Foreigner cassette out and rummaged through his tape case for something else. *Now That's What I Call Music! 3* was the winner. It was a copy he had gotten from Belchie, not a great copy, but it had the whole album, so Pete couldn't complain. "A View to a Kill" started playing. "Meeting you, with a view to a kill. Face to face in secret places, feel the chill," Pete sang along under his breath. He thought about the song and the James Bond movie, which he had watched during the Easter holidays. Roger Moore, the Eiffel Tower—which he promised himself he would climb one day, and the evil mystery of Grace Jones. She was ugly to him, but he could see there was something about her, something that could seduce the suave Mr. Bond. He sang a little louder this time, but not too loud to wake his parents. Duran Duran was so cool.

A wave of nausea crashed over him.

"Wild Boys," he said aloud. He was there again. Sitting with his back against the warm rock whilst Rudie was about to get out of his truck and change his life.

"Crap!" he shouted. He grabbed his watch from his desk and stared at it hoping that if he blinked a few times, the clock would turn back. It was twenty to four, and it was Sunday. In less than twenty minutes, Sarita's parents would stop at the shop and then the

chance would be gone. If he ran it would take ten minutes, if he ran flat out. That would leave a maximum of
ten minutes to see them, but there was a good chance
that Sarita's parents might be back before then. Last
Sunday they had arrived at ten to four.

He put both hands on his head trying to think. He
thought of Sarita, her disappointment, and Petrus—
his mind hovered over Petrus. Would he have gone on
his own? Would he have just left? How would he feel?
And what happened last week, there was a moment...

He took the tape out and searched for something
else, something safe. "Alphaville." As the tape started, he sat back on his bed. His eyes were closed.
First Sarita's soft dimples carved into her face flashed
before him, then Renate's perfect diamond-like
smile. He could smell the floral sweetness in Sarita's
silky black hair, and he could taste the strawberry on
Renate's mouth.

"No." He opened his eyes and rubbed both hands
through his hair. He had Renate now. Perhaps he
didn't need the other two anymore. Perhaps their
healing, getting over that night, was over, perhaps
it was time to just move on. He had Renate now, he
could move on. And he had Barend.

His nausea lingered. He felt like that time when he
was six and they were on holiday in Port Elizabeth. He
so desperately wanted to go on another ride at the
beachfront funfair, but his pocket money was spent.
His mom sat on a bench watching his older brothers
go down the supertube and her wallet was lying right
next to her—and it was open. A two rand note waved
at him in the breeze, and against pleas from the angel
on his right shoulder, he grabbed it, Mom none the

wiser, and went on more rides until he threw up next to a bin. Kids pointed and laughed, but his mom took him in her arms and kissed him on his forehead. Betrayal was the taste of sick in his mouth. He never told his mom, but he saved his pocket money for a long time, and one day when his mom was cooking, he snuck into her room, took out her wallet and put back the two rand, plus an extra fifty cents—because his dad always complained about all the interest he had to pay.

In the solitude of his room, he tried to reason, over and over again, but the only thought which kept repeating was that he had to get the two rands back to its owner. He had to, but he couldn't today: It was one minute past four.

POLLUTION

Venny was worried. There were only twenty minutes left before he was to receive an important message, and Sarita wasn't back from school yet. He couldn't just close the shop, his wife would ask too many questions, and life was complicated enough.

The shop was quiet, a few kids had bought Fireballs some minutes ago, but in general, this was a very slow Thursday.

Seventeen minutes left.

He would have to get to his car, drive home, unlock everything and get to his operations room to set up the radio—time was running out, and Sarita was late. It wasn't like her. She had this thing about being on time.

The door opened and the afternoon breeze puffed dust from outside into Venny's shop.

"There you are! Where were you, you're late."

"I'm sorry, Pappa. I was just helping one of the girls from school—"

"Never mind," Venny interjected. "You're here now. I need to run out for a few minutes so you must look after the shop."

"But I have two tests tomorrow, I need to—"

"It will only be for a few minutes, end of discussion."

"Yes, Pappa." Sarita slipped the bookcase from her shoulder and let it fall behind the counter.

"A few minutes," Venny reiterated and hurried out

of the door. She had that look again, he thought, the one which felt like he was physically hurting her. He wondered how she managed to do it: one look, like a dagger.

His car was just around the corner, parked in an alley under the salon. He took his keys out and checked the time: nine minutes left.

"Hello, my bunny chow buddy," a voice thundered out of nowhere.

Venny looked up. Next to his car stood a large white Toyota Hilux and leaning against it was the giant figure of Rudie. His heart sank as he thought of the last time he had seen him: the pain and humiliation.

"Good afternoon. Please excuse me. I'm late for an appointment," Venny said as he started to unlock his car.

"Always in a hurry, aren't you, Mr. Curry?" Rudie said and laughed at his joke.

Venny forced a smile and slid in behind his steering wheel, fumbling with the keys as he searched for the ignition. Rudie walked around and opened Venny's door.

"I'm talking to you." Rudie flicked his finger at Venny's ear. It stung, but he found the ignition and turned the key.

"I'm terribly sorry, I must go," he said, without looking at Rudie.

"I can't let you go. I need stuff from your shop." Rudie remained standing in his door.

"Unfortunately, the shop is closed." Venny slipped the car into reverse and pulled back. Rudie didn't expect this and jumped out of the way momentarily, giving Venny a chance to slam the door shut, slap the gear lever into drive and race away as quickly as his Datsun allowed him. In the rear-view mirror, he could see a laughing Rudie pointing his finger like a gun, right at him, and pulling the trigger. An ice-cold shiver ran down his spine.

He arrived home with three minutes left. Thank goodness for small towns, he thought, if there was even a hint of traffic he would have been screwed. He had hoped that there would have been enough time to make a nice cup of tea, but now he was in a race just to make Protea Seven's transmission. He unlocked his steel gate—his hands shaking, opened the screen door and unlocked the main door. He pulled everything closed behind him only locking the main door, before he sprinted through the living room, the kitchen and down the passageway which led to the garage. He unlocked the steel door, pulled it half-closed, snapped buttons on the radio and microphone, and adjusted the frequency. He looked at his watch: thirty seconds left. He exhaled with relief and flopped onto the small cushion.

A sickening thought entered his mind. He saw Rudie walking slowly toward his shop, opening the door and entering. Sarita was alone. Rudie walked in, took things, and Sarita tried to stop him. He started slapping her, and then punching her, sitting on top of her and punching her until she didn't move anymore.

What have I done?

"Protea Eight, come in."

Venny stared at Sarita's picture on his wall, so perfect in every way. Had he opened the gates of hell on his beloved daughter, his only child?

"Protea Eight?"

"I'm here." Venny's voice broke. "Continue, Protea Seven." He couldn't take his eyes off Sarita's picture, his mind filled with Rudie's yellow mustache, his oversized paws...*I swear on the life of my father if that white piece of trash so much as looks at my daughter I will drive to his farm and blow his brains out, what little he has.*

"The plan is in motion, Protea Eight. Your town has been authenticated."

"Okay." Venny knew this was exciting news but all he could think of was Sarita.

"We will discuss exact dates shortly, but at the moment I can confirm it will be this winter. July."

Venny drew a few deep breaths, trying to clear his mind. "Nothing will happen," he said to himself. Rudie just wanted to mess with his head, and it was working. Nothing will happen. Nothing.

"Any detail you can give me, to help me prepare, or any reconnaissance?" Venny asked, his voice still croaky.

"Negative, Protea Eight. Your task is to carry on with your normal life and not to do anything out of the ordinary." Venny thought of his drive to Rudie's farm and pulling the trigger into his sniggering face.

"Nothing out of the ordinary. Understood," Venny repeated.

"Nothing to attract unwanted attention. Protea Seven out." Then the radio went silent.

Venny stared at the radio for a few seconds. How could he follow this order if Rudie did something to Sarita? How normal could he be then?

Rudie.

He stormed out of his operations room, almost

forgetting to lock it, and begged his fingers not to fumble as he locked the house. His Datsun Laurel was trying its best to stay on the road, and a few people looked up as his golden car screeched around the corner of Main Street.

He slowed down to turn into their alleyway and prayed that Rudie's truck wouldn't be there anymore. But it was.

Sarita consumed his mind. He imagined blood covering her perfect face, her body broken.

He didn't even close his car door as he ran the short distance to his shop. All seemed calm, and he took a moment to collect himself, patting down the unruly remains of hair. He pushed on the handle to enter. It was stuck. He tried again. Locked!

He pressed his face against the window trying to figure out what was going on, but he couldn't see any movement inside. It was very dark in the shop. Sweat burned his eyes.

Venny knocked, three quick taps. Silence. Then he started hammering on the door. Still nothing, no sign of life.

Rage and fear ruptured the fault line of his mind and he turned blind. He could not see anything other than the door and a rock perched on the wall near the street.

He marched to the rock. It was heavy and warm, and its surface coarse. He carried the rock in both hands, swinging it in front of him, almost pulling him off balance, but his mind was focused and he kept going. He had to do whatever it took. *Whatever* it took.

He reached his shop door with great trouble. He kicked at the door a couple of final times, but there was neither sound nor movement. The rock was getting heavier, his arms strained, and he nearly dropped it as it started slipping from his grasp. But he adjusted his grip and started swinging it from side to side. He counted, "One...two..."

"Venkatapathi!" A shrill voice sliced through his trance-like state. The momentum of the rock was on his back heel and he dropped it. It grazed his hip and its round end tumbled into the side of his little toe.

"Damn it!" he shouted, hobbling around on his one leg, clutching his foot.

"Have you lost your mind?" Achala asked, shaking her head, standing with both hands pressed deep into her hips.

"The shop." Venny pointed to the door.

"I know what you did." Achala waved her right arm about.

"Perhaps I should take Sarita back to India and leave you and this place forever," she screamed.

"What?" Venny said, still rubbing his foot.

"You left Sarita alone in the shop."

"It was only for a few minutes."

"You left your daughter alone. Next thing—I hear her scream."

"Scream? Is she okay?"

"How could you?"

"What happened? Is she okay?"

"When I heard her scream, I ran to your shop. There was this man."

"What man? What did he do?"

"This large lump with a yellow mustache."

"What did he do?"

"For heaven's sake! Will you let me finish?"

"Sorry...what did he do? Where is Sarita?"

"This foul lump of whatshallwecallit had Sarita by the collar and he was lifting her off the ground. I screamed and shouted so much and started slapping him, but he just held her there. After a few seconds, he dropped her like a sack of potatoes, straight on the tiles. He grabbed my face like this..." Achala held her hand over her face.

"And then he said that you promised him some goods which he came to pick up. He said next time he wouldn't be this nice. He also warned us not to tell anyone; said he is friends with all the police. Venny, he hurt our daughter." Achala started crying, her voice was suddenly soft and meek.

"He just came in here, like we were nothing...you left her alone...how could you? She's just a child." She sobbed openly, not trying to stop her tears.

"I didn't know..." Venny hobbled to his wife. "I'm so immensely sorry, Achala. Believe me, I would never..." He put his arms around her and pulled her in close. She pounded her fists against his chest, but he continued to hug her until the punching stopped, and she cried on his shoulder. She gave him a few more powerless smacks on his back.

"Where is she?" he whispered.

"She's in my storeroom. I gave her tea. She's just a little girl."

"I'm sorry...I'm so, so sorry," Venny said. He let his face rest deep in Achala's thick hair. How could he pretend like this never happened? How could he just stand aside and do nothing?

A noise came from the alleyway. Rudie's Toyota Hilux was crawling closer. Venny let Achala go and stood in front of her. Rudie stopped next to them. He leaned across to look through his open window, finding Venny's eyes.

"I see you've got yourself a couple of nice mares in the stable. I'll see you soon. And next time—" Rudie turned his head toward the road for a second then back to Venny. "Next time will leave a mark."

Rudie blew a kiss to Achala and drove off.

HEALING

"What the hell are *they* doing here?" Pete asked Barend, glaring at the legendary center pairing of Gareth and John-John, parading around in full practice gear.

Barend shook his head.

"Perhaps they're just here to do fitness training with us. From what I heard they were booked off for at least another week. Besides, you're on fire at the moment, even if they came back..."

"Something's not right. Look at all the others sucking up to them, like they're kings or something," Pete said.

Mr. Theunissen blew his whistle "Listen up," he shouted. The group of first and second team boys huddled around him.

"Seconds, do one lap, then meet back here for a fifteen-minute contact session." He blew his whistle again and all the second team boys started running the long way around the school fields. The remaining boys, the first team, stood closer to their coach.

"This weekend is the big one. Vryheid High School is our toughest opponent and the one team standing between us and a fourth consecutive league title. Make no mistake, boys, they will come at us ten times harder than anything we've experienced so far this year. Every mistake, every missed tackle, every knock-on will cost us the league. They will capitalize on everything. Therefore, we will not make mistakes. We will hunt them down and feast on theirs. Boys, I will not let you off that field on Saturday until you've won. Am I making myself clear?"

"Yes, sir!"

"Now in light of this, I am happy to announce that our prayers have been answered. As you will have noticed both Gareth and John-John are here today. The good news is they are not just here for fun. The doctor cleared them, and they are ready to play on Saturday. Believe me, we will need their experience and talent against Vryheid." He paused to give the boys a chance to cheer. A few tapped Gareth and John-John on the shoulder, both smiling smugly.

"We will need to be very accurate in our execution on Saturday, so no fitness today. We will focus on set-plays and strategy. I will drill these plays into you until you forget your girlfriends and dream only of these moves."

Mr. Theunissen planted his feet apart, lifted his head. "Are we the number one team or what?"

"Yes, sir!" all shouted.

"Who's number one?"

"We are!"

"Who?"

"We are!"

"Good, now prove it. Forwards to the left, backs to the right." He blew his whistle again, and the boys dispersed.

"De Lange," he shouted and blew his whistle. Pete walked, head down, to the coach.

"The gap you plugged is no longer there. Go and report back to your coach, Mr. le Roux."

"Sir?" Pete asked.

"Move it, de Lange, you're interrupting my practice." He blew his whistle with vigor and walked away toward the other boys, without looking at Pete again.

Pete was stunned, in shock, frozen. Pete tilted his head and gawked at Mr. Theunissen standing in front of the backline players. Gareth was staring straight at him, his smile so unnaturally wide it was like something out of a cartoon.

"Piss off, junior!" Gareth shouted, and all the boys laughed. All except Barend.

Pete ambled to the far side of the sports fields. By the time he got to Mr. le Roux and the thirds and fourths, a few of the boys were shouting expletives, whistling, and gesturing exactly what they thought of him.

"Look here, it's rugby royalty," Mr. le Roux taunted. Everyone laughed and the word "wanker" echoed around the field.

"De Lange, we had a meeting and we don't think you are quite good enough for us, however, it's your lucky day. Dawid is injured, so a beautiful little space opened up on the fourth team bench—just for you." Mr. le Roux looked at his appreciative crowd and relished their response.

Pete sat on the pavilion steps for the whole duration of practice. During the bus ride home, he sat on his own in the corner and avoided any attempt Barend made to speak to him.

At home he lay on his bed, staring at the ceiling in silence. He told his mom several times that he wasn't hungry, but it was in vain. She must have sensed something was wrong because as soon as his dad returned from work, he insisted on coming in. It was the last person he wanted to see.

"What's going on, Pete?"

"Nothing."

"Nonsense. What's going on?"

"Nothing, Pa."

"I wasn't born yesterday. Talk to me. Is it about a girl?" Rikus asked. For the first time since Mr. Theunissen's poisoned darts, Pete thought of Renate. Would she drop him as quickly as the coach?

"No," Pete said.

"What then?"

"It's nothing, Pa."

"Is it rugby?" Pete didn't answer.

"Pete, what happened?" Pete remained quiet.

"Pete," Rikus said in a deeper, firmer tone.

"Ag Pa, it's those guys."

"What guys?"

"Those two first-team centers, Gareth and John-John."

"The ones with concussions?"

"Yup, they're back in all their glory. A doctor cleared them to play a week early. So I'm out."

"What do you mean, out?"

"Out. Full stop. Guess who will be warming the fourth team bench on Saturday?"

"What? Wait. Let's take it a few steps back. So, these two incumbents are back and just like that you've been kicked off the team?"

"Yup."

"And they put you on the fourth team bench, not the firsts?"

"Yup."

Rikus sat down on Pete's desk chair. He rubbed his hand across his chin repeatedly, getting more and more robust every time.

"They kicked you out?"

"Yup."

"And want to prop you on the fourth team bench?" Pete just nodded.

"Like hell!" Rikus said and got up and started walking toward the door. "What's that Theunissen's name? Tom? Dick? Harry?"

"Please don't call him, Pa! Just leave it."

"Leave it? No, no, no. They can't just chew you and spit you out like a piece of bubblegum. Theunissen is getting a piece of my mind tonight." His dad walked out of the room. Pete ran after him.

"Dad, please don't, it'll make it worse."

"You got that right! It's going to get a lot worse very quickly—for that prick. Pete, if we don't say something then these...coaches will keep on doing whatever they want, playing their favorites whilst talented boys like you are left in the cold. No, sometimes you need to make a stand. If you really believe in something and if you can see blatant injustice, then you can't just suck it up. Part of being a man is standing up to these bullies, showing them that we're not rolling over."

"But he'll say that I ran tail between my legs to my dad: can't even fight my own battles," Pete pleaded.

"Listen. He is an adult, and so am I. If this was a scrap between you and Barend, I would say sort it out yourself. But a kid taking on an adult is like bringing a knife to a gunfight. An adult needs to speak to this bloke. He thinks he can just rule his world full of kids, but out in the real world he is just another bloke." Rikus sat on the small wooden bench next to the telephone in the hall. He picked up the telephone directory and paged to the back.

"Do you know his first name?" Rikus asked. Pete scratched his right eye and wondered how he could stop this, or if he wanted to stop this.

"Sybrand," Pete whispered.

"Here it is." Rikus pointed to a name and started dialing.

Pete considered running outside, or back to his room, or pushing down the receiver, but he didn't do anything. He stood frozen as a telephone started ringing somewhere in Dundee.

"Mr. Theunissen?" Rikus said.

"I am Rikus de Lange, Pete's dad. We met briefly after the Sarel Cilliers game."

For a few moments Rikus listened in silence.

"No, wait a minute, Mr. Theunissen, let me stop you right there." Rikus's tone changed, his pitch slightly deeper, angry. "The way you treated Pete today is unacceptable. No, Mr. Theunissen, please, let me say what I have to say. I find your treatment of Pete unacceptable, under any circumstances, but especially in consideration of the vital part he played in your victories over Sarel Cilliers and Ladysmith."

Another momentary silence.

"Mr. Theunissen, I haven't finished—" The color in Rikus's face changed to a deep red. Pete had not seen that color since the time he and Barend had nearly burned down the church's derelict outside toilet block. That day both him and Barend got the hidings of their lives. He felt uneasy. He didn't like seeing his dad like this.

"What do you mean he doesn't have what it takes? Without him the Sarel Cilliers game would have been lost and who knows, perhaps even the Ladysmith game."

Pete could hear the voice on the other side getting louder.

"Cocky? Talentless stopgap? Which buffoon died and made you a rugby coach? Are you staring out of your ass?" The voice on the other end was now shouting at Rikus.

"Now listen to me, Sybrand. Your special brand of professionalism has truly been showcased during this call, I will make an official complaint to the head-master tomorrow." More shouting on the other side followed.

"That might be, but that is only if you still have a job next year. And by the way, Pete will not warm the bench for the fourth team, I withdraw him from your corrupt mob of self-serving pricks." Rikus slammed the phone down. He didn't look at Pete, but he was shaking and his color was even darker than before.

Pete couldn't move. He could only stand and wait for his dad to give him details. He wanted to hear it, even though he knew exactly what was said. Everyone knew the coach had a short temper, but to call him talentless?! This after Sarel Cilliers and Ladysmith? Pete could only shake his head, it was too much for his brain to process.

"Pete, this is going to be tough to hear, and be-lieve me it's tough to say, but you won't be playing rugby again this year." Rikus looked as though he was trying hard to compose himself.

Pete didn't respond. He knew he wouldn't play rugby again this year from the moment Gareth had shouted, "Piss off, junior!" The only thing he thought of was how he could leave this place, start as an unknown boy in a new school far away, someone with no history, no baggage.

"If that idiot is still in charge next year, we'll make a plan. You're too good not to play, but we'll cross that bridge when we get there. For now, work on fitness, increase your strength and speed, and next year will take care of itself. I will speak to the headmaster tomorrow." His dad seemed to have calmed somewhat.

"But dad, the headmaster—" Pete started.

"I know he has been keeping an eye on you. But as far as I'm concerned, you've been a diligent student since the altercation. You've been sticking to the rules ...so let me handle this."

"Thanks, Dad." Pete wanted to hug his dad and tell him how awesome he was, but he couldn't. Instead, he stuck his hand out and they shook hands. His dad had the same look as after the Sarel Cilliers game, and somehow it made him feel powerful, almost invincible. Perhaps things weren't as bad as he feared, and perhaps his connection with Renate was now strong enough to withstand this setback. Yes, what they had was special. A few weeks ago, his presence in the first team would have been a prerequisite for their relationship, but now they shared so much more. All those intimate moments, kissing, hugging, holding hands, all of that meant something. It was real. He would emerge from this stronger, and they would be stronger too. For the first time that afternoon he could feel the blood returning to his heart; life was good again, all thanks to his dad.

"Have you seen Renate?" Pete asked and turned to Barend who was sitting next to him on the bus making its way to the dance.

"She's with Philippa."

"Why?"

"She's sleeping there tonight so that she can go to the dance and not worry about getting to the sports bus in the morning. Philippa only lives two blocks from the school."

"I guess it makes sense."

"Didn't you speak to her?" Barend asked.

"It's been one of those days. I only spoke to her for two seconds. I just asked if she was going to the dance tonight, and she said 'yes,' then she had some tutoring group or something she had to go to."

Barend suddenly looked like his thoughts were drifting away with the clouds he was staring at. "Imagine Philippa's parents were out of town, and it was just us and our girls, and we all stayed over there tonight..." Barend rubbed his hands together.

"Tssh, now there's a thought." Pete felt the heat rise in him at the mere thought. "Would you? You know?" Pete asked.

"Tricky. It's so easy to say you'd wait for marriage if you have no chance in hell with the girl of your dreams. I suppose not, but if she insisted...China!" Barend grinned as only boys can. It was an idiot-grin and let out the secret that you were besotted with a girl. Pete chuckled because he knew he had the exact same grin. The same one they had mocked so many of their friends about in the past.

"Would you?" Barend asked.

"The mind is willing, but the flesh is weak, my friend," Pete said, and both burst out laughing.

The bus taking them to the dance made an unexpected stop in Hattingspruit. The driver, junior science teacher Mr. Davies, shot up out of his seat and clambered out of the bus. The kids watched him in confusion as he ran through a clearing to a large poplar tree. Before he reached the tree, his hand shot up to his mouth and in one powerful spurt, he projectile vomited against the bark of the tree. All the kids started laughing and pointing, so much so that everyone on the bus had their noses squashed against the windows to get a better view.

They were pointing and mocking, urging him on to do it all again. No one even noticed that nearly twenty minutes had flown by as they watched his ill-conceived purchase of a sausage roll from the Newcastle Street garage come back to haunt him.

When he finally made it back to the bus, one of the Standard Six girls gave him a can of Coke which she had nearly finished. Everyone laughed again. The final stretch to Dundee was fairly slow; every once in a while, Mr. Davies would slow down and a chorus of "Puke! Puke! Puke!" would reverberate through the bus.

Everyone disembarking the bus in Dundee was in good spirits. It didn't matter that the dance had started thirty minutes ago, or that there was only an hour and a half left. What mattered was that they had a fantastic story to share and share they would. Mr. Davies would be re-christened Puke-Zilla.

The dance was in full swing, the school hall dark but for a single spotlight on the stage and a few strobe lights not working as well as they once did. In the middle of the school hall, kids were shaking to Karma Chameleon, and around the outside, the windsurfing brigade shuffled and turned as best they could in their unique interpretations of the *sokkie*.

Pete scanned the room. He watched as the dancers spun by, but he couldn't spot Renate. Barend stood next to him anxiously trying to spot Philippa. Out of the darkness, Philippa appeared, her golden locks pirouetting as John-John threw her into turn after turn. She gleamed and gave a short pleasurable shrill, as he added yet another high-speed turn as the song ended. She laughed as they stopped and pretended to slap John-John on the shoulder.

Pete shot a quick glance at Barend. He was trying his best to put on a brave face, but even his natural pink hue was gone, replaced by bleakness.

"Oh, there you are," Philippa said as she saw Barend. She peeked over her shoulder at John-John and winked.

"The bus...the funniest thing happened," Barend said, but his voice was lifeless.

"Tell me while we dance," she said and grabbed his hand.

"Have you seen Renate?" Pete asked before Philippa led Barend to the dance floor.

"She's around," she said with a peculiar and un-settling grin, one he hadn't seen before. Something in her eyes burned through the feel-good buzz of earlier.

Again, he scanned the dance floor, but there was still no sign of her. He walked around the outside of the hall where small groups sat together shouting to one another over the music, and where Standard Six girls huddled together in the hope that someone would ask them to dance.

He made a full lap of the hall without a sighting. It was peculiar, but he imagined she must be in the bathroom gossiping with some of her friends, or something. He stood in the tuck shop queue and bought a Fanta Grape; after seeing Puke-Zilla drinking Coke earlier with his vomit-covered mouth, he really couldn't face a Coke.

Pete walked to the furthest corner of the hall where some of his classmates sat. He sipped his drink, all the while scanning the crowd, pretending to be interested in their conversation about robots.

Time melted away and Renate had not made an appearance. He considered asking Philippa again, but Barend was having such a good time that he didn't want to spoil it. "I Want to Know What Love Is" started playing. He loved that song and stood up, hoping that Renate would walk into the hall and take his hand. All the couples, some newly formed, including Barend and Philippa, ambled to the middle, where they engaged in slow dancing. Some looked nervous, but others just grabbed the opportunity of the shelter in the middle and started snogging, as if the survival of the human race depended on it.

Through the maze of slow dancers and snoggers, a familiar face caught Pete's eye, but only for an instant. He blinked but saw nothing except Barend, who looked like he was trying to eat Philippa's face.

Then he saw it again, clearer this time.

Renate.

He stepped closer but had to walk around the slow dancers as there was no way through. His eyes were so transfixed that he almost bumped into Michael, who shot him a strange glance, almost pitiful. He briefly wondered what that was all about but had much more important things to think about at that moment.

When he reached the other side of the hall, he saw Renate. She was wearing the prettiest and shortest of red dresses, with a thick white belt dangling on her hips. Her hair was partially taken up and teased so that it formed a waterfall of blond perfection that tumbled down her cheek. She wore heels which made her calves appear even more curvaceous than usual. And she was kissing Gareth Joubert. Not just kissing but snogging so intensely that their faces seemed to be one. His grubby right hand cupped her bum, and their lower bodies were thrust into one another.

Pete lost the use of all his limbs. He just stood there. The music faded, the other snoggers disappeared, and the lights were on. It was only him, staring at Renate and Gareth. She opened her eyes and looked straight at him, then slipped her hands under Gareth's shirt, and shoved her tongue deep into his mouth.

Barend shook Pete by the shoulders. "China! Are you okay?"

"Huh?" was all Pete managed to get out.

"I saw...I'm sorry," Barend said.

"I Want to Know What Love Is" no longer played, now Modern Talking had everyone dancing around the hall again, but Pete was still in the same spot, his eyes locked on where Renate and Gareth no longer stood.

"I need to go," Pete said. He blinked his eyes. They hurt.

"Go? Where?" Barend asked.

"Just away. Home, anywhere that is not here."

"China, I'm so sorry. Let me speak to Philippa, let's try and sort this out."

"No, I'm going to chill outside. You go to your girl, have a good time. I'll just be...I just need some fresh air."

"You sure?"

"Yeah, absolutely. Go and enjoy yourself." Pete tapped Barend on the arm and walked toward the door. He could hear people talk to him, but he kept on walking. Outside the night air was cool. He should have brought a thicker jacket as his mom warned him, but it didn't matter now. He was a little lightheaded and the loud music buzzed in his ears. Without realizing it his gaze had returned to the entrance to the hall. The wide double doors were open and inside the pupils of Dundee High were having a great time, well, almost all of them. Then Renate and Gareth appeared standing in the door, holding hands.

Pete had to get out of there. Fast.

He walked around the corner from the school's front entrance to a telephone box. He loathed himself for doing this, but his mind had stopped working and this was the only thing he could think of.

He dialed the number and slipped the coin in.

"De Lange."

"Pa," Pete said, hesitating.

"Pete, are you okay?"

"I hate to do this, Dad, but can you please pick me up from school?"

"Now? What's wrong?"

"Yes, please, Dad. I'd rather tell you in the car. Is that okay?"

"It's a thirty-kilometer drive, Pete, and I had a tough day at work. I had to tell two good foremen that we are letting them go, that they will no longer be able to provide for their families. This restructuring is really taking its toll at the mine. On me. Can't you just come back with the bus?"

"I know it's crazy at the mine at the moment. Sorry, Dad, but please, just this once?"

There was a pause. He could hear his mom ask his dad something in the background.

"Where are you?" his dad asked.

"Just outside the main gates on the corner of Tatham and Oxborrow."

"I'm on my way."

Pete's dad arrived twenty minutes later. In the distance, the music still filled the night, along with the hum of excited teenagers. It was quiet in the car, the radio was off, and Pete's dad focused on the dark road in silence.

Pete wanted to tell his dad everything, but the only thing that would acheive would be to make him look like a complete and utter loser, a waste of sixteen-year-old air, so he leaned his head against the cold window and stared at the stars lighting up the sky.

"Sarie Cloete," Rikus said out of the blue.

"Who?" Pete asked and sat upright, his face cold and sore from leaning against the window.

"Sarie Cloete. Now there was a fine specimen." Pete just stared at his dad as if he had lost his mind.

"I was in Standard Nine, and she had long reddish-brown hair. Her face was like an angel's. I swear, at night she sparkled. Anyway, she was perfect, the most beautiful thing I had ever seen. I was more scared of her than granddad's cane. She seemed to walk on air, and all the boys were in love with her, but no one dared ask her out. So, one day, after a long pep talk from one of my friends, I finally gathered enough courage to talk to her. I was shaking. I wanted to run away but something dragged me forward, and before I knew it, I stood in front of her." Rikus had a distant smile.

"Up close she was even prettier. She had these minute little freckles right on the tip of her nose, and her eyes were dark blue, like the deep sea. I can still remember how dry my mouth was, and there was this sickening taste.... Anyway, I somehow asked her out, and until this day only the Lord knows how." Rikus shook his head in disbelief.

"Back then, there was this roadhouse near our neighborhood, called Lollipops. If you wanted to impress a girl, you took her there for a milkshake. So, miraculously she said yes, and the wheels were in motion. I borrowed money from my dad. Things were so cheap back then, but it felt like I asked him for a million rand. I was quite embarrassed."

Rikus stared out of the window for a moment, taking in the passing dark landscape. Then he wiped the windscreen above the steering wheel with the back of his hand, as if it was misting up.

"Before I had too much time to ponder, Friday afternoon rolled in and at four on the dot, I stood there in my smartest shirt imagining I was Elvis Presley or someone. I clasped the coins my dad had given me until they were hot and sweaty. I waited there for almost an hour like Billy no mates before she showed up. The funny thing is, I forgave her immediately. She looked a picture in her polka dot skirt, her lips as red as a rose—man, I tell you." Rikus raised his eyebrows and glanced at Pete. "She looked like a movie star."

In the car's dark cabin Rikus's eyes lingered on his son for a moment.

"She asked for a vanilla milkshake, so I bought two, one for her and one for me. I kept looking over my shoulder, and every time she was still there, every time getting prettier. I was nervous as hell, but ex-cited!" Pete was mesmerized looking at his dad, he looked like a seventeen-year-old telling this story.

"I mean, I was on a date with my dream girl for crying out loud." Rikus took a deep breath, his smile looked as if he was right back next to her. "I took the milkshakes to her. She smiled and I melted. To my sur-prise, she took both milkshakes. I didn't question it in that moment, I was new to dates and thought it might be a *thing*. But then she turned and walked away with the milkshakes. I followed her, wondering if she was taking me somewhere more private, but no such luck. A group of her friends was waiting around the corner. One of them was this black-haired guy with a leather jacket on. She just handed my milkshake to him. And right there in full view he pulled her close and kissed her. They all pointed at me and laughed, calling me all sorts of things. I couldn't move—like my feet were glued to the pavement. I needed that moment to be undone, I felt cheated, but the teasing just got worse and worse. My legs eventually showed signs of life again and I walked home, feeling very sorry for myself for about two years, swearing off girls forever."

Rikus went quiet for a moment, watching the beams of an oncoming car.

"In hindsight, I probably missed out on quite a few nice girls because of Sarie Cloete." After the oncoming vehicle passed, Rikus glanced at Pete. "She did a real number on me. Even now, thinking about that moment makes me want to dunk her face in that vanilla milkshake. What I'm trying to say is, I left school, went to university, and on my first day on campus this clumsy girl with a short black bob walked right into me. We both fell flat on our backs. She didn't say sorry or anything, she just started laughing hysterically, so much so that before I knew what had happened, I was laughing along. People stopped and stared, but we just laughed, tears rolling down our faces. It was your mom, that girl with the hysterical laugh, your own lovely mom."

A sudden flash of joy danced across Rikus's face.

"I guess my point is, girls in high school are not real. They are figments of our teenage imaginations. We put them on pedestals and raise them up to heights which are impossible to attain, and they inevitably disappoint because they cannot be who we think they are. They are just girls. Pretty, yes, but just girls, going through similar stuff you are."

He waited for the words to sink in, then. "Just remember, once school is over, the world becomes a big place. Someone like that Renate girl—" Pete almost pulled a muscle in his neck as he flung his head toward his dad in shock. "I'm old, not blind. I saw you two after the Sarel Cilliers game. I saw the way you looked at her."

Pete let his head drop, slightly embarrassed. He had no idea that his dad saw them.

"Like I was saying, in the world beyond school, beyond Dannhauser and Dundee, Renate is just a tiny, average fish in an ocean of some amazing fish. The currents will take her, don't you worry about that."

Rikus gripped the steering wheel with both hands and shook his head. "You've had a shit week, my boy."

Pete had never heard his dad swear. He looked at this man who looked like an older, taller version of himself and wondered if his dad's story was true and if he would ever get over Renate, if he would ever meet someone better than her.

They approached the train bridge leading into Dannhauser. Pete didn't want this drive to end. Every part of his being wanted to tell his dad everything, about Rudie, Petrus, and Sarita. But his mouth remained unmoving, a cavern protected by impenetrable rocks.

He was seven years old again, and his dad was his hero, the man who could do it all, the strongest and the smartest. He looked at his dad now: The invincible warrior had taken a beating from father time, and he no longer looked like a knight. But perhaps he liked this version even more. One thing he knew for sure was that he never wanted to disappoint this man again.

NOTHING

"Pete!"

"Pete!"

The dim morning light struggled through the light green curtains. The alarm clock was difficult to make out, 06:44?

"Pete!" The knocking grew louder. It wasn't a dream. A dull pain had taken possession of the area just behind his forehead.

"I'm sleeping," Pete said, but some of the sounds got stuck in his mouth.

His dad opened the door.

"I'm sleeping. It's Saturday." Pete pulled the duvet up to his ears.

"We have a surprise for you," Rikus said.

"Can I have it in three hours?"

"No, Pete. We are going to the mountains today. Your mom called yesterday and there is a chalet available at Thendele tonight," Rikus said.

"Can't we leave a little later?"

"Come on, sleepy. Get your butt out of bed. We're leaving at 07:30, on the dot." Rikus left the door open as he walked out.

Sleep wouldn't surrender though and dragged him away to a rugby field that lay empty. Frost covered the grass, and one pair of footprints led to the Ladysmith High School pavilion. Someone whispered in his ear. He couldn't quite make it out. It sounded like a girl or a woman.

"Pete, we're leaving in twenty minutes." His mom's voice pierced the sleep bubble.

Pete raised his head slightly. "I'm up."

Pete curled up on the backseat of their spearmint-colored VW Passat. He almost fell asleep numerous times, but then the discomfort forced him to change position.

Only after they stopped at the Busy Bee shop in Ladysmith for a few snacks, did Pete slowly start to wake up. Almost every kilometer beyond Ladysmith the countryside changed, from the aloe covered hills proudly parading their burnt orange arrow points stretching out, to the watery expanse of Spioenkop Dam, to the farmland around Bergville, which formed a tapestry in shades of yellow, brown and dusty green, toward the dramatic horizon—the Drakensberg in all its glory.

The road swept into the heart of the mountains. In the distance, the gloriously majestic Amphitheatre winked: the crown jewel of the Drakensberg.

A familiar excitement nested in Pete's belly. Ever since he could remember, this was one of his favorite places in the world. He loved everything about it, from the Zulu villages along the twisty roads, with their meticulously crafted thatched rondavels, children waving and smiling at you as if you were family, the thin lines of smoke curling out into the bluest morning air, to that moment of pure anticipation when you arrived at the gates of the Royal Natal National Park.

As you left the thatched gatehouse behind and reached the top of the hill, the Amphitheatre, the snaking Tugela River, and deep green patches of forest hiding in the folds of the mountains greeted you. The curves and shapes of the mountains and rocks were perfect, and Pete knew that in the shadows of the mighty mountain hid a tiny silver slither, a shy giant, who only stepped out when it rained. His eyes searched the deep curves of the Amphitheatre, but it would not reveal his favorite, not yet at least.

"Have you spotted the Tugela Falls?" Pete's mom asked.

"Not yet, I'm looking. I think it's hiding from me."

"It's the drought. It will probably only be a trickle at the moment," she said.

"I'll find it, don't worry about that."

After a quick pitstop at the main reception to buy firewood, they drove next to the Tugela River to where the road becomes a two-track concrete path. The concrete path was steep and bent around the side of a hill, with Rikus having to focus intently to stay on the concrete. At the top, Thendele lay in wait: a few dozen thatched chalets all with uninterrupted views of the Amphitheatre. Pete reconsidered his earlier thought, this wasn't one of his favorite places, this was his favorite. He dreamed of traveling the world one day, climbing the Eiffel Tower, seeing the Pyramids, California, Hawaii, the Amazon, but he couldn't imagine that there was anywhere else on this whole planet more splendid than what he could see right there.

"It's a clear day." Rikus pointed to the intense blue painted across the sky.

"If we're going to see Halley's Comet anywhere, it'll be here," he said, smiling broadly.

Pete realized what his surprise was. It wasn't an

outing to his favorite place, it was the prospect of the thing he had been dreaming of for most of his life, to the see the Halley's Comet his grandad had described.

Since reported sightings of Halley's Comet started at the end of January, Pete had occasionally gone out into the garden at night with his dad's binoculars. But he had not seen a thing. Experts said it was a bad year for it, some suggested it had to do with where it was passing in relation to the earth, others said it had something to do with the position of its tail. But all he knew was that it didn't cover the whole sky; this wasn't his grandad's comet, this was just, nothing.

The truth is, however, with everything that had happened since the start of the year, Halley, his biggest childhood dream, had been pushed to the furthest reaches of his mind. He looked at the sky and wondered how something so important to him, that consumed so many hours of thoughts and dreams, just lost significance, lost its allure. Just because life happened. But being here lit a spark in him, Halley pushed forward and the excitement in his grandad's eyes became alive again. *Tonight,* he thought, *tonight's the night.*

"I brought a magazine which shows you exactly where to look," his mom said.

"We will find that bloody Mr. Halley's comet even if I have to drive my Passat up those mountains," Rikus said.

"Language, Rikus," Deanne reprimanded. Rikus just smiled at Pete, looking more like a naughty school kid than his dad.

After unloading the car and eating a few cheese-and-tomato sandwiches they locked the chalet and started walking down the hill to the start of the Gorge. It was a route they had walked many times, a lengthy route, which could easily take six hours there and back. The route, as the name implied, followed the Tugela River into a gorge at the foot of the Amphitheatre, where the Tugela Falls crashed and cascaded over ancient rocks and became a beautifully understated river, which meandered across the breadth of Natal until it reached the warm waters of the Indian Ocean.

Pete loved the Gorge. There was always something to look forward to. The initial part was quite flat, the river's soothing rumbling against the millions of age-smoothed pebbles and rocks, your faithful companion. The first major sight was the Policeman's Head. Sheer sandstone rock, expertly crafted by the wind over millennia into the shape of a British bobby, hat and all, eyes, nose, everything. Pete always wondered if he would ever see a real bobby, standing statuesque against the walls of Buckingham Palace. It would be amazing to see, despite his grandad's stories of old, about the red-necked *souties*, and how brutal they were during the Anglo-Boer war. Being surrounded by nature at its unspoiled best made him wonder what it must have been like during the war. Waiting behind rocks and molehills for someone who wanted nothing more than to kill you. His mind jumped to the bomb in Newcastle, where a man wanted nothing more than to kill them, and wondered, which war was worse? An official war, or this undercover, half-war, where power stations and people were blown up at random.

"Dad, if you were black, would you have fought against Apartheid?" Pete asked as they left the Policeman's Head behind and the first yellowwood forest approached.

"Jeez, Pete, I don't know. That is quite a strange question."

"I was just wondering about what drives people to do things, like in Newcastle?" Pete said.

"Anyone who intends to kill innocent people is a lunatic," Deanne said, a frown digging into her forehead.

"Not just terrorists and stuff. I wonder if we were black if we would be part of some anti-apartheid movement, whether peaceful or otherwise?" Pete said.

"Just remember the blacks think differently than us. We consider things more logically, you could say we consider things more individualistically, whereas they are influenced as a group, and that is why it's easier for nutcases to convince them to do inhumane things," Rikus said.

"Is that a black thing? Wasn't that exactly what happened in Germany, with Hitler?"

"Yes, but that was different. Hitler was...well, also obviously a man with more screws loose than a hardware store in a tornado, but he somehow brain-washed a clever nation, because they were angry and fed up and he told them what they wanted to hear." Rikus went quiet for a few moments as they entered the cool comfort of a yellowwood forest, tucked away in the side of the hill. He stopped next to a stream and filled his bottle with the slow-moving, ice-cold liquid presented by the mountains. He took a large sip and handed the bottle to Deanne.

"Aggh, Pete, I don't know. I just heard what I said in my head, and it does sound like the same thing as what the blacks might be feeling. What I do know is that they think differently. I think it's a cultural thing."

"Don't you think it's an educational thing?" Pete asked.

"Education, no. All the blacks have schools, some just decide not to go."

"But they run for kilometers to get to school, and most of the schools only have one class, so regardless of age everyone has to attend the same lessons."

"When did you become an expert on black education?"

Pete thought of Petrus, and the picture he had in his mind of what his school must look like.

"Just some of the kids chatting at school. I don't know if all the stories are true," Pete said.

"So, to come back to my question, would you join a movement—if you were black?" Pete asked.

"I don't know." His dad stared at the ocean of green around them.

"It depends, I suppose," his dad said.

"On?" Pete asked.

"Well, if you have nothing, your kids are hungry... if the police beat you and stuff...I suppose things like that would change anyone," Rikus said.

"Therefore, we need to thank God every day for everything we have," Deanne interjected.

His dad seemed to snap out of a trance and started walking again, out of the forest and into the bright sun. He walked with renewed vigor.

"I tell you what, you know how to suck the joy

out of a beautiful walk," Rikus said with a big smile. He pulled Pete's cap over his eyes and both he and Deanne burst out laughing.

A couple of hours later Pete enjoyed the shade of a yellowwood tree, happy to have seen his beloved Tugela Falls, albeit just the trickle his mom had predicted.

His dad always said that walking in the Drakensberg was better than a session with a psychiatrist. "Bring all your troubles and a few hours in the mountains will sort it out." Pete was laughing on the inside. He suspected he'd require several months in the mountains to work through all the things in his head.

The image of Renate slipping her hands under Gareth's shirt made him want to shout at the mountains, hoping that the echoes would somehow carry to wherever Gareth was, and bounce him into the ground, face first. Not that he would take her back, not after last night, never. His thoughts turned to rugby, and he realized that by now the first team game would be over. He knew it was probably wrong to hope that his school had lost, but just once he wished Vryheid would trample Dundee, running man-sized holes through Gareth and John-John.

He could see Mr. Theunissen begging him to come back, and Renate telling him how silly she was, and how she would do anything to make it up to him.

"Right, time to head back. I want to *braai* before sunset," his dad said and stood up, arching his back. Pete was startled, he was miles away.

They filled their bottles with the sweetest water Pete had ever tasted and set off on the same route from where they had come. Pete left his thoughts of Renate, Gareth, and Mr. Theunissen behind at the foot of the waterfall. His mind was now with Petrus and Sarita. Every so often he would glance at his watch without noticing the time. Hoping with everything in him that they would be back home before three the next day. Guilt awoke in his belly: the idea that they were only good enough when times were hard, but when life was good, he didn't even go, he barely even thought of them. Would they forgive him? Had he done to them what Renate had done to him?

Had Petrus asked Uncle Gerrit about finishing Matric? Did Sarita have a boyfriend? Was she still having nightmares about Rudie? He wondered about what his dad said, that blacks thought differently than whites, and wondered why he thought Petrus understood him, even though they barely knew each other. It was in the way he looked at him. It was like when Barend looked at him, but different, as if there were no secrets or barriers. It was strange. Perhaps his dad was right, perhaps they thought differently and what he thought he saw in Petrus was just something a white person didn't understand, it was just different. Perhaps Petrus didn't read him like a large-print book, perhaps it was just something in his mind. Whatever it was, he wanted to say sorry, to both. He would be a better friend from now on.

He stopped.

"Are you okay?" his mom asked.

"Yeah, I'm just..." He started walking again, faking a smile to his parents until they faced the path again and walked toward their chalet. The thought spun around in his mind: Was he friends with a black now? And with an Indian? Did that night make them friends? Just the thought of it felt like he was breaking the law. *But farm kids were always friends with blacks,* he thought, *so it was surely fine.* And his mom was definitely friends with Christina, but he somehow doubted she would name her as one. What was the protocol? Was it okay to have friends like that? *Probably,* he thought, *as long as no one found out.* What would Barend say if he knew he spent his Sunday afternoons with a black and an Indian? Would he be cool with it, or shun him? No, Barend was solid, his best friend. He might not like it, but he wouldn't shun him, not ever.

His dad might not like it, and possibly neither would his mom. She would probably say she was fine with it, but "people will," and "we're such a small community"—her standard response to most things controversial.

After dinner, they sat around the table discussing which trail to walk the next morning, with a crackling fire in the stone fireplace keeping them warm.

Deanne took out her magazine and all three of them studied the pull-out of where exactly Halley's Comet would be at what time. According to the article, the best time was between nine and ten at night.

At nine, armed with three cups of steaming Milo, binoculars and warm jackets, they stepped out into the chilly night. The air was still, and all was quiet, except for the distinctive deep "hello" of a nearby owl. Stars spanned the whole horizon, only broken up by the large black mass of the mountains to the west. The milky way looked like a cloud of cotton wool someone had placed amongst the stars. It was breathtaking. Stargazing in Dannhauser was pretty special, but *this* was something to behold. The three of them stood next to one another, turning their heads from side to side to take everything in.

"According to the magazine, it must be around there somewhere." Rikus pointed slightly to the right above him.

"Where?" Deanne tried to follow. He pulled her close, let her stand in front of him and leaned his head against hers. He took her hand and pointed the way.

"I can't see it," Pete said.

"Here, take the binoculars," his dad said.

Pete kept on searching the night sky until his neck hurt, still nothing. He gave the binoculars back to his dad who scanned the sky slowly, with incredible patience. Pete watched him closely, and then his dad stopped. He removed the binoculars, blinked and looked through them again.

"There." He pointed straight up.

"Did you see it?" Pete asked.

"Yes, it's right there. It looks like a large star, but if you look at it closely you will see there is a yellowish shadow behind it, like a tail."

His dad handed him the binoculars again and carefully pointed to the spot. Pete looked, adjusted the binoculars and pressed his eyes hard against the binoculars' viewers.

Then he saw it. At first, he thought it was a star, but it was slightly brighter, a little hazy with a yellow tint. After a minute of staring, he spotted the comet's tail. It was short and fat and so fuzzy that it was difficult to see. He looked at it for as long as he could, until he thought his neck would snap and handed the binoculars to his mom.

His mom was delighted when she saw it, giving a shrieking yelp of joy. The owl answered back as if it saw the comet too. Pete couldn't believe he had realized a childhood dream. He had finally seen Halley's Comet, and it was almost a bigger letdown than Renate. This was not a sky being sliced open by a silver bullet, this was a mere blurry speck that in reality might just as well have been a star hidden behind a lone fleecy cloud. Perhaps they all just wanted to believe that it was the comet. But he had seen it, that was what mattered, he told himself, but then started laughing.

His mom looked amused. "What's so funny?"

"I was just thinking about grandad's stories about Halley's Comet," Pete said.

"It was one of his favorite stories." His mom's voice betrayed a distant longing.

"I compared his story with what we saw tonight and wondered what Halley's Comet story I would tell my grandchildren. I mean, the comet didn't exactly tear the black sky apart in an explosion of brilliant light."

Both his parents laughed.

"But at least I can tell them that their grandfather's bad neck comes from Halley's Comet: I looked up for so long that I could swear I heard a clicking sound, and I feared my head would be stuck like that forever. Forever searching for that bloody comet." Pete smiled, and his parents' laughter grew louder in the night.

"See, I told you not to use that word in front of Pete, now look." Deanne play-slapped Rikus on the chest.

"I'm sure he's heard a lot worse at school." Rikus winked at Pete.

"Right, let's leave Halley to continue illuminating the night sky. I want to walk to Sunday Falls tomorrow morning, so it will have to be an early one," Rikus said, still smiling, and hung his arms around Deanne and Pete, ushering them back to the chalet.

"The comet is SO bright, I hope we can sleep tonight," Pete said. His mom's face was one big smile. She pulled Pete in and kissed him on the cheek.

The drive back was always filled with melancholy. Every kilometer took them closer to reality, to all the things they left behind, all the things the mountains couldn't take away. Perhaps he should become a nature conservationist and live in the mountains forever. He liked the idea. His dad wanted him to study engineering, and his mom believed being an accountant would be a better route. He still didn't know what he wanted to do, engineering and accountancy sounded boring—too much maths to be fun. Maybe a geologist, or a journalist, something where there was some adventure, something more than maths.

Ladysmith came and went, and Pete looked at his watch. It wouldn't take longer than an hour to get to Dannhauser from there and as it was just after one, meaning there was a good chance of seeing Sarita and Petrus. The thought made his sense of guilt flare up again, but he fought it. He had to see them. It didn't matter what was said, he just wanted to lean against the pool table, drink his Coke and watch Sarita's rogue strand of hair as it defied her best efforts to keep it out of her face, and Petrus tugging his ear every time he got nervous. That's all he wanted.

"Damn it!" Rikus said.

"What's wrong?" Deanne asked.

"I think we have a puncture. I'm going to pull over."

Pete saw the pool table, the Coke, Sarita, and Petrus slowly slip away.

"How can I help?" Pete asked, leaning in between the front two seats. Both his parents gaped at him as though he was a bright green martian stepping out of a spacecraft.

"Uhh, get me the spare and the jack, please," Rikus said, taken aback.

Pete disappeared behind the back of the Passat and as quickly as he could, lifted the spare tire and the jack out. He placed it next to his dad and raced back to bring the tool bag too.

"You seem eager," Rikus said.

Pete sat on his heels to help his dad with the jack. "Aggh, you hear all these stories of people being robbed next to the road..."

"Thanks for your help, Pete. It's a shame those blood...those silly nuts were stuck. Without your help, we would have been there until midnight, so thanks," Rikus said, wiping the sweat from his brow with the back of his dirty hand. Pete half-smiled and nodded. His watch shouted at him—14:58.

Pete and Rikus were quiet the rest of the way. Deanne continued telling them about her plans for the Church Bazaar in July, which she was organizing together with the Reverend's wife. She spoke at incredible length about what a pain it was to put together the traditional post bazaar concert. Both Pete and his dad nodded at appropriate times, and occasionally not, hinting that they weren't fully engaged, but Deanne continued without drawing breath.

At 15:47 they drove into Dannhauser. The only activity on Main Street was the wilting shadow of an isolated cloud. On the right the *Naidoo and Sons* sign turned its face away from Pete, shunning him for his detestable desertion. He tried to catch a glimpse of the alleyway in front of the shop and saw a gold-colored Datsun standing outside, its brake lights on.

Sarita's eyes appeared in his mind. The luminescent hazelnuts danced a slow, sad dance. Music played, a lonesome violin mourning in the wind. *In remorse there is no escape*, Pete thought. *It becomes a second shadow that never leaves you.*

"I wonder what this guy is up to?" Deanne said. Pete cranked his neck to try and see what his mom referred to.

"Up to no good, that I can tell you. Probably just robbed a shop," Rikus said, immediately upset.

Pete saw a familiar shape come into view. Petrus was running barefoot on the pavement, wearing a dark red shirt with a faded picture on it and the safari suit shorts which Pete now knew so well. His stride was graceful and full of power, every stride propelling him forward, effortlessly.

"Perhaps he's just running?" Pete said.

"Running away from a crime, more likely," Rikus said.

Because he's black?

"He doesn't even have running shoes on," Rikus said.

"Maybe he can't afford them," Pete said.

They were driving right next to Petrus. He looked up and saw Pete's face in the car window. A smile enveloped his face, but he didn't wave as if he knew.

"What is *he* smiling at? I think I should call the police," Rikus said.

"If it's a crime to run and smile, then I'm in big trouble," Pete said.

"This is different," Rikus said.

Because he's black?

"Pete is right," Deanne said. "He is probably just doing a bit of running. Blacks love running, and on TV you always see them running barefoot, besides, he doesn't appear to have anything on him like a bag or something. I don't think he is running away with stolen goods. And it looks like he is just a kid," Deanne said.

"Don't let age fool you," Rikus warned.

When they arrived home Rikus didn't call the police, instead, he went for a late afternoon nap. Pete played with Jimmy outside, thinking of Petrus, running back home after an afternoon spent with Sarita. He thought of Sarita, her sweet soft voice, and Petrus standing Coke in hand next to her. Jealousy gave a dozen or so unexpected quick-fire jabs, right into the center of his gut. He felt guilty about feeling jealous, but he couldn't shake it; no matter how much he ran around with Jimmy, he couldn't shake it.

DRAW

"There you are!" Barend called out when Pete slipped in next to him on the bus.

"You just disappeared on Friday, I looked everywhere for you. And I called you like two hundred times over the weekend."

"There was this guy my brother knows who I spotted outside the dance. He was on his way to Dannhauser, so I got a lift with him. I didn't really want to hang around if you know what I mean? And this weekend my parents took me to Royal Natal National Park. We only got back late yesterday afternoon," Pete said and slipped his knees up on the seat in front of him.

"I thought you jumped off a cliff or something. When you didn't even show up at Sunday School, I thought there was big trouble," Barend said.

"Renate is hot, but not jump-of-a-cliff hot." Pete snuck a glance behind him to check if Renate heard, but she was fast asleep. He studied her face for a moment. Something wasn't quite right, like a coffee stain on the Mona Lisa, and he felt a little queasy.

"Jeez, Friday night must have been torture for you," Barend said.

"Mmm...like being dropped off in Chernobyl by the KGB," Pete said. Barend just shook his head.

"Philippa is really pissed off with Renate," Barend said after a brief silence.

"Say again?"

"Ja, I haven't seen her like that before. She was spitting fire."

"What happened?" Pete asked.

"You know that she is good friends with Andrea too? Well, technically Andrea and Gareth were still a couple, she just decided not to go to the dance, she had a headache or something. Anyway, so then Gareth and Renate started their public snogfest and Philippa is livid. I mean, Gareth is just a dick, her words, but Renate put her in a difficult position. Andrea will ask why she didn't try to stop Renate, but I mean, what was Philippa supposed to do? Step in and pull them apart? Seriously, China."

"Flipping hell, that sounds complicated," Pete said.

"Tell me about it. There were almost big maracas at the hockey game. Andrea tripped Renate a couple of times on purpose, you will see, her knees and elbows look like a warzone. She almost punched Andrea on the pitch. Their coach had to sub Renate just to keep the peace. Big maracas, China."

"So, you're saying there was finally a hockey match with some action and I missed it?" Pete smiled. He really liked the thought of Renate flattened in the dust, blood covering her knees and elbows. He suddenly liked Andrea, he liked her a whole lot. He had always seen her as this snobbish, pretty little thing with two brain cells, but all of a sudden, she seemed to be a woman after his own heart.

"Don't mess with chicks, that's all I can say," Barend warned, looking particularly serious.

Pete wondered why Friday night felt so long ago as if it belonged to the distant past. And why did it feel like it happened to someone else, or like it was on television? He had trouble picturing Renate's face from up close. All he had in his mind was that coffee stain version he saw behind him, sleeping.

"So, what happened in the rugby? The big one?" Pete asked.

Barend rolled his eyes. "Jeez, drama, China!" He puffed his cheeks and let out a slow breath.

"It was tight. With five minutes left the scores were tied, then their one big lock tackled John-John high, right in front of the posts. The kick went over, so we led by three with three minutes on the clock. Simple game—either keep the ball or defend for your life. They got the ball and attacked with everything they had, running hard, running straight. We tackled like demons. Then their inside center, a short stocky guy, but fast as hell, got the ball and dummied John-John. A gap opened, all our defenders were flat-footed and the try line was close. The closest person was Gareth—"

"Please don't tell me that prick made the match-winning tackle?" Pete interjected.

"Well...sort of. He was close but the guy was too quick for him, so he slid in feet first and tripped the oke. He smashed into the ground and spilled the ball. Time was up on the scoreboard."

"Is that it?" Pete asked.

"No, China, then the ref blew his whistle, awarded a penalty for the trip, calling it blatant and not in the spirit of the game, so he sent Gareth off. Can you believe it? Sent off! Anyway, the Dundee support-ers cheered Gareth as if he had singlehandedly won the Anglo-Boer war and obviously the Vryheid guys booed him like he had torched their stupid little town. Their fly-half kicked the penalty and the game ended in a draw, a flipping *draw,* China. More drama than in an episode of Dynasty." Barend's cheeks were flushed pink, and he was almost out of breath. Pete couldn't help but feel cheated. How poetic would a loss because of mistakes by John-John and Gareth have been?

"Now we have to win all our remaining games and hope that Vryheid loses one, or make sure we have a better points difference. Coach wasn't happy," Barend said.

"Well at least he almost got what he deserved," Pete said.

"And I don't think he liked his medicine," Barend said and looked away. "We'll need to figure out a plan for next year."

"What do you mean?"

"Coach said you will never be on any of his teams again after your dad complained to the headmaster. I don't think he is big on criticism," Barend said.

"So be it, I don't want to play for him anyway."

"But you're a bloody good rugby player, you have to play."

"My dad said he would make a plan."

"Do you think, like, go to another school or something?"

"I don't know. At the moment, to be quite honest, I don't really care. All of this, the rugby, the cheating bitch, it's all been a bit much. Being away from it all this weekend was awesome."

"It's just not the same without you on the team," Barend said.

"Hey, rather focus on the good things: You're established on the first team, you have your dream girl and your best friend is a complete outcast. At this precise moment, you couldn't be any cooler."

"Whatever!" Barend laughed and bumped Pete with his shoulder.

"On a serious note." Pete raised his eyebrows and gave Barend his sternest glare. "Did Philippa make a man out of you on Friday night?"

"Ha! I wish," Barend said. "I think she almost turned me into a girl—all that gossiping, backstabbing, sniggering. I tell you, on Friday I might as well have been Barendina. I had to listen to all those crazy conversations between Philippa and some of the other girls. It was like I was on another planet, China. I thought maths was hard, but chicks, now that's a whole new level of complicated."

"I think it's too late. They have already changed you. You sound like a chick, and...are those boobs?" Pete poked his finger in Barend's chest.

Barend grabbed Pete around the neck: "You want to feel them, come a little closer, feel them now." He yanked Pete's face into his chest. "You like it? Mmm?"

"Shut up, you *moffies*," Walter, the cocky red-headed Standard Nine boy behind them, sneered.

Barend let Pete's neck go and hung his arm over the seat. He looked Walter, who was older but significantly smaller than Barend, straight in the eyes.

"You're a *moffie*." He turned back and shook his head.

"Now that was a compelling counter-argument," Pete whispered.

"Do you want to taste my boobs again?" Barend

said. They giggled, leaning forward in their seats exactly like they did when they were eight-year-olds.

The bus drove through the school gates and parked under the bus shelter. Everyone dragged their sleepy bodies from the bus and made their way to assembly. Halfway there, Renate walked by and their eyes met. The stain of earlier was still there, Pete thought. Her eyes scanned Pete's face as if to find something recognizable, but then she looked away and walked on, like passing a stranger. A stinging pain shot through his gut; anger, hate, sadness, relief, pain, and nostalgia, milled uncontrollably inside him. The sight of the white bandages strapped around her knees and elbows was a strange delight, but it was fleeting. He couldn't escape the feeling of injustice.

DUSTING OFF

Pete leaned his back against the red brick façade of the Eating House. It was cold in the shade and he zipped his green Adidas sweater up to his neck. He checked the time: it was only twenty past two.

His parents had barely closed the bedroom door for their Sunday nap before he was out of the house. He couldn't wait any longer, but he had only gotten as far as the Eating House. He couldn't force himself to go to the shop on his own, so he waited.

It was still twenty past two.

After an eternity, but according to his watch only five minutes later, a strongly built black guy jogged in his direction. He wore a green T-shirt, the same color as Pete's sweater, and his usual combination of safari suit shorts and bare feet.

Pete stepped out of the shadows and Petrus's face lit up.

"Aren't you freezing?" Pete asked, but Petrus was so happy to see Pete he didn't answer. He stuck out his right hand and held his elbow with his left hand. They shook hands and Petrus made numerous clicking sounds with his tongue before he spoke.

"Eish, we were worried, we thought...we didn't know what to think."

A different kind of guilt flowed through Pete. Before him was someone who was just glad to see him, no questions asked, no blame, nothing, just pure joy to see him, and it made him feel guiltier than ever before.

They started walking. "Sarita is going to be so happy," Petrus said.

"She—" Petrus stopped abruptly, tugged his ear and walked ahead of Pete.

"She what?" Pete asked when he caught up with him.

"She will be mad if I tell you."

"Well, you have to tell me now. Is she okay?"

"Eish, that man, Rudie—"

"Don't tell me, please, please don't tell me he..." Pete put his hand on Petrus's shoulder to stop him from walking away.

"No, but he came into her shop when her dad went out and he slapped her, told her things...bad things. Luckily her mom heard her scream, so he didn't do more."

"Crap! I mean I'm glad he didn't do more, but hell, what he did was bad enough. Is she okay?"

"Mmm...I think so. She is strong, Pete, very strong, but this man, eish. It is too much, even for a strong one."

"I had nightmares about this. You know, that he would come back to finish what he started, but I never thought he would actually do it. To waltz into their shop in the middle of the day? This guy thinks he's untouchable," Pete said.

"He is." Petrus sighed. "People on our farm told me he killed one of his workers and the police did nothing. He tried to kill us, and he's attacked Sarita twice, and who knows how many others there are?"

"Didn't Sarita's parents go to the police?"

"No, he told them he was friends with the police, and apparently, Sarita's dad hates them anyway. He doesn't trust them, he says they only work for the whites."

"But they have to tell the police. This was an attack right here in the middle of town, they have to."

"We didn't," Petrus said.

"That was different," Pete said.

"The fear is the same."

"Crap," Pete said and paused under the large *Naidoo and Sons* sign. "There must be something we can do? He is like this human wrecking ball swinging freely, smashing people into pieces. We must do something," Pete said.

"Do you want to go to the police?" Petrus asked.

"Yes. But what do I say to them? I'll probably end up in more trouble than him because I didn't come forward earlier. And it will be his word against mine, a sixteen-year-old against an adult. Even if you testified as well, it's just another sixteen-year-old, and if Sarita's dad is right, perhaps they won't even listen to you."

Petrus looked up at the shop sign. "I think I might be a little bit too dark to listen to."

"Maybe." Pete stood next to him and stared at the bold letters in blue.

"We have to do something to protect her," Pete said.

"That man...eish, I will necklace him. I am not violent, but I don't think I would be able to stop myself."

"And I will be right next to you with the matches," Pete said.

"Hey! Are you going to stand outside all day?"

Sarita shouted. She was standing in the alleyway outside her dad's shop. Her wide shiny-black trousers flapped in the gusty breeze, and she stood hands on hips, in a rather dismal attempt to look threatening.

She turned back to the shop before they reached her and waited behind the open door for them. Once they walked into the dark shop, she shut the door behind them.

The shop was cold, and a very sweet scent hung in the air like a mist. Pete's eyes automatically sought out Sarita, barely noticing anything else. Her smile still carved perfectly into her dimples, the rogue strand of hair still dangled on the side of her face, and her eyes were still a mirage. But she was even more beautiful than before as if she was a sculpture and the artist had been working tirelessly to polish every curve into a flawless masterpiece. He wanted to take a knife and break the blade off in Rudie's heart. Let him bleed to death, slowly, in excruciating pain, with him watching, sipping a Coke.

"Petrus. You told him!" Sarita's smile was swallowed by a tide of sadness. Pete realized his face must have betrayed him, and Petrus.

"I—" Petrus tugged on his ear, his eyes bulging.

"It's my fault, I forced him to tell me," Pete interjected.

"I didn't want—" Sarita started but was silenced when Pete flung his arms around her. He held her for a few seconds. She was soft, and it felt like she was melting against him, so he held her tighter.

"I'm so sorry, Sarita. I will kill that man, I tell you, I will kill him."

"We will kill him," Petrus added, stepping closer

and putting his hand on Sarita's shoulder.

Sarita pulled away, wiped some tears from her eyes and walked around the counter where she took a tissue and blew her nose.

"You will do no such thing." Her voice viscid. "He is not worth it, and you are too precious to me. I don't want you to even joke about it, okay?"

Neither Pete nor Petrus responded. They looked on in silence as Sarita used the tissue to wipe away her sadness.

"I'm serious. Please don't ever do something stupid. I have to believe, or we have to believe that good will triumph over evil. We cannot battle evil with evil because then evil is guaranteed of success. We have to give good a chance." She blew her nose again.

"But we have to do something. This guy is roaming free like a leopard amongst sheep, and no one is stopping him," Pete said.

"What if there are others?" Petrus added.

"Then, my dear friends, we need to come up with a plan. But killing him is not that plan, it can never be. There must be another way, a good way."

"The police?" Pete asked.

"Probably. I don't know. My dad says they will find a way to jail us instead of him because we're not white. So my dad will never let me take this to them, and even if you did, he wouldn't allow me to testify or make a statement. I think he'd much rather take me into hiding in Swaziland."

"Eish, so what do we do?" Petrus dropped his head on his hand and stared at the floor.

"I don't know, Petrus, but when I'm around you guys, I feel safe, I feel free. So right now, until we come up with a plan, that is what I'm going to hold on to." She stepped out from behind the counter and wiped her hand over her face as if trying to repel the sadness. "Did I say how good it was to have you back here, Pete?" she said. "A triangle is only a triangle when it has three parts." Pete wondered if it was possible to drown in someone's eyes. "We missed you. Without you here we had no one to educate us about jaffles and rugby, or to complain about their school's ridiculous hair rules. We thought perhaps you married that dream girl of yours and left Dannhauser." Her words made Petrus giggle.

"Ja, now there is something that is not going to happen," Pete said in one long sigh.

"Let me get the two of you Cokes, and then you can tell us all about your girl." She smiled at Pete and turned away to fetch the drinks. Her movement reminded Pete of the flow of the Tugela River, soothing, gentle. An overwhelming warmth gushed deep inside him as if a cavity he did not know about was suddenly filled, and it kept the cold out.

Next to him, Petrus was smiling. He knew that both of them were in some way, perhaps not the same way, completely spellbound by her. He wondered what Petrus was thinking. Did he have a crush on her, did he feel brotherly love, or did he feel what he felt, something he could not yet describe? A ball of bright but fuzzy colors, spinning in different directions simultaneously, just out of reach, just too far away to see properly, to understand or touch. Then, in Petrus's jet-black eyes, a tiny figure appeared in the distance, a figure carrying two Cokes, a figure whose smile could be seen even on that small scale, and Petrus didn't even know he was looking at him. He knew then: Petrus was also trying to figure out that same bright, fuzzy ball.

She placed the two Cokes on the side of the pool table and Pete observed Sarita as she and Petrus shared a joke. Their shadows seemed to be laughing along with them in the murky light. The world slowed down and Pete swallowed hard. His mind was filled with a giant egg, a crack shot down its center, and in no time an idea stuck its beak through the crack, then its tiny little head followed, and then, lo and behold, it winked at him. There was no stopping his smile.

FUTURE

"Sarita, I think you are getting lazy." Venny flopped down in his chair. "You had a whole two hours and the counter was still covered in dust. Perhaps a visit to Dādī next week is just what is needed to get you focused?"

"I'm sorry, Pappa, I will do better next week. I'm really sorry," Sarita said and shuffled closer to her mom sitting next to her on the couch.

"You have to give the child a break, with everything that has happened and all," Achala said and wrapped her arm around Sarita. "Besides, your mom always just talks about the fire that will rain down. I tell you, sometimes I think I should help Sarita with the cleaning on Sundays."

"She is your mother," Venny said.

"In law," Achala replied.

"Anyway, I know Sarita has been through a difficult time, but...I have very high expectations." Venny dabbed his thumb against his mustache. "You are such an exceptional child—I will always expect more."

"I know, Pappa, I won't let you down again."

"You didn't let me down." He shook his head and shot Achala an accusatory glance as if it was her fault that Sarita felt that way.

Venny started running his thumb across his mustache from side to side. "Your mother and I have been talking about next year." He very nearly lost his train of thought as he saw Achala in the corner of his eye nodding in agreement for once.

"I spoke to Uncle Sanjay and he said there is this really good school in Jaipur—it's where his wife's family is from. We started talking and, well, we think it might be best if you finished school there."

"Pappa, I—"

"Have I finished talking?" Venny lifted his index finger and Sarita dropped her head.

"It's a really good school, and Jaipur has lots of culture and history, all the things you love. With everything happening in South Africa at the moment I just—*we* just—think someone with your talent will be limited here. In India, it will be our people, your people, none of this Apartheid nonsense."

"But I'm South African, not Indian. The closest I've been to India was Durban."

"You can't say things like that! You will always be Indian first. Everything here is just temporary. You are Indian by right, it's in your veins. All these so-called South Africans, the racist whites and the self-serving blacks, don't care one little bit about you. They would send you back to India on the first available ship if they had the chance and call you a sugarcane plucking, good-for-nothing coolie, telling you, you don't belong. This is not our country, Sarita, it never will be. We make do, but here we will never be more than visitors. Looking from the outside in."

"Our whole family is here, everyone is doing well, we have businesses, money, houses—" Sarita said.

"But no respect. To them, we will always just be a bunch of thieving, underhanded, cannot-be-trusted intruders."

"Do you genuinely believe that, Pappa?"

"Yes, with all my heart."

"But *you* are well respected. I've seen how the white people speak to you, with respect. I've seen how black people speak to you, also with respect. And in the Indian community people look up to you," Sarita said.

"It's all just for show. Behind the smiles and the handshakes is a cesspit of hate, thinking of ways to get rid of us."

"If it's so bad, why don't *you* go back to India? Take our whole family, jump on a boat and go. Live in Jaipur and visit museums?"

"Don't be cheeky Sarita, he's your father," Achala said.

"It's too late for us. We must make it work here. We have to face the hate, and find ways to get through each day, and perhaps somewhere find small opportunities to change things, to build a home here where we are at least tolerated, rather than accepted."

"It all sounds like doom and gloom, Pappa. It's not that bad, is it?"

"You are a child, you are sheltered from the bad things. You don't see what we see."

"But I don't want to go to India. I heard the secondary school in Dundee is really good. Can't I just go there?"

"Sarita, we don't even have family in Dundee. What in the world do you want to do out there?" Achala asked.

"It's close. I can take a bus, or a taxi or something, and still live at home—it's only for two years."

"No, Sarita. The decision has been made. You're

going to Jaipur." Venny leaned forward.

"Where am I going to stay? What will I do? Our family isn't even from that region."

"You will stay with Uncle Sanjay's wife's cousin. They said they would be happy to have you."

"They are complete strangers!"

"They are basically family. You cannot call Uncle Sanjay's family strangers, that is very disrespectful," Venny said.

"Do I have any say in this?" Sarita asked, her eyes welling up.

"As long as you are a child in my house, I will be the one making decisions," Venny said.

"You always go on about the injustice of it all, that this country isn't a democracy. Well, your own house isn't even one. How can you then complain about the government if you do exactly the same?"

"Sarita!" Achala said.

"It's not fair, I don't want to go. South Africa is my home, not India! It's not fair," Sarita cried, ran to her room and slammed her door shut.

Achala started to get up but Venny stopped her.

"She's a child. This is a big change. Give her a moment to process it. One day she'll thank us, one day when this country is torn apart by civil war and she is married to a wealthy man from a good family in India."

Achala dropped her face into her hands and cried softly. Venny reached for the packet of cigarettes in his shirt pocket, took one out and inspected it for a few seconds before he placed it on his bottom lip and lit it. He took a deep drag and watched the smoke trickle out of his mouth. Achala was still crying. *It was the right thing*, he thought, *it was the only way*.

MERCEDES

The Thursday afternoon breeze was at it's biting best, forcing Pete to slip his hands deep into his pockets. His dad appeared to be trying to decipher the shopping list his mom had given him as though it was the Rosetta stone, his forehead contorting into a deep frown. She had the flu and for the first time Pete could ever remember his mom had stayed in bed for a whole day. It was therefore up to the two men of the house to do emergency shopping. Rikus even asked to leave work a couple of hours early to help his wife. They were standing outside Kismet and his dad read through the ten items on the list as if he needed to memorize it before they could enter any shop.

"Wow, check it out, Dad." Pete pointed to a shiny black Mercedes-Benz with tinted windows. It was a 560 SEL, the first one Pete had ever seen in real life. It shone under the shy late fall sun, polished to perfection, the paragon of opulence. It came to a halt close to them.

"Do you think it's someone famous, Dad?" Pete asked.

Rikus folded the shopping list and tucked it into his shirt pocket. "Now that's a car. One day when I grow up, I'm going to drive one of those," he said. Both stared at the car in awe, wondering who had enough money to afford such a thing of beauty.

The rear window rolled down. A pale, chubby man

with a bald head, a graying mustache, and thick-rimmed glasses studied them slowly and intently. He had an air of importance, or perhaps it was just the way he looked at them, with a hint of pity.

"Excuse me," the man said in a gravelly voice.

"Yes sir, how can we help?" Rikus walked closer and leaned forward to make eye contact.

"What is this place called?" the man asked.

"Dannhauser, sir," Rikus answered.

"Why are you walking around here with your son?" the man asked.

"We're just picking up a few things from the shops; my wife's not well. Why do you ask?"

"Why are you shopping in a township? Why not go to a proper town?"

"This isn't a township, sir. Dannhauser is a town. The township is just under a kilometer that way." Rikus pointed toward the west.

"But there are blacks and Indians everywhere."

"Uhh, yes?"

"I haven't seen a single white person besides the two of you. Do other white people live here, in this *town*?"

"Yes, behind these shops, about two blocks down is the white area. We have quite a nice community. We may be small, but we have a strong farming community plus there is the mine at Durnacol—which you might have heard about, it's the second deepest coal mine in the Southern Hemisphere. All of us use Dannhauser as a business center."

"You say the white area is two blocks away, so what lies between the shops and the white area?"

"That's part of the Indian area. Their area is behind

the shops on the other side of the road right up to the township to the west and on this side of the road past the shops to this side of Church Street. The white area starts on the opposite side of Church Street." Rikus waved his arms around as he pointed to all the areas.

"What! You're living next door to the coolies?" A drop of spit flew out of the man's mouth as he spoke.

"Well, technically speaking on the opposite side of the street."

"That's against the law." The man's jowls turned gray.

"It's just the way it is here, sir. We're a small town, we don't have much space, so we rub shoulders a little bit, but it doesn't bother anyone. For us, it's quite normal."

"Outrageous! I will not let this be tolerated." The man shouted at Rikus as if he was personally responsible for the town's layout.

The window rolled up, and the car slowly moved away. Pete and Rikus turned to one another in stunned silence. The car's bright-red brake lights went on, and the window rolled down again.

"Excuse me," the man called out, but in a soft tone, as if his outburst of a few seconds before had never happened.

Rikus and Pete walked closer, more as a reflex movement rather than out of choice.

"Son, I just need to have a quiet word with your father," the man said to Pete.

Pete stepped aside and Rikus stooped over the open window. He appeared to be taken aback by something the man said, quickly glanced at Pete and then said something to the man. The window rolled up again and the stretched Mercedes disappeared down Main Street, turning heads all along the way.

"Who was that? He looked familiar," Pete asked.

"I couldn't place him, but it struck me after he called me back. That was Geevert van Wyk," Rikus said.

"Minister of the Interior?"

"The very same."

"I can't believe we spoke to a cabinet minister. And here, in Dannhauser of all places."

"Ja, he seems to be on a road trip to spread his joy," Rikus said.

Pete started laughing. His dad stared after the Mercedes which they could no longer see for a few moments before he started chuckling along.

"I know it could land me in prison for saying this, but he seems like a nasty piece of work," Pete said.

"I believe the word you are looking for is 'asshole.'" Rikus stopped laughing and swung his head toward Pete. "Don't tell your mom I used that word."

"Don't worry, Pa. With someone like that very few other words would truly capture the essence of the man," Pete said.

His dad smiled and shook his head in amazement.

"What did he ask you when he called you back?" Pete asked.

"I really shouldn't tell you."

"Come on, Dad. Who am I going to tell?"

"No one. Not even your mom, okay?"

"My lips are as sealed as a coffin."

"Our revered Minister of the Interior was scouting for a bit of action."

"Action?"

"Ja, just when I thought I couldn't dislike the man any more."

"What is he up to?"

"You know the Bellihi Motel?"

"The one on the way to Newcastle? The scruffy one?"

"The very same. The honorable minister asked for directions to get there. Merely looking for a place to rest his weary head, apparently."

"But that place..."

"Exactly. In that place wedding vows are broken more often than eggs in the kitchen, all washed down with brandy and Coke."

"Jeez." Pete scratched his head.

"You can say that again. You know, I once saw old Geevert speak, a long time ago, when I was at university. He had a full head of hair back then, and he was quite slim. He was such a good speaker, a dynamic bloke, we all liked him."

Pete mulled this over. "So do you think politics changed him, or did politics just bring out his true self?"

"That is an excellent question." Rikus stared into the distance, not focused on anything. "Your mom always says an honest politician and a square circle are the same. Neither exists."

"She comes up with some good ones."

"Yup, she's smarter than all of us." Rikus blinked his eyes several times and turned back toward Kismet.

"We'd better get the shopping done before she gets worried. She's smart, but she's also not someone to upset." Rikus winked at Pete. They walked into Kismet and Rikus gave Pete a few items to pick out, but all he could think about was that fat old man with his grubby paws all over the bar girls, swigging his brandy with his driver waving cash in the air. Politics left a bitter taste in his mouth.

After a heated debate about whether plain flour and cake flour was the same thing, they finally managed to buy all the items on Deanne's list. In the end, they bought the plain flour, with serious trepidation.

On their way back Pete played with the seatbelt, then turned to face his dad who was anxious to get home to his wife.

"How did you know, Dad? How did you know mom was the one?"

Rikus swerved off the road and onto the grassy verge.

"Where did that question come from?" Rikus said when he regained control of the car.

"I was just wondering. In the movies, it's always so obvious, like you just know."

"You know Uncle Ampie who lives on the Stofdam Road?" Rikus asked. "Well, the story goes that he went to old Uncle Bismark's farm with his horse. His dad, Ampie senior, sent him to negotiate some livestock deal. Anyway, he galloped in, and Uncle Bismark's girl stood in the middle of the road, her hands on her hips, very upset that this man chased away the doves she was playing with. She was only about three at the time, tiny little thing. Uncle Bismark's other children were all grown by then. She was a pushover try in injury time, as they say. Anyway, Uncle Ampie jumped off his horse and watched this cheeky little girl marching toward him, ready to give him a piece of her mind. By now Uncle Bismark had arrived and shook hands with

Uncle Ampie, who was about twenty-two at the time. Uncle Ampie looked Uncle Bismark straight in the eye and said, 'This is the woman I'm going to marry, take good care of her until that day.' And you know what? They did get married, about eighteen years later."

"I know the story, mom told me," Pete said.

"What I'm trying to say is, there are people who just know, even though that specific story remains a little strange to me."

"But you haven't answered my question..."

"I wasn't one of those who just knew. I liked your mom right from the start, but I didn't know she was the one. I was a first-year student. There were beautiful, smart, funny girls all around me, how could I possibly know? We spent a lot of time together, we began to understand how each other's brains worked, and four years later, on a beautiful Pretoria afternoon, I got down on one knee. Not because I knew, but because I understood."

"Understood what?"

"I understood that even though there might be other women out there, some perhaps prettier or smarter or whatever, I simply didn't want to spend the rest of my life without her. I didn't want to live a life where she wasn't by my side. So, I popped the question. Truth be told, she said 'no' the first time of asking, but eventually, I managed to break down her resistance." Rikus smiled from ear to ear.

"I can't believe Mom said 'no' to you."

"Yes, can you believe it?! She said I still had some growing up to do. Such a penchant for drama."

They chuckled pensively as they approached their gate. Pete opened his door to get out but turned to his dad. "I hope one day I will also understand."

"You will. The right woman makes you understand, not always straight away, but she will, don't you worry about that."

Pete nodded his head twice hoping his dad was right. Then he opened the gate, riding it as it swung open. His dad's face was one big smile.

RECORD

"My goodness, what girl did that to you?" Pete admired Barend's slightly swollen black eye.

"Funny." Barend was seething. "It was this stupid little scrumhalf from Kliprivier. I had the ball, and then their lock tackled me. Just a solid, low tackle, so as I fell and was just about to hit the ground, this little—" A couple of the deacons walked past the open door of their Sunday School class stifling Barend's next word. He gave them an excessively cordial smile. "Unpleasant boy," he said in an exaggerated formal accent, but mouthed the word he wanted to use to Pete. "He tried to kick the ball out of my arms. He missed and his bony shin smacked me right on the eye. It was swollen shut for the whole afternoon yesterday. If I hadn't had trouble seeing him, I would have ripped his pea-sized balls off." The pink of Barend's cheeks appeared almost neon against the dark ring around his eye. Pete couldn't help himself; he burst out laughing.

"Sure, go ahead and laugh, China, but let's see how you handle this kind of pain."

"I'm sorry, it's just—" Pete's laughter turned into a hysterical giggle. The more he tried to fight it, the funnier it became.

Barend got up, puffed his cheeks and stood by the door, looking around to see what was keeping their classmates.

Pete took a few breaths, trying to compose himself. "I'm sorry, I don't know what came over me. Come, sit. Tell me about the game," Pete said. Barend gave Pete a disdainful glare before he slowly returned to his seat, shaking his head and curling his bottom lip.

"I'm sorry, okay. Who won?" Pete could feel the giggle knocking just below the surface, but he bit his lip and tried not to stare at Barend's black eye.

"We won." Barend still sounded bitter. "But it was a lot closer than we hoped. Klip Rivier had massive forwards. I don't know what they've been feeding them there, but they were huge, fortunately also slow, but HUGE. The final score was 20-18, so Coach was as pissed as a mamba in a cage because we are now well behind Vryheid on points difference, you know: to win the league title."

Pete nodded knowledgeably but was surprised by how little he cared about the rugby. Ever since he had started at Dundee High over two years ago, almost everything was focused toward rugby, but now it was as if Barend was talking about lawn bowls or showjumping.

"How is Philippa?" Pete asked, keen to steer the conversation away from rugby.

"Good. Obviously, she was worried, but she's good. There are still all these issues between her, Renate and Andrea following...the thing. Anyway, she and Andrea have decided to come up with this plan to get back at Renate. They figure if they can..." Barend continued talking but Pete's mind muted his words. He didn't care. It shocked him that there was not a single cell in his being that cared about the words falling out of Barend's mouth. Rugby and Renate related matters felt redundant, extinct as if in some evolutionary leap those things were left behind, belonging to a different being—not him.

Barend continued to talk for another six-and-a-half minutes. Pete could only assume it must have been a detailed explanation of Philippa's plan, or perhaps he had moved on and talked about something else— it didn't really matter. He watched Barend's big lips move and curl and twist as he told his stories. There was complete passion in every word he said, and Pete wondered what he looked like when he spoke. Did others see the same emotion in his mouth and face, or were his words dry, plain, passionless?

Barend stopped and looked at Pete as though he had asked a question. Pete searched for something in the chambers of his mind, some clue as to the question.

"Yeah, well, I tell you," Pete said, shaking his head and clicking his tongue. Barend looked at him for a second, then seemingly happy with the response, fell straight back into the mute storytelling.

Pete's mind shifted to Petrus and Sarita, their shadows laughing along with them, without a definite shape, anonymous, yet unmistakably them. He thought of his dad's words and those of the minister. They all raced around his mind like horses at the Rothman's July. When his mind brought him back to the present, he realized he was staring out of the window. He quickly glanced at Barend, but he had hardly noticed, too immersed in his own stories. The other kids eventually walked in, but Uncle Willie remained standing in the door.

"Where were you?" he asked.

"Uhh?" was all Pete and Barend could utter.

"It was our class's turn to help serve tea and coffee, and both of you shone in your absence."

"Sorry, Uncle."

"It's too late for sorry. I want both of you to write a thousand-word essay about the Good Samaritan for next week's class."

"But Uncle Willie, we just—"

"No buts. If it's not in my hands next week, I will personally speak to your parents." He closed the door behind him and raised his chin with more than just a hint of self-righteousness. "Okay, Belchie, it's your turn to open with prayer."

A few hours later, Pete was helping his parents with the dishes. As always, his dad was on washing up duty, he was drying and his mom was packing away, except for the glasses which Pete had to do as she was too short.

"How is the planning coming along for the church bazaar's concert, Mom?" Pete asked.

"Slowly. We still need quite a few acts, but people seem to be very reluctant this year. You always have the same people who perform, year in year out. I can rely on them but, some of them really shouldn't be on stage—I'm sure you know who I mean?" she said. Pete thought of Auntie Nelia's annual slaughter of some Italian opera and smiled.

"What would someone have to do to enter, you know, if they wanted to take part?" Pete asked but immersed himself in drying the large green cast iron pot.

"Well, it's not the State Theatre. Someone just has

to ask me and promise that there will be no vulgarity, and they're in. Why, are you thinking of doing a duet with Auntie Nelia?" she said, and his dad laughed heartily.

"No, unfortunately, someone beat me to it," Pete said. A puff of laughter escaped his mom's lips.

"I'll keep a space for you," she said after her laughter subsided, and tilted her head toward him with a gentle smile.

"Thanks, it's just in case. I probably won't do anything, but I was just curious."

"As I said, just in case, I'll keep a space open for you."

"Thanks, Mom."

Pete stood on the small porch outside their kitchen door. Jimmy sat next to him, leaning his full weight against Pete's leg. His parents were safely in bed, but the sky was dark, as black and gray clouds rolled in from all directions and converged over Dannhauser, angry and pregnant.

Pete had read somewhere that the type of rocks in the area made Dannhauser one of the places in South Africa with the most severe electric storms. He had witnessed how lightning had sliced their lemon tree in half, and how it danced on top of the electrical cables …it wasn't your friend. He knew that if he dared to venture outside on a day like this and the lightning didn't kill him, his mom most definitely would.

But it was nearly 14:30 on a Sunday and he had missed too many *Naidoo and Sons* gatherings. He wasn't going to miss this one, there simply had to be a way. He patted Jimmy on the head, who closed his eyes and nearly fell over when Pete walked into the house. Jimmy gave Pete a disgruntled look and sighed as he curled up in the corner.

Pete scanned the kitchen for some inspiration. He held his mom's purple umbrella in the one hand and his Drimac in the other, but then he spotted something that made a lot more sense. To the left of the fridge was the poorly crafted key holder, in the shape of a giant key: his Standard Three woodwork project. On it, he saw the keys for his dad's Passat and those for their little Ford Bantam. He was a pretty decent driver. His parents taught him to drive when he was eleven, so that wasn't the issue. It was more what his dad would do...and think.

After weighing up the pros and cons for a few moments it wasn't difficult to find justification in his mind, but the logistics were an issue. He grabbed the Bantam's keys and walked toward his parents' bedroom. All seemed quiet. He walked out of the house, got a disapproving glance from Jimmy and sprinted to the Bantam which was parked under a lean-to next to the garage.

With the Bantam in neutral and the handbrake released, he started pushing it down their long drive, pushing with his right shoulder, with his right-hand steering through the rolled-down window. When he neared the gate, he pulled the handbrake and went to inspect his parents' room once again. It was as safe as it could be.

Lightning flashed just as he touched the gate. He counted aloud, "One thousand and one, one thousand and two, one thousand and three." As he said "three" a roaring thunder shook their small town. The lightning was close. He raced to open the gate and maneuvered the vehicle through. Another flash lit up the dark sky, and this time he couldn't even get to "one thousand and three."

He drove off and looked at the sky, which was now equal part darkness and blinding light as if the bolts infected one another and an attack on Dannhauser had been launched. The wind tugged at the last few remaining leaves on the trees and the branches swayed without offering much resistance.

Pete turned the lights on as he approached the bend in the road near the bus stop. To his surprise, a lone person sat huddled in the corner of the bus stop as the lightning and pellets of water attacked from all sides. There were no buses on Sundays, so out of curiosity, Pete slowed down to get a better look. In the murky light under the insufficient beams of the Bantam, he recognized the faded blue safari shorts hovering above bare feet. Petrus.

He swerved left and brought the vehicle to an abrupt stop. He leaned over to the passenger door to wind down the window.

"Jump in," he shouted as the rain became angrier.

Petrus held his hand over his eyes to see better. "Pete?"

"Yes, jump in!"

Petrus ran out from under his shelter and in one leap jumped onto the back of the truck. Pete flung his door open. The rain was cold and razor-like.

"Are you crazy, get inside," Pete shouted.

Petrus hopped off and opened the passenger door. Pete was busy wiping water from his forehead.

"Sure?" Petrus asked, still getting soaked in the

flood of swollen drops.

"Yes, damn it, man, close the door!"

Petrus hesitantly climbed in and seemed to sink in the seat.

"Have you lost your mind, the lightning would have made toast out of you!"

"Eish, I thought if I ran fast, I could beat it, but today the thunder—she was very quick." Petrus wiped his hands on his wet shorts, looked at Pete for a brief moment before quickly looking away again.

"Are you sure I'm allowed to sit up front with you?"

"Where else would you sit? At the back you might as well have a target on your head for the lightning, never mind the rain."

"It's just, I have never sat in the front before...what if someone sees us?"

"This town is dead on Sunday afternoons even when the weather is glorious. No one in their right mind would dare venture outside on a day like today."

"Except us," Petrus said.

"As I said, no one in their right mind." Pete smiled and Petrus laughed along.

"How did you get the truck?" Petrus asked.

"Well, technically my dad doesn't know, so I can't stay very long."

"Eish, Pete, you are going to get into big trouble. Just drop me right here and take it back."

"Hey, sometimes you have to take a chance to open doors. I'm going. Look, we're almost there. Do you still want to be dropped off?" Pete asked.

"It's fine, I just don't want you to get into trouble."

"We'll make it a quick visit today," Pete said.

They turned left next to the *Naidoo and Sons* sign,

slowly passed the linen shop and parked right in front of the door of the main shop.

"Isn't this too close?" Petrus asked.

"If we park elsewhere, we may as well have walked here. Come." Pete jumped out and stood under the blue fabric canopy above the shop entrance. Petrus joined him a couple of seconds later. They wiped the water from their faces, glanced at each other and knocked. It was very dark inside, and a sudden growling thunder caught them unawares. It made them jump. They stood with their backs against the door. Pete knocked again and then peeked inside. There was no movement, no light, just shelf after shelf of everything under the sun.

"Look." Petrus tapped Pete on the shoulder.

Squashed under Petrus's big toe was a little piece of yellow paper. Ink looked like veins on the back of the soaked note. Petrus bent down and picked it up, read it and showed it to Pete.

Sorry Px Px

"Crap, she's not here. We're the P's."

"They must have taken her to see her crazy grand-mother," Petrus said.

"Crap!" Pete said, clutching the sodden note in his hand as if Sarita would miraculously jump out of it.

"We must go," Petrus said, urgency and worry in his eyes. Then he ran to the passenger side of the vehicle.

Pete stood there for a few moments. The rain crashed down and bounced on the roof of the Bantam. Pete remembered the last time it had rained this hard—it was *that* night. He had walked home and Sarita's pure, unfathomable beauty was revealed by every drop that cleansed her of the mud and Rudie.

Petrus knocked on the driver's side window, waving anxiously.

Pete rubbed his cheek. He could recall every millimeter of her face.

"What do you do when you feel something you don't understand?" she asked him the week before. Her eyes penetrating a part of his soul or his inner being or whatever it was that he didn't even know he had. Her expression asked more questions than her words did, but in a language he did not understand.

"Keep prodding it until it makes sense," he answered, but her expression kept calling out to him, louder and louder until panic set in. He tried to shy away. "Or go to sleep until the feeling passes." His silly attempt at a joke cut her off and he lost her stare. She forced an unconvincing smile and started talking to Petrus. Why was he such an idiot? He could see she was asking something, but all he could do was mess it up with that stupid joke, just because he panicked.

Petrus knocked again. It startled Pete. The rain was splashing in his face.

Pete got in and started driving. He watched the rain as it covered the windscreen but couldn't erase Sarita's face. What was she trying to say to him? And when they said goodbye...he could have sworn she hugged him twice as long as Petrus. Or was it all in his mind? Her hand gently wandered across his back. Breathing became impossible, but he could not let go of her. It was all in his mind. It had to be.

"Just drop me here on the corner," Petrus said.

Pete lifted his foot off the accelerator, eyeballed Petrus. "In this weather? I can't drop you here. It's a helluva long way from your home."

"Don't worry about me, just get home so that your dad doesn't find out."

"Petrus, there is no way I'm letting you walk three kilometers in a thunderstorm. No jokes, you'll die. Forget about my dad, I knew what I was doing, but this is toying with your life."

He drove along his familiar running route, the swimming pool on his left and then the monotonous architecture of New Extension. Just before they reached the two-track farm road, the rain became so heavy that Pete had to stop the car. The wipers glided across the windscreen as best they could, but it was impossible to see anything but water pounding the car.

"I'll run from here," Petrus said.

"Sit, damn it!" Pete said, gripping the steering wheel and leaning toward Petrus. "You're always so bloody afraid of everything, but now you just want to throw your life away? Sit, we'll wait it out. I can already see a speck of brightness toward the mountains."

"I try not to be afraid," Petrus said, avoiding eye contact.

"I'm sorry, I didn't mean it like that."

"It's true though. I can see it, and my dad teases me about it. Probably hoping I will change—but I can't help it. It's like someone tied a big tractor tire behind me and I'm trying to run, but I can't move."

"Come on, you're not afraid to walk right through the white neighborhood every Sunday to meet with Sarita and me, even though you know that if the police saw you, they might take you in for questioning. And look at what you did today, you weren't afraid to run into a bloody thunderstorm to see us—I think you might be too hard on yourself."

"You're just being nice."

"Listen, I'm not trying to be nice. There are times when I wonder why a strong, tough guy like you is afraid of stuff, like talking to Uncle Gerrit about doing Matric."

"I will do it, I just..."

"You see, that's precisely my point. You haven't spoken to him even though it is something you really want. All the other things you are afraid of, you do anyway. Like standing up to Rudie, going to see Sarita on Sundays, getting into the truck today. You did these things despite your fear. Hey, we're all afraid of stuff, all of us. We worry about different things but the more we do the things we worry about, the less fear they hold. I bet you don't fear to go to Sarita on Sundays as much as that first time?"

Petrus half-nodded.

"And did it kill you to get into the truck with me today?"

"Not yet." Petrus smiled.

"Funny!" Pete punched Petrus on the shoulder.

"You're a cautious person, and that's fine, just don't let fear be the brick wall between you and your dreams. That's all I'm saying. And screw whatever anyone else thinks or says, you know what your dreams are, you know what you have inside you."

"Maybe you should become a politician. That was a good speech," Petrus said.

"It's only a good speech if someone listens."

"I listened. You're right...it's just hard, but you are right."

"You can do it, Petrus, I believe in you, and I know Sarita does too."

"Thanks, Pete, it means a lot to me."

"Hey, that's what friends are for," Pete said without thinking. He watched helplessly as the words left his mouth and drifted unstoppably toward Petrus.

His blood turned cold.

The words might as well have been a punch on the chin. Petrus's head flung backward in shock. Both were mute as their stares found each other and the rain smashed with renewed vigor onto the Bantam.

"Are we friends?"

"Uhh...we're uhhm...I..." was all Pete could muster.

"I don't think whites and blacks can be friends." Petrus let the words linger and Pete tried to swallow, but the aridity in his mouth had reached Atacama levels.

"My friends at school say the best we can do is tolerate each other. That's all. We are too different, whites are too selfish, holding on to their European ways. When I was young, we played with some of the white kids on the farm. We didn't realize they were different at first, and I don't think they did, but our parents told us not to get too buddy-buddy with them—they're different, so be careful. And as time went on, we heard that so many times that we believed it. I suppose the white kids must've been told similar stories and once we all started going to school, we were no longer kids running, playing, and getting into trouble together. Suddenly we were black, and they were white—like we had potato sacks over our heads and suddenly they were lifted. We played less, we laughed less, our names changed from Petrus and Phineas to boy and kaffir. Our parents said, 'I told you so' when we cried about it, and we learned a new lesson: that we all had a place, and our place was away from the whites. We drink coffee out of rusty tin cups and live in huts with no electricity, and we wear clothes that were thrown out by the whites—*that* is our place."

He took a deep breath before he continued, "But it isn't all bad. Aikona." Petrus clicked his tongue a few times. "We have food, a house, clothes, money, work, everything—as long as we remember where our place is, and our place is in the corner, far enough so that you cannot see us, but close enough so that we can clean your shoes if you stepped in dog shit." There was an irrepressibility in Petrus's voice, his words crashing against Pete like the rain outside.

"My father and *baas* Gerrit work very closely together, but they are not friends. They have respect for one another, sometimes they might even like each other, but they both know their place. When *baas* Gerrit needs something from the town he gives my dad the keys to his truck—not his best one, but he trusts him enough to know that he will do his job and the truck will be returned without a scratch. But when they go together, my dad doesn't sit in the front with *baas* Gerrit, that's not his place, no, the passenger seat remains empty and he sits at the back, in the cold, rain, wind, whatever, it doesn't matter; that's his place. And they're all happy, it works. Everyone with their own place works." Petrus stopped and looked out of the passenger side window. Pete could not move his lips or any part of his face. The digestion of the words was slow, and he was thankful for the pause.

"Now today you ask me to sit in the front with you. I look through the window and I can see you are white, but you want me to sit in the front. My dad has worked for *baas* Gerrit since he was a boy, and he has never sat in the front with him. It makes me confused. That day we met, eish, I was angry. You called me *kaffir*. You looked at me like you would look at a stinking toilet. I was so angry, I wanted to pick up a rock and smash all your teeth out until you couldn't call me that word anymore, and until you stopped insisting that I call you *'baas.'* I hate that word: *'baas.'"* Petrus clenched his fist.

"But I didn't pick up that rock. I put my hands behind my back and said, 'Yes *baas*, sorry *baas*,' because that was my place."

Pete felt like getting out and running away. But something stopped him. Curiosity? The veil that was lifting over the anger of the guy next to him? The veil over his own head?

"When we were hiding from Rudie behind that rock, it was the first time I touched a white person since I was a little boy. It was right here." Petrus pointed to a spot on his forearm.

"It felt like someone had taken a burning stick out of the fire and pressed it against my skin. I know it's crazy but that's what it felt like. Like it was a sin, a crime of sorts." Pete thought back to that moment when their arms touched. He had ripped his arm away, and he felt the same burn, the same sense of wrongdoing.

"And then we met Sarita, or rather, we saved

Sarita. But we still had our places. You were white, I was black, and she was Indian. All three of us just played our parts, we worked together, and then it should've ended, right?" There was a fire burning in Petrus's eyes, a fire Pete had not seen before.

"All I wanted to know was that she was okay. That's all. Meeting with you here, even going to see her with you, it all felt like I was sinning, but not a big sin, just a little one. Because we all still had our places—I was black, you white and she Indian, and we only met to check if she was okay, then we would all go back to our places. But we didn't."

Pete watched as a ray of light tried to force its way through the clouds. The rain became less intense. Petrus stared into the distance, the fire in his eyes growing.

"We went back, over and over again. It was almost like the fear-thing you spoke about, every time we went back, I felt a little less black, you looked a little less white and Sarita a little less Indian. Last week when I walked in there, Sarita didn't look Indian to me anymore, I couldn't figure out what she was. She wasn't black or white like us, she was just—I don't know—Sarita.

"Now this week I sit in the front of a truck next to a white boy. He gives me advice, listens to me, and when he looks at me, I don't think he sees a stinking toilet anymore. He looks at me as if I'm just me, normal, like him, the way Sarita looks at me.

"I look at your arms and face and I can see they are white, I can see it. But when I look at you, I don't see it. I have no idea what you are anymore. I'm looking for the white, but it's not there. I'm confused." Petrus exhaled into his fist, his eyes unblinking.

"I have many friends at school, but, eish, there is something about being here with you, something which makes me fear less." Petrus gave a little shake of his head. "And that with a person who used to be white. What does that say of me? Am I sinning, is this a crime? Why am I not in my place, because I know my place, I've been taught from a young age. I know it well. I know all the roads there, every brick, every mud-covered floor. I know my place so, so well. But here I am, in a place that I don't know, a place that is not mine...and I like it, I like it a lot.

"Here in this truck you're not white, and I'm not black. But I'm afraid to go back to my place. What if this place goes away, or it never existed? What if tomorrow you are white again like those kids when I was little?

"As I'm sitting here next to you, I know I don't know you well, but well enough to know you are not just my friend, but my best friend. But what happens when you go to your place and I go to mine? What happens tomorrow when the rain doesn't force me inside? Will I have to sit at the back like my dad? Is that my place?" A single tear rolled down Petrus's cheek. He gazed to a faraway place beyond the patches of brightness struggling to chase the rain away.

Pete's hands rested on the steering wheel. There was a glow warming inside him, not fear, or angst, but something good. He recalled the day he sat with his grandad for the last time. They spoke about Halley's Comet and how fast cheetahs were, but although the words bore little significance those moments had felt precious. Like he wanted to bottle them and keep them safe, keep them forever, not out of sadness, but out of joy. This moment felt like that.

"We both know outside this truck people will see us as black and white." Pete's grip tightened around the steering wheel and he took a deep breath. He wanted to cast away the bonds of his words. "People will put us in our separate places. It will be hard because this kind of thing is not *normal* to them. We won't be able to play rugby together for the school or have sleepovers, but what they think isn't appropriate doesn't change us—or what we have right here in this truck.

"Petrus, I never thought I'd say this, but you are my friend. And I promise that as long as I live and as long as it's within my power, you will never have to get in the back of any truck I drive. My friends sit in the front with me. This is your place, nowhere else." Pete studied Petrus's eyes, and the amalgam of emotions in them, desperate to be transformed into something different—new. He thought about what Petrus had said and smiled.

"What?" Petrus asked.

"No, I was just laughing. When I look at you, I see someone who has black arms and a black face, but I have no idea what color you are either." Petrus smiled, head bowed.

"I have to go, the rain stopped," Petrus said.

"Can I drop you closer to home?"

"No thanks. I need to run, have time to think."

"I understand, I think I need to do the same."

Petrus opened the door and got out. He stood with the door open and leaned in. "I'll see you on Sunday?"

"Wouldn't miss it," Pete said and stuck his hand

out toward Petrus. Petrus looked at it, then in Pete's eyes, his broad smile illuminating his face. They shook hands for a few seconds before Petrus turned and ran down the two-track road, gaining speed with every step, like his grandad's cheetah.

All the way home Pete ruminated about all that was said as the vehicle crept along the sodden streets. He had never thought of things like that, he had never really placed himself in someone else's shoes. Deep in thought, Pete opened the gate, drove through, closed it behind him and parked under the lean-to. Just as he locked the car and turned, Rikus stood in front of him, arms folded.

"Pa!" Pete exclaimed, staggering back into the car door.

"Explain, and make it a good one," his dad said, but his face didn't give anything away, just a blank stare.

Pete could feel his heart beating against his chest. He felt a little lightheaded and the keys were heavy in his hands.

"Uhhm, well..."

"Uhhm well, what?"

Is it possible for a brain to explode?!

"Uhm, just before it rained, I saw one of my friends running in the street, so we had a chat, then it started pelting down and he had to get home. I didn't want to disturb you. You guys were sleeping, and I know your naptime is precious, so I just thought if I took the truck, just to take him home and out of the lightning, it would be okay. I know it was stupid, I'm sorry. I deserve to be caned."

"You were gone for a very long time."

"The rain was so heavy that I couldn't see in front of me, so I pulled over and waited for it to calm."

"And who is this so-called friend?"

"It's a pal who lives down New Extension way."

"Does this *pal* have a name?"

"Uhh...Petrus," Pete whispered.

His dad had that look of disappointment which always felt like a stab in the gut.

"Petrus, you say?" His dad's eyebrows tightened. Pete nodded. "My guess is it's probably Petru or Petra. If you want to impress girls with your driving skills, then just ask me. I know what teenage hormones are like. Just ask me, Pete, for crying out loud, just ask me! Your mom was worried sick."

"Yes, Dad, sorry, Dad."

"Go wait in the bathroom, you do deserve a caning. But don't tell your mom about the girl, okay, that stays between us." Rikus winked, and Pete made the long walk to the bathroom where Rikus gave him three strikes with the cane across his bum, but not nearly with the same venom as usual. Afterward, Rikus tapped him on the shoulder and said with the same regretful look he always had after a caning, "It's just that we worry, that's all."

"I know, Dad, I'm sorry," Pete said and disappeared into his room.

PLANS

It was strange to see Petrus, Pete thought. A week before they had sat next to one another in the truck. A lot of things were said. Prickly things. Things that stuck. And here he was again, in his familiar shorts, even though it was freezing, and a jersey that should never have been allowed out of the 1950s. But this was not the same guy Pete had called the k-word that night. This was his friend, Petrus. A lump in his throat appeared and he couldn't say anything when he stood in front of him. He nodded, and as if Petrus was going through the same thing, he nodded too. They walked side by side to *Naidoo and Sons*, both focused on their feet, both with hands in their pockets.

Five meters away from the shop the door suddenly flung open. They looked up, and out stormed Sarita. There was no time to blink or move, within the blink of an eye she hurled her arms around them, hugging them both while she dangled in between them. She squeezed them closer. She held them for a few seconds then pulled back, her smile melting away the wintery cold.

"Come," she said, and by the time they had followed her into the shop, two Cokes were waiting for them.

"I'm sorry about last week. It was my grandmother's birthday, and I was expected to go. It was terrible, I mean I love her and all, but it is so difficult to be around her. She looks at me with these wide eyes, her pupils dilated, and says, 'The fire will burn, no one can stop the fire, the fire will burn.' Not in English, in Hindi obviously, but she says it over and over again, first to me, then my mom, and then a hundred times to my dad." She sighed but her smile was still there.

"Sounds like a great birthday!" Petrus said.

"Wish we were there," Pete said, and all three laughed from the gut.

"Did you get my note last Sunday?" Sarita asked, tucking her rogue strand of hair behind her ear.

"Yes, thanks," Pete said.

"It was raining so hard, it was crazy. Pete stole his father's truck and gave me a lift," Petrus said.

"You stole your dad's truck? Pete!" Sarita said, her mouth agape, pretending to be deeply shocked.

"There wasn't much of a choice, the thunderstorm was bad. Luckily, I saw Petrus, because for some reason he believed he could outrun lightning," Pete said, and Petrus looked away, laughing shyly.

"Did you get into trouble? Did your dad find out?"

"Well, when I got home my dad was waiting for me. I got the fright of my life."

"Serious?" Petrus suddenly stopped laughing and leaned his head forward.

"Yeah, can you believe it? I thought they would still be sleeping."

"What happened?" Sarita said.

"Let's be honest, he wasn't particularly happy, but at least he didn't ground me or something like that, he just gave me a hiding."

"Shoh-shoh! Eish, I'm sorry, Pete. It's my fault, if you didn't give me a lift you wouldn't be in trouble,"

Petrus said.

"Hey relax, it wasn't that bad. I think my dad held back. He thinks I went out to see a girl, so he wasn't really mad at me. He just said to tell him in the future. I think he was hoping I had moved on from the whole Renate saga."

"Have you?" Sarita asked almost before he had finished his sentence, then flashed a pretend smile and half-shrugged. "You know, moved on from her?"

"Renate who?" Pete responded, smiling.

"What did you tell your father?" Petrus was still worried.

"I sort of told the truth. I said I saw a friend of mine running and he got stuck in the thunderstorm, so I took him home, New Extension way. All of that is true of course, except I led him to believe that my friend was running in the street outside our house." He shrugged. "But really, why get bogged down by minor details?"

Pete looked up at the neon light above him. "Recently my dad has started treating me differently, better, almost as if he doesn't see me as just a young boy anymore. He surprised me. I suppose I just always thought his mind worked a certain way, but the more we talk, the more I realize we might not be so different after all."

"My dad definitely still sees me as a little girl. I don't foresee a time when he would ever accept that I am capable of thinking for myself," Sarita said. "Once he's made up his mind whatever he says is law. You can jump up and down as much as you want, it makes no difference. What's worse is that even when I can see that my mom doesn't agree with him, she won't oppose his decisions. It's very frustrating. I think if he was given half a chance, he would lock me away until he could find a rich man for me to marry."

"Perhaps it's because you are an only child *and* his daughter. From what I've seen, dads tend to be very protective of their daughters," Pete said.

"It's true," Petrus said. "My brothers and I can more or less do what we want, but my dad always wants to know where my sisters are. And they get into big trouble if they go out without letting him know."

"Maybe, it's just..." Sarita sighed. Then it looked as though she shook off the bad thoughts and smiled. "Anyone fancy a chocolate bar?"

Time petered to a near halt for the three hidden away in a dark shop. They compared notes about the silly rules at their respective schools, joked about the oddities in the shop, but mostly laughed, sometimes for no reason at all.

Out of the blue Saita said, "Guys." Both looked up.

"Nowadays my head is filled with such random thoughts. But I suppose this is probably the only place on earth where I can ask random questions." Neither Petrus nor Pete seemed to be following her.

"I started thinking about next year and where I might be, and then I started thinking about the bomb in Newcastle and the stuff on TV and the Struggle and the government and all the rest of it, and it made me wonder where everything was headed. You know? South Africa?" They remained silent, waiting for her to continue.

"I know we have joked about it, but do you guys think we will have a black president one day? Like in, a proper democracy?"

Neither of the two guys could answer straight away—as if the question had rendered their lips and thoughts useless.

"Martin Luther King said, 'The arc of the moral universe is long, but it bends toward justice.' So it's inevitable, isn't it?" Sarita said and then sat against the pool table.

Petrus shook his head. "My dad said you shouldn't dream dreams that could hurt you." Sarita opened her mouth to say something but Petrus beat her to it. "What do you think, Pete?"

He didn't know. It was as if everything he was ever taught prohibited the mere thought of it. As if it was sinful.

"If one listens to old P.W., then something like that will never happen."

"But you want it, right? Democracy?" Sarita said.

"Pfff...of course." Pete shied away and took a large bite out of his chocolate bar. Did he really want it? What would it mean: democracy, a black president? Still, could it be worse than now? State of Emergency, sanctions, bombs, hatred?

"I think our first black president should be some-one who wasn't part of the Struggle. Someone who can start with a clean slate," Sarita said.

"*If* this battle is won, those who fought would want that seat. They won't give it up," Petrus said.

"Probably," Sarita said, her enthusiasm gone.

"Burdened with eternal optimism, hey?"

She turned to Pete and a smile slowly started to form, like she was shocked that he remembered her words, then she bit her lip and looked away.

Seemingly unaware of the others, Petrus stared

at the ceiling. Then, almost like he was talking to himself, he said, "Pete's right, the government will never allow it. Things are the way they are."

Later Petrus bounced the cue ball, whilst Pete explained the principles of the game to him, but neither had noticed that Sarita had become very quiet. She stood at the end of the pool table, her hands locked in front of her.

"Guys." They both looked up and sensed a seriousness about her.

"Another random question?" Pete asked. He waited for her to smile but her face remained stark.

"Sort of," she said. "You know *that* night?" Pete and Petrus straightened up. Petrus let the cue ball drop from his hand.

"I've been...I still get nightmares. It got better but ever since I *saw* him again, they are back. Worse. Things are changing, my life is changing." She pursed her lips, her thoughts seemingly transporting her to a place of great sadness. Pete and Petrus exchanged a glance but remained quiet.

"At the end of this year I...could be anywhere. The point is it won't be here. Dannhauser doesn't have a secondary school that runs to Matric, so I'll be sent away—somewhere. I can't take these nightmares with me. Wherever I might go, they need to stay behind. So, I wanted to ask for your help?"

"Anything," Petrus said, and Pete nodded which made his fringe—which had started to take shape again—look like a bird flapping, trying to escape captivity.

"I want to go back. I want you to take me back,

please?" she said, her eyes wide and round.

"Back?"

"To...?"

She nodded and straightened her back.

"I must go back there, to face it, and hopefully, to bury it, or some of it at least. But I cannot do it without you, please, you have to help me?"

"Eish, it will be difficult," Petrus said.

"Perhaps during the school holidays? Yes, maybe we can all make up a story and meet there," Pete suggested, nibbling the corner of his bottom lip. "It's difficult during term time. Parents are always watching you carefully just in case you're not pulling your weight with homework, but during the holidays, parents, well mine at least, are just happy to have me out of their hair."

"I'll have to work," Petrus said.

"Me too," Sarita said. "But it is easier than during term time, especially if it's just a one-off and not a regular thing. Do you think you'll be able to get away, Petrus?"

Petrus took a protracted moment to answer. His face exposed the torment inside.

"Yes," he said as if the word physically hurt him.

"Okay! Wow, that would be so fantastic, thank you. We'll do it during the holidays. It's only three weeks away." She bounced up and down.

"Yup, it's just a shame that those three weeks are filled with exams," Pete said.

"Are you worried about the exams?" Petrus asked.

"You know, not really. This year was so messed-up that exams feel like the least important thing in my life," Pete said, which made the others chuckle.

"We've already started. Half the exams are finished," Petrus said.

"Jeez, that's early. How did it go so far?" Pete said.

"Good. I think better than last year."

"It's because you are clever. In fact, that goes for both of you. That's why I'm not worried about you two in the slightest," Sarita said, waving her hands and smiling.

"I bet you are top of your class, a super student of sorts," Pete said.

"Not if you ask my dad," Sarita said, inspecting one of her fingernails.

"Does he have high expectations?"

"More like impossible expectations." For a moment she seems distracted, her thoughts far away, then she suddenly seemed to snap back to reality. "He's very funny; he always manages to bring politics into everything. He says to me we need to be thirty percent better than the whites and twenty percent better than the blacks and coloureds. And then he leans forward and even puts out his cigarette." Sarita mimicked her dad's every move.

"He whispers and says, 'The news is, the whites are getting seventy percent and the blacks and coloureds eighty, so you have no choice, my girl, it's a hundred percent or you've lost before you've begun.' So you see, even if I get ninety-eight percent my dad will have this look, one that's telling me I failed by two percent."

"My goodness, that's tough!" Pete said.

"My parents are happy with anything above sixty percent," Petrus said.

"I can tell your dad a secret." The right side of

Pete's mouth curled into a smile. "A lot of the whites in my school are well short of the seventy percent mark."

"And we have forty children in my class and only two are getting above eighty," Petrus said.

"So, it seems your ninety-eight percent is good enough after all." Pete winked and Sarita covered her mouth laughing.

Pete paced around a bit. He could see the slow-moving clock of earlier was suddenly making up for lost time and this Sunday's *Naidoo and Sons* visit was almost over. A drop of sweat slid slowly down his temple; it felt cold against his skin.

"I see we need to go." Pete pointed to the clock.

"Just two more minutes, please?" Sarita asked with praying hands.

"Yeah, I actually wanted to tell you something," Pete said, in a deeper tone.

"Me?" Sarita pointed to her chest.

"Both of you."

Petrus stepped closer. "What is it?"

"I've been thinking, about, well—everything. Mostly about us, and Dannhauser, *that* night, you know, the whole lot. It's amazing how much time you have to think if you don't play rugby." Pete forced a laugh at his joke, but the anticipation in the others' faces urged him on.

Pete slowly exhaled through his nose. "I have a plan," he said. He clenched his teeth and felt how excitement and fear bounced around inside him in equal measure.

"You can't start like that and then stay quiet. Tell!" Sarita took two steps closer, Petrus was right next to her.

344

"Okay, but please stop me if you think it's crazy," Pete said, smiling nervously.

PART FOUR

THE WAY TO IMMORTALITY

Venny slurped his tea. It was piping hot and just right—sweet and strong. He had recently changed the bulb in his operations room, and it transformed the whole space. It was no longer as dark, and the yellow hue which reminded him of old photographs was gone. This was more business-like, more appropriate for someone on the front line of the Struggle.

He gave the room a proper clean, spent hours filing the newspaper clippings, documents, and photographs. This is what he imagined it must look like in a KGB office, everything in its place, labeled and efficient. He liked it but didn't feel quite at home yet. A part of him loved the amateur secrecy of hiding in a garage and talking about all his great ideas, collecting articles, writing a few himself. But playtime was over now. This was the real deal.

There were a few things, however, he couldn't bring himself to change, like his chair, the cushion—which he hated and thought about changing every time he saw it—the radio of course, and the two things on the wall he could never take off: the newspaper clipping of the Indian woman being beaten by the police, and his beautiful Sarita.

He leaned over his table to have a closer look at the Indian woman. It was as if the baton never stopped beating her. The black-and-white photo was grainy like it was fading. He couldn't let that memory fade.

Regardless of whatever else happened, that was the one thing he would never allow. He stroked his hand across the face of the woman, wishing he could protect her, wishing he was there that day.

He stood back and caught the tear that escaped his eye, wiped it off on his pants, and slurped his tea again.

The room seemed bigger now as if he had expanded his operations, and the smell was different. Cleaner. He lifted Sarita's picture off the wall and smiled. That face, every perfect millimeter of it, was his world. It was her school holiday. But whilst other children were playing silly games and loitering about aimlessly, she was in the shop working, smiling to customers, stacking the shelves, doing inventory, cleaning. There was no break for her. No games to play. "Hard work builds character," he said aloud. There will be plenty of holidays once she is married to a wealthy, upstanding man.

She was so proud the day before. She ran in with her mid-year report card, the school had just shut for the winter break and excitement was like a glow around her—almost infectious. Achala thought it was a good report card. She hugged her and promised her things, but Venny could not lie to her. Of course, an eighty-nine percent aggregate is good for Standard Eight, but good was no longer good enough, nowadays good was bad. If you wanted to succeed as an Indian, and as a girl, you had to be excellent—perfect even. Eighty-nine percent will get you a hug from your mom, but in the real world, you will just become a number, a random Indian number. So perhaps he was too hard on her when he said he was disappointed and that she was better than that. Her tears broke his heart. But that was the thankless job of being a father. His dad taught him that, and that same tough love made him the man he was today. He would not be able to live with himself, or face others, knowing he had sent a girl with unending potential into the world as merely average. No, he did the right thing, and one day she would go on her knees and kiss his hands and say: "Thank you, Pappa."

He put the picture back on the wall and sat down in his chair, holding the cup in both hands to warm them.

"Protea Eight, come in." He almost spilled his tea. He calmed himself, put the cup on the floor, wrapped the earphones over his ears and flicked the microphone on.

"Hello, I mean, Protea Eight confirmed, here, present..." He rolled his tongue in his mouth and moved his lips to wake his face.

"Protea Eight, I have your orders." Venny had reached for his tea but stopped half-way. His arm dangled beside him, his eyes felt as if they would pop out of their sockets, and he was certain his heart just stopped.

"Password?"

Venny searched his mind. Suddenly every chamber of it seemed to be empty. He knew there were two passwords: one to indicate that it was safe to talk, the other warning that it was not safe, sparking a fictitious order.

"Protea Eight?"

"Bulawayo...Bulawayo," Venny said, sighing, thankful that his mind had finally released the word.

"Received, authenticated." Protea Seven paused and there was a faint rustling of paper in the background.

"The order follows, but to reiterate, no notes, this must be memorized."

"Of course," Venny said, hoping his brain would be able to retain the information, whilst he silently pushed the pen and paper in front of him to the side.

"Date: Friday 18th July. Exact time to be confirmed but between 18:00 and 20:00. Target: the Lion's Club Hall, Renier Street, Dannhauser. You will be given a team of trained operatives to carry out the order. Starting next week, you will receive deliveries of videos on Wednesdays at 09:00 from a company called Video Direct. The contact is Simon. They will be delivered in small crates. Each crate has a false bottom. The merchandise needed for the order is stored therein. Keep these safe. I cannot reiterate this enough: The merchandise is highly volatile. The operatives will join you on Sunday 13th July. You will shut your shop for the week, and they will use it as the base to prepare. Your shop will reopen on Friday 18th July. Business as usual. After the order is fulfilled you will not speak to or hear from them again, and they will ensure that no traces are left to connect you to anything. It remains your duty to dispose of any potentially incriminating items. Order received?"

"Yes, thank you. Just a couple of questions. My shop never shuts, except on Sundays, how will I be able to shut it, for four days?"

"Be creative, that's why you were chosen. I've seen your shop; it's crying out for some sprucing up."

"Good idea, good idea." Venny could just see

Achala's questioning face, her unending questions.

"Anything else?"

"Yes, purely out of curiosity, why is the Lion's Club being targeted? They have not been traditional enemies, have they?"

"We're not targeting the Lion's Club. That night the Northern Natal annual general meeting for the Afrikaner Brotherhood will take place in the Lion's Club Hall."

Venny rubbed his mustache. "The Broederbond?!"

"Correct. The brain trust behind this devil we are fighting. This will be one of the most important missions our organization has ever planned, so only success is an acceptable outcome. Protea Seven out."

"Protea Seven?" Venny asked, but the transmission had ended. He flicked the microphone off and stared at the radio. He thought about the Afrikaner Brotherhood, or Broederbond as they referred to themselves, shaking his head. They were nothing more than a bunch of racist white elitist pricks who thought they had the divine right to play puppet masters to the country just because they were born into the right families, had the right connections, the money. They had all sold their souls a long time ago. He could just visualize them getting together in dark rooms, whispering to one another, making decisions that destroyed the lives of millions, all for power and money. If he pulled this off, he would be an icon of the Struggle. He would be immortal. Not Achala's nosy disapproval or anything else would stand in his way. This was Venny Naidoo's moment. And it was going to be perfect.

THE RETURN

"Are you going out?" Deanne asked, busy kneading bread. Pete was standing at the fridge. He pulled the zipper of his green Adidas sweater up to his chin and clutched his warmest jacket under his arm.

"Yes, a bunch of us are going to give Halley's Comet one last chance," Pete said.

"I thought the comet had left us alone for another seventy years?"

"More like seventy-six, so I'll be ninety-two then. They said on the news last night that there might be a surprise final sighting on the western horizon tonight, like a last hoorah. I just wanted to see if grandad's Halley was still out there."

"You looked so captivated by the tennis on TV, I didn't think you'd move a muscle?"

"Lendl is crushing that guy. I think this is his year—he just needs to beat Becker."

"What about Kevin Curran?"

"Aggh Ma, I told you last week he was knocked out in the first round."

"Oh, that's a shame, I like him. So, who are you going with?"

"A bunch of us decided to go, but I don't think I'll be late—it's freezing."

"Yes, no silly stuff, you hear me? And I want you back here by eight, I'm making pancakes later."

"Thanks, Mom, see you later." Pete rushed out the

door. The shock of the cold was startling. Jimmy was curled up in the corner and Pete pulled his doggy blanket over his shivering body. He acknowledged Pete's kindness with an affirming groan.

Pete put his jacket on and the gloves he kept in his pockets, Even so, the cold still cut to the bone. It was difficult to believe it had just hit six o'clock; it was pitch dark, with only the distant glow of stars coloring the vast sky.

Without thinking about it, Pete started running. It made the cold slightly more bearable. Each breath formed a balloon of white mist in front of him, and he wondered if that would freeze and fall to the ground like tiny icicles. He was an ice-machine, he thought and smiled. But it was too cold to smile.

When he stopped, he checked the time: 18:10. Exactly on time. He stretched out his hand, groping around in the dark for the rusty gate of the public swimming pool to lean against.

There was no one there. He searched every dark shadow, but nothing moved except the fog-like breath escaping his mouth. Doubt besieged him and with it those thoughts that always attacked him when he stood still, without any structure or reason. He couldn't understand it, he could barely stay awake through maths class, but leave him alone in the dark or let him lay in his bed and his thoughts exploded in every conceivable direction.

His mind took him back to the previous Sunday's get together in the shop. In fact, all the Sundays in the shop and everything else that brought him to this moment, standing in the dark, became one all-consuming thought. All the conversations, the laughter, the crying. Petrus...Sarita.

A sinking feeling formed in the pit of his stomach. He had to get her out of his thoughts. But she was always waiting there for him.

He could see her smile. Then he shook his head and took a few steps toward the street. He implored another thought to supplant the thoughts of her.

He tried to think about school and Halley, but nothing seemed to work. Then Petrus's face flashed before him. He was grateful for the interruption, but it didn't last long, because without permission his thoughts jumped back to that day listening to Petrus in the pouring rain, and then to Sarita, and every word she had ever said to him. He could see them clearly in his mind: black and Indian. His shoulders felt heavy. All these lines in the sand, all the do's and don'ts, were all one big mess, and he was dangling in the middle like some kind of idiot, not knowing which way to fall.

One Sunday Sarita declared: "Fear is behind every bad decision." Perhaps that was the problem; a part of him was still trapped by all the fear spewed out on the news day after day about the Red Scare, the Black Scare, every bloody color brought with it another scare.

But this wasn't who he was anymore, was it?

Then he started thinking about Sarita again. "They should bring in a law that when you turn sixteen you must go and live in a different community for a year. Call it an exchange program," was her proposal. He couldn't help but laugh—Sarita and her random ideas.

"If you went to live with Petrus's family for a year, Pete, just imagine all the things you would learn. You would get an idea of what it's like to live in his shoes. And his family would start to understand you. Don't you think that would be awesome?" She turned to them, gleaming. It was only later that he registered what she said because in that moment he was completely bewitched by the magical powers of her eyes.

He let the idea wash over him again; a year with Petrus and his family? It sounded quite nice, in a strange kind of way. But what if it wasn't Petrus's family, but complete strangers living in some village in the middle of nowhere?

"Eish, I don't know who would struggle the most? Us, the whites, coloureds, or the Indians?" Petrus remarked. "But one thing is for certain; we will all struggle."

"But just imagine the impact it would have on everyone?" Sarita said.

"Even if the government said we must do this, do you really think your dad would let you live with whites or blacks?" Petrus asked.

"Of course not, he doesn't even want me to talk to anyone outside our family. But a girl can dream." She walked up to the pool table and stroked her hand over the green baize, her face suddenly solemn. "What's the alternative? How do you change a heart?"

There was despair in her eyes. It made Pete think of Rudie and what so nearly happened. He wanted to protect her against everything that brought despair, against all bad things, but how? That night it was pure luck that they escaped. Her face flashed before him again, from that first time he truly saw her in the rain, to the tears, the joy, her dimples, and of course: those eyes.

Then he recalled her answer to Petrus's question about whether or not she had a boyfriend: "Boyfriend?" she exclaimed and started laughing. "There is not a single boy in my school who I would date." She turned to Pete. "Trust me, I am not interested in anyone *there*." Her face spoke in that strange language again, the one he did not understand. Or perhaps he did understand, but he was too afraid to.

Stop it, Pete. He looked up at the stars searching for something. An escape? Punishment? Permission? He shook his head again. His thoughts disturbed the order of things arbitrarily, at least the way he imagined the order of things to be. It was all the fault of that damned night—that was the door which let in all the unwanted guests. And now he was on his way to fiddle with that same bloody door again.

"Psst." Pete almost fell on his back. His heart was in his mouth. He frantically looked around him for any form of movement, a shadow, a tiny bit of vapor, anything, but there was nothing.

"Psst." There it was again. He so wished he had brought a torch.

Then a hint of vapor appeared from the darkness. Movement. Coming from behind some overgrown shrubbery. A figure. Its dark shape was difficult to distinguish against the equally dark surroundings. Pete squinted.

"It's me, silly."

"Me who?" Pete asked.

"Me me," the voice said, and Pete started laughing.

"Me who, me me. That sounds like two cats chatting." He giggled, all the tumultuous thoughts evaporated in an instant as if they never existed.

"You're late."

"No, I wasn't, my watch said 18:10," Pete said.

An arm hooked into his. In the shadows hidden under her jacket's hood, he could see her shimmering smile and a hint of those dimples.

"I think your watch is wrong." Now he could feel her smile.

"Come, I have to be back by eight," Pete said and pulled her hood further over her face.

They walked on the sidewalk, keeping the trees and the street between them and any prying eyes of the residents of New Extension. Sarita's arm remained hooked into Pete's, as if that made her invisible, there, walking with a white boy, in a white neighborhood.

Pete didn't know what to do. Should he unhook her arm? What if someone saw them? What if people talked? But the feeling of her warmth next to him, and her eyes seeking reassurance every few meters made him feel powerful, able to break anything or anyone who came in her way.

The road next to the fishing dam was difficult to navigate in the darkness, but one hesitant step at a time they made it. The stars sparkled, and even in the near-complete darkness, they seemed to guide their way, so that soon a familiar silhouette appeared, statuesque, at the top of the hill.

"I was getting worried," Petrus said, shaking Pete's hand before getting a very firm hug from Sarita.

"Jeez, it's cold," Pete said. Petrus just nodded, rubbing his hands together. He didn't have gloves, but Pete was relieved to see that he was wearing a jacket and proper pants, and most shocking of all: shoes.

"So you do own shoes?" Pete teased.

"I don't like them but tonight my toes might freeze off if I don't wear them."

Pete laughed. His sides hurt from the cold.

"This is the place." Sarita had walked away from them and stood on the spot where Rudie had pinned her down.

"Right here." She turned to them and pointed. They joined her and stood on either side of her.

"Are you okay?" Pete asked.

She didn't answer. Her body was shaking a little and streams of tears began to roll down her face.

Pete and Petrus both held her, flanking her sides. Not a word was spoken.

When the final tear dropped into the newly formed puddle on the ground, she fiddled in her pockets and produced a small yellow piece of paper. She kneeled and placed the paper on the ground, ironing it out with her hands. She sat like that for a while, and Pete and Petrus questioned with their eyes, their mouths firmly shut.

She took two small stones lying on the ground and pinned the paper down. She looked at it one last time and pushed herself up. The boys helped her to her feet.

Pete desperately wanted to ask but didn't know if it was appropriate. He was physically biting his tongue.

"What is that?" Petrus asked, to Pete's relief.

"It's a poem. It's me letting go."

"A poem about your feelings?" Petrus asked.

"Yes. I put all of them on that piece of paper, all the things I could never say to that man. All the things he made me feel, all the nightmares, the tears...they're all there now, buried in this place."

The three of them stared at the piece of paper pinned down by two stones, lying next to a puddle of teary mud, for quite some time.

Pete looked skywards. Rudie's face appeared in his mind's eye, sketched among the stars. He saw the yellow mustache and heard the fiendish laugh. His face was large but scattered amongst the stars and soon Pete had to blink several times to recognize him, and then he faded to nothing until only the stars remained.

The trio left the piece of paper behind and sat on the rock behind which Pete and Petrus hid months before. Here they studied the majestic black outlines of the Drakensberg. A contented silence pulled them closer together. Frozen in time, as one.

The year played in Pete's mind like a movie, and he tried to fathom how these two absolute strangers, in every sense of the word, were now sitting next to him. And why it felt as normal as breathing. He was sitting shoulder to shoulder with an Indian girl and it didn't feel like a sin anymore. He shook hands with a black guy, and he didn't want to wash his hands straight away anymore. He wondered what the others were thinking. Did they also wonder whether they had landed in a parallel universe where they were friends with a white guy all of a sudden?

"Look!" Sarita broke the silence, pointing to the horizon. Pete and Petrus both almost fell off the rock.

Just above the mountains, the dark night was pierced by a light, like a flashlight from beyond the heavens. Its beam was short but breathtaking in silvery gold, etched above the ancient curves of the mountains.

"Halley," was all Pete could muster.

They watched the comet as its brightness changed to a softer glow, the tail became shorter and it seemed altogether more distant. Pete couldn't help but think of his grandad's Halley, and now he had seen a glimpse of that, like a gift through time itself. Without realizing it, his eyes were wet, and soon two thin lines on his face shone in the fading splendor of Halley.

Sarita glanced at him, her head tilted. Something in her smile made Pete feel as though she too knew his grandad. *She was so incredibly beautiful,* he thought. She rested her head on his shoulder and wrapped her arm around him tightly. He felt lightheaded and in his trancelike state kissed her on the top of her head, right in the splendor of her silky hair.

Petrus looked at them with a wry smile: He saw the shock on Pete's face, and that he had forgotten how to blink.

Sarita lifted her head and sat upright again, giving Pete the subtlest of smiles that warmed his insides like a fire. She folded her arms around both boys. She pulled them in close, holding them tight.

"Thank you," she said. "You didn't just save me, you set me free."

They hugged her from both sides. Petrus gave Pete a mischievious glance. He kissed Sarita on her head without breaking eye contact with Pete. Pete knew straight away that he was mocking him for his earlier shock. Pete smiled, feeling a whiff of embarrassment, but then he met Petrus's mocking gaze and kissed Sarita purposefully on her head. Petrus responded with two more kisses on her head, to which Pete replied with two of his own, and soon they were peppering the top of her head with so many kisses that she cried with laughter. She laughed and wriggled so much that she fell off the rock, managing—just—to land on her feet.

The boys jumped off and stood next to her, giggling. She play-slapped both on their shoulders.

"Now I understand what the term, 'killing with kindness' means." Their giggles echoed in the night.

"I don't want tonight to end, but my dad will kill me if I'm not home very soon," she said, her smile fading.

The realization that this magical evening was over left deep, sad, footprints in Pete's soul. It was as if this was a new beginning, a blank page. They were back where it started, but they were more: much, much more than then.

Petrus hugged Sarita and she responded by planting a forceful kiss on his cheek, which made him cry with laughter like a baby being tickled.

"I'll see you on Sunday." She rubbed his arm with her hand. "Thank you for tonight."

"Hey, guys, listen. I also wanted to say thanks for tonight...but also for your help with my plan," Pete said. "Thanks for believing in me, not telling me I belong in the nut-house or something. I appreciate it, really."

"You're welcome." Sarita said. "But we never said you don't belong in the nut-house." Pete grabbed her in a playful headlock. She snort-laughed.

"We'll work on it Sunday, same as the last few weeks?" Petrus asked.

"Yes, I think it's almost there...with only three weeks to go there isn't much of a choice, it has to be ready," Pete said.

"It will be." Petrus shook Pete's hand, waved, and ran down the hill toward the distant lights of the farmhouse.

Pete and Sarita walked slowly over the farm road, but once they arrived at the tarred stretch, Sarita pulled her hood over her head and started jogging. They ran and laughed like it was the first night on earth, like the whole world lay in wait for them, and nothing but that moment mattered.

"I guess I'll see you Sunday," Pete said, out of breath as they reached the entrance to the side street beyond the library. Sarita battled to catch her breath. She didn't answer, instead, she was standing with her hands on her knees until her breathing calmed. Then she straightened up, took Pete's wrists in her hands and stood on her toes so that her face was right up against his. He blinked slowly. He tried to swallow. His heart made an audible noise—or at least he was sure it did. Her eyes locked into his, he found himself suddenly naked, exposed before her. His mind shut down as he beheld her face. He was burning up. As if it could never be cold again. Even under the dimness of the nearby streetlight, she looked angelic, way beyond pretty, beautiful, magnificent.

Her face moved in and her cheek brushed against his mouth. Her lips pressed softly, deliberately deep into his cheek, lingering, and then she withdrew, quicker than lightning. She turned and without looking, ran back down her street until the darkness took her. Pete took his glove off and held his hand on his cheek. He could still feel her warmth on him.

He recalled the Reverend's words, that it was a sin

to lust, and against nature and moral decency to have a relationship with a person of color. But feeling her lips against his skin, smelling the sweetness of her hair, and seeing those eyes, and what they did to him, didn't feel like a sin or against nature. It felt...right.

For a while he just stood there, holding his fingers against his cheek. How long he could not tell. Later, when his mind's fog lifted, the cold of the night had crept into the deepest parts of his bones. He took one final look at where the darkness took Sarita and then he sprinted home. One minute to eight he walked through the kitchen door. He called his parents, and the three of them stood in the garden, eating warm cinnamon-sugar filled pancakes and watching Halley's final farewell.

SNAP

It was Sunday. Pete and Barend did what most of the children did during the holidays after church: They loitered, waiting for their parents to finish their cups of tea and coffee and the driest biscuits on earth.

After pottering around the church, Pete and Barend settled on the steps at the church's side entrance. They were bathed in beautiful, bright sunshine, but the sun was weak, and the breeze biting.

"So, do you think the coach will be fired?" Pete asked.

"Well it is the first time in what, three or four years, that we haven't won the league—I don't know. The headmaster was at that last game and at one point I thought he was going to run onto the field himself, he was pissed off as hell."

"I still can't believe you lost to the Agricultural School. No one loses to them," Pete said.

"Tell me about it. I have no idea how it happened. Perhaps it was the pressure. We heard Vryheid High beat Klip Rivier earlier in the day, so we knew exactly what to do: beat the farm school by twenty-seven points and we win the league. I mean, like two years ago we beat them by fifty points. We just wanted to score tries, all the time, then we started making mistakes, knocking on, missing tackles. Before long we were passing to the opposition more often than to our own teammates. It was just a crazy game. Almost

SNAP

like we were watching it on TV, and we couldn't do anything about it. I thought Coach was going to have a heart attack. Jeez, I can't believe we lost to those farm implements, I tell you, China."

"Well, I suppose it's probably better than beating them by twenty-five points and losing the league by one point," Pete said.

Barend shook his head. "Tell that to Mr. Theunissen."

"I think I just might." Pete smiled. The idea of walking into Mr. Theunissen's office conveying his heartfelt condolences sat comfortably in his imagination: "You had a good run, sir, all the best for the future in your new role as street sweeper!"

"I think it might have worked out in your favor— I'd be shocked if you didn't walk straight into the first team at the start of next season, even if he is still there," Barend said.

"We'll see." Pete pulled the sleeves of his jersey over his hands to warm up.

"And you and Philippa? These days the two of you are joined at the hip, how are you going to survive the two-and-a-half weeks away from each other?"

"Oh, I haven't told you?"

"Huh?"

"She came to visit yesterday."

"Here, in Dannhauser? I thought everyone from Dundee was too good for our humble little town?"

"Yup, she braved it out here in the Wild West. Her parents came to drop something off at her mom's half-cousin's or something, so she spent the afternoon with me."

"Ooooooh," Pete teased.

367

"Stop it." Barend punched Pete on the shoulder.

"The news is, she asked if I wanted to go away with them. They're going to Amanzimtoti for two weeks. Her parents came to speak to my parents and everything."

"Jeez! Seriously?"

"Oh yeah, me and my girl on the beach in Toti, my China." Barend stretched out his arm as if he held Philippa by his side.

"That is next-level stuff. You can't get married without your best man, just remember that." Pete gave Barend the sternest expression he could muster.

"I know you're joking but let me tell you a little secret." Barend got up and inspected the area. When he felt satisfied that they were alone, he sat right next to Pete.

He whispered: "It's her sixteenth birthday next Saturday, and she said there is only one thing she wants." Then Barend went quiet as he gazed into the distance.

"What?" Barend was taking way too long for Pete's liking.

"She wants to do *it*," Barend said with a smile almost tickling his ears.

"It? As in it *it*?" Pete asked.

Barend nodded with glee.

Pete dropped his chin onto his hand. "Dude..."

"I know I said I wanted to wait until marriage."

"Yeah, so much so that you pledged it in front of fifty other kids at last year's church camp," Pete reminded him.

"Yes, I know, I remember. But China, when it is staring you in the face and pulling you in, it's impossible to say no. It's Philippa, China. If I don't, someone else will be the first, and I can't live with that."

"You're sixteen, it's not like all women will abandon earth if you decided not to."

"Perhaps, but I think Philippa will. She asked me if I wanted to and I said 'yes.'"

"We all want to, but we don't actually do it," Pete said.

"You're wrong. We live blind, China. Everyone's doing it. It's not just pricks like Gareth and John-John who do it. Normal guys like Alistair, Gert, Jan: they've all done it."

"Bullshit, those guys haven't even seen a woman topless without stars on her nipples."

"It's true. I didn't hear it from them, Philippa told me. It's the eighties, man, kids our age...it's almost expected of us."

"I think it's all a bunch of nonsense. I bet you that I can count the number of kids at school who have had sex on one hand," Pete said.

"Okay, lets count," Barend said. "Just those we have no doubts about. Klayton and his long-time squeeze, Poppy. Lawrence with all the girls from Glencoe, Hermien, John-John, Gareth, Andrea, Renate—" Barend put his fist in front of his mouth and looked away.

"I'm sorry, that slipped out," he said.

"Renate? With Gareth?" Pete asked, surprised that there was something inside him that felt like a fish-hook being tugged through his guts.

"Yes, and no. Gareth recently, but Philippa told me there was this guy in the city she has been seeing on and off since primary school. They crossed that bridge last year if you know what I mean."

"No! No way," Pete blurted out. He was shocked. Feeling a little sick—more than a little. *Why?* he wondered. And why did he feel betrayed somehow? It was ridiculous, wasn't it?

"No, Pete said again. His voice meek.

"We all live our own lives and choose what we choose. She's no longer part of your life, let her hump around like a rabbit, it doesn't matter, does it?" Barend said.

"I know, I was just...surprised. I didn't see that one coming at all." Pete scratched his head with both hands, desperate to shake this lingering bitter aftertaste in his mouth. "Well, enough of rabbits and whatever they do. Tell me, Toti; what's the weather like there?"

"Warm, for winter. We'll be able to swim and tan and stuff."

"Cool." Words dried up in Pete's mouth. He looked down at his fabric loafers. The cold was slowly starting to grip his toes and he wiggled them to make sure they still functioned.

A black man wearing a torn blue overall and a gray blanket around his shoulders walked from the street onto the grassy sidewalk about fifteen meters from them. He stopped and took his large, mangled leather hat off, and held it against his chest. He was dirty as if he hadn't seen a bath for years, and his bottom lip quivered.

"Please my *baas*, I'm very hungry. I'm just asking for a small piece of bread, please my *baas*? God bless you, my *baas*." He gripped his hat tighter, dropped his head and shuffled his feet as if he were petrified of standing still.

"Bugger off, you rotten piece of trash! Go! *Suka wena!*" Barend shouted and smiled with pride. Pete was stunned.

"Why are you pulling your face like that?" Barend asked.

"It's nothing." Pete looked at the man, hesitating for a moment.

"Let's just give him a break. He's just an old man and it's winter. He's probably just tired of being cold," Pete said.

"What? That good for nothing over there? Look at him, China, he is dirtier than the rats at the dump. We'll catch some disease if we get close to him. He's just here to check out the place, believe me, he's here to see if there is something to steal." Barend looked disgusted. "Bugger off, you piece of—" Barend jumped up and pretended to throw something at the man. The man fell flat on the ground.

Barend bent over backward with laughter. "Did you see that, did you see how he fell, like a bullet hit him, China? Where the hell is Belchie, he would have wet himself!"

"Come on!" Pete said. "Look at the poor bloke, he's freakin' old. Look at how he is struggling to get up. Leave him alone already."

"It's only because he's been sniffing glue all day. And when did you suddenly turn into a kaffir-brother?" Barend's right fist nestled in his side, his forehead an explosion of frown-lines. "I thought we were friends?"

"What has friendship got to do with it? He's just an

old man!" Pete pointed to the man, now on his knees.

"*Kaffir*-brother!" Barend stormed closer until he was right in Pete's face. "You're nothing more than a *kaffir*-brother. Is that why you always come up with excuses if I want to do something on Sunday afternoons? Is that your special time with your mud hut dwelling buddies?"

Pete pushed Barend hard. He stumbled back but didn't fall, then sucked his bottom lip into his mouth, and glared at Pete as if he was about to storm him.

"Maybe I am a *kaffir*-brother!" Pete shouted. His voice almost breaking. "So what? So bloody what, China?" Pete flung his arms wide open. For a moment it was as if Barend had forgotten that he wanted to storm him.

"But he's a black," Barend said stunned.

"And? What? He's a hungry old man. Dude, this building behind us is a church. Aren't we supposed to help people?" Pete said.

"Yes, but our people. Ones like him will just take and take and take. And when there is nothing left to give, they will rape our women and kill us. This is reality, China, snap out of it! They are planting bombs in Newcastle, Durban, Pretoria, the bloody country is in a State of Emergency because of boys just like him who are taking and taking and killing and raping. You're either one of us or one of them. No gray people are walking the streets, just black and white, China. Just black and white. So, if you pick their side, in my books, you are worse than them. They think like animals; so simple minded they can hardly help it, but you, you know better. So, think long and hard, China, once you choose them, you'll have the blood of innocent white people on your hands. Think!" Barend jabbed his forefinger against his head.

"I'll see you when I get back. And I hope my best friend, Pete de Lange, will be here because I don't know where the hell he is today!"

With that Barend turned and walked away. Pete's mouth was swimming with so many words that he thought he would have to throw up to get rid of them all.

"Eish, sorry, *baas*." The black man was standing again, and waved apologetically, shaking his head. Then he started walking away toward the street.

"Wait!" Pete shouted. The man stopped. His wide damp eyes revealing his uncertainty and fear.

"Just wait there," Pete said and sprinted around the church.

The grown-ups were chatting away and didn't even notice when Pete tilted the whole tray of leftover biscuits onto a paper plate and poured milk into a polystyrene cup. He raced back. The man stood frozen on the same spot where Pete had left him.

Pete came to a halt right in front of the man, out of breath. He then held the plate and the cup out to the man.

"I'm sorry...about him," Pete said, his voice hoarse.

"No, no, no, my *baas*. Sorry is a bad word. You never say sorry when you are doing the Lord's work."

"My name is Pete."

"My name is Klaas."

"Nice to meet you, Klaas."

"*Baas* Pete, today you changed the world. A tiny little bit." Klaas held his index finger and thumb a fraction apart. "But it is better now." Klaas smiled, revealing his few remaining brown teeth. He then walked away without saying another word, munching the driest biscuits on earth, as if it was a feast fit for a king.

Pete cried. He didn't know why, but it just came, it overwhelmed him. Later, Klaas was so far down the street that he could no longer see his dirty leather hat. But Pete kept staring in his direction until his tears ran dry.

RENOVATION

"Achala, I am not asking. If we want to move the business forward, we need to continually renew. Look at the paint, it's peeling everywhere." Venny stood in his shop opposite Achala who was shaking her head and looking at him as if he made her sick. He hated that look but saw it often these days.

"We will lose a whole week's business—how will we afford that, and the materials and these men? They don't even look like decorators," Achala said.

"So, what do decorators look like, according to you? Huh? This is not a discussion, it's happening. Your shop will trade. I will put a sign up, and we will make the money back through new customers in no time. The shop will be open again on Friday."

"You know—" She stepped closer to ensure the men walking in and out of the shop bringing in their gear wouldn't hear her. She whispered, "Boys are notoriously slow. Who says you will be open on Friday? I'm worried this will go on for weeks and they will rob us blind in the process."

"These ones are different. We can trust them. I'll make you a deal: If this shop is not open for business again on Friday, I will stop smoking."

"Ha! You will never stop. But accepted, it's a deal. If for nothing else I would like to see you suffer..." She paused, and Venny wondered what was going on in her head, "...Trying to quit," she finally finished her sentence.

"Dad, Mom, what's going on? I thought you were on your way to Dādī?" Sarita said, standing in the door. "And who are these men?" she added as if trying to hurry everyone up.

"Sarita, we are not going to Dādī today," Venny said.

"But it's Sunday?" Sarita said.

"Your wonderful father here has decided to waste his meager profits on this bunch of *decorators* that look like they have just escaped from prison, to redo his beautiful shop, in lovely shades of purple."

"Achala, enough now!" Venny said.

"Sorry, is it pink, not purple?" Achala said, biting the corner of her bottom lip.

"As you can hear your mother is not happy. In business, we need to look fresh, so there will be a little bit of renovation this week. But Friday it will be business as usual, with a new look."

"I thought you always said people didn't care about what shops looked like, they only cared about products and price?" Sarita said.

"Times are changing, child. One day you'll understand."

"I'm not three years old you know. I take business economics at school, I'm not a complete idiot," Sarita said.

"Don't talk to your father like that." Achala tilted her head toward Sarita.

"But you...aggh, what does it matter." Sarita sighed and swung her head away. She looked up at the clock and her whole face turned a grayish color.

"Uhhm, I'll take the rubbish out." She grabbed the

black bag next to the counter and disappeared out of the shop.

"She is right you know. She is smarter than both of us. You can't treat her like a child anymore," Achala said.

"She'll always be my little girl," Venny said, a smile threatening under his mustache.

"Your little girl is almost grown up now, you need to get that into your thick head."

"I'm not ready to let go yet. As long as she is under my roof—"

"Yeah, yeah, yeah. Same old story. I'm going home." Achala threw her right hand in the air and walked out of the shop.

Venny studied the four men carrying paint and crates into his shop. They were large men. Their faces told a story of bitter battles and suffering, and Achala was right, they didn't look a thing like decorators, but for redecorating the Lion's Club Hall with blood, they were perfect.

"I can't believe it's less than a week to go?" Petrus said as they walked away from the Eating House.

"It's crazy isn't it, the time has flown by," Pete said.

"Do you think...?"

"It will be ready? Yes. If it will work—who knows?" Pete said.

"I guess this time next week, we'll know," Petrus said.

"Yeah," Pete said, staring out toward the *Naidoo and Sons* sign in the distance.

"How do you feel? Do you think you will be—" Pete started but his train of thought came to a screeching halt as they saw Sarita race around the corner with a black bag in her hand. She was quite clearly distressed and kept looking over her shoulder.

She dropped the bag near some bins and jogged toward them, her plait swinging like a pendulum behind her.

"You have to go," she whispered, not looking at them, but looking over her shoulder, as if she was being chased.

"What's wrong?" Petrus asked.

"My parents are here, you have to go. Turn around now, go!" She waved them away with both hands.

They turned, tail between their legs and started walking, but Pete stopped and looked back at her.

"Saturday?" he asked.

"Yes, yes, I know what to do, everything. Just go," she said and jogged back toward the shop.

"That was weird," Pete said.

"I think if her parents are around, we should probably not be seen together," Petrus said.

"Yeah, the last thing we need now is tongues wagging, hey?" Pete said. The mere thought made him shudder. He shook his head quickly and then asked: "How about a run Wednesday?"

"I'll be there," Petrus said and sprinted away from Pete.

Pete ambled back home. The energy he had earlier had all but vanished. He was tired, weary. Everything in his week was geared toward their Sunday get together, most waking moments consumed by things he wanted to say, things he wanted

378

to ask. And he wanted to see her. That smile. Feel her softness against him when they hugged. Even Petrus. He never even asked him whether he had the talk with Uncle Gerrit, as was his plan. The sadness growing in him ground him down and when he finally reached home, he collapsed onto his bed and slept, a dreamless gloomy afternoon sleep, which brought no rejuvenation.

FRIDAY, 18TH JULY

Venny had never felt so warm in his life. He turned off the heater behind the counter, took off his sweater, rolled up his sleeves but the sweat kept coming and the heat rose as if he had lava in his core. Outside, the easterly wind was particularly biting, slicing right to the bone, but even standing outside the shop for a few minutes didn't cool him down. He looked at the clock above the door like he had been all day. It was 16:41. All around the clock the walls featured a fresh coat of paint his pretend decorators had applied in between preparing the Soviet manufactured explosives. The shop didn't look that much better in his opinion, but it did appear brighter, and several people complimented him on it, except Achala of course. She referred to it as an embarrassment to the painting profession, but he knew that even if Michelangelo himself had painted it, she would have complained about the amateur he hired.

The team of decorators was due to arrive at 17:00 just as the shop closed. They would then get everything together and leave for the Lion's Club Hall at 18:45. It was a three-minute drive, so that would give them roughly seven minutes to set up, and then brighten the dark night at 18:55. Everything had gone well, everything was ready, it was going to be perfect.

"Pappa, what else do you need me to do?" Sarita walked out of the storeroom with a broom in her hand.

Crap, he had forgotten all about her.

"I'm having a meeting with someone at five, could you please go to Kismet before they close and buy me a carton of Gunstons, and then go straight home from there?"

"But Pappa, it's so cold. Can't we take the car?"

"I'll need the car later. Just do as I ask Sarita, don't be difficult. Here, that is more than enough, and bring the change and receipt." Venny slapped a twenty rand note in her hand. "And go straight home afterward, okay, it'll be dark soon."

"Yes, Pappa." She took the money, shoved it in her jacket pocket and left without looking at him.

He looked up at the clock again, and then outside. Dark shadows ushering in the night shifted across Dannhauser. His mouth was dry, and when he tried to light a cigarette he couldn't, his hands were shaking too much.

"Take control, Venny, you can do this, you were born to do this," he muttered to himself. He shook his hands and rolled his neck, then he tried again. This time his hands just about managed to be steady enough to light his cigarette, albeit only the one side. He dragged hard on his Gunston, and the tip glowed in bright orange. The smoke swirled inside him and he could feel the courage swell up, and the fear subside.

He exhaled slowly.

He was ready.

A frigid gust sliced right through Sarita as she stepped out of Kismet. The flurry of cold pricked her cheeks like dozens of small needles. Sometimes she didn't understand her dad—correction: Most of the time she didn't understand him. It would have only taken him a few minutes to take her home, it would have made no difference to him whatsoever. He would have been back well before his "five o'clock meeting." Just some excuse, she was sure.

The gust tugged at the carton of Gunston Plains she had to buy for her dad. The smell of those cigarettes was like oil stains at the back of her nose, it was always there. She promised herself she would never smoke and never ever marry someone who did.

Thoughts of her dad and his cigarettes fluttered away with the next gust. The freezing nip reminded her of the night when they saw Halley's Comet. Her mind replayed every part of that night, the sounds, the smells, the cold, the warmth, Petrus...Pete. Before she knew it, a smile had wiped away any trace of resentment and irritation she had since leaving the shop. Joy filled her. It warmed her. She was no longer on a quiet street in Dannhauser, but on a cloud which was as far away as it was tangibly close.

She did not hear it until it was too late. The truck's door swung open. That very familiar door. Familiar seat. Familiar face. Familiar yellow moustache. Familiar malevolent eyes. That door which she had escaped once but which she always feared harbored promises of an inevitable return. She prayed it wouldn't but somehow knew this day would come.

It was the end.

He was upon her. His strength and speed surprised her as much as it did that day in January. Rudie's grip impossible to break. She kicked and writhed as best she could, but he was a lion, and she a hare. There would only ever be one winner. And one loser.

It was the end.

The fear was still there, but it had turned into the most incredible sense of euphoria he had ever experienced. It was as if he had a power so great in his hands, that he could tear up streets and lift buildings from their foundations. The feeling gave him focus, certainty and he knew without any consideration of doubt that they would succeed. They weren't going to become gods, they already were.

Around the shop everything was ready. Venny was impressed by the attention to detail this thuggish-looking team of his gave to everything. Every device was checked five times, every gun cleaned and loaded—it was a thing of beauty. They were all dressed in black, with black balaclavas tucked into their pockets for the operation. Venny declined the offer to carry a pistol like the others. Once, four years ago, he had attempted to shoot a gun for the first time, but he was terrible at it. Tonight, his wit, leadership and above all, the explosives, would be his bullets. Besides, the guns were only ever meant to be a contingency, and tonight, nothing would go wrong.

"Five minutes, gentlemen," Venny said, before lighting a final cigarette. It tasted sweet, and he tried to imagine just how spectacularly sweet the first one after their success would taste. He licked his lips.

The men loaded everything into black sports bags and kept their pistols hidden inside their jackets.

It was a cold night, but the air was filled with adrenaline, and he could see pearls of sweat on the foreheads of all the men.

"Remember, there is a State of Emergency in the country. The police are a little edgy. Luckily in Dannhauser, the police are probably a few beers strong by now, and I don't expect any of them on patrol. But just in case, lay low in the car. We will park half a block away in Palmiet Street. From there it's an easy escape out, in any direction. Any questions?" Venny asked.

The four men shook their heads as one. There was a dullness in their eyes, a kind of knowing, and in them, Venny knew there was no turning back; they were prepared to die tonight.

Out of nowhere, a loud knock rattled the door. Venny almost fell on top of one of the sports bags holding the explosives. The four men drew their pistols. Then another knock followed, louder, urgent.

Venny's breathing was shallow. He was a little lightheaded but realized his obvious fear was a sign of weakness to the others. So, he lifted his hands as if to say they should calm down and crept to the door. He peeped outside but couldn't make anything out in the darkness.

"We're closed," he said, his voice trembling.

Another knock followed, and this time he was more assertive in his. "We're closed."

"Protea Eight," a voice whispered from behind the door.

Venny looked at the men behind him. Their pistols pointing at the door.

"Protea Eight," the voice called again.

"We don't sell proteas, this is not a flower shop," Venny said.

"Open up, this is Protea Seven—I have urgent instructions regarding tonight."

"Protea Seven?"

"Affirmative, now let me in."

Venny's mind raced. What if this was a trap, and twenty soldiers stood outside? There would be a firefight, but it would be over in no time and he would be shredded like a block of Swiss cheese standing in the middle.

"Password?" Venny asked.

"Bulawayo. Open up."

Venny looked back to the men and gave them a reassuring nod. He then slowly unlocked the door and opened it a fraction. To his relief, there was no squadron, only one very short black man with thick glasses and a patchy beard.

Protea Seven pushed him out of the way and entered the shop. Venny shut the door behind him.

"Abort, gentlemen, abort," Protea Seven said.

"What do you mean, abort?" Venny said.

"I mean there will be no operation tonight."

"Why not?"

"The Afrikaner Brotherhood meeting was canceled. If we strike tonight, we'll blow up an empty hall. It will attract unwanted attention without any significant impact. Therefore, we must abort."

"Do we know why the meeting was canceled, was there a leak?"

"We're working on it. Currently, intelligence suggests the district leader is in hospital, but that could just be a front. We are trying to ascertain whether our plans were intercepted. So, men, get rid of everything. You'll need to leave tonight." He straight-ened his back and turned to Venny. "Protea Eight, there will be radio silence until this has been inves-tigated. The search will start for a new target. It is a shame about this one, it would have been perfect, but now we'll have to start from scratch. From what I've heard, the focus will shift to the Free State. Operation-wise, Northern Natal will go dark for a while."

Venny thought the sky was going to shatter and crush him to death. His moment was being taken away from him. Stolen. And to top it all he might never have another shot. If they were transferring their focus to the Free State, Northern Natal would be forgotten, his days of freedom fighting would be over. He looked at the men on the team. The dull determination that filled their eyes was now replaced with dejected, lost stares.

"What if there was another target?" Venny said, his lips pursed.

"Another target? Here? Nothing of significance ever happens in Dannhauser. This was a one-time op-portunity, and it's gone now. Move on, Protea Eight."

"Isn't the purpose behind all we are trying to achieve to bring fear and terror into the hearts and minds of ordinary whites? To show them nowhere is safe? That change was the only way, and death await-ed if they tried to fight it?" Venny asked.

"Well yes, but there's nothing here. How will we ever send a big message like the one you are talking about, out in a place like this?"

Venny inhaled as deeply as he could. "There is one thing," he said and exhaled.

"Don't waste my time. We are all vulnerable standing here amongst the merchandise. I only came to deliver the message. So, you have thirty seconds."

"In small towns, nothing is more sacred to the whites than their annual bazaars. Everyone is there, every white face in the area. They *braai* and laugh as if life was one long party. In the evening they have a concert. I can only imagine that it must be a breeding ground for their white propagandist crap, but the point is they will all be crammed into one building. If we strike—"

"A church bazaar?" Protea Seven asked. He realized he raised his voice and quickly pretended to clear his throat.

"Yes, imagine, we are talking about hundreds of people. It will send a message to every white community in the country that they are no longer safe, no matter where they are."

"But we need to get out of Dannhauser, especially if we've been compromised," Protea Seven said.

"Dannhauser's church bazaar is tomorrow. We're ready. Look at us: We have the team, we have the merchandise. Just say the word and it's done. Tomorrow night this time, we will make the biggest statement yet," Venny said.

"It's risky. Very risky. With so many people...let me have a word with those further up the chain. For now, stay put, await instructions. Protea Eight, be at your radio at 07:30 tomorrow, I will confirm then," Protea Seven said, turned and slipped out of the shop.

A dull ache shot up Venny's spine and nestled at the base of his skull. He felt nauseous and scanned the room for a bin to throw up in, but then he saw the four men in front of them, waiting for instruction, and something in their eyes suggested respect, respect for him. He fought back the sick as best he could.

"Hide the merchandise in the back, then disappear. Come here just after 13:00, that is when the shop closes. I will have the instructions then," Venny said, with his nausea still hovering. The men went about their business swiftly and left in silence. That left Venny alone in his shop. A sudden cramp tugged at his gut. He ran outside and vomited a few times until there was nothing left. The cold air burned his lungs, and he looked up at the star-clad expanse above him. It looked as though the stars were all watching at him, judging him. Had he lost his mind?

THE BAZAAR

An icy blanket of frost greeted the few brave souls who camped in the church's large grounds in anticipation of Saturday's festivities. By the time the sun decided to illuminate the ice-covered town the first fires were already crackling, and the aroma of brewing coffee filled the morning air. There was not a cloud in the sky, nor a whisper in the air; it promised to be a cold day, but a wonderful one. A day where a symphony of people shared food and company, putting aside quibbles and sharing a drink, if only for a few hours.

The sun had not even started melting the frost when the roar of vehicles woke Dannhauser. Cars, trucks and even a couple of small lorries entered the church grounds and people started setting up their stalls in the pre-designated areas. Like ants with one clear goal in mind, they offloaded, arranged, carried tables, pitched gazebos, only occasionally stopping for a sip or two of piping hot coffee, lovingly prepared by the ever-dutiful sisters of the congregation.

These sisters were the true heartbeat of the Bazaar, but they were not to be messed with—they ran a tight ship. Everything went through them: from the allocations of stalls to decorations, tokens and how much and what type of oil should be used in the *koeksisters*. "This was purely to keep everyone happy," they would say, outwardly smiling but unable to hide the not-so-well-disguised threat.

Ultimately it all culminated in the day's grand finale: the Bazaar concert. This year Deanne de Lange along with the Reverend's wife was responsible for the concert. It wasn't just a role, but an announcement that one had made it to the very top of the sisters of the congregation hierarchy. Deanne had earned her stripes by flipping pancakes for ten straight hours every bazaar, for more years than she cared to re-member. She ran the stall with military precision, and every year it was one of the most successful stalls. This year, with her elevation to the right hand of the Reverend's wife, Eunice, a spinster with an insatiable appetite to please, was to be the new leader of the pancake brigade.

Pete was proud of his mom. She worked so hard in preparation and especially on the day of the bazaar, that every year without fail, she would be in bed with a terrible cold almost as soon as the last person left.

This year she seemed a little more relaxed. The Reverend's wife had developed the concert into a fine art over the years, so there was very little to do. Every concert followed the same routine, starting with a hymn performed by the pre-primary kids, and fin-ishing with a rousing rendition of the Call of South Africa. She told Pete's mom that it didn't really matter what happened in between, as long as no one was on stage for longer than ten minutes. To her, losing the crowd to boredom was the eighth and deadliest of all the sins.

Like most teenagers, Pete hated the bazaar. It was the same every year. The same people sold the same things in the same stalls year after year. There was very little to keep teenagers occupied once the gluttonous safari around the food stalls brought them to a point of near nausea. The little kids had a bouncing castle and treasure hunt and an array of other games, but the teenagers had only two things: target shooting with air rifles, and target throwing with knives. Although it was fun, it never lasted long, because before long a few of the farmers would have warmed themselves up nicely at the mampoer stand and would then take over the air rifles and knives, to prove once and for all who the best farmer was, or something. For teenagers, that meant going back to overeating and hanging around on bales of hay.

This year was different though. As always, he was there early to help his dad set up the *braai* stand he worked at every year. But his mind was only on one thing: the concert. He was happy to help his dad as it kept him busy, but he knew as soon as all the stalls were set up, and the bazaar was officially opened at ten, his day would be a long tedious one, waiting for the evening.

Then, of course, there was Barend. Although the school had started again on Wednesday, they had not spoken a word to each other. Barend used the junior bus again, and at school, he was always on Philippa's arm. It was as if he was trying to punish him. But, having replayed that doomed Sunday over in his mind a million times, he knew Barend was at fault, and he prayed that he would have come to the same conclusion during the holidays—so that they could just move on, be best friends again.

As he predicted, the minutes and even seconds

were crawling along. At times it felt like it was going backwards, from that moment when the Reverend opened the bazaar with Scripture reading and prayer. People started eating as if they had been starving themselves for weeks. There was a lot of handshaking, patting on the backs and the usual array of old ladies prowling in search of children to slop wet kisses on.

It was nearly midday when Pete first spotted Barend. To his surprise, Philippa was by his side and he wondered if she would still be considered cool if she was seen in Dannhauser—for a second time, no less! With them was Renate, who now seemed closer to Philippa than ever, which was far too confusing for his brain to understand, after their supposed spat. He wasn't even going to attempt to make sense of it: Some intricacies of the female species were beyond all male comprehension. On Renate's arm was a boy he had never seen before, and he wondered if that was the one from the city, her first. He decided to avoid them until he could speak to Barend alone, but the four of them paraded around like show horses, always side by side, never separating—they even went to the toilets in pairs.

Venny shut the shop a few minutes early. Luckily Achala's linen shop shut at twelve so she was busy cooking at home with Sarita, so there was no risk of her usual interference. Exactly at 13:00, the four men knocked on the door. There was an eagerness in their eyes that told him everything he needed to know about what they would choose if this was a democratic decision.

He put his half-smoked cigarette out and took a sip of the cold tea that was left on his counter. It tasted vile.

"Just as Protea Seven promised, I received orders this morning at 07:30." He took another sip of the tea, and it was even worse than the previous sip. The same nausea of the night before hovered in his throat. But the men's eyes were so full of hope, so full of pure, unquestionable commitment, it repressed the urgency of his queasiness. He looked them in the eye, one by one.

"We got the green light. The church bazaar is ours." He could feel his right leg shaking a little bit and started pacing to hide it.

"The concert starts at 18:00 and goes on until about 20:30. There is a break at 19:00, so we want to strike before the break, at 18:40. Meet me here at 17:00. I'll brief you on the building and all the details. In essence, it will be the same plan as last night, we just have a bigger hall to contend with and multiple entrances, so it will be high risk. There are a lot of people, so I repeat, it will be high risk. Does anyone feel uncomfortable with this?" Venny asked.

The men shot a quick glance at one another and then their leader simply said: "We're in."

The men left and Venny closed up, walked to his car and sat behind the wheel. He had gloves on, but his hands were shaking so much that he struggled to grip the steering wheel.

He played Protea Seven's monotone message in his mind.

"Negative Protea Eight, the operation is canceled

in its entirety. Release the team, go dark. Command does not consider religious targets viable at this point."

What did they know? It was okay to blow people's brains out in a shopping center, but not in a church hall? What was the difference? This would rattle the whites in bones they didn't even know they had. No, history wasn't made by those who followed orders, it was made by those who made decisions, and lived by them. He was doing the right thing. Protea Seven might disapprove, but once Command had seen the impact his decision made, any minor disregard for Protea Seven's order would be forgotten, and he would be hailed a hero. Something like this could spark the end of the whites, drive them back to their European pig farms. He lit a cigarette but just watched the heat burn away the paper until a long ash cylinder fell at his feet.

History was made by those who made hard decisions. History was made by those who made hard decisions, he repeated over and over in his mind.

Finally, Barend was separated from the herd. The other three entertained themselves with the knife throwing, while Barend left to replenish their pan-cakes supplies. Pete intercepted him just as he joined the queue.

"Howzit," Pete said.

"Hey," Barend said, looking away.

"How was the holiday?" Pete asked.

"Nice."

"Cool," Pete said and slipped his hands into his pockets.

"So, did you and Philippa...you know?" Pete asked with a teasing smile.

"It was a good holiday, okay," Barend said.

"What, are you just going to leave me hanging?" Pete said.

"Yes, that's the way it is now."

"The way it is now? What are you talking about?" Pete asked, but Barend's head was completely turned away from him like he was too detestable to look at.

"Ah, look who's here," Philippa called out from behind them.

"Everyone's favorite little kaffir-brother." Renate and her new boyfriend who stood beside her, burst out laughing.

"So, this is the oke?" Renate's new toy asked Barend.

Barend glanced at him quickly and then looked Pete straight in the eyes.

"Yup, that's the one." Barend's eyes had no life in them, except loathing, and that hurt more than the words. Pete had nothing. No words would form in his mouth, just a dry, bitter taste.

"Let's go look for the white queue, it smells like a mud hut here," Philippa said. The other three laughed as they walked away. Barend turned to follow them and bumped his shoulder against Pete's. He glared at Pete up and down and then wiped his shoulder as if a bird had soiled it, to the great delight of the others. Pete was left standing in the queue; others around him looked at him as if he had suddenly contracted leprosy. He walked away to the far corner of the grounds and sat on a tower of hay bales. People went about their business, people he had known his whole life, but they all looked like strangers, like he was parachuted into a foreign country or planet, and he was the only one of his kind.

In the distance, he saw a familiar face in the ocean of strangers. His dad walked to him with two *boere-wors* rolls in his hands. He climbed up the bales of hay, carefully balancing the rolls. At the top, he sat next to Pete and handed him one.

"It has everything on it, onions, tomato sauce, and mustard," Rikus said.

"Thanks," Pete said and took a bite.

"Quite a view from here," Rikus said and Pete just nodded, looking at the people who now appeared faceless, almost shapeless.

"I heard you and Barend had a bit of a scrap. Do you want to talk about it?" Rikus asked.

"Not really," Pete said.

His dad took a bite and chewed for a long time.

"You know, people say things they don't mean all the time. Mostly because they don't understand and then they react in the only way they know how— saying something stupid, hurtful. It's the way we're brought up. From a very young age you are taught two things: to be proud, and not to question things. Things are there for a reason, and it is not our place to challenge them. I was brought up that way, and I'm afraid I've brought you and your brothers up the same way. So, we end up with a nation that is too proud, or stubborn, to change. You can change a house, it takes planning, hard work and lots of money, but it can be done. A mind on the other hand...is not so easy."

Rikus put the rest of his *boerewors* roll down next to him and turned slightly toward Pete.

"Tell me what happened? You guys have been best friends for so many years, inseparable. I really would like to know why he attacked you like that out of no-where? Friends fight, that is normal, but not like that."

The *boerewors* roll lost all its taste, but Pete held on to it and focused his eyes on the white bread wrapped around the blackened sausage, covered in blood-red tomato sauce.

Pete drew a deep breath and started telling his dad about that Sunday, about the old man and about how Barend called him a kaffir-brother.

"I really thought he would have calmed down over the holiday, so I went to him today to make peace, but then he and his girlfriend called me all sorts of names ...treated me like I had the plague. Now everyone is staring at me like I'm some sort of freak."

"That asshole. Sorry," Rikus said, clenching his jaw, before taking a deep breath.

"Pete, no one who looks at the world with kindness will ever be seen as a freak. At least not in the eyes of the Lord. Unfortunately, the same cannot always be said of people. I'm sorry you had to go through that. I wish I could take it away.

"I want you to know Mom and I are so incredibly proud of you. You are such an amazing son, we're very proud." Rikus's voice broke a little, and he reached for his roll and took a large bite. Pete felt like he want-ed to hug his dad. He had never looked stronger than in that moment.

"You know, only yesterday, I saw a girl who was

first grabbed and then slapped by someone right there in the street outside Kismet, in broad daylight. This guy didn't give a damn, like he was untouchable. I shouted at him, and he made up some story that she stole his cigarettes. Ha! Like she was even capable of smoking, never mind taking something from his over-sized, grubby paws.

"Of course, like the coward he is, he walked away. I had to help her up. It was this Indian girl, long black hair—sweet looking, probably not much older than you." A piece of the bread got stuck in Pete's throat, it was dry and heavy. Sarita?

"She's a slight little thing, but a tough cookie, let me tell you. She got up and thanked me and apologized for the inconvenience. Imagine that, apologizing for being attacked!

"But that wasn't the end. That bloke who attacked her wanted to finish what he started. Thankfully, we're not talking about the sharpest tool in the shed here. He must've thought I'm blind or an idiot or both be-cause he just parked his car down the road in a small car park. I saw him drive in there and I could still see the hood of his truck. He just waited for her." Rikus rolled his eyes. "Lots of plans in that piece of trash's head. Nasty plans.

"So, I took her to her home. Crazy thing is, even though there weren't many people on the street, I still got a few colorful glances because I dared help an Indian girl up, comfort her, open the door for her, and heaven forbid! let her sit in the front with me. Today I actually heard one snide remark about my mis-deed. Mixing with *them*. Getting chummy-chummy with *them*. But what are we supposed to do?" Rikus shot a quick glance at Pete before he focused all his attention on his hands. Rubbing them together more for inspiration than for warmth. "Should you have left Barend to abuse that old man, or should I have left the girl in the claws of that monster? No, Pete, we couldn't. Doing the right thing isn't always the acceptable thing in the eyes of the world, if you know what I mean."

"Yeah, I think so." Pete picked at the hay, tried to hide the panic in his voice. "Uhhm, what happened to the girl?"

"I took her home, I must say they have a very nice house. Her dad is a shop owner I believe. She is really sweet, there is something almost...I don't know... something about her—she is one of those people who oozes happiness. I know it sounds odd, especially after she was attacked." Rikus shook his head. "Strange." Rikus seemed to be far removed all of a sudden.

"Sarita." Rikus said after a long pause.

"What?" Pete called out.

"Her name is Sarita. You know what's funny? In a small town like ours, an attack on the street like that is supposed to be a big thing, but I haven't told anyone about that here today, because I can't trust them enough to look beyond the fact that she is an Indian and I gave her a lift and let her sit next to me. Never mind the fact that a rabid wolf like Rudie is prowling the streets. And it's not even their fault, it is how we are brought up. We make such a big deal about the little things, that the herd of elephants in the room are just ignored, even though they are destroying everything."

"Did you say Rudie?" Pete asked.

"Ja, you know Uncle Rutger's son, the guy that was in the army for a long time?"

"Yes, I know him," Pete said, biting hard on his bottom lip.

"You know, with people like him, what he did yesterday and the stories about him killing farmworkers and who knows what else, there are moments when I almost understand the anger of these so-called freedom fighting terrorists. If you are subjected to that kind of thing long enough, maybe all of us would change," Rikus said.

"I much prefer the Martin Luther King school of peaceful demonstrations and non-violence," Pete said, but his mind could only see Rudie's yellow mustache in Sarita's face.

"Mmm. I suppose these guys are just so fed up with being kicked around that something in them snapped. But how can you ever justify gunning down innocent people like that day in Newcastle? Or blowing up restaurants and offices? It's all a bit of a mess, Pete, but all we can do is the right thing. We can't change the world, but we can make sure we're not part of the problem. We'll get our reward. Most probably not anytime soon, but somewhere in the future it will be waiting for us."

They sat in silence for a few minutes. The sun was starting to wilt as the evening approached and the day's meager warmth was fast replaced by a tangible coldness.

"I'd better go. We'll have to finish up before the sun goes down," Rikus said.

"Can I help?" Pete asked. His dad seemed shocked

by the offer but accepted gratefully. They climbed down the bales of hay and Pete helped dispose of all the rubbish, wiped down the tables and packed away half-empty bottles of condiments—anything to take his mind off the devil.

The men stood in front of him. They no longer looked like oversized thugs, but like soldiers—his soldiers. They wore their black uniforms, and they lived and breathed every word he said. He knew now these men would die for him, they would die for Venny Naidoo.

Venny's right hand kept fiddling with the pistol that rested in his jacket pocket. On this day he couldn't show any weakness, and if that meant carrying a gun, so be it.

"The church hall itself has two double-door entrances on either side of the building. The one faces the church and the other the field, where most of the stalls will be. At the rear of the building, there are two toilets. People will have to walk around the outside of the building to get to them because the only other way is across the stage, which wouldn't happen during the concert.

"The toilets are our biggest risk: Some baby or kid that needs to piss could expose us. For that reason, we will only plant one explosive on that side. We'll split into five groups, each covering a specific section. Spade, you will take the front right, Axe, you will take the front left, Bull, you will take back right, and you will plant two mines next to one another. I want that to be the core of the blast. Bones, you will take back left, and I will plant one in between the toilets at the rear.

"There should be a window of about ten minutes between 18:30 and 18:40 from when the slow ones finally make their way into the hall, and before the ladies who make the refreshments pop out. That's our slot. We will be waiting nearby at 18:25, at 18:31 plant the mines, and then five minutes later—we'll light up the sky. Questions?"

Venny almost felt as though someone else was talking, like he was a general and his troops were about to embark on the final battle for earth. The feeling was indescribable.

Spade raised his hand. "Will there be a hiding place for us after planting the bombs, before detonation?"

"Spade, you and Axe will hide in the street, as you are at the front of the building on the street side. It would be too dangerous to join us. Try to get a little further away, closer to the car. The rest of us will hide behind the cars parked opposite the toilets, on the church's side. After the blast, we will sneak away using the cars as cover. There will be so much chaos that I am confident we can get away unnoticed.

"Remember to activate the timer on the explosives as soon as they are planted, that will give us five minutes to get away from the blast zone." Venny smiled. "And then they all go boom!"

"Shouldn't we just plant them and go, why wait for the blast?" Bones asked.

"You guys can go, but I want to be close in case there is a detonation issue," Venny said, but he knew they could see that he just wanted to be there, a first-hand witness of his handiwork.

"I'll wait with you," Bull said.

"Good, so Bull and I will meet you at the car. If we are not there within five minutes after the explosion, just go. Park the car at my house and disappear," Venny said.

The four men nodded, happy with the plan. Venny looked at his watch, it was 17:57. A knot of excited terror churned in his gut. He did feel a little sick, but also like he could run outside, spread his arms, and fly.

"You're going to be great, I know it. Break a leg, okay," Deanne said, squeezing Pete's hand.

"Thanks, Ma. And thanks for the sheets."

"I have been looking for a reason to get rid of them for a long time, besides, Christina did all the hard work, you should thank her."

"I did. She's quite something," Pete said.

"That's for certain," Deanne said, smiling a bitter-sweet smile.

"What time am I on?"

"Six-thirty. I will see you afterward. I have to get things started otherwise the poor Reverend's wife's heart won't take it. I love you," Deanne said, brushed her hand over Pete's cheek and paced toward the stage.

Pete looked at his watch but didn't register the time. His mind was riddled with doubt and fear, and everything in between. He walked outside in the cold evening air. It was pitch dark, and the cool air in his lungs calmed him somewhat.

"Good evening, Pete," Captain Burger said, standing right next to him.

Pete forgot how to speak. He wanted to hold his wrists out so that he could just be arrested and forget about the world in the sanctity of a prison cell.

"Have you seen any good crimes lately?" Captain Burger said with a broad smile revealing too many wrinkles to count. Pete was sure he would either vomit or faint, most likely both and then he would choke to death on his vomit and he would die without anyone ever knowing.

"Rudie kidnapped an Indian girl called Sarita and tried to rape her and when we tried to stop him, he shot at us. It happened in January. I'm sorry I didn't tell you—" Pete's mouth suddenly lost all moisture, and his eye was itching like it had never done before.

"Slow down, Pete. What?" Captain Burger placed his hand on Pete's shoulder and leaned closer. "Those are serious allegations. Are you talking about Uncle Rutger's Rudie?"

"Howzit, Captain, howzit, young Petrus." Rudie walked toward them from the bright lights of the hall's veranda, cupping a cigarette between his thumb and middle finger.

"I must go," Pete said and walked away as quickly as he could without running. He could hear Captain Burger calling out after him, but soon he was in the toilet, standing over the bowl waiting to throw up. But nothing came.

"Ladies and gentlemen, please take your seats; the concert is about to begin." His mom's voice echoed over the microphone. He could hear the shuffling of people and chairs, coughing, kids calling out and he knew he had to pull it together. He'd have to deal with Captain Burger later.

The Reverend's wife appeared on stage and welcomed all in her usual array of well-crafted adjectives. She told everyone that this was the most successful Bazaar ever like she did every year, and she was particularly proud that in a tough year, a year of drought and terrorist attacks, people still came together and poured their effort and hard-earned money into the church. It was a touching speech, and more than a few damp eyes shimmered under the neon lights.

After her speech, the lights went out and the curtains opened. A bright spotlight illuminated the twenty tiny kids on stage, each cupping their hands like the sopranos of old, exactly like they were told.

Like every year they received a standing ovation. People loved them. However, the same could not be said of Aunty Nelia who came on after them. She was doing some Italian operatic piece a grave disservice. A few men sought ways to slip away to have a cigarette but were stopped by threatening glances from their wives.

Thankfully a comedy sketch by five primary school boys lifted the mood. The crowd loved it and roared with laughter, cheering excessively as the curtains were drawn.

When the laughter subsided, the Reverend's wife took the stage, praising the wonderful comedic talents of these young stars.

There was no one around. The streets were deserted. Not a car could be heard, and no lights were on in any of the houses. The only beacon of brightness was the light streaming out of the church hall.

They left the car a block away behind a few trees, out of view. Now they were walking in the darkness with their sports bags in hand, pistols on the hip, with complete focus. They stopped just outside the church, Venny gave them the signal and they all covered their faces with balaclavas. He pointed to Spade and Axe to go around on the right, to the front of the building. He shook both their hands before they set off, shoulders low like foxes.

The other two followed him as they snuck from car to car, to just outside the church hall. They could hear the laughter inside, but there was not a soul in sight. The toilets were no more than twenty meters from them. He pointed Bull and Bones to the sides they needed to go to and then jogged with his back stooping low toward the toilets. The only thing he could think of was how much he wanted a cigarette. He could almost taste the sweet Gunston perfume stroking his insides, but he had to remain focused, ready, alert.

There was an outside light above the men's toilet but as luck would have it, a wonderfully dark patch above the ladies' toilets. His senses had become heightened. Everything around him disappeared. His ears pricked for the faintest creak, but all he could hear was a woman making some announcement inside the hall.

He lifted the explosive out of the bag. His hands were surprisingly steady. He stuck the device right in the heart of the dark patch and with great care, let go. He took a step back. It stuck.

He drew a deep breath and exhaled slowly. His thoughts took him to the newspaper clipping above his desk in his operations room, of the Indian woman being beaten by a policeman. He thought of her face: the absolute despair. Then he remembered what she really looked like when she wasn't being beaten by police. He recalled her near blue eyes that could scan every millimeter of his soul with one glance. He could feel her touch, her smile. It was his most precious and wonderful Ruhi. He should have been there that day when she protested, he should have been there to protect her, to save her from being taken away like an animal. To die.

"This is for you, Ruhi," Venny whispered and pulled the wire on the side of the device. He looked at it one last time and then ran, without looking or seeing anything around him. He ran with everything his short legs had until he flopped down behind a blue 1978 Ford Cortina. It took him a few moments before he realized Bull and Bones were there too. They gave him the thumbs up and Bones slipped away, leaving him and Bull to be spectators of their own concert.

"Next up is a performance simply titled *Shadows*. I for one am very excited, so please put your hands together and give a warm Dannhauser welcome for our young performer. *Shadows*, ladies and gentle-men." The Reverend's wife waved to the stage as if she was a magician's assistant, and she was rewarded with a half-hearted round of applause.

The curtains opened and the front of the stage was completely covered by a few sewn-together white bedsheets. A bright light illuminated the bedsheet canvas to make it appear as if it was the source of the light. A few heads turned, a few questions whispered, a few shoulders shrugged: This was not one of the usual items in the concert, and a buzz of excitement grew as the canvas stood blank for a few moments.

"Tonight, I am going to reveal one of the world's greatest secrets." Pete de Lange's voice cut through the expectant silence. He was nowhere to be seen; it was only the illuminated white canvas on stage.

"All these years they have been among us since time began, yet we have never known their secret. Until now. When you walk down the street, have you ever noticed your shadow?"

A few kids in the crowd excitedly whispered stories about their shadows to each another until their parents hushed them.

"Of course, you have seen them, but have you ever asked yourself what happens to them while you are safely tucked away in your bed at night and sleeping peacefully?" The children were quieter now, their eyes glued on the canvas.

"Last night, I woke up in the middle of the night. All was quiet, everyone asleep. I needed fresh air, so I stepped outside, but something moved, and I ran, fearing the worst, but knowing that if it was an intruder he had to be chased away. Ladies and gentlemen, it wasn't an intruder.

"Behind the back wall of our garage, with the stars sparkling in the sky, I saw a shadow, hiding. I looked around but there was no one, just a shadow. I called out: 'Hey!' But it remained unmoving. So, I stepped closer."

The kids were now sitting on the edges of their seats, and a few adults too. There was not a sound to be heard, except the buzzing of the speakers.

"All of a sudden he jumped up!" A shadow appeared behind the canvas that looked like it was inside the sheets. People gasped and a few children shrieked. A man-sized broad-shouldered shadow filled the stage, standing nervously, twitching, as if it wanted to run away.

"I said, 'Wait, don't run. How do you do that? Where is your...person?' He looked afraid and I walked closer as slowly as I could. He bent down a little, petrified, then I said, 'What's your name?' The shadow stood up again and he whispered so softly that I had to ask again. He said, 'Iri, my name is Iri.' I said to him, 'How could it be?' And this is what he told me:

"He said that late at night when people are asleep, shadows are set free. They always feel, and they always know, even when people do horrible things, but at night, they are free, and life is worth living. I asked him where he was from and what he was doing there, and then he told me his story."

The crowd stared at the statuesque presence of the shadow on stage. No one moved and suddenly everyone wanted to hear Iri's story.

"Iri comes from a place far away. It is called Dannbauser." The crowd laughed, thankful for some release of tension.

"It is a strange place, everyone has gray skins and massive eyes. There is a river that runs through town, called the Tupela." A few people chuckled.

"On the one side of the river all the rich people lived in big fancy houses. They drove cars similar to what we know as a Mercedes-Benz. They didn't do much work, but they have always had money, passed on from generation to generation. They were known as the Luteras. On the other side of the river lived the Kuttas. They lived in tents and slept under trees. There was no money and very little food. They worked from morning till night for the Luteras, but often for little more than a piece of bread.

"This was the way it always was since the day before forever began. Luteras and Kuttas never mixed, never spoke, unless a Lutera gave a Kutta an order."

For a moment it was so quiet in the hall one could hear a pin drop.

"On a lovely bright summer's day Iri was casting a shadow for his person, a Lutera man named..." Pete hesitated for a moment. "...Rudie," he said muted, as if he was asking for permission.

"They strolled along the edge of the river toward the only bridge that connected the two parts of town." Pete's voice had regained its power. "Rudie was a bad man, but he was big and strong, and everyone feared him." The crowd laughed as the shadow flexed his muscles like a bodybuilder. Sitting right in the middle of the audience, Rudie slid down in his seat, peering around, spotting one or two people looking at him. He pulled his cap lower over his brow.

"In the corner of his eye, he saw a beautiful Kutta girl picking flowers on the opposite side of the river." The shadow of a girl appeared in the bottom right-hand corner of the canvas, pretending to pick flowers. The man's shadow turned toward her.

"Iri glanced at the magnificent shape of the girl's shadow and wondered if one night he would be able to find her. But Rudie, big, bad, evil Rudie, had other plans. He wanted to steal her, make her his slave, make her work in his cellar all the hours of all the days until her beauty was no more. Kuttas did not deserve beauty, and he would take it away.

"So he snuck across the bridge so that no one saw him." The male shadow hunched and crept melodramatically. But the crowd didn't laugh, they were too anxious to learn what was going to happen.

"She was singing a song, mesmerized by the beauty of the wildflowers." A girl's voice started humming a melody that no one in the crowd knew. It was as haunting as it was beautiful.

"She didn't see Rudie until it was too late. She tried to run but he had her. He grabbed her tight and regardless of how much she kicked, this evil man was just too strong for her." One of the moms contemplated whether her five-year-old daughter might be too young for this story as the shadow of the girl kicked the air behind the canvas, but she remained, unable to move.

"The girl's shadow pleaded with Iri in their secret language, which people can't hear, 'Please do something, please do something.' But what could he do, he was only a shadow?"

Pete was silent for a minute, then continued:

"Shadows have to follow every single movement of their people, no matter how bad, or how much they don't want to—they have no choice. Iri became so frustrated and mad that he wanted to scream, but all that came were his shadow tears dripping on the ground. You might have seen them; when they fall to the ground they turn into prickly thorns. He cried and cried but nothing helped. Rudie carried the girl toward the bridge. The girl's shadow kept pleading: 'Help, help, please help.'

"But what could he do, he was just a shadow?

"At that moment the sun was directly behind them and Iri saw himself against the bridge. For once he was bigger than Rudie! He looked at the girl and then at her shadow, and something deep inside him stirred, something he had never felt before. With everything he had in him, he clenched his shadow teeth, and closed his shadow eyes and pulled, and pulled. When he opened his eyes, he was shocked: He stood apart from Rudie, free. He waved and flapped his arms like a madman. His arms looked like giant eagle-wings spread against the bridge. Rudie was startled and dropped the girl as he searched the skies in confused terror for this evil winged monster. Then he spun around and ran as fast as he could, across the bridge and straight into his house where he locked the door behind him.

"Iri was there, back with Rudie. His freedom short-lived, but it didn't matter, he had saved her." A few moments of silence followed, the audience's hearts racing.

"Now Iri and the girl's shadow, Suri, are best friends. Every night when Dannbauser is asleep, they run to the bridge where they smile and weep together.

"That, ladies and gentlemen, is Iri's story. So tonight, when you're cozy in your bed, and sleep takes you away, dream about your shadows, as they go out and play. But just remember one thing, and this Iri asked: When you cast your shadow, do what's right and don't be like Rudie who leaves a trail of prickly thorns in his wake." Behind the illuminated bedsheets the two shadows moved to the center of the stage holding hands and then bowed twice.

The crowd sat in silence for a few moments before Deanne jumped to her feet and applauded with great vigor, followed by Rikus, and Aunty Eunice, the Reverend and then everyone else. The only two people who remained seated were Captain Burger and Rudie. Captain Burger glanced across to a stark-looking Rudie, their eyes meeting briefly before Rudie looked down at the drink in his hand and took a large sip.

The curtains were drawn, and Pete pulled down the sheets as quickly as he could, rolled it into a make-shift ball and cast it into the corner of the stage. He handed the microphone back to the Reverend's wife, who gave him an approving smile, and then raced behind the stage, dancing down the steps which led to the corridor behind the toilets.

His two shadows waited for him there. They were covered from head to toe in suits made with great skill by Christina out of old bedsheets. The only thing sticking out was their eyes, and in them, Pete could see both shadows smiling gleefully—the one very dark pair of eyes, and the other those most amazing translucent hazelnut ones, which took his breath away every time.

"We did it," Pete said.

"It was so amazing," Petrus whispered.

"You guys were sensational, thank you so much," Pete said.

"I wouldn't have missed this for the world. I think along with the Halley's Comet night this must be the best day of my life," Sarita said.

It was funny to see only their eyes sticking out, they looked so different, yet unmistakably them, unmistakably his friends.

"Do you think anyone could tell who we were?" Petrus asked.

"No chance, they were captivated. That's the beauty of small towns, it doesn't take much to amuse people," Pete said, smiling.

"You are too hard on yourself. That was brilliant. You are a genius, seriously," Sarita said.

Petrus looked over his shoulder. "We must go before people see us," Petrus whispered.

"I know, I wish you could stay, but I know," Pete said and looked at his watch. "Thank you for taking this massive risk for me. I wish I had the words to express how much this means to me. You guys are amazing."

Petrus raised his hands. "That's what friends are for."

"It was more than a pleasure, it was a privilege. And to do this with you two, my best friends, is something that will live inside me forever. I'm going to cry,"

Sarita said.

"Don't cry, you'll wet your bedsheet," Pete said, and the three of them chuckled in muffled silence.

Petrus stuck out his hand and Pete grabbed it. They shook hands and spent a silent moment looking at one another. Pete nodded.

"I asked *baas* Gerrit about doing Matric," Petrus said as an afterthought.

"What?" Pete called out a little louder than he should have and looked behind him guiltily. "That's great! What did he say?"

"He said yes. I'm doing Matric. It's going to be through the post, but he said that would be a better quality Matric anyway. I'm doing it."

"That is the best news! Well done," Pete said.

"I'm so proud of you, Petrus, you are going to do so well," Sarita said.

"Oh, before I forget," she added, "here." She took two folded pieces of paper out of a hole in her sheet and handed one to each.

"What's this?" Petrus asked.

"Just something small. Read it later."

"Okay, I'll see you outside," Petrus said to Sarita, curled his hand around the piece of paper and slipped through the men's toilet to the outside.

Pete slipped the piece of paper in his pocket and stepped closer to hug Sarita, but she stopped him. She pulled off her white face-hugging mask and smiled at him, her dimples even more beautiful than usual. His heart was racing. All he wanted to do was take her in his arms and kiss her until the universe ceased to exist. But he fought the urge as best he could.

"You are beautiful, you know? Absolutely beautiful," Pete said and tried to swallow. "I heard about yesterday, about *him*, I'm so sorry."

"It was your dad who saved me, wasn't it?" she asked.

"Yup."

"A family of heroes, it seems. My heroes." Her eyes fixed on his. "Pete, yesterday, I was afraid, but now I'm not afraid anymore. He is just a big ugly monster and I think somewhere between Halley and the white sheets tonight I finally locked him away in a cupboard. And I threw away the key. Life is so much better without fear. Besides, I now have a father-son team of heroes to protect me." She smiled shyly casting her eyes to the floor.

"I...I, you are just so...I think you are the...I think I am...I am..." Pete tried, but Sarita shuffled closer, so close that it felt as if she was part of his skin.

"Me too." She smiled. Their eyes met, the world shut down, noise, color, everything except her. His hand searched for her face, then his fingers pulled her closer. He could no longer contain the yearning inside, like a fire, igniting everything around it. Her eyes shut, but he kept his open. He did not want to miss any of this. Their lips met. It was like an electric shock, not one that hurt, rather one that brought you back to life. It sent blazing bolts of energy to every cell in his body. Her lips were soft, sweet like plums and warm. It quenched a deep thirst he did not know he had. She pushed her body into his and he pulled her even closer. The earth stopped turning. He was a hot air balloon and she the fire. He was ready to lift off. And never come down.

416

Footsteps.

They ignored it. Locked in the moment. So close that Pete thought they could never be split apart. Forged together, there behind the stage, she dressed in white sheets, he overcome by her.

The footsteps became louder, urgent, from the stage coming toward them. They pulled apart, gobsmacked. Her face was glowing, and she was short of breath. She jumped forward and kissed him again. Lingering. His heart stopped. When she slowly released her lips from his, she gently stroked her fingers over her lips as if she wanted to capture him there for all eternity. She whispered a barely audible "wow." A look of complete wonderment on her face, her eyes almost asking if this had truly happened. Pete smiled back, the same wonderment filled him, he nodded as if to confirm to both of them that this wasn't just a dream. Then, as the footsteps reached the set of four steps leading to the passageway where they stood, she winked, pulled her mask over her head, turned and disappeared through the ladies' toilet. A couple of boys almost ran him over, but he hardly noticed. He was certain he was going to lift off and float to heaven. Her taste lingered in his mouth, all the way back across the stage and out on the side, where he joined his mom and dad in the fourth row from the front. They both smiled at him with pride, but all he wanted to do was shout his unbridled joy out to the mountain tops. He wanted to grab the microphone and proclaim what magic had just happened. But he sat quietly smiling, carefully touching his lips every few seconds–recalling the moment she whispered "wow," recalling every single aspect of the most enchanting moment the world had ever known—and watched as the Koekemoer family performed their annual *Sound of Music* tribute.

"Shit! Why is it taking so long? They should have gone off thirty seconds ago," Venny whispered to Bull.

"Let's give it a minute, perhaps the timers aren't too accurate," Bull said.

"We don't have a minute, soon people will start coming out, and then they might notice the devices, evacuate, call the army, and all will be in vain."

Venny was now so desperate for a cigarette he was willing to blow his cover.

"Patience, Protea Eight," Bull said.

"Don't talk to me about patience. I've waited for this moment for over five years. I cannot accept failure, it has to happen and it has to happen now!" Venny stood up, but Bull pulled him back down with such force that he landed on his backside.

"You're going to get us killed. Look." Bull pointed toward the toilets. A figure wrapped in white sheets stood outside, pacing anxiously.

"Who the hell is that, some Ku Klux Klan wannabe? What are we going to do now?" Venny asked.

"We wait till he disappears, then we have to go."

"No! I will not go until that bloody bunch of white racist scum are blown to pieces," Venny said.

"We'll be in pieces if we don't get away right now. These devices are old Soviet issued mines that have been passed from one country to the next for who knows how long, perhaps they don't even work anymore. It's better to get out now and live to fight another day."

"There won't be another day. Not for me. The Struggle will continue, but Dannhauser will be forgotten, it will just be another small shithole full of pricks like me."

"Crap, I think people are starting to leave. There's another one," Bull said. Venny watched as another figure dressed in white walked out of the toilets, the ladies' this time.

The two figures talked, and then hugged, before the one that was out first ran toward the darkness of the field on the opposite side of the church hall. The other figure ran toward them.

"If he gets too close, I'll have to shoot." Bull said, resting the shaft of the pistol against his forehead.

"It's a she," Venny said, watching on as the figure ran toward him. There was something familiar in the unrestricted, joyful, childlike run of this woman. He knew it, he knew it well.

"Sarita?" he whispered.

She came closer, her arms swinging freely, and although her face was covered, he could sense her smile, her unbridled joy. The world slowed. Bull and his gun faded, so did the car behind which they were hiding, the church, the hall, it was just him and his little girl and she was running toward him.

Then an immense, all-engulfing light flashed behind her like a moon exploding. He knew it must have been loud, but he didn't hear it. He watched as the wall where he had placed the mine slowly disintegrated and bricks, mortar, and glass were sent into the cold winter air like arrows of hate.

He wanted to call out, but his mouth had no feeling. He wanted to jump up and run to her, but his legs lay lifeless under him.

A single red brick appeared out of the blinding light.

It shot through the darkness like a rocket. He had to stop it, but his voice was mute, and body lame. He couldn't stop it. Even though he could see its target, he couldn't. Mute. Lame. The brick piercing the darkness struck its white, sheet-clad target, and then fell to the side. As if it was innocent. Harmless.

"We have to go," Bull pulled on Venny's arm, but he could not look away. The bedsheet had a red spot now and red was spreading.

"We have to go." Bull plucked him off his feet and ran with him draped over his shoulder. Venny looked back, his senses flickering, sounds slowly filling the night—screams, cries, shouts. And a bedsheet stained with blood.

"It wasn't her. It wasn't her. It wasn't her," Venny kept mumbling all the way to the car.

"Are you unharmed, are you okay?" the Reverend asked as he made his way through the stunned mass of people standing outside the church hall, bunching close together.

He saw the white-and-red figure lying under a tree, and he saw one of his elders running toward it. Then he started running too, for the first time in twenty years. Seconds later he dropped to his haunches completely out of breath next to his elder who kneeled beside the body.

The elder looked at him as though asking for permission. He nodded. Then, as gently as he could, the elder removed the bloodstained mask. Blood was like a sticky syrup in the person's long black hair. With shaking hands, the elder slowly rolled the body over.

"Oh, it's a coolie," he said with a sigh of relief.

"There are more bombs. Get out! Everyone, get as far away as possible," Captain Burger shouted from the hall. People scattered like a herd of impala being chased by lions. The Reverend looked in shock at the elder as he jumped up and ran away. Then the Reverend bent down, took the lifeless body of a young Indian girl in his arms, and ran for the second time in twenty years.

RUBBLE

It was nine o'clock. A bitter wind howled outside, flaying open the rubbled remains of the church hall's toilets. It was cold in the church, but there was not a single empty seat. Everyone who had been shocked into disbelief the night before sat in black and gray jackets, waiting for something: hope perhaps, or sense.

Pete didn't want to go to church, but like all the others, he was there, not knowing why, not understanding the tear inside him, a chasm, growing every second, taking with it everything in its wake—his heart, his soul.

The pain was unbearable like he had swallowed razor wire and it sat in his gut, and a heavyweight boxer was pounding away at him, every blow slicing him apart. He couldn't sleep, nor did he want to. He had to hold on to her for as long as he could.

When the first whispers of the victim reached him, he knew.

"Would you believe it, it was an Indian girl?" people said. It could only ever be Sarita, the most perfect being he had ever met. And why would it not be? They tried to cheat nature, pretended for a moment as if nothing but them mattered, nothing but happiness. But clearly, it mattered.

He was angry, strangely and although he wanted to be, not with God. He wanted to shout in the church and up to the heavens, "Why?" But he couldn't, this wasn't God's work. It was the work of the devil, whispering in the ears of monsters, and they ripped her away from him. Or perhaps it was all his fault. If it wasn't for him, she would have been at home, safe, and no one would have died. He could have met up with Petrus in the afternoon outside the Eating House and gone to her. She would have opened the door smiling, giving them Cokes...and the chasm inside him kept growing.

He wondered if he would just flop to the ground like a plastic bag, empty, used, once the chasm had devoured everything inside him. But first he had to find them, the monsters, he had to. He scratched his right eye and ran his fingers through his hair. She would hate revenge, he thought. But how could he let this go? How could he just stand aside and let this go?

He hadn't even noticed the Reverend walking up to the pulpit, nor did he realize that the opening prayer was over already, and he hadn't even joined the other men and boys as they stood.

"Brothers and sisters of the congregation," the Reverend started, and Pete looked up at the old man with large black circles under his eyes, hoping for something that would make all this pain go away.

"Today, I won't keep you long. This is a time to be with your families, with the ones you love." The words were like another boxer joining in, punching away at his gut. Pete dropped his head.

"Last night our church, our community, was attacked. It was a cold, cowardly act by those who had been seduced by evil. But I am not here this morning to speak about them, although we must pray that the Lord enters their hearts so that they would never commit such acts ever again.

"There were six explosive devices planted around the church hall last night. If all six had detonated as they should have, this church would have been empty today. Our community would have been wiped out. But by some miracle, and may I say, through grace alone, not by our good virtue, were we saved from this great catastrophe. And we should go on our knees every day we are spared and thank the Almighty for His grace, His amazing grace.

"Except for a few scratches and bruises, not a single person from our congregation and community was hurt—that is a miracle. But lest we forget, one of the bombs did explode. With great force, it reduced the rear of our church hall to rubble. But it is only bricks and mortar. In this church, there are no idle hands and therefore it will be rebuilt. No, the damage from the explosion was far greater, infinitely so, than mere bricks. It stole a young life." The Reverend stopped, his voice was almost breaking, and he took a sip of water, his hands quivering. Pete cried openly. He sat with his head in his hands and wept. Deanne shuffled closer and rested her hand on his back.

"Last night I had the torturous privilege to hold her lifeless body in my arms, as I carried her away amidst the threat of further peril. Her face was calm, almost smiling, and there was a peace about her. It was almost...angelic.

"She was beautiful and young, but her body was dead in my arms. I had never felt so powerless. A life filled with promise, so cruelly taken away. Her name was Sarita, Sarita Naidoo, and she was sixteen years old." The Reverend's eyes were pink with tears. Pete had sunk even deeper into his hands as if hearing her name made it more real like the final illogical hope was taken from him. His mom kissed him on the shoulder, and in the distance, on the deacon's pews, she saw Rikus wiping away a tear.

"I met her mother this morning. Her face told me more than her words ever could. She is a broken woman. Her eyes had no life as if the switch inside her was turned off. I prayed with her, but she did not hear, not because she is Hindu, but because the pain had made her blind, and deaf.

"Brothers and sisters, I am telling you this because I feel ashamed. I feel like I have failed God and failed you. A child from our extended community died last night, forty meters from where I am standing right now, and you know what our reaction was? We were relieved. Because it wasn't one of *us*...it was one of *them*. Thank the Lord it was one of them, we thought.

"How dare we! Are we somehow better in the eyes of the Lord? Are we not all the same before Him? How dare we be relieved about the death of a beautiful young girl and who gives a damn if she was Indian or white!

"Shame on us. Shame on me, and shame on you. Tonight, we should kneel in front of the Lord in thanksgiving for His grace that saved us, but we should tear our clothes and weep before him that we have so greatly sinned that we counted ourselves as better. Worst still, as if our lives supposedly count more than those of others. Pray hard, weep hard, the Lord is merciful, but we have sinned greatly." The Reverend's voice was softer now, trembling as the tears rolled over the wrinkles on his face.

"On Wednesday afternoon, the Naidoo family and the rest of the Indian community will lay Sarita to rest. Let us act like Christians for once and support them in their time of grief.

"I know they are different, pray to a different god, eat different food, have different color skin, but the grieving is the same. The pain...the same.

"Let us go there and show them the body of Christ." The Reverend grabbed his mouth and took a few moments to compose himself.

"The funeral is at four o'clock. Don't go because some old fool on a pulpit asked you, no, ask yourself: Would Jesus have gone, or would He have turned a blind eye?

"Close your eyes." The men did not have time to react before the Reverend started praying.

"Lord, be thou merciful to me a sinner. Amen." The Reverend wiped his tears away and walked down the steps and out to his chambers. The congregation sat in silence for a few moments, taking in his words. Auntie Betty shuffled closer to the organ, dabbed her tears away with a handkerchief, and started playing "Silent Night."

Pete listened to the melody as she played, and even though it was July, it felt right. He could see Sarita's face clearly now, for the first time since she was taken.

She was perfect.

He fell onto his mom's shoulder and cried as though he would never be able to stop. Deanne stroked his hair, and after the song had finished playing and people left in silence, Rikus joined them and put his arms around Pete and Deanne.

THE ROCK

After the church service had ended Pete went to his bedroom. There was no Sunday School, no coffee or tea after the service and all but a few had left for their respective homes the moment Auntie Betty's rendition of "Silent Night" had ended.

Pete could not eat. In fact, he didn't even know if his mom had cooked lunch. He went straight to his room and his parents let him be. His mind had seemingly seized up. Thoughts trickled slowly and with great difficulty, like, thick, stinking, unrefined molasses.

The only thought he could decipher among the thick darkness of his thoughts was the face of Petrus. He had to see him. He had to. As soon as possible. There was no question about it.

When Pete awoke it was Monday already. He had no idea anyone could sleep for that long. Stranger still, he had no idea someone could sleep for that long and be just as tired as when he went to bed. Perhaps even more.

His parents allowed him to stay home from school. He was immeasurably grateful but didn't think he was able to express this to them. But he suspected they knew.

When 16:00 rolled around he was already at the rock. Standing about ten meters away from it. Staring at it. The multitude of images crisscrossing his mind became a blurry patchwork. His mind could not retain a single image. There were too many.

As he stood there, he wondered how he got there. Did he run? Walk?

A new image appeared. A silhouette. He had trouble decerning it against the images spinning in his mind. Was it real? Was it a memory?

"Pete!"

He kept staring at the source of the sound—the silhouette coming closer. No matter how hard he tried—even squinting, tilting his head—he could not make it out.

"Pete!"

"Pete!"

The third "Pete" was like a fist into an opaque mirror. The glass shattered, light started streaming through, the images in his mind dissipated, the blurriness gone, the spinning too. He could see again. The silhouette was not an imagining. The sound not an echo of some past conversation.

Petrus was in front of him. Standing a few feet away. Uncertain. His eyes puffy, tired, moist.

It was too much for Pete. He could not look at the only person in the world he thought he wanted to see. The tears in Petrus's eyes were too real. Said too much. Said things he was not prepared to hear.

The tears came. But not alone. It brought with it sobbing, his whole body shook, his legs became wobbly and the hard, beaten earth under his feet became a spongy, tottering mess. Like the mud in the dam, that night when it all began.

Petrus's hands shot to his face, covering almost every inch of it. Yet tears still seeped through the gaps between his fingers, the pain hidden behind his hands just as evident as if he had not covered his face.

They stood there, feet apart, weeping, with the rock in the distance and the mountains on the horizon cloaked behind a dark veil of cloud. Like it was weeping too. The sun hidden somewhere behind this veil, not able to face this great hurt.

Eventually the ground under foot firmed somewhat. The sobbing subsided, the tears stopped rolling but remained welled-up in his eyes. But none of the pain had disappeared. In fact, Pete longed for those few glorious moments before Petrus arrived when everything was a blur, and his heart didn't feel like it was being hacked out with a panga.

Petrus wiped the tears from his face, but only half succeeded. He sought out Pete's gaze, gestured with his head toward the rock and started walking. Pete followed.

They did not sit on the rock, just stood next to it, afraid to touch it. "My grandfather had a heart-attack when I was nine," Petrus said, his eyes fixed on the uneven stubbly surface of the rock. "I asked him when he came back from hospital whether it was the most pain he had ever experienced." A tear escaped Petrus's eye, he swallowed, the grief gushing up, he drew a short breath. "My grandfather laughed, said 'no.' He said it was nothing compared to the pain he felt when his twin sister died when he was still a boy." Tears were again streaming down his face. Somehow, he managed to continue speaking. "I now understand what he meant." He looked up at Pete, biting his lip. "I feel it," he said, then punched his fist against his heart twice. "I feel it."

"I'm so angry," Pete said. "I'm so, so angry." He glanced at the horizon, searching in vain for the mountains hidden behind the grayness. "I just want to—" He took a few steps away from Petrus. The proximity too much for him. It was making words impossible to articulate. Then, out of the deepest part of him, he screamed. It didn't sound like him, but he felt it reverberate inside him, scraping his throat. He screamed again, and again. And again.

Petrus remained standing, next to the rock, shaking his head, pursing his lips, feeling each scream as if it were his own.

"It's not fair," Pete shouted when his last scream evaporated into the still air. "It's not fair!" His voice was croaky and cracked. Petrus shook his head more and more until something broke, his face contorted.

"Why wasn't it me?" Pete said. "Hell, why was it anybody? None of the other bombs exploded, why did that one?"

"No," Petrus said, raising his head a fraction, "it should have been me. If I had stayed with her, walked her home...something, I could have protected her."

Pete shook off the idea. "No, no, no. Then both of you would have...no. It's my fault. If I hadn't come up with that stupid plan of involving the two of you in the concert, then—"

"Pete," Petrus said, the tears stopped, he walked up to Pete and touched his arm so that Pete would meet his pressing gaze. "It wasn't stupid. It was right. It will always be right."

"How can it be right?" Pete asked, flapping his arms and hands open. "What's right about it? She is—" He still couldn't bring himself to say it. "Look what happened. Nothing is right about what happened, Petrus. Nothing. And it's my fault."

Petrus placed his hand on his hair and dug his fingers into his scalp, rubbing it in a circular motion, with each rotation he pressed harder. "What do you think Sarita would say if you asked her if she would do it all again?"

Pete knew the answer. Petrus didn't even have to ask. But he couldn't, wouldn't accept it, even though he could see Sarita's reaction to that very question, her utter disbelief that they even considered not going ahead with the plan.

"That's not the point," Pete said, "if she had left right away—"

"Pete, no—"

"I kissed her," Pete blurted out. The tears which had momentarily ceased were back. All the pain of before compounded into that one utterance. "If I hadn't kissed her, then, then—"

"You kissed?" Petrus's mouth was slightly agape.

"I know, how ridiculous, how selfish."

"Did she kiss you back?"

Pete was startled by the question, staring quizzically at Petrus. "Well, yes."

Petrus couldn't hold the gaze, his face lapsed into his hand, grief rising up from him like a mist. It looked like he wanted to say something but couldn't. Pete waited. He had no idea if he had just done something wrong, said the wrong thing. At this point his mind was having trouble decoding the most basic of messages, which this one wasn't.

Petrus finally spoke through his sobs. "She told me the night of the concert, when we met up before it started, that her heart had betrayed her mind, her common sense. Those were her exact words. I knew exactly what she meant; she didn't need to explain. So ..." Petrus wiped the tears away with his right hand. "I'm just happy. That's all. Happy for her. Happy for you. For that moment."

It was all too much. The weight of Petrus's words. The concert, the bomb, the last six months. The kiss. Everything struck Pete down. He dropped to his knees, forehead against the very soil where he had first seen her. He thought he could feel the warmth of Petrus's hand on his back, though it was impossible to tell. Everything was just too much. He missed her too much for it to even make sense.

THE BRIDGE

Pete sat on his bed. He was wearing a black jacket, and he had already put his gloves on. He was rolling the stem of a yellow rose in his hands, watching the petals flopping as it turned around and around.

Then he put the rose down, gently, and picked up the sheet of paper Sarita gave him. He stared at it without seeing any words for a few moments until the ink slowly started seeping through his haze. He could not tell how many times he had read it, or how many times he would again. She was in those words and therefore it felt like the single most precious item in the world. The most precious in the entire history of the world.

"Are you ready?" Rikus asked, standing in Pete's door. He wore a thick gray, woolen jacket, and he was checking his pockets for gloves.

Pete carefully lay the piece of paper down on his pillow, wiped away his tears and bit his bottom lip. He then gave a single nod without looking up.

"I received a call from Captain Burger; he arrested Rudie," Rikus said softly, before sighing and adding in a barely audible tone: "But they are still searching for those who planted the bombs."

Pete still didn't look up. He knew this was good news, that the devil was in custody, but the pain did not relent, not even for a fleeting moment. It was just too great.

Deanne was waiting in the kitchen. Her knee-length coat was checkered in black, gray and white. She tried to smile, but her mouth would not play along, and she kissed Pete in his hair as he stood next to her.

The three of them remained silent as they drove through the white area, and alongside the white cemetery, then out on the Durnacol road, before Rikus turned onto the little dirt road flanked by a guard of honor of leafless eucalyptus trees. The road was in a state of disrepair and the Passat struggled, but Rikus remained quiet, his face unmoved by the bumps to the car's chassis.

To the left, there was a rusty farm gate propped open by a large rock. The sign on the gate read: *Indian Cemetery*.

The grass was pale yellow and sparse as the cemetery swept up toward the top of the hill. On the crown of the hill cars and people were visible, Rikus turned toward them.

He parked to the side under an acacia tree. They sat there for a few moments. Pete's gaze was locked on the yellow rose resting in his glove-clad palm.

"Pete," Rikus said finally. "This is one of those times in life when words fall short of doing anything. I know you are hurting, and I will not pretend to understand what you are going through because pain is different for everyone. All we want you to know is that we love you. We don't just love you because we have to, we love you because of who you are." Rikus paused, his gaze dropped, Deanne placed her hand on his lap and smiled.

"You are a special, special boy—or man, really. You have honored us as parents, even though we have done nothing to deserve you—you are a gift." A tear escaped Rikus's eye but he did not stop it. Instead, it carved a path over his pale cheek.

"There will be people who won't like what you did at the concert on Saturday, but they don't understand. Hell, for long, I don't think we understood, but somehow God placed a sixteen-year-old son in our lives with so much wisdom that we are in awe. You showed us that we have spent so long looking straight ahead that our necks became fused and we missed everything else around us. You unfused our necks.

"So, I doubt if anyone else will say it today, but us just sitting here is a little bit of a miracle. You did that. You and Sarita, and your friend, Petrus—who we are looking forward to meeting. The three of you brought people together who didn't believe they belonged together. Yet here we are.

"We just want to say thank you, Pete. That's all. If for no one else, for us. We are so proud." Rikus pulled a handkerchief out of his pocket and wiped his face.

Deanne turned to face Pete, her eyes were puffy and red. "We love you so much."

"Mourn her death, Pete, she deserves that." Rikus waited until Pete's eyes met his. "She deserves all our thoughts and prayers, but don't get stuck there, you have to celebrate her life—not death. That way her life will continue to have power, holding on to grief will just stop you from being."

"Okay," was all Pete could muster. He was now almost used to the pain inside him. He imagined that at any given moment his heart would ignite, and it would burn out, engulfing all of him with it.

Rikus cleared his throat. "Right," he said. They

left the car and walked toward the others. As they approached, they saw a group of about a hundred Indians standing to their right. All dressed in their traditional clothing, weeping around the wooden casket-like box perched on top of a mountain of dry firewood, and framed with colorful flowers and ornaments.

To their left were only two people, dressed completely in black: the Reverend and his wife. They joined the Reverend who only nodded, gripping his Bible as if he too would perish if he let go of it.

"Is anyone else coming?" Rikus asked.

"Only the Lord knows," the Reverend said distantly. Without looking at Rikus and without any of the usual strength in his words, he added: "Now that Rutger and his cronies have accused me of treason and left the church, I don't know anymore." His gaze glanced past Rikus before staring up at the morose clouds above them.

"The Lord will provide, Reverend." Rikus placed his hand on the Reverend's shoulder, but he didn't seem to notice.

They stood in silence opposite the weeping family and friends of Sarita, who occasionally snuck a peek toward them, but mostly avoided eye contact as if they were not really there.

In the center of the mourners stood a middle-aged man with a salt and pepper mustache and long fluffy black hair lifted by the breeze to reveal his baldness. He was well known to all: It was Venny Naidoo, the shop owner. But today he was not that, he was a mourning father. He seemed paler than the Reverend, and he ignored all around him, even his wife's questions, as his eyes remained unmoved from the casket.

Pete stared at the rose in his hand and squeezed it gently one last time before he stepped forward and placed it standing upright against the casket. It was colorful and fragrant in contrast to this dreary day, *a little bit like her*, he thought. A stinging pain punctured his heart, and he fought the tears as best he could.

Shortly before four, a steady hum sounded from where the eucalyptus trees guarded the road to the cemetery. Everyone turned to the noise coming closer. A few people whispered as the sound of car doors closing rang out through the cold air. Then heads appeared as they came up the hill, and soon almost a hundred people, nearly a third of the Reverend's congregation, joined him and the de Langes to the left of the casket.

Pete did not know what a Hindu priest was called, but a man dressed in orange-and-white robes and a turban spoke in a language he did not understand. He listened and imagined what the priest was saying, all the wonderful things about Sarita and that perhaps she would be reincarnated as a flower. For once he wished reincarnation was something he believed in. He wouldn't want her to be reincarnated as a flower though, or a tiger, but as her. The exact same her.

Alongside him, all the white people stood with their heads bowed. It was clear to see that the ceremony, the strangeness of their language and ways, made them uncomfortable. But there they were, dressed in the darkest winter clothing they had, mourning with these familiar strangers the loss of someone they most likely had never met but felt inseparably linked to.

The priest stopped and everyone looked up. To the other side of them, from the darkness of a nearby black wattle forest, a song rang out. A choir of melodic voices drifted across the barren earth to where they stood in the freezing cold. As the group of nearly a hundred and fifty people approached, some of their faces became visible. Men, women, and children sang in beautiful harmony, and the Zulu hymn floated up to the gray-and-white cloud covered heavens.

The first recognizable face was that of Christina. She walked right in the front, raising her hands as she was singing, occasionally clapping along with the others, her whole body feeling and believing every word she sang.

Pete could feel his body shaking, but it wasn't from the cold. The hymn filled him with a warmth he hadn't felt since before that hated moment. The harmony of voices woke something inside him, something living and growing, soothing and calming against the darkness of his vast chasm. It tasted a little like hope.

He looked to his mom on his left. Her eyes were fixed on Christina and tears flowed freely, her bottom lip quivering.

The hymn ended as the group of black people plugged the gap between the white and Indian groups at the foot end of the casket. Everyone shuffled closer to one another, and soon the three very distinct groups of mourners formed a circle around Sarita's casket.

Christina stood right next to Deanne, their shoulders touching. They looked at one another and then Deanne took Christina's hand, squeezing hard, not letting go.

Pete scanned the crowd of black people for a face he wanted to see more than anyone, the one person in the world that understood. And then he spotted him, standing on the edge of the group of black people next to an old Indian lady. Petrus stood broad-shouldered, his jaw muscles flexing with two shimmering lines on his face.

Their eyes met. Without thinking or waiting, Pete stepped out of the line of white people, smiled at his mom and Christina and walked straight toward Petrus. Petrus did the same, breaking free from the safety of his people to the empty space between the crowd and the casket.

When they were standing opposite each other Petrus's dad wanted to bring his son back, but his wife stopped him. Pete took his right glove off and held out his hand to Petrus. Petrus looked at the white hand protruding from the black jacket for a moment, and then back to Pete's eyes. He placed his hand in Pete's and then as one, they both fell into an embrace, weeping without reservation on each other's shoulders. The warmth he felt during the Zulu hymn was growing with every tear dampening Petrus's tattered old jersey. He could feel Petrus's fists pulling him closer as he too released the hurt. For a moment he thought of the white faces watching them. For now, in front of witnesses, he would forever, and without question, be a kaffir-brother. But it did not matter, not now, not ever. His best friend was crying on his shoulder and in his moment of greatest grief, no one else mattered. He pulled Petrus closer, and the warmth grew.

Rikus put his arm around Deanne and no longer hid

his tears.

The priest stepped forward. He cleared his throat a couple of times and said: "Friends, I am indeed speechless, and as the Indians here can attest, that is not something which happens often. We as the Indian community are truly blessed by the presence of our white and black friends. I am sure Sarita would have loved this."

Pete's eyes were fixed on Sarita's mom, he couldn't help it. He saw something of his own torment in her: Grief hung like a millstone around her neck. But a sudden noise snared his attention: A few *hadedas* had flown up, complaining as they flew over the crowd, across the gray-white sky before disappearing in the black wattle forest. The priest stopped talking and everyone stared in a near-mystical trance at this mournful fly-by.

Their cries had barely died down before the deep gurgling of large-sized vehicles could be heard coming closer, at speed. Achala's whole body drooped, she looked toward the noise as if it had drained the last microscopic droplets of lifeblood she had.

Doors shut and soon forty soldiers raced toward them. The soldiers were in full uniform and armed with machine guns. Leading them was a man with a square jaw and blood-red mustache, holding his weapon out in front of him like he was carrying a baby that he wanted to return to its mother.

"Stop!" he shouted.

The crowd stared in muted shock at these uniformed men running toward them. A few black people retreated several meters, but no one ran.

"What is this?" the Reverend asked, walking closer

to the army man carrying the rank of major.

"Under the State of Emergency, group meetings such as this are strictly forbidden. I will give everyone one minute to disperse or you will all be arrested on the spot," he shouted past the Reverend.

"This is a funeral, Major. We are here in peace, mourning the tragic loss of a young life," the Reverend protested.

"It does not matter. You are meeting unlawfully, disperse immediately and return to your homes."

A few of the black people started creeping away at the back.

"Wait! No one is leaving," a voice came from within the white crowd. Out stepped Captain Burger.

"I am Captain Burger. I can attest that this is not a political gathering. We had a terrible tragedy on Saturday, and the community as a whole has come together out of respect for the deceased."

"My orders are clear," the major said in a slightly less aggressive tone.

"Major, the Lord's house was attacked last Saturday, but we as a white community were spared," the Reverend said as Captain Burger took his place next to him. "It was a miracle. Yet we grieve. We grieve for Sarita Naidoo. She died not because of any fault of her own but by the hands of those who worship evil. I asked my congregation to come here today to show our support for our extended community, but also to give them a place to grieve, to let go of the anguish which has crippled us.

"Reverend Dlamini of the black church has done the same, so we are just here, weeping because an innocent sixteen-year-old girl lies in that casket,"

442

the Reverend just about managed to say before his voice started croaking.

"I am sorry, but—" the Major started.

"I take full responsibility for all these people," Captain Burger interjected. "If anything happens, take my badge and throw me in prison. Major, we're almost done here, please afford us just a few more minutes. After that, we will all go home."

The Major peered over his shoulder at his men, and then back at Captain Burger.

"Okay. But then everyone goes," he conceded with a sigh. "The State of Emergency's rules are very clear."

"A few minutes, that's all we ask," Captain Burger assured him.

The Major made an impatient gesture for them to continue before ordering his troops to take a few steps back.

Achala stood frozen, staring at the Major as if her brain had stalled. Then her knees suddenly gave way from under her. Her face choking in the immovable sorrow as her body collapsed on the ground.

Next to her Venny stood frozen. He didn't seem to be aware of anything around him, his wife, the casket—anything—as if covered by a shroud. The Reverend and the Hindu priest walked closer and helped Achala to her feet.

Then the Reverend's wife started singing:
"Amazing grace! How sweet the sound
That saved a wretch like me!
I once was lost, but now am found;
Was blind, but now I see."
By the second verse, the whole congregation sang

together with their eyes closed, and by the third verse, the Zulu congregation joined in, singing in Zulu.

Everyone from the Indian community held each other, as they listened to the beautiful symphony of languages pouring love out over them, and they wept smiling.

Pete looked over his shoulder and saw the shadow cast by the people surrounding Sarita. It was one, uninterrupted shadow. No breaks, no holes, just one perfect shadow. He smiled at Petrus standing next to him.

Another man wearing a white robe and an orange cloth tied around his waist walked around Sarita three times, sprinkling liquid. Then the priest handed him a handful of straw, which he lit and placed on the side of Sarita. The dry wood took to the flames happily and grew mighty within seconds encasing Sarita's casket, bright as the sun.

Pete could not watch her burn so he walked away, followed by Petrus. They stood together, some way away, backs turned to the raging flames. They stood in silence. There were no words to say.

Venny walked into the house carrying the urn with Sarita's ashes. He placed it on the coffee table in the living room and turned to Achala.

"Make sure you release her into a river," he said.

"What are you talking about, we'll do that together," she said.

He looked his wife deep in the eyes; their twenty years together flashed before him. He saw the good times and the bad and realized that virtually all their best memories contained Sarita. And he killed her.

"I need to go out," he said.

"In this weather?" she said. "I won't be surprised if it starts snowing. Come, let me make you a nice cup of tea."

"No, there is something I must do. Something I should have done a long time ago."

"Venny," she tried.

"Whatever happens, you must remember that everything I did, I did for Sarita and you. I was a fool. I believed I was something I'm not, and I paid the price. The most expensive price any man could ever pay."

"What are you going on about?"

"Achala, I loved Sarita with all my heart. She was my little girl." Tears came for the first time that day for Venny.

"And, in my own way, I love you too." He walked to Achala and kissed her for a few intimate seconds, then he rushed out of the door, leaving her standing there in utter confusion.

"Venny, what are you doing out in this weather? How can I help?" Captain Burger said as he opened the front door to his house.

"I want to surrender."

"Surrender?"

"I killed my little girl," Venny screamed sobbing.

"Venny, listen, I know this was a traumatic day, and I'm sure if it was my daughter, I would feel responsible too. But it wasn't your fault, how could you have known? It's a horrible thing, but it's not your fault."

"I wish you were right." Venny sniffed and wiped

his tears away with his sleeve. "But...I did kill her. I planted that bomb, the one that killed her. I was behind the attack. I wanted to destroy the white regime so much, I was blinded by hatred. But all I achieved was to destroy myself. Captain Burger, you have a gun. I beg you, go and get it and blow my bloody brains out. Please let it stop, I'm guilty. Take away this pain. Please?"

CHRISTMAS

Pete sat on his bed. He was wearing a black jacket, and Pete wrapped his last Christmas present and placed it on his bed. It was four-thirty on Christmas Eve and his brothers would be there soon after their stint of holiday work. He was excited to see them. There was so much to tell them, but probably, even more he could never tell them. The thought of listening to hours and hours of stories about university life, however, sounded like the ideal Christmas to him.

First, there was something he had to do, a gift to deliver. He put his running shoes on, gave Jimmy a quick pat on the head on his way out, and ran the route, the one he could practically run with his eyes closed.

Everything was familiar but seemed happier and fresh in the warm pre-Christmas glow. A few festive decorations even made the New Extension houses look somewhat better than their usual morose self. He laughed out loud as he ran past the little fishing dam and thought of Renate. He was so in love that he couldn't even distinguish a dragon from a princess. He could only shake his head.

His route ended as always at the top of the hill. There, waiting for him was a broad-shouldered guy called Petrus. They shook hands and shared a joke before they sat on the rock and stared out toward the Drakensberg.

"Any news about Rudie?" Petrus asked.

Pete reluctantly met Petrus's expectant gaze, bit his bottom lip, and shook his head.

"No, that...*man* is out on bail again. He appealed against his conviction and they somehow granted him bail." He looked up at the bright blue sky above them.

"Eish, what if his appeal is successful? Then we'll be back at square one." Petrus sighed.

"Captain Burger said it won't be. According to him, Rudie is wasting the state's time and money. Apparently, his appeal is not worth the paper it is written on."

Petrus clicked his tongue. "He better be right. He must."

Pete wrapped his arms around his legs and stared at the dust on Petrus's feet for a few silent moments.

"I still can't get over Sarita's dad," Pete said.

"I know. What a crazy year."

"Completely crazy." A small bird buzzed by them and they watched it as it disappeared into the horizon.

"Hey, I brought you a Christmas present," Pete said.

"No, Pete, don't, I didn't—"

"Shush! I've been waiting to give this to you for a while." Pete took a photograph out of his pocket and gave it to Petrus. It was of two shadows on the church hall's stage, holding hands on a white canvas.

"Iri and Suri," Petrus said.

"Together forever," Pete said, with a bitter-sweet smile.

"Eish Pete, this is...the best gift." Petrus gently touched Sarita's shadow with his fingers.

"You're welcome, my friend. Let's make it our

business to ensure she is never forgotten," Pete said.

"I could never."

"I know." Pete nodded deep in thought. "My brothers will be home soon, I'd better go. I just wanted to give you that."

"Thanks, Pete, it means so much to me," Petrus said, clasping the photo in both hands. "I miss her," he added.

"Me too," Pete said, breathing deeply and closing his eyes for a moment. "So incredibly much."

Petrus rolled his bare feet across the uneven surface of the rock and stared at the photograph in his hands. Then he leaped off the rock, glanced at the sun before turning to Pete.

"Do you want to go for a run after Christmas?" he asked.

Pete climbed down from the rock and wiped the dust from his shorts.

"Absolutely. And in the New Year, I'm going to teach you how to play rugby," Pete said.

Petrus smiled. "You can teach me rugby as soon as you can run faster than me."

"Deal," Pete said, and they shook hands.

"Merry Christmas, Pete."

"Merry Christmas, Petrus."

THE MEANINGS OF
SOUTH AFRICAN TERMS
USED IN THIS BOOK

A **Aikona**: *no, or to decline, in Zulu.*

Apartheid: *system of governance based on segregation of people based on skin color.*

Appies: *abbreviated term for apprentices.*

B **Baas**: *boss*

Bakkie: *pick-up truck*

Bliksem: *crass way of saying "to hit/punch" someone, or a term used to say someone is a bad person, "he is a bliksem," or used as an exclamation. The word is derived from "bliksemstraal" which is a bolt of lightning.*

Boerewors: *thick beef sausage with a coriander-based herb mix.*

Braai: *barbeque*

C **Chappie**: *brand of individually wrapped chewing gum.*

Coolie: *derogatory/racist term for a person of Indian origin.*

Corporal Punishment: *For more information read the following: https://section27.org.za/wp-content/uploads/2017/02/Chapter-19.pdf*

D **Danie Gerber**: *legendary South Afrcan rugby player, he was a center.*

Drakensberg: *largest mountain range in South Africa, spanning most of central South Africa, and in particular separating Kwazulu-Natal from its neighbors, The Free State and Lesotho.*

Dutchman: *derogatory term for an Afrikaner, used by white English-speaking South Africans*

E **Eish**: *an exclamation.*

G **Group Areas Act**: *an act introduced during the apartheid era where white, Indian, black, and coloured people were given separate designated areas to live in cities and towns.*

H **Homelands**: *another idea from the apartheid era, which gave approximately six percent of the total area of South Africa to black tribes to govern themselves, as a way of diluting a common resistance movement, and easing tensions at home and abroad.*

Howzit: *informal greeting.*

K **Kaffir**: *derogatory/racist term for a black person.*

Klipspringer: *very agile small species of antelope.*

Koeksisters: *baked syrupy treats.*

Kombi: *term used for a minibus or traditional VW type MPV's.*

L **Laager**: *circular formation of ox-wagon - prevalent particularly during the Great Trek of 1838.*

Lowveld: *area of outstanding natural beauty surrounding and including the Kruger National Park.*

M **Mampoer**: *home-distilled liquor using a variety of fruit or vegetables.*

Moffie: *homosexual*

N **Necklacing**: *execution of someone (tribal/informal justice) by putting a tire around their necks laced with petrol and lighting it.*

O **Oros**: *a brand of orange squash.*

Ousie: *term for a black woman, either as a maid, or generic term, slang term meaning old sister.*

P **Panga**: *long-bladed machete*

Pap: *a starch made from corn flour. Staple of many South Africans.*

R **Red neck**: *derogatory term for white English-speaking South Africans (see below under 'souties')*

Rock spider: *derogatory term for an Afrikaner, used by white English-speaking South Africans*

Rondavel: *circular home, usually with a thatch roof, and traditionally made from mud.*

S **Shaka Zulu**: *notorious and successful Zulu king of the early 19th century*

Sokkie: *a type of dance, where two people dance together, shuffling, and turning to the music, also sometimes referred to as bokjol or windsurfing.*

Sosatie: *marinated cuts of meat on a skewer, often flanked by capsicum, onions or dried apricots.*

Souties or Salties: *derogatory term for the English in South Africa, particularly when complaining about the country and telling everyone how perfect England is.*

Also in reference to the Anglo-Boer War, and the term "red neck"—used because the African sun scorched the necks of many British soldiers during the war.

State of Emergency: *an act whereby the head of the government enforced a type of martial law in times of increased unrest.*

Stoep: *veranda*

Studying through the post: *term that was used to describe distance learning.*

T **Township**: *informal black settlement, usually with temporary structures as homes.*

Tsotsis: *term for criminals/bad people.*

V **Voetsek**: *term to chase something away, mostly dogs.*

W **Wena**: *Zulu term meaning "you."*

Wors: *sausage.*

AUTHOR
HANNES BERNARD

 Hannes Barnard is a South African-born author of both English and Afrikaans novels. He debuted in 2019 with the YA novel, *Halley se komeet*, which he translated into English as *Halley's Comet*. In 2020, *Wolk*, his apocalyptic YA adventure, was released, and coming up in 2022 is his crime novel, *die wet van Gauteng*. When not writing, traveling, or planning his next adventure, Hannes works in marketing. He has called England and Seychelles home but now lives in Johannesburg with his wife.

9 781946 395559

Dirección editorial
Ana Laura Delgado

Cuidado de la edición
Sonia Zenteno

Revisión del texto
Rosario Ponce

Diseño
Ana Laura Delgado
Mabel Totolhua

© 2009. Javier Malpica, por el texto
© 2009. Enrique Torralba, por las ilustraciones

Primera edición
D.R. © 2009. Ediciones El Naranjo, S. A. de C. V.
　　　　　Cerrada Nicolás Bravo núm. 21-1,
　　　　　Col. San Jerónimo Lídice, 10200, México, D. F.
　　　　　Tel/fax + 52 (55) 56 52 1974
　　　　　elnaranjo@edicioneselnaranjo.com.mx
　　　　　www.edicioneselnaranjo.com.mx

ISBN 978-607-7661-03-0

Impreso en México • *Printed in Mexico*

PARA NINA

Un diario sobre la identidad sexual

Javier Malpica

Enrique Torralba ILUSTRACIÓN

ediciones
el naranjo

18 de agosto de 1995

Querida Nina:

*Hoy fui a comprar este cuaderno
con un dinero que le tomé prestado a Frida... tu hija.
También me compré un gran helado,
uno de vainilla.
No estaba muy bueno.
Regresé a la casa.*

*Frida me dio una tunda por haberle tomado dinero. No le importó que
le dijera que compré un cuaderno para la escuela. Aunque era mentira,
ella no podía saberlo.*

Me castigó y tuve que ver dos horas de telenovelas contigo.

"Siempre quise escribir un diario." Ésas fueron las palabras de Nina unos meses antes morir. Tenía noventa años. Estaba postrada en su cama debido a una fractura en la cadera. La muy bárbara se había subido a la azotea de la casa de una vecina con la intención de impermeabilizar el techo.

—Mamá, ¿por qué no le dijiste a tu amiga que llamara a un especialista? —la reprendió Frida (mi madre) con su natural tono de: "¿Por qué avergüenzas a la familia?".

—¿Y permitir que pagara por algo tan sencillo? Yo subí las montañas más altas del mundo. ¡Por Dios Santo!

—Tú nunca has subido ninguna montaña. Ni siquiera has salido de esta ciudad.

—Yo recorrí el Sahara con sólo una bolsa de dátiles en mi chamarra.

—Lo que tú digas, mamá.

Nina, mi abuela, no había sido una gran exploradora, ni mucho menos. El único desierto que conocía era el Desierto de los Leones, y lo más alto que había escalado en su vida era la Torre Latinoamericana (y lo había hecho en elevador, como cualquier persona con dos gramos de cerebro lo haría). Nunca fue a los Himalayas ni al Nilo, pero creía que los conocía. Tampoco se había tirado de un paracaídas, pero ella estaba más que segura de que lo había hecho. Nunca conoció al príncipe de Dinamarca, aunque juraba que había tenido un romance de miedo con él.

Te lo diré claramente: mi abuela era una vieja loca.

Nunca supimos el porqué de esa desbordada y alucinada imaginación. Nunca supimos cuándo fue que las tuercas de su cerebro se aflojaron sin remedio y perdió todo contacto con la realidad. Pero ese día que cayó de la escalera y se dio directamente contra unos arbustos —afortunadamente para ella, pero desafortunadamente para el precioso jardín de su amiga—, nos mandó llamar a mi hermana y a mí a su lado. La anciana estaba convencida de que unas pirañas (como te lo estoy contando) le habían mordisqueado la pierna y que no viviría mucho tiempo.

—Jamás debí aceptar ese trabajo en el Amazonas. Nunca puedes confiar en los peces carnívoros.

—Nina, te duele la pierna por la caída —le aclaró Claudia.

—¿Y crees que no lo sé? Como sea. ¿Qué hacen aquí?

—Tú nos mandaste llamar —dije con algo de temor.

La verdad es que a veces me daba miedo la abuela. Nunca he sabido lidiar con locos, por muy de la familia que sean. Y con Nina no podías saber en qué momento su mente iba a montar una motocicleta y se iba a dirigir a toda velocidad rumbo a Fantasilandia.

—Pues claro que los llamé. ¿Creen que olvido las cosas o qué? Los llamé para decirles algo muy importante. Algo que sólo ustedes pueden entender. Alguna vez se lo dije a su madre, pero siempre fue muy estúpida para entenderlo. Eso pasa cuando le regalas rosas a los tlacuaches. Y su madre será muy mi hija, pero es un tlacuache estúpido.

No hay que escandalizarse ante este comentario de mi abuela. Hay familias ejemplares que pueden ser retratadas para la portada de una revista o para la etiqueta de un *shampoo*; familias en las que todos los miembros se llevan bien: todos tienen el cabello sedoso y sus casas están tapizadas con las hojas del manual de Carreño. Pero hay familias que son todo lo opuesto. Nada lindas; familias con el cabello descuidado, en las que las abuelas no tejen chalinas, ni las mamás cuidan celosamente del hogar; familias en las que la abuela llama estúpida a su hija y la hija desea en secreto el coma diabético de su madre. Así era mi familia. ¡Qué le vamos a hacer!

Frida y Nina nunca se llevaron bien. Y nosotros nunca nos llevamos bien con Frida. Tal vez el odio es algo que se lleva en la sangre. Tal vez es algo que está en nuestros genes.

Así que en el momento en que Claudia tenga hijos, estará en serio peligro de llamarlos estúpidos, si no por la genética, sí por aquello de seguir la tradición familiar.

—¿Y qué secreto es ése, Nina? —preguntó mi hermana, orgullosa de no ser una estúpida ante los ojos de una persona tan cuerda.

Yo temía que nuestra abuela loca quisiera revelarnos dónde estaba escondido el tesoro del rey Salomón, y que nos hiciera jurar que iríamos hasta el otro lado del mundo a buscarlo (con lo que me fastidiaba viajar), pero no, en vez de eso nos dijo lo del diario.

—¿Un diario? —se me alcanzó a salir con un clarísimo tono de incredulidad.

—No es una buena idea confiar en la memoria —explicó Nina—. Dicen que cuando recuerdas, lo que en realidad haces es recordar recuerdos.

—¿Qué? —dijo Claudia un poco harta de oír locuras, aunque en realidad ella siempre se ha hartado fácilmente, no sólo con las locuras, sino casi con cualquier cosa que pruebe su paciencia.

—Quiero decir que si quieres recordar la última vez que tuviste sexo con un brasileño, no recuerdas el sexo en sí, sino el último recuerdo que tuviste de esa relación. —Mi hermana y yo no pudimos evitar soltar una pequeña risa, la mención del sexo, o cualquiera de sus temas afines, siempre ha hecho que los niños ya sean de ocho u once años (como era nuestro caso) emitan risitas. A Nina esto no le importó, así que continuó—: Cada vez que recuerdas algo lo estás cubriendo con una capa de telarañas. Así que con los años, bailar tango se vuelve tan oscuro como un bosque cubierto por la niebla.

Nina hizo una pausa y me pidió que le alcanzara su tónico (así le decía a su anforita con brandi). Recuerdo que hacía un frío terrible esa noche. Ella continuó:

—Si hubiera llevado un diario y hubiera escrito sobre cada montaña que escalé o cada tango que bailé, ahora podría leerlo, podría verlo en mi mente y volvería a sentirlo todo de nuevo... Creo que la última vez que tuve sexo con un brasileño fue en Berlín... ya no sé si se siente algo en el estómago cuando tienes un orgasmo. No sé. ¿Tú lo sabes? —le preguntó directamente a Claudia, que no tuvo otra que mirarla con temor por unos dos segundos, tal vez deseando en su interior que le hubiera preguntado mejor por el clima.

—No lo sé, Nina. Apenas tengo once años.

La abuela nos ofreció de su tónico. Claudia no dudó en tomar un trago. A mí, francamente, el brandi nunca me ha entrado, lo supe desde esa primera vez, cuando tenía seis años, que la abuela (quién más) me ofreció un poco dizque para que dejara de llorar. Había visto *Dumbo* y no soporté que encarcelaran a la madre del cursi elefantito.

—Háganme caso niños. Hay vidas, como la de su madre, que aburren hasta a Dios, ésas no merecen ni un párrafo en una revista de cocina. En cambio hay vidas tan maravillosas, como la mía, que deberían ser relatadas en un diario. Y así va a ser con ustedes. Yo lo sé. Sé que no son ordinarios... Lo sé. No dejen de escribir acerca de su extraordinaria existencia.

Un día después, comencé a escribir mi diario. No sé por qué. Siempre me fastidió escribir, para mí era como hacer la tarea de español. Pero también siempre fui muy impresionable. Cuando tenía ocho años podías decirme que los baños de leche podían quitarte los lunares y yo lo creía. De hecho lo creí, y Frida me dio una tunda monumental por desperdiciar tres litros de leche en mi absurda vanidad. "¿No sabes que hay niños en África que se mueren de hambre?", me dijo la muy hipócrita. Nunca le importó que la gente muriera de hambre, así viviera en Zacatecas o Madagascar. Lo que le importaba era que no iba a tener leche para su dichoso pan francés de todas las mañanas. Yo, en cambio, tenía que vivir con mi horrible lunar en la mejilla. Bueno, pero lo que estaba diciendo es que yo era tan impresionable, sobre todo a los ocho años, que tal vez decidí empezar un diario tan sólo porque no quería olvidar, como mi abuela, si un orgasmo se sentía en el estómago (si es que llegaba el momento en que supiera qué demonios era eso). O tal vez fue lo que dijo Nina de que yo era extraordinario. Lo que sí sabía era que tenía un pequeño problema. Yo no tenía grandes eventos que recordar. No había subido montañas como mi abuela loca lo había hecho (aunque sólo hubiera ocurrido en su imaginación). No había bailado tango, ni había tenido sexo. Y a los ocho años tampoco estaba entre mis planes más urgentes averiguar sobre esas experiencias (ni la del baile, ni la del sexo). Esa tarde, me las ingenié para robarle unos pesos a Frida de la cartera. Fui a la papelería y escogí un cuaderno forma italiana de doscientas hojas con una preciosa portada color índigo. En la noche me encerré en mi cuarto y anoté en la portada del cuaderno: Para Nina.

Ése sería el nombre de mi diario. Imaginé que todo se lo contaría a mi abuela la chiflada, la única persona que siempre tuvo fe en mí. Después lo abrí y escribí la primera fecha, y lo que sería el primer capítulo de esa extraordinaria vida que era la mía: *18 de agosto de 1995...*

Pero el gusto no me duró mucho. Bastó que anotara ese primer párrafo para convencerme de que eran las peores líneas que se hubieran escrito jamás en toda la historia de la literatura, y si no me crees regresa a la primera página y lo verás.

Después de escribir tan maravillosos acontecimientos, pensé que Nina no sólo alucinaba con los Alpes y exploraciones submarinas, también alucinaba al creer que mi vida era digna de ser contada. Ya me veía convertido en un anciano decrépito, acomodándome los anteojos, leyendo esas palabras y sintiendo una vergüenza tal que me haría saltar por la ventana para así terminar con tan emocionante existencia. Pero cuando uno recibe una humillante tunda por un cuaderno con un color tan nostálgico, no queda otra que darle otra oportunidad, no sólo al cuaderno, sino a la vida gris y abominable que le ha tocado en suerte. Tal vez al día siguiente ocurriera algo grande, tal vez al día siguiente me encontrara con un extraterrestre, tal vez un oso polar atacara la escuela o tal vez Bono —mi máximo ídolo— apareciera por la calle firmando autógrafos.

Pero al día siguiente nada de esto pasó, así que decidí esconder el cuaderno y esperar hasta que algo verdaderamente emocionante me ocurriera.

Casi diez años tuvieron que pasar para que me armara de valor; hurgara entre mis cosas del clóset y tomara otra vez ese cuaderno. Este cuaderno. Ya no tiene doscientas páginas (alguna vez tomé unas hojas para apuntar teléfonos y recetas), pero el color índigo sigue igual de brillante. En la portada aún encontré esa dedicatoria: "Para Nina". Quién lo diría. Diez años después. Justo cuando estoy por cumplir los dieciocho. Y es que creo que ahora sí tengo algo que contar.

Día en que te cuento sobre mi verdadera naturaleza

Soy mujer.

¡Ya lo dije! ¡Por fin se lo he confesado a alguien! Y ni te escandalices, porque si no es a ti entonces a quién se lo cuento. A quién. Tú dime. Además, es absurdo que un diario se sorprenda (aunque no haya tenido noticias de uno en diez años). Para eso está. Para escuchar las cosas más terribles y pantanosas, y esto cuando mucho tendrá un poco de lodo. Bueno. Tengo que reconocer que yo mismo me he ruborizado un poco al confesártelo. Pero creo que es natural. No es fácil decir que uno es mujer, cuando toda su vida ha cargado con una anatomía masculina y el nada femenino nombre de Eduardo. Y claro, tú te preguntarás cómo es que de pronto, a los casi dieciocho años, este bruto se vino a dar cuenta de algo así. Pues para que te lo sepas, esto no es nuevo, no podría ser nuevo. Es algo más viejo que tú. Y eso que tú también tienes tus años. El caso es que esto que te digo es algo que he cargado por mucho tiempo y que no me había atrevido a enfrentar, pero que ahora reconozco plenamente. Es algo que supe casi desde que nací. O al menos desde ese día memorable.

Tal vez por ahí debí haber empezado. Por ese primer recuerdo. Si mi abuela pudiera escucharme, le daría otro coma diabético.

Cuando tenía cinco años y la tía Lola me preguntó qué quería ser de grande, yo le respondí con toda naturalidad, desfachatez y seguridad: "Mujer". La señora emitió una absurda carcajada que me dejó ver sus dientes retorcidos y amarillos (¿Puedes creer que hasta hace unos años todavía los tenía así?, la muy tacaña jamás pudo gastar un poco de su fortuna, porque si algo tiene es dinero para ponerse una sonrisa de comercial de pasta de dientes, y en vez de eso ha preferido, durante todos estos años, seguir gastando todo en su estúpida colección de peluches y en cajetillas y cajetillas de cigarros, los causantes de tan linda dentadura). Perdón. Estoy divagando (otra vez)... El caso es que la tía Lola sonrió. Entonces, asumiendo que yo no había entendido la pregunta, intentó aclarar:

—No, querido. Me refiero a qué profesión te gustaría tener, ¿te gustaría ser bombero, doctor, futbolista?

—Pues... secretaria.

La vieja se puso más blanca que la mascarilla de mayonesa que usaba a veces por la noche (y que por cierto nunca le sirvió), al tiempo que tosía (tal vez por efecto de la última dosis de nicotina). Hubieras visto la cara que puso. Peor que si me hubiera convertido en un demonio del Apocalipsis o en Saddam Hussein (que era el villano de la época y que ahora ya no tiene nada de temible, lo han ejecutado y es a lo mucho un pobre espectro barbón patético).

No le tomó ni un segundo darse cuenta de que yo no bromeaba. Sobre todo con aquello de ser mujer. No sé qué le molestó más, si lo de ser secretaria o lo de ser mujer. De pronto debió imaginarme con un vestido sastre de mala calidad, lentes cuadrados, unas medias corridas y mordiendo un lápiz corriente, y seguro que hasta ganas de vomitar le dieron, pero las buenas costumbres y su nebulosa inteligencia sólo le permitieron darme una palmada en la cabeza y emitir otra sonrisita forzada (de ésas que suelen poner las tías cuando la moral y el buen gusto han sido vapuleados y han quedado en calzones) y un "Ay, pero qué Eduardito éste".

Así que ya lo ves, yo a los cinco años era sabio. Tenía una voz femenina atrapada por una fuerza desconocida y oscura. Pero ahora, después de años de cautiverio, por fin sientes en tus páginas mi auténtica y maravillosa voz, y aunque no me lo digas, casi podría apostar que debes estar bastante contrariada por estos años de silencio. Espero que no te moleste que tu nombre siga siendo el de mi abuela. Pero hablarte así, como si hablara con la mismísima Nina, me hace sentir más en confianza. Nina era la única persona que hubiera tolerado escuchar las confesiones de alguien que se ha descubierto viviendo con los genitales equivocados. ¿Ves? Ya no me he ruborizado al usar la palabra genitales. Ella me confesaba cosas que ni siquiera ahora podría entender, pero veía en su rostro, en las tres arrugas que corrían por sus mejillas cuando me contaba sus locas aventuras, que para ella lo importante no era que yo la entendiera, sino que la escuchara. Eso es lo importante. Saber que tú me escucharás ahora. Para mí, Nina, eres como la hermana gemela de mi abuela. Esa abuela que apenas me conoció. Esa anciana a quien tuve la oportunidad de escuchar muchas veces, pero que nunca tuvo la oportunidad de escucharme a mí. Y ahora que puedo, quiero que me conozca a partir de ti. Quiero que sepa todo de mí a través de esta nueva Nina. Esta Nina que no tiene la piel arrugada, pero sí casi doscientas páginas en blanco. Así que no te extrañes si a veces me dirijo a ti como a mi diario, y a veces como si efectivamente fueras mi querida abuela esquizofrénica.

¿Puedes creer que casi te arrojo a la basura cuando tiré los viejos cuadernos de la secundaria? También casi me deshago de mi álbum de fotos. Me entró una angustia cuando hice el tiradero. Es que debes saber que odio tirar cosas; parte de mi personalidad (no sé si defecto o virtud, yo creo que defecto). Tengo una terrible manía por coleccionar chácharas y ropa. Ya ni siquiera uso todas mis chamarras, pero no puedo soportar la idea de tirarlas. Si aún están buenas tienen que seguir en mi clóset. Tampoco me es posible regalarlas. Ni siquiera he podido donar unas cuantas a esa pobre gente del huracán. Claro, unas chamarras seguro les harían bastante bien, pero no puedo. Ya sé lo que estarás pensando. Si éste ya está cambiando, pues que se deshaga de su ropa vieja. Lo que pasa es que he descubierto que además de mujer, soy un egoísta de lo peor. Sí. Eso pasa. Una vez le presté a mi hermana mi chamarra favorita de mezclilla y me la devolvió con una mancha espantosa de grasa. Yo creo que por eso no puedo prestar nada. Por supuesto que hay que reconocer que Claudia es bien conocida por dejar todo lo que toca hecho una desgracia. Nada más hay que ver su cuarto. Bueno, yo creo que ni una expedición de exploradores del *National Geographic* se atrevería a entrar ahí sin un mapa. Como sea, esta vocación mía de hormiga ridícula debe también desaparecer. Pero ésa será otra historia.

Me estoy desviando del tema principal. Otro de mis defectos: divago mucho. A veces puedo estar platicando con alguien de la entrega del Óscar y de pronto, sin previo aviso, empezar a platicar de la escasez de agua. Dios mío. Creo que es algo que le debo a mi abuela. Sólo espero no confundir algún día las aceitunas con las bujías. Pero de que soy disperso, lo soy. ¿Ves? Lo volví a hacer. Bueno, decía que el tema principal de esta primera confesión es: el cambio.

¿Qué, no te lo he dicho? Pues sí. Quisiera cambiar. Quisiera no sólo reconocerme en mi verdadera sexualidad, sino atreverme a ir más lejos. Quisiera ser mujer de cuerpo completo. ¡Claro que tengo miedo! No soy tonto, sé que para ser completamente mujer deben pasar cosas evidentes en mi anatomía, pero no me corre prisa. No te asustes, no pretendo tomar un cuchillo y eliminar mi masculinidad en cuanto termine esta página. Salvajadas, no gracias. Es algo que debe ir paso a paso. No es algo que se pueda tomar así, como un vaso de agua. Es una decisión muy difícil y sé que debo irla madurando en mi cabecita. Es algo que no se puede tomar así, como un hidalgo de tequila, tan a la ligera. Para nada. Sé que es algo que debe maquinarse, como los planes de las peores villanas de las telenovelas. Algo que debe pensarse muchísimo.

No he decidido aún cambiar por completo, pero la sola idea me emociona. Estoy dispuesto, querida Nina, a averiguar contigo si realmente debo dar ese gran salto. Así que sólo me queda una pregunta, una vez que yo me he reconocido... ¿Qué sigue?

Día en que te cuento cómo encontré mi verdadero nombre

Hoy ha nacido Victoria Citlali Dorina de la Concepción.

Después de haberlo pensado mucho, Nina, decidí que uno de los primeros pasos que debía seguir era el de cambiar mi nombre.

No fue fácil. Había tanto de donde escoger. Me encantan desde los nombres comunes, como Fabiola, Adriana, Diana, Elena, hasta aquellos que no le gustan a la mayoría de las personas, como Cordelia, Úrsula, Fernanda o Déborah. Me agradan los nombres extranjeros, como Jennifer, Madeleine, Midori o Gretchen y los mexicanos como Xóchitl o Eréndira. Pero eso sí, me fascinan casi todos los nombres de mujer, por eso no pude decidirme a escoger tan sólo uno. En realidad, todos los sustantivos femeninos tienen una música y una delicadeza, que casi podrías jurar que despiden un maravilloso perfume (aunque se oiga muy azotado). No es lo mismo el chocante sol que la pálida luna, no es lo mismo el molesto viento que la gentil brisa. No es lo mismo el deprimente aguacero que la cálida lluvia. Ahora que lo pienso, también pude llamarme Lluvia o Niebla, pero lo *hippie* no va conmigo. Y aunque mi nombre es pomposo y largo, para ti, querida Nina, seré simplemente Victoria. Sí, como la Victoria que triunfa, como la sexy y madura Victoria Abril, como la glamorosa Victoria Secret o como la real princesa Victoria de Suecia. Pero, eso sí, nada de Vicky, ¡por favor! Cursilerías, no gracias.

Día en que te cuento sobre mi primera confesión

Y hoy, Victoria Citlali Dorina de la Concepción tuvo una primera misión. Matar a Eduardo. Qué trágico se oye (¡*my God*!). Como de fotonovela barata.

Como sea, hoy Victoria tomó su retrato (el de Eduardo), lo sepultó en el pequeño patio de atrás y le llevó un ramo de rosas (siempre le gustaron las rosas). Y no lo hizo porque lo odiara. Nunca podría odiarlo. Por casi dieciocho años compartieron el mismo cuerpo, la misma vida. Odiar a Eduardo sería odiarse a sí misma de algún modo. Victoria lo mató porque era necesario hacerlo. Porque hoy, que ella ha comenzado a existir, es claro que no podrá compartir más el cuerpo con él. Dos personas no pueden ocupar un mismo espacio. Es una ley de la física matemática universal. La *victoria* sólo puede ser de uno.

No te imaginas lo difícil que fue. Una cosa es confesártelo a ti. Después de todo no eres sino pulpa de árbol procesado, lo que hace que hablar contigo sea como hablar con una planta (no te ofendas, pero si lo piensas bien, así es). Claro que si de verdad lo piensas bien, en realidad a quien le estoy contando todo esto es a mí mismo, tú no eres sino una representación de uno de los niveles de mi conciencia (no sé cual de todos, pero así es). Eso diría algún psicólogo ridículo.

Bueno, planta, conciencia o nostalgia por mi abuela, una cosa es decírselo a uno de los tres y otra muy distinta a un ser humano completamente ajeno. Y es que me puse a pensar que Victoria Citlali no puede existir si no existe para otros. Así que decidí hablar con la persona que creí que después de Nina podía entenderme mejor: mi hermana Claudia. Después de todo, ella es lo que se dice una rebelde de nacimiento y si alguien cercano a mí sabe algo de crisis y cómo enfrentarlas, es ella.

Claudia siempre fue para mí una especie de *wonderwoman*, si es que me entiendes. Siempre se las ha ingeniado para lograr todo lo que quiere y no ha necesitado usar un lazo de la verdad ni un avión invisible para ello. No importa que para lograr sus metas, siempre deje todo en completo desorden (como aquella ocasión que arregló la lavadora y las manchas de grasa en el suelo jamás se pudieron quitar). Recuerdo esa primera vez que, teniendo doce años, se acercó a Frida y le pidió que la dejara tomar clases de actuación. Frida le dijo algo así como:

—¿Actriz? ¿Quieres volverte una ramera?

—¿Una qué?

—Ninguna hija mía va a ser la concubina de nadie.

—¿La concuqué?

Frida no se molestó en explicarle que para ella todas las artistas, incluyendo a Meg Ryan y Doris Day eran unas prostitutas exhibicionistas, así que se encargó de terminar la discusión poniendo en duda el talento de mi hermana:

—Tú no puedes ser actriz, para eso hay que tener la capacidad de engañar a la gente. Eso es lo único que saben hacer esas mujeres desvergonzadas, hacerle creer a la gente que son unas blancas palomitas, cuando en realidad son unas zorras libidinosas.

Claudia quiso convencerla de que tenía talento, de que ella no era una zorra promiscua y me pidió que la ayudara. Una tarde le presentamos a Frida una escena en la que una mujer histérica, que interpretaba mi hermana, corría de la casa a su esposo, que represento yo (Dicho sea de paso que no sirvió de nada que le pidiera a Claudia que me dejara actuar mejor de hija embarazada, y que los ensayos resultaran de lo más molestos, ya que mi hermana quería que mis líneas me salieran perfectas y estuvo varias veces a punto de arrancarse el cabello ante mis múltiples equivocaciones).

Frida se molestó..., no, es más justo decir que se puso furiosa, pues era obvio que Claudia estaba interpretándola a ella corriendo a nuestro padre. La castigó por impertinente, mala hija y una serie de adjetivos arcaicos y pasados de moda. Y remató diciendo:

—Si al menos me hubieras engañado, pero ya ves... ni para eso tienes talento.

Más tarde, Claudia se las ingenió para que Frida le diera el permiso para estudiar actuación. Por eso la admiro, ella nunca tuvo miedo de retar a nadie, ni siquiera a Frida. Ésa fue la razón de que la escogiera como la primera persona que se enterara de la existencia de...

—¿Victoria Citlali qué?

—Dorina de la Concepción

—...

Esos tres puntos indican un gran silencio, lo que me hizo decir:

—¿Qué tiene?

—Nada.

—¿Qué?

—Nada

—¿Qué?

—Me gusta nada más Victoria.

—Está bien (Sabía que no iba a entender mi magnífica extravagancia). Nada más no me vayas a decir Vicky.

—Oye, ¿no serás solamente homosexual?

—Te digo que es más que eso. Siempre me he sentido como atrapado en un cuerpo que no es mío.

—...

Más silencio inexplicable de mi hermana.

—¿Qué piensas?

—¡De poca madre! Siempre quise tener una hermana (Claudia siempre ha sido un poco "mal hablada" diría Frida, o "pinche grosera", diría mi abuela, pero qué se le va a hacer, es parte de su *charme*, diría yo).

Esta gran revelación, como podrás entender, nos llevó a ponernos a recordar cómo era todo cuando éramos chicas...

Y digo aquí éramos "chicas", porque acabo de decidir que si me voy a llamar Victoria, debo empezar a asumir mi género hasta para escribir, así que lo repito: cuando éramos chicas, yo solía ver con envidia la ropa y los zapatos que le compraban a Claudia. Le confesé a mi hermana que era yo quien a escondidas maquillaba a sus *Barbies* y les cambiaba los vestidos. "Con razón. Y yo que creía que había una niña fantasma en la casa", me dijo un tanto divertida. La verdad es que Claudia difícilmente jugaba con sus muñecas y por eso el misterio de sus *Barbies* maquilladas apenas si llegó a molestarle. Ella prefería jugar beisbol en el parque, hacerse raspones y dejar completamente inútil su mejor ropa.

También le dije que desde que yo me acordaba, algún lugar escondido en mi interior deseaba que alguna de las playeras o pantalones vaqueros que la tía Lola me compraba se tiñeran mágicamente de lila o al menos de morado. Pero luego me decía a mí misma (tanto por los colores en la ropa, como por lo de las *Barbies*): "¿Qué te pasa? Esos gustos son para las viejas...". ¡Vaya palabra! Me asusta pensar que fui tan ordinaria y corriente como para haber usado alguna vez esa expresión. Pero así era. Yo era un hombre y debía comportarme con dureza y frialdad y no hacer ninguna de las cosas que las mujeres hacían... como llorar en las películas. ¡Ay! De eso mejor te platico mañana, que ya se hizo tarde y me choca que Frida venga a tocarme la puerta para pedirme que apague las luces. Sí, Nina, casi tengo dieciocho años y todavía molesta con eso, pero no creas que lo hace por cuidar mi sueño, lo hace para ahorrarse unos pesos en el pago a la compañía de luz.

Día en que te cuento cómo me hundí de un modo peor que el Titanic

Llorar en las películas

Cuando era una niña atrapada en el cuerpo de un niño, eso no era un problema, pero después, cómo me comenzó a dar lata. Desde que llegué a la adolescencia, cada vez que voy al cine, tengo que comprar de esas palomitas gigantes y ponerme a comer como compulsiva para evitar que salgan los lagrimones. La primera vez que no pude contenerme de plano fue con *Titanic* (ya antes me había pasado con *Dumbo*, pero ésa no cuenta, pues no hay niño o niña que no tenga un pequeño trauma con esa película o con *Bambi*). Si te contara. Bueno, sí te voy a contar. Total, ya pasó... Resulta que nos llevaron a Claudia y a mí, Frida y el Número Cuatro... Creo que aquí tengo que explicarte quién es el Número Cuatro... Lo que pasa es que mi hermana y yo numeramos siempre a todos los novios de Frida. Todo empezó con el gordo del Número Uno (ya no recuerdo ni cómo se llamaba), yo tenía siete años. "El aroma del cadáver de tu esposo aún ronda por los pasillos y tú ya sales con otros", le dijo mi abuela a Frida cuando ésta comenzó a salir con el panzón repugnante (Nina había olvidado que el esposo de su hija no había muerto, sino que ésta lo había corrido, pero eso era un error recurrente, así que...). Frida le contestó: "No son otros, es sólo uno... uno". Y repitió varias veces ese número. Fue entonces que sin sospechárselo, el pretendiente de Frida quedó bautizado: Número Uno. Tal vez Frida iba a intentar sustituir a nuestro padre, pero no iba conseguir nunca que llamáramos a sus horribles novios por su nombre... Y de decirles "papá", ni hablar.

Pero te decía que fuimos al cine con el Número Cuatro —él no era en realidad tan malo, nos llevaba al cine, a la feria y hasta nos compraba ropa—. En ese tiempo yo tenía, deja hago cuentas..., once años. Apenas despertaban en mi mente mis primeras inquietudes sentimentales, o sentimentaloides, debería decir.

Y pensar que yo antes me burlaba de mi hermana cuando lloraba en las películas. Es lo único que puede quebrar (hasta la fecha) a Claudia. Toda hierro ella, pero si ve un amor *hollywoodense* imposible en la pantalla, se rompe como una de esas tazas corrientes que compró Frida en el súper.

¡Cómo me burlaba de Claudia cuando lloraba! Hasta que ocurrió ese bochornoso episodio de *Titanic*.

Fue terrible, yo estaba emocionada, pues pensaba que vería una película de maravillosos efectos especiales, donde un gran barco se partía a la mitad, quedaba suspendido con la popa apuntando al cielo, se hundía y en el proceso morían cientos de personas, aplastadas, ahogadas y congeladas. Yo creía que de eso se trataba. Jamás me imaginé que en medio de toda esa espectacularidad estaba escondida una historia de amor. Luché contra mis sentimientos durante las más de tres horas que duró la infeliz película. Fue un martirio. Sólo las palomitas me ayudaron un poco. Pero cuando en la última escena los amantes vuelven a reunirse, me quebré por completo. Tuve que salir corriendo al baño. Me encerré en un privado y no podía parar las lágrimas. Seguía comiendo palomitas y ni siquiera eso me quitaba la tristeza. No importaba que me dijera cosas como: "Pero ¿quién puede creer que una anciana más vieja que Nina va a recordar, después de ochenta y tantos años, una aventurilla de amor que duró menos de una semana? ¿Nada más porque la pintaron desnuda y tuvo sexo en la bodega de un trasatlántico? ¿Qué me pasa?". El llanto parecía detenerse con esos pensamientos. Pero entonces recordaba a Kate saltando del bote salvavidas de regreso al barco y diciéndole a Leonardo: "Sí tú saltas, yo salto". Y luego a Leonardo haciendo que ella prometiera que iba a seguir su vida... y cuando él muere... y ella no se da cuenta de que él deja de respirar... y ella llora y promete... y él se hunde para siempre en el azul profundo... con la mano en lo alto... y ella silba y... y... y... ¿ya ves? Aún ahora, estoy a punto de lagrimear, ¿no te digo?

Cómo se burló Claudia (aunque ella también lloró). No le importó entrar al baño de hombres a buscarme, con tal de reírse de mí. Cuando salimos, le hice jurar que no le diría nada a Frida ni al Número Cuatro. Todo quedó en un supuesto dolor estomacal. "Claro, te acabaste tú solo dos bolsas tamaño gigante", dijo Frida, molesta porque gracias a mí había hecho el ridículo frente a su cuarto novio... aún lo recuerdo.

Sí. Siempre hubo cosas que me hacían sospechar de la existencia de Victoria; esa mujer que estaba escondida en mi cuerpo. Pero la vida, en cuanto te ve con el cabello corto, usando pantalones y orinando de pie, se empeña en que debes cumplir con ciertos papeles, no sólo debes permanecer como roca ante una película romántica, sino evitar la más pequeña lágrima cuando te caes de la bicicleta y disfrutar de juegos que sólo los gorilas o seres con un IQ menor de cien, disfrutarían; como las luchas, las canicas o...

&/&#&"/&(#&& ¡Carajo!... No se puede tener privacidad en esta casa. Ya vino Frida a molestar. Para ella, una persona que se encierra en su cuarto sólo puede estar haciendo cochinadas. Lo que es tener la mente cochambrosa... Quién sabe qué creerá su roñosa mente que... bueno, mejor le sigo mañana. Es imposible seguir platicando con mal humor, y ahorita estoy que no me calienta ni el sol de Mexicali.

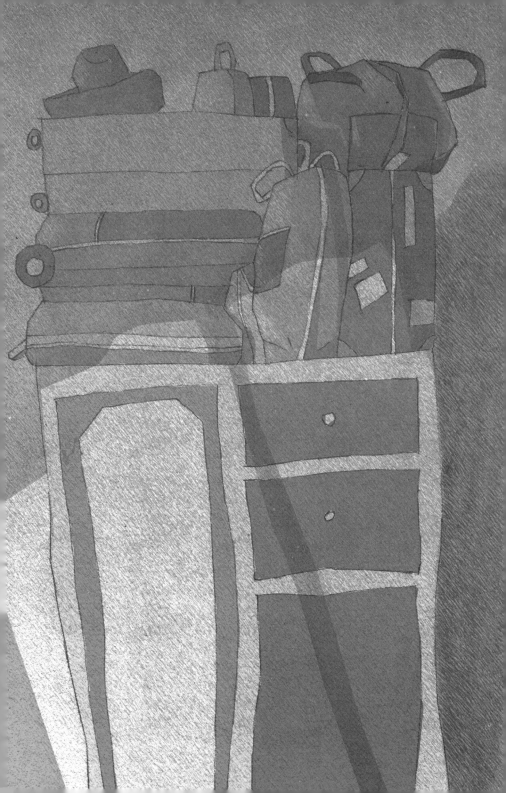

Día en que te cuento acerca de mis manos mágicas

El futbol. Odio el futbol. Y eso sí que va perfectamente con una mujer. Ni siquiera mi abuela soportaba la fiebre que despertaban eventos como los campeonatos mundiales: "Son sólo ocho tontos persiguiendo una pelota junto a otros ocho tontos" (Realmente, Nina, nunca tuviste idea del número de jugadores o de cualquier otra cosa relacionada con el juego). El problema es que por años he tenido que jugarlo. Y yo creo que nunca me resistí, y hasta intenté que me interesara, justamente porque sentía que debía gustarme. Era como darme inyecciones de masculinidad. El futbol era otra de las cosas que impedían que me encontrara a mí misma. Sin que me diera cuenta, ocultaba a Victoria de la Concepción con cada patada que le daba a la pelota. Ahora que lo pienso, usando mis neuronas femeninas, creo que lo único que sí me gusta del futbol es que es uno de los maravillosos deportes donde puedes ver hombres en pantalones cortos.

Pero te decía que he tenido que jugar futbol. ¿Por qué? En realidad todo empezó por culpa de Claudia. Siempre me hacía jugar con ella. Ella me pateaba la pelota, mientras yo tenía que ponerme como portero. Le encantaba sentirse cada uno de los jugadores de la selección. A Claudia la enloquecía el futbol. Hasta tenía una playera del Cruz Azul, su equipo favorito, que Frida le escondía, pues, según ella, "El futbol es para hombres y lo que es peor, para hombres corrientes y más cuando se trata de un equipo de cementos". A mí no me parecía un deporte de gente vulgar, pero sí medio bárbaro. De hecho, al principio me daba miedo. Pero yo me repetía: "Se supone que soy hombre, entonces me debe gustar patear balones". Tanto me lo repetí que llegué a acostumbrarme, no a la idea de ser hombre, sino a jugar ese deporte. La primera vez que Claudia pateó un balón directo hacia mí, recuerdo que me dio terror que me fuera a pegar esa pelota mugrienta en pleno rostro, así que puse las manos justo frente a mí, y cerré los ojos. Cuando me di cuenta, la pelota estaba atrapada entre mis dedos. Ese día Claudia me lo dijo: "Tienes las manos mágicas de Michel Prudom". Yo no tenía idea de a qué se refería, pero me imaginé que había querido decir que mis manos eran las de todo un portero. Yo más bien creí que sólo tenía los dedos demasiado largos. Pero en vez de que mis manos recibieran un trato más fino y que yo hubiera sido impulsada como pianista, no, mi hermana se encargó de hacerme todo un guardameta, todo un Prudom. Así que cuando entré al bachillerato y el maestro de deportes nos puso a jugar futbol, como un requisito indispensable para aprobar el curso, no pude negarme. La otra opción significaba un examen extraordinario consistente en hacer tantas sentadillas y lagartijas como para que te diera un infarto. Yo odiaba el ejercicio extenuante y sin propósito, por eso preferí unirme al equipo de futbol. El entrenador —un tipo que jamás entendí qué hacía de maestro de Educación Física si tenía la figura de un elefante marino— no tardó en darse cuenta de que poseía manos mágicas. De nada me sirvió decirle que no se dejara engañar, que en lo que yo realmente tenía talento era en la cocina y que prefería esa actividad extracurricular. Así que en menos de lo que te lo escribo, ya estaba yo convertido en el portero oficial del equipo. Y no fue nada fácil; ya que, como debes saber, un portero no sólo debe atrapar balones, sino atreverse a enfrentar jugadas tan peligrosas como salir a cortar centros o barrerse como verdadero salvaje, con el riesgo de que le rompan una pierna. No tienes idea el esfuerzo que tuve que hacer. Me daba TERROR (así, con "mayúsculas subrayadas") cuando un tipo se acercaba con el balón y no tenía defensas cubriéndome. Me daban ganas de demandarlos por hacer que me jugara la humanidad por un tonto deporte. En más de una ocasión yo hubiera dejado sin problemas que anotaran gol con tal de evitarme un raspón, pero esa voz maligna en mi interior me decía: "No puedes ser cobarde. Eres hombre. Ve por la pelota". No sé cómo (porque casi siempre cerraba los ojos), pero lo hacía. Y aunque te parezca raro, nunca me lastimaron. Y eso que me daba verdadero pánico que me pasara algo, y dicen que cuando más aterrorizado estás, más llamas a la desgracia.

Pero yo me hacía la ruda, fingía que no me importaban los raspones ni ensuciarme, y que disfrutaba sudar como albañil.

Eso hizo que nadie sospechara que por ahí, debajo de ese suéter de color morado —lo único bueno de todo este asunto— estaba Victoria que, con cada partido, prefería cerrar los ojos y esconderse en algún lugar entre mi estómago y mi hígado.

Día en que te cuento sobre la fecha en que casi muero atado a una alambrada

Como recordarás, Claudia me dijo que tal vez yo era homosexual. Pues yo le tuve que explicar que lo que a mí me pasaba era más profundo. Era una cuestión de identidad. ¿Entiendes? Le dije que sí, que creía que me gustaban los hombres, pero como le gustarían a una mujer. Un homosexual está contento siendo hombre y así le gustan los de su mismo sexo. Yo soy mujer, y como tal lo más normal era que me gustaran los hombres, pero no descartaba la posibilidad de que me gustaran las mujeres, o sea que Victoria podía ser una mujer lesbiana (todo un lío). Le expliqué a Claudia que ser heterosexual u homosexual eran cuestiones de preferencias. Le expliqué que así como a uno le puede gustar U2 (a mí, evidentemente) a otra persona le puede gustar Metallica (a mi hermana, evidentemente). Y ella pareció darme la razón cuando le pregunté: "¿Si tú fueras lesbiana, te cambiarías el sexo sólo porque te gustan las mujeres?", y ella me contestó: *"Touché"*.

No podía culpar a Claudia por pensar así. De hecho yo siempre tuve que cuidarme para que Victoria no apareciera cuando estaba en presencia de otros hombres, ya que corría el riesgo de ser calificado de marica o, peor que eso, de puto (vaya vulgaridad).

Eso me pasó el día que conocí a Rodrigo. O más bien el día que "realmente" conocí a Rodrigo.

Fue jugando futbol. O más bien, después de jugar futbol. Fue el día que entró al equipo un chavo, que digo un chavo, un megagalán: Carlos Rico era su nombre. Aunque no me lo creas así se llamaba... bueno sí, es mentira, la verdad yo así le puse. Se llamaba Carlos Rincón. Yo, que en aquel entonces era conocido por todos como un aguerrido portero, tenía que contener los impulsos de Victoria. Tenía que hacer esfuerzos sobrehumanos para no quedármele viendo como tonta. Y no es que me dieran ganas de besarlo o algo así. Era sólo verlo. En clase me era difícil mirar hacia el pizarrón cuando le tocaba exponer algún tema. Era como estar ante un maravilloso paisaje y estar obligada a ver infomerciales por la televisión. Siempre luchaba por no verlo. Pero ese día, la bruta de Victoria no pudo más. Estábamos cambiándonos en los baños y de pronto sin saber cómo, me quedé mirándolo. Me quedé viendo fijamente cómo se ponía las calcetas. No pienses mal. ¿Qué puede haber de sexy en un tipo poniéndose las calcetas? El caso es que mis ojos se quedaron ahí, ¡zas!, como dos agujas prendadas de una bola de estambre. Y debieron ser dos agujas muy puntiagudas porque, de inmediato, Carlos Rico volteó hacia a mí. Ni siquiera pude reaccionar a tiempo. No sé qué cara de idiota he de haber tenido, que hizo que su rostro de caballero andante se transformara en el del peor microbusero de la colonia Guerrero. Y la que se armó.

—¿Qué me ves?

Yo seguía embobada.

—¿Qué me ves, eh, maricón?

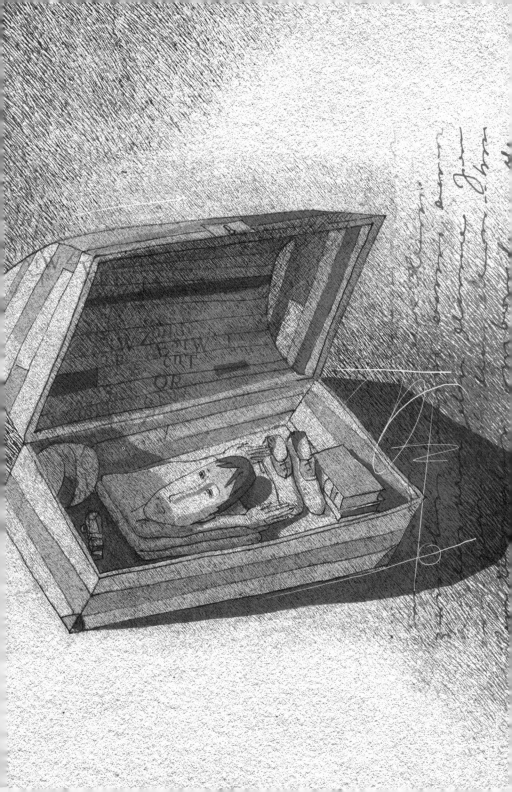

No importa cómo veas a un hombre. Si tus ojos se quedan en él por más de cinco segundos, supone que tu intención es violarlo enseguida. Si eres mujer (digo, de carne y hueso) no hay problema, el tipo se siente más soñado que el ángel guardián de Brad Pitt, pero si eres hombre...

Se me lanzó encima. Victoria estuvo a punto de gritar. Pero apenas pudo balbucear algo absurdo, algo tan absurdo que no puedo ni ponértelo aquí. Apenas si puedo recordar cómo me lanzó un golpe en plena mejilla que me hizo caer al suelo. Me dolió tanto, que creí que me iba a desmayar. Entonces, ya en el suelo, sentí de pronto que su cuerpo me caía encima, mientras seguía repitiendo: "Responde, maricón. Responde maricón...". Victoria debió haber pensado: "Hasta aquí llegaste, y todo por golosa".

En ese momento lo único que pudo enfocar mi mente fue una película que acababa de ver unos días antes. Una de ésas que están basadas en hechos de la vida real. Era una película sobre un pobre homosexual al que mataban dos muchachos (bueno, debería decir, dos bestias), tan sólo porque se les antojó matarlo. Lo golpearon, lo ataron a una cerca de alambre y lo dejaron agonizando ahí. El muchacho gay, todavía llegó al hospital y permaneció varios días en coma. Todo un escándalo. Entrevistaron a la gente del pueblo. Nadie quería siquiera hablar de ello. Es extraño, pero todo el poblado parecía sentirse culpable. Claro que había quienes lo negaban y decían cosas como: "No lo mataron porque fuera gay, sino porque algo debió hacer, les robó su dinero o tal vez los insultó, ¿o qué, los gays no insultan a los demás?". También estaban los cínicos, los que decían orgullosos barbaridades como: "El odio es uno de nuestros valores" (y esto lo dijo una viejita que podía pasar por abuela tuya en sus peores años).

Y recuerdo que pensé: "Menos mal que no vivo en Wyoming, porque habría tenido que montar a caballo o marcar reses, en vez de jugar futbol, para ocultar a Victoria". Y es que simplemente no hubiera podido ser vaquero: una vez Frida me llevó a una granja y yo estaba aterrado. No podía acariciar ni a un conejo, tenía miedo de que confundiera mi dedo con una zanahoria; y ni hablemos de las vacas, para mí eran como pequeños dinosaurios pintos diabólicos.

Todo eso recordé en unos segundos, mientras sentía los golpes de Carlos Rico en mis brazos, que por instinto había cruzado para cubrir mi rostro. Pero entonces sentí como su cuerpo se alejaba de mí. No porque se hubiera arrepentido o hubiera tenido suficiente, sino porque había llegado alguien a rescatarme.

Me hubiera gustado decirte que fue un caballero azul, un galán de barba partida, ojos verdes y negra cabellera. Pero no.

Era Rodrigo Méndez. El defensa central del equipo.

Si buscas en un diccionario ilustrado la palabra "sexy", seguramente no te encontrarás la foto de Rodrigo Méndez como ilustración. Hay muchos adjetivos para describirlo, pero "atractivo" no es uno de ellos. De hecho me gustaría decirte que es un tipo ordinario, uno de esos que tendrías que señalar para referirte a él, pero no. Rodrigo no puede pasar desapercibido, simplemente porque un metro ochenta y más de cien kilos de peso en un ser humano, nunca pueden pasar desapercibidos. Rodrigo, como todos los seres voluminosos, ha tenido que cargar con apodos tan desagradables como: gordo, mantecoso, globo, *porky*, ñoño, y varios más. Sin embargo, también es cierto que gracias a su estatura, nadie se atreve a meterse con él. Tiene el tamaño de un refrigerador de ésos que están en las gasolineras. No es muy rápido para correr, pero ni falta que le hace, como defensa no tiene problema para impedir el paso a alguien. Y es que ¿quién puede pasar por encima de un refrigerador de gasolinera? Rodrigo tiene además una voz profunda y potente, y un modo de apretarte la mano cuando te saluda, que tú juras que te va a fracturar un hueso. Juega futbol americano y he sabido que ha mandado al hospital a uno que otro inocente. Además de que como defensa central no es precisamente un inofensivo ratoncito. A mí siempre me había dado miedo, y tengo que reconocer que me intimidaba estar cerca de él. Victoria siempre tenía que ser cuidadosa. En más de una ocasión tuve la pesadilla en la que iba saliendo a la cancha hecha toda una Victoria Dorina, en medias y calzando tacones, cuando Rodrigo Méndez, al ver tal aparición, hervía por dentro, me tomaba de una pierna y comenzaba a tirar de ella, dispuesto a desprenderla, pero justo cuando comenzaba a rompérseme la media, yo me despertaba sudando, fuera de mi cama, con la pierna torcida envuelta en la sábana y en una posición bastante incómoda.

Cuando Rodrigo me quitó de encima a Carlos Rincón pensé que tal vez las intenciones de mi defensa central no eran salvarme sino, como en mi sueño, desmembrarme sin ayuda de nadie.

Pero no fue así. Le propinó un fuerte empujón a mi atacante al tiempo que le decía:

—¿Y a ti, qué te pasa?

—Ese maricón —dijo mientras me señalaba.

—¿Y cómo sabes que es maricón?

—Me estaba mirando.

—Y yo te estoy mirando, pendejo. A ver, dime a mí maricón.

Lo siguió empujando contra la pared como si fuera una pelota de volibol con la que estuviera practicando. Entonces, Carlos empezó a rogar que lo dejara, con un clásico e imaginativo: "Ya ahí muere, ahí muere". Rodrigo lo tomó de la camisa y le dio un fuerte empujón. Y mientras Carlos abandonaba el lugar a medio vestir, Rodrigo le gritó: "Tú eres el pinche maricón... A la chingada, pinche pendejo". No sé si el mareo que me dio entonces tuvo que ver con haber participado en una escena de tanta violencia o con el hecho de pensar que yo sería lanzado contra el techo. Pero en vez de triturarme, Rodrigo me tendió la mano y me preguntó si estaba bien. Yo me senté en la banca y me quedé un momento callada, entonces Rodrigo y su grave voz llenaron el silencio vaporoso que se había hecho.

—Odio que esos tipos se metan con nosotros. Lástima que los más guapos sean los más imbéciles.

Querida Nina, me quedé más muda que una difunta decapitada. ¿Había escuchado bien? ¿Rodrigo había dicho "nosotros"? ¿Había dicho "guapos"? ¿El refrigerador de gasolinera era gay? No pude pensar nada inteligente. Sólo se me ocurrió:

—Pero... yo no soy...

—¿Cómo?

—Digo que yo no soy homosexual...

—¿Cómo no vas a ser, si te vi mirándolo? Y déjame decirte que no tienes mal gusto.

—Pero... te juro que yo no soy...

Tal vez fue que en ese momento, como ahora, estaba convencida de que no era homosexual. Quizá si me hubiera dicho: "Oye tú, mujercita", entonces sí que me hubiera sentido aludida. Probablemente fue por eso que lo miré con ojos de "estás equivocado". Seguramente fue por eso que cuando Rodrigo me miró, entonces sí que se puso furioso, respiró hondo, me tomó de la camisa, igual que a Carlos y me dijo:

—Nada más dices una palabra de esto y te hago pedacitos y te tiro al pinche escusado.

Rodrigo me arrojó con la misma facilidad con la que hubiera arrojado la envoltura de un chicle, y yo me quedé ahí en el suelo, sin poderlo creer: el tipo más rudo de la escuela, el único que usaba sus manos como cascanueces, era homosexual.

Una leve sonrisa, Nina, se dibujó en mi cara.

Claro que no fui una ingrata o algo por el estilo. Para nada. Al día siguiente le pasé una nota en la que le agradecía que me hubiera salvado la vida y le juraba que jamás revelaría su secreto; y mi juramento lo hacía por la tumba de mi abuela y de mi madre (Ya sé que Frida aún está viva, pero me gustó la imagen de ella bajo tierra).

Para mi fortuna, Rodrigo es una buena persona, cero sexy, pero agradable, y se le pasó rápidamente el enojo. Fue así que nos hicimos amigos.

Día en que te cuento de mi segunda confesión

Desde que Rodrigo y yo nos hicimos amigos, he sido una especie de confidente suya, no sé si me entiendes. Gracias a mis pláticas con Rodrigo, he descubierto algunas cosas de él, unas muy profundas y otras muy ordinarias, como su gusto por el futbol que él me refirió:

Mi gran sueño siempre fue llegar a ser el primer delantero de la selección que llevara a su equipo a levantar la copa del mundo. Cuando era niño, soñaba con que le anotaría tres goles a Alemania en la final. También me soñaba jugando para grandes equipos. Los martes y los jueves soñaba que jugaba con el Bayern de Múnich, y los lunes, miércoles y viernes soñaba que jugaba para el Liverpool. No sé por qué, pero así era.

Ése fue el modo en que se hizo tan fanático al deporte de las patadas. Pero me contó que un día dejó de soñar. El día que cumplió doce años y su mamá le compró una báscula, tan sólo para que se diera cuenta de que ya pesaba ochenta kilos y que si no hacía nada, el único modo en que jugaría futbol iba a ser a través de los videojuegos.

Fue entonces cuando empezó a intentar seguir una dieta, de eso también me contó:

Pero lo hice a escondidas de mi papá. Ya sé lo que me hubiera dicho: "Esas dietas no sirven, ¿crees que no las he intentado yo todas? Todos en mi familia siempre hemos sido gordos. Ni siquiera el ejercicio nos ha servido. Tu abuelo era gordo, tus tíos pesaban más de cien kilos cada uno y a tu tía Cristina le decían todos La Tina... co. No hay nada que hacer". Y tal vez tenga razón, ya he intentado la dieta de la luna, la de los vegetales verdes, la de cero grasas. Siempre con el mismo resultado. Doscientos gramos menos. Doscientos pinches gramos.

Me explicó que durante diez días se limitó a comer lechugas, espinacas y apio para bajar apenas lo que pesa mi libro de matemáticas (el delgado). También me confesó que en una ocasión hizo ejercicio durante un mes todos los días; se levantaba a las seis para correr en el parque y después con un par de pesas, que se fabricó con dos latas grandes de chiles jalapeños rellenas de cemento, hacía varias series de levantamientos en la noche, pero el resultado siempre fue el mismo...: "¡Doscientos gramos! ¿Puedes creerlo? La única buena noticia era que no subía más. Pero ¿doscientos gramos?", me contó desesperado.

De todas las confidencias que me hace Rodrigo, las que más me gusta escuchar, Nina, son las más íntimas, como cuando me dijo: "¡Rafa! Aún lo recuerdo y la piel se me pone... Desde la primera vez que lo vi y tuve ese vacío en el estómago, lo supe. Ésa fue la vez que descubrí que era homosexual".

Rodrigo se enamoró del dependiente de un videoclub. Fue hace apenas dos años, él (Rodrigo) tenía catorce (Rafael, que así se llamaba, debe haber tenido unos diecisiete). El videoclub estaba cerca de la casa de una prima suya que vive en el otro extremo de la ciudad. Ese día la acompañó, pues ella quería ver la última película de

Julia Roberts (iba a decir que qué cursi, pero creo que no soy la más indicada para opinar). Dice Rodrigo que en cuanto lo vio se quedó paralizado, el corazón le comenzó a latir tan rápido como una batidora y la cabeza le comenzó a hervir. "¿Hervir?", le pregunté. "Sí", me dijo. "Era como si un fuerte calor que naciera en el estómago, quisiera salir por mi cabeza y no pudiera hacerlo." "Tal vez simplemente te habías insolado." "No, era amor." (Rodrigo sí que podía ser muuuuyyy cursi).

Claro que, como te podrás imaginar, Nina, y como normalmente ocurre en estos casos de amor apabullante, mi buen amigo no pudo dirigirle la palabra al dependiente, del que no averiguó ni el nombre. Lo único que se le ocurrió fue regresar al día siguiente, sacar una credencial e ir todos los fines de semana —que era cuando trabajaba su amor platónico—. Todos los viernes hacía un viaje de hora y media para llegar al video, fingir como que escogía películas, cuando en realidad sólo le echaba el ojo a su galán a través de los estantes, salir con películas que nunca veía y tomar el camión a su casa; otra hora y media de camino. ¿Y sabes qué fue lo peor, Nina? No. Lo peor no fue que tuviera que hacer el mismo viaje dos días después para tan sólo devolver las películas. Lo peor fue, claro, que el bestia de Rodrigo nunca le dirigió la palabra al mentado Rafael. "¿Nunca hiciste nada?", casi casi le recriminé. "Tanto como nada, no. Le escribí un recado en un video que regresé un sábado con todo y multa. Era una declaración de amor." "¿Y qué pasó?" "Nada. No me atreví a regresar."

No cabe duda de que el amor es una cosa muy complicada, Nina.

"Entonces todos tus viajes y las películas que no viste no sirvieron para nada", le dije. "Claro que sirvieron. Cuando dejé esa nota tuve la seguridad de que era gay."

.

Tengo que confesar que Rodrigo me dejó callada. Nadie mejor que yo sabe lo que significa por fin descubrir quién eres, después de ojeras espantosas, resultado de horas de insomnio con el cachete pegado a la almohada (y eso que, en ese momento, yo todavía no estaba segura de la existencia de Victoria). Pero pude entender a Rodrigo. Pude entender lo traumático que debió de ser para él descubrir que a partir de ese momento tenía dos caminos enfrente: o se encerraba en el clóset y ponía sus más profundos sentimientos bajo un uniforme de futbol o, bien, se asumía y anunciaba su condición, gritándolo a los cuatro vientos contaminados de la ciudad, arriesgándose a ser rechazado, ridiculizado, discriminado, y resignándose a escuchar que la gente lo llamara desde maricón hasta puto, pasando por puñal, mayate, hüilo, ¡ah!, y lilo.

Claro que, como te imaginarás, Rodrigo escogió el primer camino.

Y no lo puedo culpar, sobre todo después de haber visto la película ésa del homosexual asesinado.

Pero, a todo esto, lo que yo quería platicarte era otra cosa. Como ya te he contado y como te puedes imaginar, me he hecho buena amiga de Rodrigo, fue por eso que decidí que ya que él me había tenido tanta confianza al contarme sus intimidades, no podía callarme más.

Ese día, Rodrigo se había hecho un nuevo corte de cabello.

—Rodrigo, tengo que decirte algo.

—Ya sé. Estoy terrible. Le dije a Lucy que no me cortara el fleco, pero nunca me hace caso.

—Para nada. Te queda bien. Te hace ver más delgado.

Creo que exageré un poco... o mucho. No creo que exista corte de pelo que le haga ver más delgado. De hecho no creo que ningún ser humano con la talla de Rodrigo pudiera verse más delgado por algún efecto de ilusión óptica; así usara ropa con rayas verticales, ropa suelta o un traje negro en medio de un callejón oscuro. Es increíble, Nina, cómo somos vanidosos los seres humanos. Si alguien nos dice que un suéter se nos ve bien, se convierte inmediatamente en nuestro mejor amigo (me refiero al suéter), si alguien te dice que te ve más delgado, no consideras que lo más seguro es que el tipo tenga una avanzada miopía y nadie se lo ha dicho, porque, ni te has puesto a dieta por más de dos horas, ni tampoco has hecho una miserable lagartija en los últimos dos meses. En vez de eso, asumes que el hada madrina de Claudia Schiffer vino y sin consultarnos nos hizo el milagrito. Otra vez estoy divagando. Pero ya que estamos en eso, te pregunto, Nina, ¿te imaginas cómo usa Victoria el cabello?

Mi abuela (o sea, tú) siempre me dijo que le encantaba mi pelo. "Si yo tuviera tu cabello hubiera sido una gran modelo de *Vogue*", me decía, "y no simplemente una conejita de *Playboy*" (ya sabes, otra de sus alucinaciones). Y la verdad tenía razón, mi cabello siempre ha sido sedoso, brillante y fácil de peinar. Sí, todo un paradigma de los anuncios de acondicionador. Cuando era chica, Frida se encargaba de cometer el crimen de dejármelo como de militar. ¡Yo lo odiaba! A veces me metía al baño y al mirarme al espejo, me imaginaba con una gran cabellera ondulada y encrespada como de Whitney Houston y pensaba en lo bien que podría lucir mi rostro (con todo y mi lunar). Pero cuando cumplí los quince años, las cosas cambiaron: le pedí a Frida como regalo que me dejara usar el cabello largo. Claro que se opuso, ella no podía ver a Victoria, así que el cabello largo era sinónimo de *hippie* mugroso, pero le dije que si no me regalaba esa pequeña extravagancia, entonces tendría que regalarme un *iPod*. Tú sabes, esas maravillas tecnológicas que te permiten tener en una minúscula cajita todos los discos de U2 y de Radiohead. Por supuesto que tal aparato no es una bagatela (como diría mi abuela), así que cuando Frida supo el precio, tuvo que decidirse por la cabellera. Si hay algo que pueda ponerla en verdadero estado de coma, es el tener que gastar dos pesos de más en sus hijos. Tacaña podría ser su primer apellido; Moralina, vendría después. Frida Tacaña Moralina, para servirles (podría decir ella al presentarse).

Ya llevo tres meses con el cabello largo y Frida todavía no se acostumbra a verlo, siempre que llego a tomar mi desayuno con el cabello suelto, noto cómo se esconde tras de su taza de café, comienza a temblar, y siempre, invariablemente, me dice: "No pensarás irte así a la calle, ¿no?". Entonces lo ato con una cola de caballo y salgo con una sonrisa. Querida Nina, si no fuera por Rafa Márquez y otros personajes de cuya masculinidad nadie se atrevería dudar, nunca hubiera podido tomar este *look* originalmente reservado para las chicas. Además, agradezco estar inscrito en una preparatoria donde ni el corte de pelo, ni la ropa son cuestionadas en un estúpido reglamento. Lo único que exigen es la pulcritud, cosa con la que estoy completamente de acuerdo. Mugrosa, nunca.

Lo que más me gusta de mi cabello es que una vez que estoy en la privacidad de mi cuarto, puedo deshacerme de la cola de caballo y con un cepillo encrespármelo para darle volumen y ver una mayor aproximación de lo que es la verdadera Victoria.

Rodrigo será muy gay, pero usa el cabello de un modo que la misma Frida hubiera premiado con un beso. Nada sexy, para que me entiendas. Todavía no sé por qué le dije semejante mentira sobre su ordinaria cabellera, tal vez quise hacerlo sentir bien, o tal vez no tuve la suficiente crueldad como para decirle lo que realmente pensaba. Lo cierto es que Rodrigo dudó y me preguntó con suspicacia:

—¿Realmente lo crees?

—No.

Después de todo sí tenía yo un poco de crueldad en las venas.

Afortunadamente, Rodrigo era un acérrimo militante de los optimistas, así que sonrió y de inmediato cambió el tema, o más bien regresó al asunto original:

—Y ¿qué querías decirme?

Tuve que llevarlo aparte. Lo que le iba a decir no lo podían escuchar ni las palomas que a veces rondaban el patio de la prepa:

—¿Qué?, tienes una cara, porterito...

Rodrigo sólo se atrevía a decirme porterito u otros apodos bastante ridículos, cuando no podían escucharlo ni las palomas.

—Soy mujer.

—...

....

....

....

....

....

....

Para que pudieras entender el gran silencio que se hizo en ese instante tendría que poner una página entera vacía y no sólo un párrafo lleno de puntos, pero no quiero desperdiciarte demasiado.

Finalmente, Rodrigo habló:

—¿Qué?

Entonces le expliqué todo el asunto.

Rodrigo no pudo contenerse y gritó como si efectivamente su corte de pelo lo hubiera hecho perder dos kilos. ¡Qué oso!

—Lo sabía. Lo sabía.

—¿Quieres controlarte?

—Eres mujer....

—¿Por qué no lo gritas? Creo que no te escuchó mi madre.

¡Mi madre...!

No quiero saber que pasaría si se lo cuento, Nina...

Día en que te cuento sobre la confesión de Claudia

Aún recuerdo la escenita que ocurrió exactamente hace seis años.

¡Cómo no estuviste ahí!

Claudia esperó hasta tener los quince años para darle a Frida una noticia apabullante.

Frida estaba feliz de que su "pequeña brujita" (Frida le había puesto ese apodo, que, por supuesto, Claudia odiaba) hubiera alcanzado la mágica edad de los quince años. Estaba pensando en hacer una gran fiesta que organizaría el Número Ocho (este novio era lo que se dice bastante pudiente, y aunque no lo creas, gracias a un negocio de anuncios luminosos).

Estábamos comiendo una sopa instantánea y tacos descongelados (el único tipo de comida que podía hacer Frida sin ocasionar una movilización del cuerpo de bomberos), cuando Claudia, sin levantar la vista del plato, dijo:

—Madre...

Yo sabía que algo fuerte se venía. Sentí un nerviosismo extraño que me hizo temblar. Nunca he podido evitarlo, las situaciones tensas me ponen en un estado muy poco conveniente. Por lo general sólo me tiembla una de las piernas, pero cuando la cosa se pone escalofriante, entonces, me tiembla el labio u otras partes de mi anatomía.

En ese momento me temblaron los dos labios y el dedo índice de la mano derecha.

A Frida no le hubiéramos dicho madre, ni por hipocresía o equivocación, ni siquiera en el festival del diez de mayo de la escuela, claro, si es que se hubiera dignado a ir. Y ella lo sabía, por eso no se alcanzó a llevar la cuchara a la boca.

Las dos —madre e hija— se quedaron paralizadas y tan mudas como dos paredes.

—Soy lesbiana —dijo por fin Claudia.

Me quedé de a seis, de a cuatro y hasta de a nueve, Nina. ¿Claudia era homosexual? Era cierto que mi hermana no era lo que se podría llamar un modelo de la feminidad, que su gusto para vestir no la iba llevar a ninguna pasarela y que tal vez ella hubiera disfrutado más mi posición de portero que yo misma (o que muchos hombres), pero de eso a que le gustaran las mujeres había como mil kilómetros. Además, yo la había visto suspirar por uno que otro hombre, por eso me tomó por sorpresa. Pero lo importante, Nina, no eran mis dudas, ni la sorpresa que me provocó; en ese momento lo único que pude pensar fue en la posible reacción de Frida. Mi hermana le había dicho a su madre que era lesbiana. Y lo había dicho así como así. Ya no eran sólo los labios y mi dedo, sentía que hasta el cerebro me temblaba.

Frida se quedó estática. Después con delicadeza llevó la cuchara a la boca, tragó la sopa y se limpió los labios.

Claudia y yo nos miramos. ¿Acaso no iba a decir nada?

Entonces sin que mi hermana lo esperara, Frida la tomó de la oreja y le dio tal tirón que creí que se quedaría con un pedazo de carne en la mano.

Claudia apenas si se inmutó. Ya estábamos acostumbrados a esos comportamientos esquizoides de Frida, sin embargo, no pude evitar sentir un leve miedito.

Mi hermana sólo se llevó la mano a la oreja y se sobó.

Frida tomó un sorbo de agua y dijo:

—Es la última vez que tolero que se hagan bromas pornográficas en la comida... —Y después de una breve pausa, con la mayor naturalidad del mundo, continuó—: Dime, mi brujita, ¿quieres que hagamos la fiesta en un salón o en casa de la tía Lola?, ya ves lo mucho que te quiere.

—¿No escuchaste lo que dije? Soy homosexual.

En ese momento sí que me aterré. Seguro que vendría otro tirón o una furiosa cachetada que era siempre el segundo golpe de Frida. Pero entonces miré sus ojos. Por fin la mujer había tragado bien el bocado amargo: su hija, su brujita, estaba hablando en serio.

Frida dio un fuerte manotazo en la mesa, se levantó y comenzó a murmurar:

—¿Es otra broma tuya, Claudia? Mira que si es otra broma... te juro que...

—Ya te lo dije... me gustan las mujeres.

—Pero ¿cómo es posible? Eres una niña. A una niña no le pueden gustar las mujeres.

—Tengo una novia... se llama Julieta.

Frida comenzó a dar vueltas por el cuarto murmurando una receta que Nina le había hecho aprender de niña. Una receta que jamás fue capaz de hacer. Siempre que entraba en una crisis se ponía a dar de vueltas y a murmurar cómo preparar un soufflé de zanahoria: "se cuecen las zanahorias y se aplastan. Se hace una salsa blanca espesa con la mantequilla...".

—Te lo quise decir, para que no te enteraras por otros.

—No te estoy escuchando. Esto no puede ser cierto.

—Me gustaría invitar a todas mis amigas a mi fiesta de quince años.

—Ninguna hija mía puede ser una loca promiscua...

—¿Te imaginas? Una fiesta llena de chicas besándose entre sí.

—Cállate, Claudia.

En ese momento Frida levantó la mano. Por un momento creí que la azotaría contra la vitrina del comedor (la que seguíamos pagando con un 10% de interés), o que de menos la arañaría como gata salvaje. Pero se detuvo, yo creo que temía romperse una uña y arruinar su manicura (Claudia tuvo la fortuna de decírselo un miércoles de manicura). Entonces Frida se llevó las manos al pecho fingiendo un ataque de asma, del corazón o epiléptico, lo que fuera. Cualquier cosa melodramática y fulminante.

—¡Dios mío! ¿Qué pretendes con esto?

—Tenía que decírtelo.

—¿Por qué tenías que mortificarme ahora?

—¿Cuándo querías, cuando tuviera cincuenta años?

—Tal vez hubiera sido lo mejor. Ninguna hija decente le hace esto a su madre.

—No es el fin del mundo...

—Es el fin del universo...

Un silencio espeso comenzó a cubrirlo todo. Era tan, tan espeso que por un momento hasta la vista se me nubló. Entonces Claudia dijo:

—Tienes razón, Frida. No soy lesbiana. Todo lo hice para engañarte... Te engañé, ¿verdad? —El silencio que siguió fue aún más espeso que el anterior. Claudia continuó—: Vas a firmar el permiso para que pueda entrar al grupo de teatro de la prepa. Y lo vas a hacer como un regalo por mis quince años.

Me quedé pasmada. Mi hermana tenía la capacidad para convertirse en una gran actriz. Y se lo había demostrado a Frida. Si nuestra madre tenía palabra y memoria, tendría que apoyarla en esto.

Indignada, Frida se levantó (Ella también era toda una artista, podía acabar en el suelo tras apenas un minuto de rabieta y sin hacerse el menor daño), firmó la hoja que Claudia había puesto en la mesa, la miró con desprecio y le dirigió la que sería la última frase por mucho tiempo.

—Yo ya no tengo hija...

Se arregló el cabello, se sentó y continuó comiendo.

En ese momento, Frida dejó de hablarle a mi hermana.

Casi seis meses duró "la ley del hielo" que le aplicó mi madre a Claudia (Tú la conoces y sabes que no miento). Si quería comunicarse con ella, siempre lo hacía por mi conducto. Lo cual era un verdadero fastidio, Nina.

La verdad es que en esos meses envidié como nadie a mi hermana. Pocas veces la he visto tan feliz.

Después madre e hija tuvieron que volver a hablarse, no recuerdo por qué, creo que una firma de boletas estuvo involucrada, y las cosas volvieron a la terrible normalidad.

Pero no creas que ese tipo de eventos no volvió a ocurrir. La personalidad explosiva de Frida mezclada con la rebeldía de mi hermana han ocasionado estas rupturas en varias ocasiones. Algunas veces han durado unas tres semanas (como cuando Claudia decidió que estudiaría teatro a nivel profesional); otras, unos tres meses (como cuando mi hermana se peleó con la tía Lola contra todos los deseos de Frida); y otras, unos cuatro meses (como ahora, que mi hermana le notificó a Frida su deseo de irse a vivir al extranjero con su novio). Pero nunca un pleito ha alcanzado el maravilloso récord de aquel otoño. Quién sabe, tal vez este año lo superen.

El caso es que si Frida reaccionó aquella vez como lo hizo con una noticia falsa, ¿te imaginas, Nina, qué pasaría si le digo lo que le dije a Claudia y a Rodrigo? Ella no se pondría a saltar de alegría como ellos. Seguro que le provoco un soponcio auténtico, uno que la haga quedarse ciega y paralítica de un solo golpe.

Aunque la verdad, si Frida me dejara de hablar por uno o dos años, no sería tan malo. Mi madre, como dice mi hermana: "Calladita se ve más bonita".

Pero como te decía, Nina, tuve que controlar a Rodrigo para que me escuchara y entendiera:

—Se lo dije a Claudia y te lo digo a ti. Soy mujer, no homosexual.

—O sea que eres transexual.

No era la primera vez que oía la palabra, pero era la primera vez que la oía asociada a mí, por eso me quedé callada, sin saber qué decir.

Día de una explicación científica no pedida

Transexual, Nina. Supongo que siempre que alguien se topa con esa palabra, piensa en una cosa: operación de cambio de sexo. O sea, un corte criminal, ya sea para eliminar tetas o testículos. Y eso pensé cuando Rodrigo me preguntó si yo era transexual; y casi estoy segura de que él pensó en lo mismo. ¿Quería yo eso? No lo sé. Sé que me llamo Victoria, que soy mujer, que me gustan los vestidos, que idolatro a Bono, que no puedo evitar llorar en películas románticas, pero no sé si eso signifique que tengo que deshacerme de cierta parte de mi escultórica figura.

Hoy por la tarde, justo después del entrenamiento de futbol, fui a la biblioteca y averigüé algunas cosas. Entonces entendí un poco de por qué soy como soy.

Frida y mi padre... tuvieron sexo. Difícil de hacerse a la idea, de veras. Frida desnuda y a merced de un hombre no es algo agradable ni para la imaginación. Difícil ver en mi mente al hombre del que apenas tengo una imagen vaga. El caso es que debió ser una noche de septiembre. Tal vez hacía frío. Tal vez Frida bebió un poco de vodka

—desde que recuerdo siempre ha tomado vodka—. Tal vez mi padre, que debió ser un romántico con toneladas de paciencia (cualidades que no tenía, ni tiene, su esposa), la llevó a cenar. Tal vez le regaló alguna flor. Tal vez por el efecto de las copas, ella cambió y se convirtió en una mujer dulce y hermosa. Entonces mi padre, sin poder resistirlo, la comenzó a besar, primero en los dedos de la mano, después en el cuello. Tal vez Frida comenzó a reír. Mi padre entonces quizá la llevó hasta la cama, sin que ella pusiera un gramo de resistencia. Pudieron haber pasado tantas cosas, pero eso sí, esa noche tuvieron sexo. Y estoy segura de que si el momento no fue romántico, al menos debió haber sido tan cálido como un día de carnaval brasileño.

No usaron condones, y Frida, como podría decir algún cursi novelista, era una flor abierta, esperando a ser fecundada. Un solo esper... (Siempre me ha parecido horrible esta palabra, suena como a una especie de dinosaurio, pero es peor decir semilla, así que la diré). Un solo espermatozoide de mi padre encontró esa pequeña esfera viajera en el útero de Frida e inició todo.

Desde ese primer segundo de mi existencia, por un truco de intercambio de la genética, dos cromosomas que definieron mi sexo fueron XY. La naturaleza decía que yo debía ser hombre, pero algo pasó. Mi cuerpo y mi cerebro, gracias a las hormonas segregadas por Frida, comenzaron a recibir kilos de información. Así, mis genitales se formaron (bastante bien, debo decir) y en mi mente, la sensación de pertenecer al género de los gladiadores, de los que hacen la guerra, de los que golpean esposas, debió haberse instalado, pero no fue así. Mi cuerpo y mi cerebro registraron cosas diferentes. Una mezcla inadecuada, una impregnación no del todo acertada en ciertos puntos de mi mente, me hicieron ser diferente... en mi mente ya era Victoria.

Fue gracias a...

Perdón que te dejara por un momento, Nina, pero sonó el teléfono.

Era Rodrigo. El muy loco sigue entusiasmado por mi comentario. Y se le ha ocurrido algo. A ver qué te parece.

—Ya sé cómo podemos averiguar si eres transexual.

Eso fue lo que me dijo, casi gritando por el teléfono. Por un momento tuve miedo de que Frida estuviera escuchando. A veces le da por descolgar el auricular que está en su cuarto, pero recordé que ella había salido con el Número Doce (me parece que a una exhibición de cosméticos).

Rodrigo insistió:

—Ya sé lo que debemos hacer.

—¿De qué estás hablando?

Rodrigo me habló de algo muy especial, Nina. No me atrevo todavía a contarte de qué se trata. Ni siquiera sé si lo que trama mi amigo será posible. Será este viernes y si salgo viva, entonces, prometo contarte todos los detalles, pero por el momento te dejaré con la angustiante duda.

Espero que no seas tan impaciente como yo. Ya sabes que a mí no me puedes dejar con la duda de nada, de hecho, si tú fueras de carne y hueso y me dijeras algo como "luego te cuento", primero te ataría de pies y manos y te encerraría en una caja, antes que permitirte que huyeras sin decirme de qué se trata. Pero como tú eres un diario, tendrás que soportar esta crueldad, pequeña, pero crueldad al fin, de ocultarte este tremendo chisme por unos días.

¡*Ciao*!

Día en que mi vestido finalmente sale de paseo

Llegué a casa de Rodrigo muy temprano. El brazo derecho, desde el hombro hasta el dedo meñique, me temblaba mientras subía por el elevador. Iba abrazando la maleta morada que llevaba. Dicen que cuando una hace cosas así (me refiero a aferrarse ridículamente a un objeto) es por inseguridad. Y tienen razón, yo estuve insegura todo el tiempo. Sentí nervios cuando me metí al cuarto de Frida, aprovechando que ella se había ido a vender sus tiempos compartidos. Una de las piernas me tembló cuando abrí su clóset. Experimenté gran ansiedad cuando salí de la casa. Ya en el taxi tuve espasmos en las dos piernas. Me sentí ridícula y estuve a punto de pedirle al chofer que mejor me llevara a un bar. Y lo hubiera hecho, pero no tengo la edad adecuada y ni credencial de elector que me hubiera permitido olvidarme del asunto con un par de tequilas. Sin embargo, algo en mi interior me decía que no podía ser tan cobarde, que ya le había prometido a Rodrigo que iría. Y por alguna razón desconocida, que hacía temblar mi vientre (jamás me había temblado el vientre antes), me sentía obligada a hacerlo.

Los números en el elevador iban cambiando y yo, aprovechando la soledad en esa caja de metal, me repetía una y otra vez, tal como me había recomendado Nina que hiciera para tomar valor: "¡Vamos Victoria, tú puedes! ¡Vamos, tú puedes!".

Cuando la puerta del departamento se abrió, apenas lo pude creer. Ahí, ante mis incrédulos ojos, apareció. Fue una imagen de ésas que se te meten al ojo como un dardo se incrusta en un tiro al blanco. Una mujer entrada en carnes, qué digo entrada en carnes, una tipa bastante gorda, que lucía un corsé negro con holanes, unas medias negras de red y tacones de charol, se apoyaba en el quicio con actitud realmente de dar miedo. De pronto, me sentí en una película italiana vieja, de ésas en las que las prostitutas venidas a menos intentan sacar a sus hijos del hambre infame. Apenas me atreví a mirarla otra vez al rostro. Ella se echó sobre el hombro una estola lila que le caía sobre el pecho. Yo estaba más que incómoda y las palabras que un instante después salieron de mi boca sonaron igual a las de un mocoso que va a pedir un par de huevos con la vecina: "Perdón, señora, ¿vive aquí Rodrigo Méndez?". Como respuesta lo que obtuve fue una sonora y burlona carcajada. Estuve a punto de reclamarle a la vieja hipopótamo ésa y decirle que si quería burlarse de algo se mirara en un espejo, pero entonces reconocí la voz. Era Rodrigo. Mi amigo estaba convertido en la tía gorda de Liza Minelli. No podía creerlo. Si me hubiera atrevido a mirar con detalle, lo hubiera reconocido sin duda. Claro que sabía que podía encontrarme con algo así, pero la verdad es que cuando Rodrigo me invitó a que nos coláramos en una fiesta travesti, creí que él a lo mucho se atrevería a usar una peluca, nunca me imaginé que fuera a disfrazarse de ese modo, y menos me imaginé que pudiera abrirme la puerta vestido así. Estaba demostrado que yo era una novata en estas cosas.

—¡Qué bárbaro, Rodrigo... mírate nada más!

Por un momento temí que mis palabras hubieran sonado como a las de una madre neurótica que ve a su hijo embarrado de vómito. Pero afortunadamente no.

—¿A poco no estoy perfecta?

Era la primera vez que oía a Rodrigo referirse a sí mismo como una "ella". Tal vez por eso sólo me salió una sonrisa que intentó ser lo más aprobatoria posible. (*Oh, my God*, si Rodrigo hubiera sabido lo que realmente estaba pensando).

Me apresuré a entrar en cuanto me invitó a hacerlo, no quería pensar en el oso que sería para Rodrigo (está bien, en el ridículo que sería para mí) si alguien pasara por el pasillo. Ni siquiera una mosca aguantaría la risa.

Lo curioso es que Rodrigo apenas si se había inmutado. Casi podría jurar que quería que los vecinos salieran a verlo. Más tarde entendería por qué.

Pero te decía que me invitó a pasar.

—¿Cómo es que no estás lista? No pensarás ir sin la vestimenta adecuada, ¿o sí?

—No esperabas que viniera desde mi casa vestida así.

—Pues de aquí no sales sin un buen par de tacones, porterito, quiero decir, porterita.

Como comprenderás, Nina, no iba a ser nada fácil. Le pedí a Rodrigo que me permitiera usar su cuarto para cambiarme.

Al principio estaba muy temerosa. ¿Qué le diría a la madre de Rodrigo?: "Qué tal señora, soy una gran amiga de su hijo, sí, escuchó bien, soy una amiga de su hijo, no se deje engañar por mi presencia masculina, en realidad soy una mujer, una mujer atrapada en un cuerpo dotado con la manzana de Adán y también con sus testículos. Un pequeño error de la naturaleza, de Dios o de quien a usted mejor le plazca. El caso es que su hijo y yo vamos a ir a una fiesta travesti. Sí, claro que aún somos unos adolescentes, sí, muy próximos a los dieciocho, pero no se preocupe, nos colaremos. Además, dice su hijo que ya maquillados, apenas se notará que estamos en la edad en que aún pedimos permiso a nuestros padres para ir al cine. Yo sé que no tendrá inconveniente en darle a Rodrigo permiso. No será nada terrible, sólo habrá hombres sudorosos usando medias, *lipstick* y tacones, algunos no serán nada discretos, pero nada para apurarse. Bueno, mucho gusto en conocerla...". Beso, beso.

No. Definitivamente no habría sabido qué decirle, pero después Rodrigo me confesó que sus padres estaban de viaje y que no regresarían sino hasta el día siguiente. *Thank, God!*

Me sorprendió ver el cuarto de mi amigo. Era la primera vez que entraba al cuarto de un gay. La verdad es que esperaba ver *posters* de modelos de Calvin Klein, paredes pintadas de fucsia con un techo rojo salmón, revistas pornográficas masculinas y juguetes eróticos regados por el cuarto, pero no. Ya sé que tener diecisiete años y vivir con padres heterosexuales tenía que ver con ello, pero no había ni la más leve pista de su "alegre" orientación: el cuarto podía haber aprobado una rigurosa inspección de Frida. De hecho me pareció asquerosamente limpio (si es que algo así es posible). Las paredes eran blancas y lo más colorido que había era el edredón con motivos de las chivas del Guadalajara (el equipo favorito de Rodrigo). Todo estaba perfectamente ordenado y el piso parecía sacado de un anuncio de limpiador con olor a bosque noruego.

Puse entonces con cuidado sobre la cama mi próxima indumentaria.

Quitarme mi atuendo masculino fue fácil, pero ponerme el vestido de Frida... Estuve un buen rato... tal vez quince minutos, que a mí me parecieron como tres horas, mirando esa prenda, esas medias y la peluca que Rodrigo me acababa de prestar (él insistía en que debía convertirme en una rubia a lo Marilyn, no sé si por lo de mi lunar en la mejilla), y casi me imaginé contemplando el cadáver de una mujer (Marilyn, *of course*, después de lo de las pastillas). Por un momento me pareció que estaba a punto de robarle el cuerpo a una pobre desconocida que ahora flotaba como un fantasma por ahí.

Finalmente lo hice.

La experiencia de meterse en esa ropa, con toda la intención de lucirla en público, fue... ¿qué te puedo decir que no suene ridículo?, fue simplemente lo mejor de todo. Por un instante sentí como si lo hubiera hecho toda mi vida y no sólo cuando no había nadie en la casa, en forma clandestina. La sensación de la seda era algo que nunca había probado y me hizo construir una ridícula crítica instantánea a la ropa interior masculina: ¿por qué las trusas y los *boxers* no son fabricados igual? Me sentí como la vez que comí mis primeros pistaches. Frida siempre nos los prohibió y de pronto en una fiesta los conocí, sentí que comía el néctar con el que se hartaban los dioses lujuriosos del Olimpo. Desde entonces han sido mi placer culpable (tengo siempre una bolsa escondida en mis guantes de portero de repuesto). Como nunca antes, entendí que la posible razón de la existencia de los travestis es simplemente reconocer una cosa... la ropa femenina se siente mejor... y es mejor.

Y todavía no conocía la ropa interior...

Cuando me miré al espejo, te juro, Nina, que me dieron ganas de presentarme con esa mujer que estaba frente a mí. Afortunadamente yo era lampiña, si no, hubiera tenido que someterme a la tortura medieval que yo sabía que era la depilación. Por un momento me sentí frente a mi hermana gemela. Y tanto me gustó la imagen, que podría

decirte que me asustó —hasta sentí que mi famoso lunar me hacía ver sexy—, y casi hubiera jurado que podría engañar a quien quisiera.

Rodrigo estuvo insistiendo, como no tienes idea, en que me pusiera algo parecido a lo que él se había puesto, pero el vestido que yo le había tomado a Frida me hacía ver justo como yo quería verme.

Tampoco le hice caso a mi amigo con lo de la peluca. Tenía mi maravilloso cabello, que sólo requería un cepillado vigoroso para lograr el efecto deseado.

En cuanto Rodrigo me vio, me dijo el mejor cumplido que me hubiera podido imaginar. Ni a Casanova se le hubiera podido ocurrir: "No hay duda. Eres una mujer".

Me deberías haber visto. Ni siquiera Frida podía haber lucido tan bien en su propio vestido como yo.

De veras que no te he revelado cómo es que entré tan fácilmente en el vestido de Frida. No, no fue cosa de brujería, ni de una suerte endemoniada. Sucede que ya en varias ocasiones me había probado los vestidos de Frida. Sólo eso. Pero ésta era la primera vez que efectivamente usaba uno. Ya imagino la cara que estarás poniendo. Una cara de "¿cómo pudiste entrar en la talla de Frida?". Una cara de "¿cómo es que siendo ella tan mal proporcionada de carnes y teniendo una figura tan lamentable pudo compartir un vestido con alguien tan esbelta y de tan buen ver como tú?". Una cara de "¿por qué no usaste mejor uno de los vestidos de Claudia si tienen casi la misma complexión, peso y altura?". Esta última cara de sorpresa te la puedo quitar al darte una fácil y simple explicación: Claudia no usa vestidos y los que usa están para que cualquier diseñador respetable llore.

Ésa es la razón, querida Nina, de que haya empezado a probarme los vestidos de Frida. Claro que, aunque nuestras estaturas fueron casi iguales desde que cumplí los quince, pronto me di cuenta de que nunca llegaría a ganar las carnes de Frida, y ni pensar siquiera en engordar para que me quedaran sus vestidos. Grasa, no gracias. Sólo había una solución. Sin que Frida se diera cuenta, llevé a una costurera en un mercado lejano a la casa, dos de sus vestidos menos feos (tampoco creas que Frida tiene un gusto envidiable). Le di las medidas, mis medidas, *of course*, a la vieja artista de la aguja y el alfiler e hice que los arreglara. Ya te imaginarás la consternación de Frida al ver que no entraba en dos de sus vestidos favoritos, nunca se le hubiera ocurrido la opción de que tenía una hija atrapada en el cuerpo de un hombre con el irresistible impulso de usar faldas y medias, y que se había encargado de hacer que sus prendas quedaran tres tallas abajo. Por el contrario, le echó la culpa a los panes franceses de las mañanas y a las galletas con chocolate de las tardes, y comenzó una dieta absurda acompañada de cinco minutos de ejercicio en un ridículo armatoste que vio en la televisión, que prometía quitarle cinco kilos en una semana con un esfuerzo tan absurdo que le permitiría, al tiempo de que hacía ejercicio, ver la televisión, tejer un suéter o escribir una novela.

Pero estaba en otra cosa más emocionante (perdón, pero volví a divagar).

Al salir de su casa, Rodrigo resultó ser un poco más cuidadoso. Se puso un gran abrigo y me pidió que no taconeáramos demasiado, pues "no queríamos que se dieran cuenta los vecinos". ¿Por qué de pronto se había vuelto tan pudoroso? Resulta que la escenita desfachatada de cuando me recibió en el pasillo, exhibiéndose a los cuatro puntos cardinales, se debía a que en ese piso no estaban ocupados los demás departamentos (de ahí su falsa valentía).

Los tacones, Nina... No. Eso sí que no lo entendí. Al pararme frente al espejo mis piernas se veían levantadas y torneadas, pero al comenzar a caminar... Yo que creí que tenía práctica suficiente... Claro, no te he contado, pero cuando era pequeña me gustaba tomar los zapatos de Frida y de mi abuela (es decir, los tuyos) y ponerme a caminar por toda la casa. De hecho, sin que Frida lo hubiera notado, cuando Nina murió me quedé con unos de sus zapatos. No los usé por mucho tiempo, pero mientras me duraron me causaron un particular placer cuando me los ponía y caminaba un poco de aquí para allá. Hacía mucho que no me metía en unos zapatos de mujer y ahora introducirme en esos nuevos tacones de Frida estaba resultando toda una tortura digna de la Inquisición.

Y eso que con Frida había sido afortunada, digo, con eso de los zapatos. Frida siempre resultó ser una mujer de pies grandes. ¡Cómo le fastidiaba eso! Número 27 en México, diez en Estados Unidos y 42 en Europa. Yo en secreto me preocupaba junto con ella al ver lo difícil que le era conseguirnos, digo, conseguir zapatos. Sin embargo, así tuviera que encargarlos a una amiga que hacía un viaje al extranjero, siempre los obtenía. A veces, la muy vanidosa, se sentía princesa egipcia, o algo así, e intentaba entrar en zapatillas más pequeñas, pero siempre terminaba con dolores terribles de pies.

Ahora yo compartía ese dolor. Los tacones que le tomé resultaron ser más chicos de lo previsto.

Yo, que iba tan soberbiamente vestida, no me imaginé sentir tal sensación de desnudez cuando pisé la calle. De verdad que creí que la leve brisa nocturna que nos recibió me arrebataba todos mis trapos y me dejaba ahí toda expuesta. Sentí que todos nos veían. Al menos las dos parejas que cruzaron nuestro camino. Y así, sin más, le rogué a Rodrigo, con las únicas palabras que podían liberarme de esa angustia.

—Un taxi, poooor favooor.

Afortunadamente Rodrigo estuvo de acuerdo. Ya era un poco tarde y era lo más conveniente si queríamos llegar allá con todos nuestros miembros (es decir, manos, pies y demás) en su lugar. La verdad es que yo estaba exagerando. Con las mascadas, los anteojos y los abrigos, era difícil que alguien se metiera con nosotras. (¿Debo decir nosotras?, no sé, aún con sus dos kilos de maquillaje y su peluca, Rodrigo me parecía todavía bastante... bastante... Rodrigo).

Nina, dicen que el hermano del asesino de Lincoln rescató al hijo de éste cuando cayó entre dos carros de ferrocarril, unas semanas antes de que el presidente fuera balaceado. También dicen que Shakespeare y Cervantes murieron el mismo día y que Mark Twain nació en un año en que apareció el cometa Halley y murió cuando el mismo cometa volvió a aparecer.

Todas esas coincidencias increíbles, pero ciertas, no se comparan con lo que te voy a contar y que merece de igual modo la manoseada expresión de "aunque usted no lo crea".

Resulta que había tal congestionamiento, que Rodrigo y yo, temerosos de que toda nuestra economía fuera a quedar en manos de un taxímetro, comenzamos a considerar seriamente bajarnos y optar por el nada agradable Metro.

Yo no estaba segura..., ¿no seríamos objeto de burla?, ¿no nos encontraríamos con la liga de la decencia y seríamos linchados y a falta de alambrada, amarrados a las vías o a un torniquete del Metro? Pero Rodrigo me convenció:

—Vamos. Ni tu madre te reconocería. Será divertido.

—¿Y qué tal que se meten con nosotros? (Ni hablar, tengo que decir "nosotros", Rodrigo aún no me parecía muy ella, así que seguirá siendo él para mí).

—Son sólo cuatro estaciones.

Bajamos las escaleras, y aunque yo ya había adquirido cierta destreza, mi amigo se veía peor que una garza embarazada.

Por suerte, ya era tarde y no había mucha gente en el Metro.

Con cada paso que dábamos más confiada me sentía. Contrario a lo que desearía una mujer coqueta que ha vestido una buena parte de su vida maravillosas faldas abiertas, escotes y zapatos de aguja, yo no esperaba miradas, sino todo lo contrario: mi sueño era pasar totalmente desapercibida, encontrar la fabulosa etiqueta no de *pretty woman,* sino de *ordinary woman.*

Pero el calor que hacía en los vagones del Metro me hizo atreverme a algo. Quitarme el abrigo. Digo, no había peligro, mi vestimenta no era la de una cabaretera como la de Rodrigo, así que me atreví a dar el gran paso... Miré alrededor. No hubo cataclismo. Nadie gritó: "Llévenlo a la alambrada y línchenlo". ¡Qué alivio! Entonces sentí la curiosa mirada de dos hombres que se sostenían del pasamanos. Tuve el súbito impulso de volverme a poner el abrigo. Pero entonces, Rodrigo me dijo algo que cambió mi percepción por completo:

—Vaya..., le gustas a los cabrones.

Era cierto, Nina. Intenté indagar en la mirada furtiva, sobre todo en la del joven que leía un periódico, y pude descubrir una chispa de

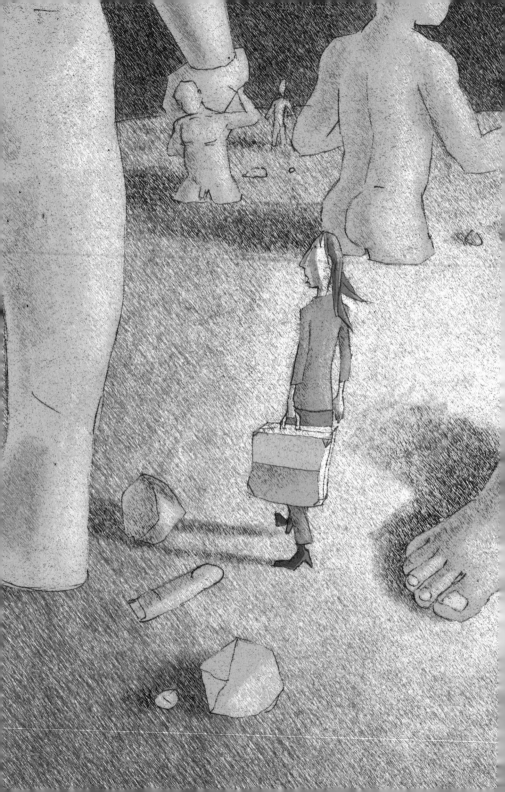

lujuria, esa chispa que viene directamente de esa parte libidinosa del cerebro y que te hace desear no precisamente un pedazo de pastel... pero algo parecido.

Me dieron ganas de quitarme la mascada, de lucir mi rostro en todo su soleado esplendor, pero entonces recordé el exceso de maquillaje que Rodrigo y yo nos habíamos aplicado, recordé las palabras de mi amigo:

—Vamos a divertirnos, ¿no? Hay que atascarnos. Hay mucho lodo y no precisamente de una marca de segunda.

Y no sólo fue un atasque de rubor, también fue una exageración el volumen que alcanzó nuestra boca con los kilos de lápiz de labios aplicados, y ni qué decir de la longitud de nuestras pestañas postizas.

Pero con todo y la vergüenza colorada que comenzó a instalarse en mis mejillas, miré al individuo que posaba su mirada en mi anatomía y de pronto hice algo inesperado...

Le sonreí... Él también me sonrió. Mi primer coqueteo. Soy una loca, pensé. ¿Qué estoy haciendo?, ¿y si me habla?, ¿y si me pide mi teléfono?, ¿y si me pide matrimonio?, ¿y si...?

Entonces mis pensamientos se vieron rotos... así, rotos por una voz escalofriantemente conocida:

—¿Dónde compró ese vestido?

Sentí todos los horrores del mundo: las voces de la Inquisición, el demonio y sus secuaces, Hitler y la SS, todos mezclados en un solo espantoso sonido.

Era Frida.

Bueno, en realidad no era Frida, pero como si lo fuera. Se trataba de Liliana Cantarel, una de las mejores amigas de mi madre, compañera de la prepa y la persona que le había regalado el vestido que ahora me engalanaba.

Por fin pude entender eso de que "hasta las medias se me corrieron". Suerte que estaba sostenida del pasamanos, porque sentí que me daba un desvanecimiento, un desmayo de ésos que sólo les dan a las embarazadas. Imagínate. Yo ahí tirada en medio del cochino vagón y la gente rodeándome y creyendo un posible embarazo. Yo en el hospital sola, sin nadie que me defendiera (pues Rodrigo también se habría desmayado y la amiga de Frida se habría encargado de huir y escurrirse de la escena que ella misma había provocado), y entonces en cuanto el doctor pidiera que a la pobre mujer que se había desmayado entre Etiopía y Eugenia le quitaran las ropas, todo el personal médico, incluido un anestesista y una chica haciendo su residencia, se encontraría con una gran... bueno, una impresionante sorpresa... pero ahí no terminaría todo, al otro día, la noticia en los diarios sensacionalistas sería todavía más sorpresiva: "Travesti se desmaya en el Metro y es confundido con una mujer embarazada...". Como para que yo misma me dejara de hablar. Y todo por no haber resistido una terrible aparición. Afortunadamente, como te decía... la soporté. Me afiancé al tubo metálico y le ordené a todo mi cuerpo que por esta vez no temblara como cable de luz ante la visita inesperada de una parvada de gavilanes.

—Perdón, es que yo regalé un vestido igualito.

Nina, la voz de Liliana, sus palabras y su mirada de gavilán... hicieron que por poco me diera el soponcio. Si bien era certísimo que Liliana y yo nos conocíamos poco y que ella se topaba conmigo y mi cara cuando mucho una vez al mes, yo estaba casi segura de que en cualquier momento podría reconocerme. ¿Cómo sales de una situación así? Tú dime. El desmayo; no, definitivamente no iba a salir en el *Alarma*. La nota roja, no gracias. Salir corriendo. *Don't make me laugh*. ¿A dónde podía llegar?, ¿al otro lado del vagón? Lo peor es que el cobarde de Rodrigo me había abandonado. Él ya estaba en el otro lado del vagón. Obvio que no podía haber reconocido a la amiga de mi madre. Si a la propia Frida apenas la había visto una vez, cuando me llevó un libro de matemáticas a la casa, pero era muy posible que mi rostro de horror le hubiera hecho pensar que lo mejor era poner metros de distancia y garantizar su seguridad; tan sólo por aquello de las malditas dudas. Y si él temió algo malo, ¿qué podía esperar yo, que llevaba soportando toda una vida al lado de la amiga de la mujer que ahora no dejaba de mirar el vestido que alguna vez pagó seguramente a un precio no muy bajo en una *boutique* exclusiva? La única salida que podía existir era la más peligrosa...

—¿En serio? (Me salió un poco grave la voz)... Hmjjjj (carraspeé)... ¿En serio? (Ahora la voz era parecida a la de mi tío Gustavo fingiendo ser mujer. Estaba perdida).

Entonces fue cuando ocurrió:

—Sí. Se lo regalé a una amiga...

Milagro... ¡Gracias, santo patrono de las causas gays...! Me atreví a mirarla. Sonreía. Esa aliada del gran buitre de las montañas llamado Frida, sonreía. No me había reconocido. Si hubiera tenido un poco de control de mí misma, me habría dado cuenta de que con una mascada encima y unos lentes color *antipaparazzis* como los que llevaba, era difícil que se percatara de quién era yo. El caso es que de pronto, por una razón incomprensible del comportamiento humano ante situaciones de alto riesgo, me divirtió la situación... así que tres punto cuatro segundos después me sentí más confiada, tanto como para esgrimirle un cantarín:

—¿Verdad que está divino?

—Lo curioso es que me dijeron que se trataba de un diseño original.

No sé qué me pasó, pero no pude resistirme, así que le dije:

—¡Ay, querida! Sé a qué te refieres. De seguro también compraste un bolso que hacía juego con él y te dijeron lo mismo.

Me estaba jugando el pellejo.

—Ya no se puede confiar en la gente.

—No te preocupes, querida, me parece que de cualquier modo tienes un gusto exquisito...

No sólo le di una entonación casi casi de peinadora de Liz Taylor a cada una de mis palabras, además me atreví a tocarla levemente en el hombro.

Liliana dejó de tocar la tela de mi —de su— vestido y por primera vez me miró directamente al rostro, yo bajé la cabeza.

—¿No la conozco de algún lado?

No pude evitarlo, me dio un ataque de tos. Uno ligero, que me permitió decir:

—¿Va mucho a Guanajuato?

—No.

—Pues fíjese que yo casi no salgo de mi pequeña hacienda de cien hectáreas. Sólo voy a la ciudad cuando me invitan a un evento social importante, usted sabe, como cuando el gobernador quiere tomarse una copa conmigo... ¿conoce a alguien de la alta sociedad guanajuatense?

La ex compañera de estudios de Frida negó con la cabeza.

—Entonces no creo que nos conozcamos.

—Sin embargo, casi podría jurar que la he visto antes.

—En realidad tengo un rostro común, querida, eso debe ser.

No sé qué pasó. No me lo explico. Pero el nerviosismo me hizo querer acomodarme los lentes, y justo en ese momento esa estúpida temblorina me atacó y... *Oh, my God!*... Ahí van los lentes oscuros.

Como una tonta me llevé la mano a los ojos y grité, como si la luz del sol (que obviamente no podía haber en un vagón del metro) me lastimara igual que a una vampiresa.

Estaba perdida, pero en eso, escuché la voz de Rodrigo y sentí cómo me colocaba los lentes.

—¡Ay, querida! Debes tener más cuidado.

Liliana estaba de una pieza, como solía decir mi abuela al referirse a alguien petrificado y con la bocota abierta. A juzgar por la posición en la que tenía el brazo, podía adivinarse que Rodrigo le había arrebatado los lentes justo de la mano.

Para Liliana debió ser obvio que mi amigo no era la tía de Liza Minelli, además la voz ya lo había delatado, y lo hubiera delatado de cualquier forma, así hubiera estado oculto en un clóset y hablando a través de una botella.

—Pero si usted... si... no...

Imaginé todo lo que pudo haber estado pasando por la cabeza de la amiga de Frida... toda una carambola de choques neuronales... Seguramente jamás se había imaginado que pudiera estar tan cerca de un travesti de la talla de Rodrigo.

Yo aproveché su consternación para arreglarme la mascada (que por efectos de un enfrenado sorpresivo del tren subterráneo, se me había ladeado). Liliana apenas pudo decir, justo cuando llegamos a la estación y se abrían las puertas del carro:

—¿Vienen juntos...?

—No. Pero nos bajamos juntos.

Rodrigo no pudo resistir la tentación y le dio un fuerte apretón en uno de los cachetes antes de que abandonáramos el vagón.

Nuestra intempestiva huida debió dejar a la vieja amiga de mi madre impresionada, pero ella parecía haberse quedado paralizada por algo aún más serio: había sido tocada por un travesti..., es decir, había sido tocada por la perversión, la lujuria y hasta posiblemente por el portador de millones de virus escalofriantes... No sé Liliana, pero si Frida hubiera sido la de las mejillas magulladas seguramente habría llegado a la casa a darse un baño con todo y cloro mientras recitaba la receta del *soufflé* de zanahoria. Y después, si no hubiera estado peleada con Claudia, habría ido derechito a contarle su desagradable encuentro cercano del tercer tipo, pero, básicamente, habría tenido que guardarse sus impresiones y tener horribles pesadillas. Y la imagen, tengo que decirlo, me hizo sonreír.

Esperamos el siguiente Metro. Aún tenía una espantosa taquicardia ocasionada por pensar en lo cerca que estuvo Liliana de ocasionarle un paro cardiaco a la aún desconocida hija de su amiga. El idiota de Rodrigo no paraba de reír (y eso que no tenía completamente clara la situación). Tuve que darle un bolsazo para que cerrara la bocota y dejara de llamar la atención. Y encima, la media se me había corrido, y yo no tenía idea de cómo había sucedido.

Por fin salimos a la superficie a respirar el aire veraniego. Fue entonces cuando se aplicó una de las leyes de Murphy citadas precisamente para travestis: "Querida, prepárate, porque tus primeros tacones siempre coinciden con tu más larga caminata".

Rodrigo copió mal la dirección y aunque estábamos en la calle correcta, teníamos que caminar varias cuadras para encontrar la fiesta. Teníamos que ir desde el número 150 hasta el 750. Es decir, que estábamos en serio riesgo de provocarnos unas tremendas ampollas.

Fue en el camino, cuando Rodrigo me confesó que nadie lo había invitado a la famosa fiesta.

—¿Un anuncio? ¿Te enteraste por un anuncio?

—Pero no cualquier anuncio, tranquila. Lo saqué de los clasificados de la revista *Gay Parade*.

—¿Y por qué no me lo dijiste antes?

—Porque sabía que si te lo decía no te animarías.

No sabía qué pensar, sólo me quedó respirar hondo... uno, dos, tres..., y pensar con optimismo. Supongo, Nina, que pudo haber sido peor y que Rodrigo podría haber obtenido el dato de la fiesta de alguna pinta en el baño público de una gasolinera. Claro que el optimismo se puede correr junto con tus medias, si tu compañero entaconado se empeña en ayudarte:

—Y yo no iba venir a mi primera fiesta travesti solo.

—¿Tu primera fiesta travesti? ¿¡Tu primera fiesta travesti!?

Nina, los vecinos de toda la calle, desde el número uno hasta el 900 supieron en ese momento que íbamos a nuestra primera fiesta como travestis.

Estuve a punto de dar la media vuelta, pero ya íbamos a la mitad del camino y cuando Rodrigo se arrodilló implorando que no lo fuera a dejar abandonado, tuve que ceder; claro que el resto del camino me dediqué a manifestarle mis claras ganas de darle con el tacón de los zapatos en pleno ojo.

—Tú me dijiste que tenías experiencia en esto.

—Nunca te lo dije. Tú lo asumiste así.

—Uno no invita a alguien a una fiesta travesti como se invita al cine y tú así lo hiciste.

No sé con quién estaba más molesta, Nina, si con mi mentiroso compañero, con mi media corrida o con mis tacones. Sólo perdoné a Rodrigo porque prometió que nos iríamos en el momento en el que yo lo decidiera. Además, juró por la memoria de Freddie Mercury defenderme en caso de que algo terrible me amenazara (y nadie que se viste como algo parecido a Liza Minelli puede jurar por la memoria de Freddie Mercury en vano).

Sólo esperaba que Rodrigo resultara tan buen guardaespaldas como defensa central.

Hubo una fuerza superior a la vergüenza de tocar la puerta de un departamento del que escuchas que provienen los mayores éxitos de la música disco tocados a todo volumen: un fuerte dolor de espalda, ocasionado por recorrer media colonia Del Valle en calidad de garza espinada. Un solo pensamiento me martillaba la cabeza, tanto como las punzadas en mis pies: "Una silla, por favor, una silla".

Rodrigo todavía se quedó unos segundos sin decidirse del todo a tocar.

—Pues ya estamos aquí.

—¿Vas a tocar de una vez? —me oí decir casi al borde de la locura prehomicida.

Por fin la puerta se abrió y una voz nos dijo:

—¿*Voulez vous couchez avec moi?*

No me lo vas a creer, Nina, pero era…

—Cristina Aguilera —gritó mi compañero casi como una adolescente histérica, dando saltitos y toda la cosa.

Otra cosa que el idiota de Rodrigo nunca me dijo. Era una fiesta travesti, sí, pero no una cualquiera, sino una de celebridades. Claro que no me refiero a que una serie de celebridades hubieran decidido hacerle al travestismo, sino a que una serie de hombres en mallas, medias o pantalones ajustados habían decidido emular a sus artistas favoritas.

La que nos abrió no era Cristina Aguilera vestida como hombre, no. Era un estudiante de contaduría llamado Luis Manríquez (después lo supe), idolatrando a la rubia de sangre latina.

Apenas entramos y Cristina Aguilera nos preguntó quiénes éramos. Yo creí que Rodrigo diría entonces que se había vestido de Liza Minelli en proceso de engorda, pero no. Era Catherine Zeta-Jones en Chicago. Quedé tan azorada que cuando me preguntó quién era yo no pude decir nada. Fue el bruto de Rodrigo quien se atrevió:

—Ella... ella es Camila... Camila Parker.

¡Camila! ¡Camila Parker! Todo ser humano sabe que si existe la definición de una mujer fea, odiada y completamente alejada de la definición de sensualidad o voluptuosidad es Camila Parker (al menos eso dicen todas las revistas de moda). ¡Y el imbécil de Rodrigo me había comparado con ella! Apenas estaba recuperándome de la impresión, cuando Cristina Aguilera nos introdujo al resto de la fiesta; es decir, anunció nuestra presencia a más de treinta travestis.

—Señoras, *Ladies, pay attention, s'il vous plait.* Por fin llegaron: Catherine y Camila.

—¡Hola Catherine! ¡Hola Camila! —gritaron más de treinta travestis.

¡Oh, mein Got! Diría la tía Lola si se sintiera alemana. Cómo sería la impresión de verme comparada con la mujer que había usurpado el lugar de Lady Di, que hasta los dolores de pies y espalda desaparecieron y fueron sustituidos por un malestar en todo mi ego que me llevó a tomar el gordo brazo de Rodrigo y propinarle tal pellizco que él no pudo dejar de emitir un bastante varonil quejido:

—¡Ay! ¡Qué pasa!

—¿Camila? ¿¡Camila!?

—¿Qué querías que dijera? Estás usando un vestido de tu madre. Por Dios.

Nunca le iba a perdonar a Rodrigo que me hubiera hecho ir a mi primera fiesta travesti como una ñoña destroza hogares.

Pero resulta, Nina, que no pasó mucho tiempo para que conociéramos a Thalía, Madonna (*of course*), Britney Spears (cuatro de ellas), y debo decir que algunas superaban a las originales. ¿De dónde sacaban esos cuerpazos?

Claro que había algunos totalmente pretenciosos y fuera de la realidad, como era el caso de Rodrigo. Había una Selena, tan excedida en carnes, que tuvo que ponerse un gafete para evitar que le siguieran preguntado, a cada metro que se movía, a quién estaba homenajeando. Había otros que, más conscientes de sus límites y sus alcances, optaban por personajes como la Doña (a sus ochenta años) o la Tigresa (a sus setenta años). Había uno que aprovechando su parecido con Margaret Thatcher, se vistió como ella y parecía su hermana gemela (cosa que no creo que le hubiera envidiado ningún otro ser de este planeta, ni siquiera la verdadera hermana de la Thatcher).

Algo era cierto, Nina. Todos estaban divertidísimos. Orgullosos de encontrarse dentro de esas ropas y cubiertos de maquillaje.

Sin embargo, debo confesar que no todo resultó como esperaba. Yo estaba segura de que en tal ambiente, pronto encontraría a mis almas gemelas, trillizas y quintillizas. Estaba convencida de que encontraría a mis compañeras de dolor.

Pero esa tarea pronto se convirtió en una búsqueda más difícil que la de encontrar a un fanático del Necaxa.

Resulta que cuando me acerqué a Madonna, en vez de hablarme de su verdadera identidad, que créeme, intenté abordar con propiedad y con la mayor gentileza posible, me comenzó a hablar de su última gira, de lo maravilloso que había sido ser madre, de su incursión como escritora de libros para niños y del distanciamiento con su esposo. Justamente en el momento en que recordaba a Guy y estaba a punto de llorar, y con ello, tal vez, embarrar con su maquillaje corrido mi anticuado, pero limpio vestido, decidí dejar a la reina del pop y buscar otra plática menos trágica.

Rodrigo, mientras tanto, reía junto a su gemela, otro burdo intento de Catherine Zeta-Jones (sólo que ésta iba como la Catherine del Zorro, ¡Imagínate!).

Me acerqué entonces a quien en ese momento me pareció de entre todos los asistentes el que podía ser el más sensato de los travestis: un intento regular de Penélope Cruz.

—¡Qué tal! —saludé.

—¡Nada! ¡Que estoy como la ostia!

—¿Por qué...?, ¿qué pasa...?

—¿Os parece poco? Tom se ha matrimoniado con esa tal Katie. Yo me pregunto, cómo puede andar con ese crío. Si yo hasta me he operado las tetas... Y para qué. Lo único bueno que me ha pasado es que Pedro sigue dándome grandes papeles.

Yo no podía creerlo. ¿También Penélope? ¿En qué clase de fiesta estaba? Tuve que hacer otro intento.

—Espera. Yo me llamo... Victoria.

—¿No eras Camila?

—Quiero decir que en verdad me llamo Victoria.

Yo creo que Penélope finalmente pudo ver en mi mirada mi profunda consternación, porque unos segundos después se encargó de iluminar mi atribulada cabeza:

—Querida, ¿no te dijeron?

—¿Qué cosa?

—En esta fiesta debemos ser totalmente lo que representamos.

—¿Quieres decir...? —No atiné a terminar la pregunta, que más que una pregunta era una manifestación verbal mientras mis neuronas se hacían a la idea de lo que acababa de oír.

—Así es más divertido —concluyó Penélope.

Debí de haber puesto tal cara, que Penélope no pudo evitar decir, ahora sí con una voz totalmente normal:

—¿Eres primeriza?

No tuve que decir ni "claro", "por supuesto" o "¿qué, no se nota?". Penélope lo entendió inmediatamente en la ligera mueca que hice con mis labios.

—Mi nombre artístico es Luana.

Estreché la mano de Luana.

—Mira, no vayas a creer que siempre es así... Lo que pasa es que para nosotras es tan emocionante sentirnos en estas ropas que lo tomamos como una gran fiesta. A veces hacemos reuniones en las que platicamos de nuestras cosas, pero hoy es un día en el que nos gusta jugar y pretender que somos alguien a quien admiramos.

—Entonces me sonrió y me dijo de nuevo con la voz de mujer sevillana—: Anda, ponte maja y vamos a divertirnos. ¿O qué, nunca antes habías ido a una fiesta de disfraces?

En ese momento decidí que lo mejor que podía hacer era seguir el consejo de Penélope (digo, de Luana). Si no iba a encontrar a alguien con quien compartir mis dudas y penas, al menos me la iba a pasar bien. Al poco tiempo ya no me importó explicar (totalmente instalada en Camila Parker) que nunca fue mi intención provocarle algún daño a Diana y que mi amor por Carlos —"Charles", tenía que decir— era totalmente desinteresado.

Por un momento pensé que tal vez debería abandonar la fiesta y reunirme con Luana y sus amigas en otra ocasión menos carnavalesca y plantear mis inquietudes, pero fue entonces cuando Rodrigo me dijo:

—¡Vente! ¡Ya va a empezar el *show*!

Efectivamente, Nina. La mayor parte de las magníficas vestidas estaban esperando ese momento.

Un pequeño espacio adaptado por el anfitrión (una versión bastante aceptable de Shakira) sirvió como escenario, incluso unas luces teatrales iluminaban el lugar donde un pedestal con micrófono esperaba a los artistas.

Comenzó la presentación y el derroche de lentejuela con el *show* del dueño del balón. Para qué te niego que a partir de ese momento me comencé realmente a divertir. Y no tardé en unirme a mis nuevas amigas para corear y bailar cada uno de los éxitos de la colombiana. Y así ocurrió con cada uno de los cantantes, que de cualquier manera eran en su mayoría apoyados por un *playback* (muy necesario, por cierto, ya que la cantidad de desafinados, urgidos de unas buenas clases de canto, eran muchos).

La única nota penosa de la noche la brindaron las dos Catherinas (o sea, Rodrigo y acompañante), que no daban una. Aunque debo decir que me sorprendió que los dos parecían conocer bien los pasos de la canción cabaretera *And all that jazz* de la película *Chicago*.

También Penélope tuvo una no muy afortunada interpretación de una canción de Joaquín Sabina.

Y la sorpresa, al menos desde mi muy particular punto de vista, la dio Jennifer López. Tengo que decir que cuando la vi apersonarse en el escenario, por un breve instante, pensé que la verdadera "J. Lo" estaba efectivamente frente a mis ojos. Hasta el magnífico trasero era igualito. Y al bailar, ¡qué bruto! El hombre bajo esas entalladas ropas, sí que se había deshecho por completo de su testosterona. Sólo una mujer auténtica podía bailar así. Al menos, sólo una mujer podía mover la cintura y las caderas de ese modo.

Otra sorpresa se dio cuando subió al escenario alguien que no venía pero para nada al caso: un tipo de cabello rizado, sin demasiada gracia y, más bien diría, sin un gran atractivo, que hizo una imitación de Gustavo Cerati. Y a pesar de haber hecho una interpretación que hubiera sido calificada por cualquier oído algo educado de más bien mediocrona, el muchacho fue sonoramente ovacionado y al menos no hizo el oso. Inmediatamente se me ocurrió, Nina, que el admirador del vocalista de Soda Stereo debía ser el novio de alguna de las divas, posiblemente de la anfitriona.

Pronto yo ya estaba completamente en ambiente y las pocas cubas que me había servido me estaban poniendo en un ánimo de verdad jocosón. Fue entonces que ocurrió.

De la nada, apareció sin previo aviso:

En la puerta como una reina. Como una diosa. Preciosa (tal vez con más de una cirugía en el rostro). Esbelta como una garza (y lo quiero decir como un piropo). Con un ceñido vestido color plateado que a kilómetros de distancia debía parecer el brillo de una estrella: Nicole.

Es cierto, Nina, que no había modo de que ocultara sus grandes manos, sus anchos hombros y un cuello un poco grueso. No había duda de que estábamos ante un representante del sexo masculino, pero eso no le quitaba que fuera un muy respetable intento de ser el reflejo de la maravillosa actriz australiana.

Parecía que todos los asistentes se hubieran quedado presos de un hechizo marca Hollywood. Por un breve instante la música calló. Pero Nicole con pasos seguros avanzó hasta el escenario. El cantante en turno (una entusiasta Ana Torroja) se retiró mientras pasaba tímidamente el micrófono a la rubia. Haciendo una señal, Nicole pidió la música. Los compases de la pista de *Something stupid* empezaron a sonar. Y así, sin *playback*, mostrando toda su vibrante voz, Nicole se robó la noche.

Los aplausos de treinta y cinco hombres entallados se dejaron escuchar. Yo había contado a los asistentes y eran treinta y seis. Efectivamente, Nina. Una de las invitadas no aplaudió. Y cuando te diga quién fue el envidioso, yo creo que no me lo vas a creer.

Nicole agradecía con una elegante reverencia cuando de entre las sombras, surgida de no sé dónde, Penélope, cual archivillana de Batman, saltó como una gata que ataca al veterinario.

Las pelucas fueron las primeras en salir volando. En cuanto Penélope se fue contra Nicole, se quedó cual piel roja con toda la cabellera. Desafortunadamente para Penélope (Luana, debería decir), Nicole fue más rápida y tomó el verdadero cabello al intento de clon de la española. Varias de las chicas se cubrieron con las manos sus asustados rostros. Fuimos Gustavo Cerati, Shakira, Rodrigo y yo los que nos atrevimos a evitar que las uñas de las dos rivales llegaran a arañar algo más que el maquillaje de la otra. Fue entonces, al intentar separar a la fiera Luana, que escuché los más increíbles insultos. Cuando logramos que Nicole dejara el maltrecho cabello de Penélope (listo para una intervención de urgencia de su estilista de confianza) y pudimos distanciarlas, comenzó la inusual batalla de las divas:

—Suéltenme —gritaba Luana a la que no me era tan difícil contener, gracias a la ayuda de Rodrigo.

—No me suelten a esa loca.

—Aparte de traidora eres una cobarde.

—Yo no sé qué le pasa a esa demente.

—No te hagas la idiota, que no te va.

—Deberían encerrarte en el manicomio.

—Tú me quitaste a mi hombre.

—Yo no te quité nada, él se quiso ir conmigo.

—Tú sabías cómo lo quería.

—Él nunca te quiso.

—Claro que me quería.

—Él me quiere a mí.

—Me quiere a mí.

—Suéltenme que la mato.

—No la vayan a soltar.

Por un momento creí, Nina, que efectivamente ese afán por imitar a sus admiradas artistas había tocado los niveles de la esquizofrenia y que las falsas Penélope y Nicole se estaban peleando por Tom Cruise. Incluso llegué a temer que se apareciera la señorita Holmes y que aquello se convirtiera en una real pelea de lucha libre (al menos las cabelleras para apostar ya las tenían). Pero no, se trataba sólo de una extraña coincidencia. Sí, estaban peleando por un hombre, pero no por el agente especial encargado de efectuar misiones imposibles, sino por un trombonista portugués llamado Yanuario Díaz. Resulta que Penélope y Nicole, debo decir, Luana e Irene (nombre artístico de Nicole) trabajaban en un espectáculo travesti y habían sido las mejores amigas hasta que la música se interpuso. El novio de Luana, que vino desde la península ibérica para juntarse con su corazoncito, se vio deslumbrado por la rubia apariencia de Irene y a base de mentiras la conquistó. El tal Yanuario le había contado a Irene que Luana le había sido infiel y que él por eso había decidido romper.

Finalmente, después de que todas sus amigas les pidieron que se tranquilizaran y mejor se tomaran un té, las rivales se convencieron de que el verdadero cabrón desgraciado de la historia era el lusitano y de que la amistad de ellas no podía romperse por un tipo con nombre de calendario.

—Perdóname, amiga, ya sabes que te quiero mucho.

—Perdóname tú a mí.

—No, tú perdóname.

—No, tú a mí.

—No, tú.

Las dos reconciliadas amigas decidieron (no sé si en son de broma) que lo mejor que podían hacer era ir a darle una golpiza a Yanuario, acompañadas de varias voluntarias, entre ellas Margaret Thatcher y Celia Cruz, o sea, Marina y Jennifer (nombres artísticos).

Fue finalmente al calor de los tequilas que siguieron después, que pude platicar un poco con Mayra (es decir, Shakira) y con Lucía (es decir, Ana Torroja) y descubrí que eran de lo más divertidas y sensibles. Me di cuenta de que la gran mayoría de ellas trabajaban en *shows* travestis y en bares y preferían usar sus nombres femeninos adoptados. Pero también me percaté de que había unos cuantos que no tenían ningún problema en referirse a sí mismos como Mario, Pedro o Luis y en contarme que trabajaban en oficinas, en despachos o en agencias.

Todos nos adoptaron de la manera más cordial que te puedas imaginar. Era evidente que Rodrigo y yo éramos los más jóvenes de la fiesta. Pero a nadie le importó, incluso les pareció simpática nuestra primera intromisión en una fiesta travesti. Y pronto se referían a nosotros como las "nuevas reinas".

Dos de las personas más interesantes que conocí esa noche se llamaban Mario y Pedro (uno había interpretado a Martha Sánchez y el otro a una cantante que no pude identificar) y de hecho eran una pareja gay, que después de confesarles mi primera y prejuiciosa impresión sobre los travestis (algo así como: "Cuando entré, creí que no iba conocer a nadie real"), me dijeron mientras me servían un tequila:

—Querida, que no te confundan nuestras ropas.

—No somos para nada banales.

—Somos de carne y hueso.

—De mente y espíritu.

—La gente cree que sólo nos la pasamos pensando en pantimedias y pelucas.

—Y que nos la pasamos en la fiesta.

—No siempre estamos en la fiesta.

—Definitivamente, no siempre.

—Aunque no sería tan malo.

Ambos rieron.

—Ahí donde lo ves, Mario es un extraordinario pintor.

—No exageres.

—Claro que lo eres.

—Bueno, supongo que eso me obliga a decirte que Pedro es dueño de una librería y que está ahora organizando un festival gay.

—Un festival de cultura gay.

—Cine y exposiciones, ya sabes.

Me sentí mal, Nina. Tengo que reconocer que por un buen rato había tenido el prejuicio de pensar que toda esa gente (tal vez un poco influida por la naturaleza de la fiesta) estaba sólo empeñada en ser otra persona y que no podrían entender a alguien como yo que buscaba precisamente encontrar su verdadero yo.

Estaba equivocada.

Es cierto que estaba rodeada de personas, un poco estrafalarias, pero muy sensibles e interesantes.

Y todos, finalmente, estamos siempre en la búsqueda de nosotros mismos, ¿no?

Aún así, cuando la fiesta estaba por terminar, yo no podía evitar sentir que todavía me faltaba algo. No había encontrado a nadie con una inquietud igual a la mía.

Y justo cuando estaba por sacar a Rodrigo de una divertida charla (al menos eso me indicaban sus risas) con Luis (¿Cristina Aguilera, debería decir?) y pedirle que ya nos retiráramos, ocurrió que el supuesto cantautor argentino, es decir, el imitador de Cerati se me acercó y todo cambió:

—¡Hey!, quería agradecerte por tu ayuda.

—No fue nada, no te fijes (supuse que se refería a mi intervención en la pelea).

—No, en serio gracias.

Se hizo un silencio que no supe enfrentar, así que hice lo que normalmente acaba haciendo una en esos casos de vacío mental: mentir.

—Me gustó mucho cómo cantaste.

—Me llamo Alejandro.

No me sorprendió que no me dijera el inevitable "Soy Gustavo Cerati, pero me puedes decir Gus". Me sorprendió otra cosa. Hubo algo en su voz, Nina, que me hizo sentir que algo raro pasaba con ese muchacho de escasa barba. Yo creo que fue un sexto sentido, intuición de mujer, creo yo, lo que me llevó a continuar con la charla y lanzar una extraña pregunta:

—¿Y vienes con alguna de las chicas?

—No. Vengo solo. Pero no soy travesti.

La verdad, Nina, no entendí. ¿No era ésta una fiesta exclusiva? ¿No era ésta una fiesta de travestis? Si venía solo, ¿sería que...? Mi gesto debió tener tal expresión desconcertante que, seguramente, Alejandro se sintió obligado a hablar:

—Soy transexual.

¡*Oh, my God*, Nina! Ahí estaba, de carne y hueso, un ser que no contento con su identidad sexual, había entrado en terapia psicológica, había decidido someterse a inyecciones y toma de hormonas y finalmente había entrado en la sala de operaciones para modificar su apariencia.

Es cierto, se trataba del caso opuesto al mío, una chica que había decidido que las flores, las muñecas y la compra compulsiva de zapatos no era lo suyo, que prefería el deporte extremo y eructar después de un buen trago de cerveza.

—Yo... yo...

No acertaba a encontrar la palabra correcta. No podía decir que yo era transexual, que deseaba serlo, que me interesaba el tema... Aparentemente sólo había una forma correcta de decirlo:

—Yo... soy mujer.

—Quieres ser mujer.

Estaba clarísimo que Alejandro no iba a tener las dudas que yo tuve al verlo a él. Por ningún lado se me notaban las partes que me corresponderían en caso de ser efectivamente una mujer, ni siquiera si esas partes se hubieran debido a los implantes o a la progesterona. Pero yo insistí:

—Soy mujer.

Alejandro sonrió.

Día en que te cuento la terrible y triste historia de la cándida Alejandra y sus desalmados padres

No pude resistir la tentación, Nina. Tuve que pedirle a Gustavo, digo a Alejandro, que me concediera una cita. Era más que evidente que él me había entendido, que en algún momento de su vida se había enfrentado a mi problema, que Alejandro había nacido llamándose Margarita, Dalia, Brisa o Violeta y que al sentirse atrapado en un nombre tan florido, había decidido no sólo cambiar su sexo, sino su vida.

La cita fue en un café de chinos, justo en el centro de la ciudad.

Alejandro iba vestido con unos pantalones negros de algodón, una playera casual, un saco *sport* y unos zapatos negros que deslumbraban por su perfecto lustre. Cómo lo envidié. Es cierto que yo tampoco iba tan mal vestida. Traia unos *jeans*, fina playera y un suéter sobre los hombros, pero no dejaba de ser un atuendo masculino, por más que yo quisiera aligerarlo de testosterona. Cómo lo envidié. Debía sentirse tan bien usando las prendas de su sexo.

No pude sino agradecerle infinitamente por haber aceptado un café y contarme sobre su experiencia. Me hubieras visto, Nina. Estaba tan ansiosa que, al estar sentada, casi caigo en el irresistible juego de quitarme los zapatos por debajo de la mesa.

Tuvimos que romper un poco el hielo y entre café y bísquets, comenzamos por hablar de la entretenida fiesta, de las interpretaciones y de la inesperada pelea entre Luana e Irene. Fue un poco después que le pedí que me contara su experiencia. Y he aquí lo que Alejandro me confió:

—Es un poco difícil mirar hacia atrás. Una de las cosas que más agradeces cuando te sientes en tu verdadera personalidad es que ya no tienes que ver con ese viejo tú y ese pasado. ¿Por dónde empiezo...? Bueno, como te dije, nací con cuerpo de mujer, bajo el nombre de Soledad.

(Vaya que lo compadecí, Nina, hay nombres femeninos que no deberían existir por deprimentes y absurdos).

—Soledad a secas. Ni siquiera un María que me pudiera sacar del inevitable: Chole. Y mis padres, bueno..., desde pequeño me decían princesa... lo odiaba.

(No pude evitar pensar en Frida y sus cursilerías con mi hermana al llamarla "brujita").

—Te juro que aunque tenía apenas tres años, lo recuerdo como un gran trauma. No podía entender qué me veían de princesa. Lo que más odiaba era ese gusto por vestirme con holanes y mallas. Recuerdo cuando en una fiesta infantil mi madre me quiso vestir de Blanca Nieves, lloré. Ella creyó que mis lágrimas se debían a que yo en realidad hubiera preferido ir de Cenicienta. No los culpo. Tú recibes un bebé con una vagina en lugar de un pene y lo primero que vas a hacer es ponerle un mameluco rosa. ¿Cómo podían saber que dentro de esa niña había en realidad un niño? Aunque creo que desde que yo era pequeño ellos notaron algo. Siempre pedí que me cortaran el pelo casi como muchacho. Afortunadamente me tocó una moda en la que a muchas niñas les cortaban el pelo chiquitito.

También tengo que agradecer por la existencia de los *jeans*. Yo no sé qué hubiera hecho si toda mi vida hubiera tenido que seguir sintiendo esa desnudez que te provoca la menor brisa que se cuela por entre tus piernas cuando usas falda. Y por si eso fuera poco, cuando me compraban muñecas ni las tocaba y cuando me compraban juegos de té o planchas, los destrozaba.

(Sí que había coincidencias entre nuestras historias. A mi mente llegó la imagen de aquellas muñecas que recibía Claudia y que ni tocaba. Yo siempre iba a su cuarto cuando no estaba y me ponía a jugar con ellas. Tenía que esconderme en el clóset. Las *Barbies* me encantaban. Les intercambiaba los vestidos y a veces hasta las maquillaba. Un día Claudia llegó inesperadamente. Tuve que quedarme encerrada en el clóset. Pensé que se iría pronto y se me hizo fácil quedarme ahí parada conteniendo la respiración, pero no fue así. Era imposible quedarse petrificada ahí sosteniendo diez muñecas. Intenté encontrar una mejor postura, pero la *Barbie* exploradora y la *Barbie* novia se me escaparon de las manos. Al intentar recuperarlas, las demás muñecas cayeron y yo con ellas. Claudia pegó tremendo grito. No la culpo, hice un escándalo peor que los que hace Frida cuando llega la cuenta de la luz y se pone a tirar cosas. Lo que no esperaba es que Claudia saliera corriendo y gritando. Eso me dio la oportunidad de abandonar mi escondite y desaparecer. Luego me enteré de que le había dicho a mi abuela y a Frida que había un fantasma en su cuarto. Y yo no iba a desmentirla, *of course*.

Todo eso lo recordé en un segundo, no creas que me quedé ahí con cara de tonta y babeando mi bísquet. Nunca dejé de prestar atención a la confidencia de Alejandro).

—Nada de muñecas para mí. Desde que recuerdo me gustó salir a jugar a la pelota en el parque. Me encantaba el beisbol y era mejor que muchos niños, por eso aprendieron a respetarme. Marimacha fue el primer insulto que recuerdo haber oído. Y curiosamente no me importó tanto. Que me llamaran así, para mí, al menos significaba que no era la princesita dulce que todos esperaban que fuera. Pero lo que sí me molestaba era que ellos me consideraran una niña que aspiraba a ser niño. No se daban cuenta de que yo en realidad era un niño. Una vez hasta me peleé a golpes con un chistoso que me dijo que las niñas eran unas lloronas. Casi le digo que yo no era una niña, pero sólo me salió decirle que él era más llorón que yo. Y lo bueno fue que pude demostrarle que yo tenía razón; en cuanto le di ese golpe en la nariz, que lo hizo sangrar abundantemente, empezó a pedir a gritos que me alejaran de él. Todos pensaron que yo estaba loco, aunque más bien debieron pensar que estaba loca.

(Ay, Nina, con cada cosa que me contaba Alejandro más identificada me sentía. Yo que en un principio creí que nuestros problemas no tenían nada que ver, pero me estaba dando cuenta de que la cochina aceptación social empieza siempre en la infancia. También pude percatarme de que eso de que los niños pueden ser muy crueles, es una ley de la naturaleza, más poderosa que la ley de la gravedad, yo diría que los condenados escuincles son hasta sanguinarios. Segregarnos unos a otros parece estar también en nuestros genes. Es una lección que no necesitan enseñarte unos padres nazis. ¿O será que todos tenemos padres con complejo de raza superior?).

—No fue fácil mi infancia. Sexto año y secundaria los hice en un colegio de niñas. Mis padres seguramente querían que aprendiera a ser mujercita. Fue un infierno. El uniforme era tan incómodo que ni siquiera a las niñas les gustaba. Y en segundo de secundaria sufrí muchísimo cuando me gustó una niña nueva. Luchaba contra mí mismo por no mirarla o estar cerca de ella, pero fue en vano. Un día no pude evitarlo y la besé. Fue todo un escándalo. Llamaron a mis padres y la directora les dijo que tendrían que expulsarme pues una institución como ésa no podía aceptar lesbianas.

(Ahí sí que no teníamos la misma experiencia. Yo aún no había sido flechada por esa cosa llamada amor. Mi atracción por el tal Carlos Rincón no podía contar sino como una amarga situación, un desliz de vestidores. Y no puedo evitar pensar que no hubiera sido del todo malo llevarme un besito de recuerdo).

—Tenía quince años y odiaba mi cuerpo. Mis pechos eran grandes y mis caderas no eran precisamente estrechas. Me esforzaba por esconder mis formas. Una vez me oprimí tanto los senos con un vendaje (que yo mismo me puse), que casi acabo en el hospital. Mis padres se enfurecieron como nunca. Mi mamá lloraba como histérica y mi padre no me dirigía la palabra.

(¿A quién me recordaba esa madre histérica?).

—Estaba muy confundido. Me sentía algo así como un monstruo. Por suerte para mí, mis padres ya estaban tan decepcionados y hartos que decidieron mandarme aquí a la capital con mi tía Susana. Fue mi salvación. Para mi suerte ella había estudiado un año de psicología antes de encontrar su verdadera vocación: la historia. Cuando supo todo lo que me había pasado y de mis inclinaciones, se dio cuenta de lo que realmente me ocurría. Me dijo de inmediato: "Tú no eres lesbiana. Es más, creo que no eres mujer".

Gracias a su ayuda fui al psicólogo y pronto se concluyó que yo era posiblemente un transexual en potencia. De inmediato me aconsejaron que comenzara a usar la ropa que mejor me acomodara. Por primera vez me hice el corte de cabello que yo quería. Después de un tiempo mi psicóloga concluyó que podía comenzar a tomar hormonas. Las fuertes dosis de testosterona me comenzaron a hacer crecer la barba y a aplanarme ligeramente el pecho, al menos eso creía yo. La vez que pedí al estilista un corte totalmente andrógino y me miré en el espejo (mi principal enemigo durante toda mi vida), fue la primera vez que de verdad comencé a gustarme.

Estaba decidido a ir más adelante.

Primero me hice la mastectomía y me liberé de mi copa c. Y luego vino la decisión más difícil de todas... la histerectomía. Hace un año, después de muchas sesiones psicológicas y hormonales, finalmente me quitaron los ovarios, trompas y útero.

(Aquí, Alejandro hizo una pausa muy significativa. Al principio no entendí por qué, pero bastó que lo escuchara por otro minuto para que mi mente se iluminara. Y vas a ver que tú no necesitarás más allá del siguiente párrafo para que estés en las mismas).

—Creo que fue lo más difícil de todo. Renunciar a un hijo propio. De algún modo sabes que si te quedas con esa parte de ti, es posible que tengas un hijo de tu propia sangre, pero también me di cuenta de que yo no estaba dispuesta a dejar mi identidad de hombre por nueve meses de embarazo. Me recomendaron que congelara mis óvulos, pero después pensé que mi vocación maternal no era tan fuerte y que bien podía, en caso de desear un hijo, adoptar, o que mi pareja femenina lo tuviera.

(Era cierto, Nina, era una decisión muy fuerte: renunciar a tener un hijo propio. Si yo decidía eliminar mi máquina de producir esper..., bueno, tú me entiendes —sabes que odio la palabra—, tendría que pensar en adoptar a un pequeño desamparado —que lamentablemente nunca faltan—. Y tal vez ésa sería mi decisión, porque no me parecía nada atrayente la idea de un niño congelado, ni que fuera yogur).

La revelación de Alejandro parecía haber terminado, y mi cabeza estaba hirviendo de inquietudes. Primero tuve que deshacerme de una duda superinquietante. Nunca creí que fuera yo tan morbosa, pero tenía que preguntárselo, si no, esta historia no estaría completa, al menos no para mí.

—¿Y tienes....?

No pude decir la palabra. Como una escuincla persignada, sólo acerté a señalar su entrepierna.

Alejandro sonrió y me dijo:

—No lo necesito. La faloplastia es una operación muy difícil y aunque la metadoioplastia es una opción más viable, la verdad no tiene los resultados fantásticos que uno quisiera. Las hormonas hacen crecer tu clítoris y supuestamente lo hacen parecerse a un pequeño pene, con injertos de tu propia piel lo convierten en un miembro apto para orinar, pero la verdad es que no puede compararse una cosa con la otra. Al menos en el aspecto visual y funcional. No creo que valga la pena, por el simple gusto de orinar de pie, someterme a una operación así. Además de que esa cirugía no se practica en cualquier hospital y es muy cara.

No pude evitar imaginarme que él debía de tener razón; formar un pene no era cualquier cosa, no se trataba de agarrar un trozo de plastilina y darle la forma deseada.

Tampoco pude evitar sentir que el fabricante de seres humanos debía de tener un sentido del humor un poco macabro. No podía pensar en una paradoja más incómoda que la que estábamos representando Victoria y Alejandro en ese momento en un café de chinos del centro. Una mujer encerrada en el cuerpo de un hombre deseando deshacerse de un pene, un pene que con toda seguridad le habría encantado tener al hombre encerrado en el cuerpo de mujer que tenía enfrente. Todo fuera como quitar y poner, con gusto le hubiera regalado, ahí mismo, mi magnífico miembro a mi nuevo amigo.

Después de encender un cigarro y comenzar a fumar, continuó:

—El día en que esa operación permita obtener un pene con todas sus funciones..., y me refiero al sexo, entonces, ya veremos. Pero por el momento estoy bien así. Además mi pareja es comprensiva. Podrías decir que técnicamente practicamos el sexo como lo harían dos mujeres, pero lo importante es lo que sentimos.

Me quedé, como decía mi abuela: de una pieza, anonadada y atolondrada. No lo había pensado. Que un médico me hiciera una vagina (por mucho que resultara ser el hermano gemelo de Miguel Ángel o hubiera tomado unas clases de escultura o artes plásticas), no quería decir que iba a permitirme tener orgasmos femeninos, de esos que dicen que hacen que todo el cuerpo te hierva... y como la operación de implante de útero y ovarios aún no existía, pues de tener hijos ni hablamos.

Fue entonces que le conté a Alejandro mi triste e inusual historia. Todo eso que ya te he contado a lo largo de muchas páginas. Y aunque no dije nunca la palabra consejo, aconsejar, recomendar o algo parecido, Alejandro entendió que eso era lo que yo estaba buscando.

—Antes que nada creo que estás evitando todavía tu problema. Lo primero que debes hacer es comenzar a transitar como mujer. Nada mejor para darte cuenta de cómo te sientes. La mayoría de los transexuales odiamos la ropa del sexo con el que nacimos. Y fíjate que estoy usando la palabra odio. Por eso no somos simples travestis. Ellos pueden transitar por la vida con los dos tipos de vestimenta. Para nosotros no es sólo una cuestión de gusto o comodidad, es un asunto de identidad. Después vendrá el resto, es decir, el tratamiento psicológico y hormonal.

Cuando Alejandro mencionó la palabrita, un escalofrío recorrió toda mi sensible y dulce piel: psicólogo. Tal vez para Alejandro había sido una experiencia afortunada, pero para mí, la palabrita era una combinación de algo así como Freddy Krueger mezclado con *Scream* y *Vestida para matar*.

La verdad es que hasta ahora no he tenido la experiencia de tratar con un psicólogo. Una vez estuve a punto de ir con uno. Fue cuando Frida me descubrió aplicándome un poco de su lápiz labial frente al espejo del tocador. Yo tenía siete años y al verme, ella gritó, se escandalizó y amenazó con llevarme con "un médico para gente enferma de la cabeza", pero al final prefirió evitar que alguien ajeno a la casa se enterara de mis ímpetus maquillistas y me castigó con un encierro de una semana sin televisión y sin juegos.

Lo cierto es que las historias (posibles) de doctores que recluyen pacientes para que sus familiares se adueñen de sus fortunas y de analistas que usan sus conocimientos de hipnosis para inducir un estado de somnolencia en sus pacientes jóvenes tan sólo para aprovecharse de ellos, siempre me han aterrado.

Ya sé que todas esas historias parecen leyendas urbanas, Nina, pero son posibles y a mí me pone en estado de pánico que alguien indague en mi cabecita, tan sólo para decirme que tengo algo que suene a: psiconeurotraumahisteria múltiple. No, gracias.

Estaba en estas tribulaciones, cuando Alejandro me dijo:

—Para que te decidieras a hacer las operaciones tendrías que estar ya muy segura, siempre asesorada por tu psicólogo. Conozco casos de hombres que intentaron una faloplastia y quedaron destruidos. En el caso de las mujeres es un poco menos grave. Al parecer la vaginoplastia permite que tengas orgasmos como los conoces.

Como debes de suponer, querida Nina, soy virgen... no te lo había contado porque el tema no había surgido. Ahora, armada de valor, te confieso que nunca tuve la inquietud de tener relaciones mientras

sentía que mi anatomía era equivocada. Pero también te confieso que conozco los orgasmos, conozco la experiencia que provocan muchos sueños nocturnos y la masturbación, es por ello que me preocupaba un poco saber sobre las sensaciones que podían perderse con una operación de cambio de sexo. Se me revela algo insospechado: aparentemente la vagina se forma a partir de los tejidos del pene, así que en muchos casos la sensibilidad apenas se pierde. Bueno, eso es algo que habría que pensar. Pero por el momento, el uso del cuchillo y el derramamiento de sangre —mía—, me parecen una tremenda barbaridad, indigna de considerar. Así que, aunque me anestesiaran con diez inyecciones y me garantizaran que no me iba a doler..., por el momento: no gracias.

Todavía platicamos un rato y quedamos en estar en contacto a través del *mail*, ya que Alejandro se iría en una semana a España. (Por cierto que el nombre de usuario que escogió para su correo electrónico es: *"therightman"*, es decir, Nina, "el hombre correcto". Dime si no es para entusiasmarse). Me deseó mucha suerte y puso a mi consideración el contactarme más adelante con algunas de sus amigas travestis (a algunas ya las había yo conocido en la fiesta) y transexuales. Desde una que tenía una colección de trescientos pares de zapatos hasta a la que sus abuelos le pagaron la operación como regalo de graduación. (Yo quiero unos parientes así).

Pienso que eso podría ser una muy buena idea, si es que logro pasar la primera fase. Pero por el momento ya tengo suficiente de experiencias externas. Ahora me toca a mí. Mi abuela decía que sólo se escarmienta en cabeza propia.

Y ahora sí, perdona que te deje, Nina, pero estoy muy excitada. Tengo que elaborar la misión: "Salida del clóset... de toda la ropa".

Día en que te cuento de cómo Frida perdió la voz... al menos para mí

Así que tengo una misión en puerta: descararme.

Por supuesto que no será un descaro total. En la vida me plantaría en plena escuela con mis zapatos de tacón de aguja, mi blusa floreada y una minifalda, acompañada por un buen par de medias. No voy a provocar escándalos baratos y mucho menos voy a darle el gusto al descerebrado de Carlos Rincón de que me diga algo así como: "Ya lo sabía". Tampoco voy a liberar mis prejuicios en mi casa, y a provocarle el soponcio de su vida a Frida. Pero hay un modo de comenzar a experimentar. Para eso necesito la ayuda de Rodrigo.

Aprovecharé su casa para cambiarme y acto seguido pasearé mi atractiva humanidad por zonas desconocidas de esta gran ciudad. Si algo tiene de bueno la Ciudad de México en beneficio de mis propósitos, es que colonias donde nadie me conoce, hay para aventar como confeti.

De acuerdo a mis planes, lo único que necesito es circular. Ir al cine, a centros comerciales, mirar aparadores, *of course,* a tomar un café en calidad de fémina desprotegida, para saber si me siento como toda una Victoria dispuesta a conquistar el mundo.

Apenas y pude concentrarme en la escuela. Afortunadamente, Rodrigo estuvo absolutamente de acuerdo con mi plan. Incluso pensó en que sería una buena idea acompañarme —no vestida como cabaretera como en la fiesta, no gracias, sino como todo un chaperón—. Al principio no me gustó mucho la idea, pero al final pensé que tal vez no sería una mala propuesta, al menos la primera vez.

Rodrigo se portó como un gay de lo más considerado y galante. No puedo negarlo. Nuevamente dejé libre mi cabellera y la esponjé con *mousse* y un buen cepillado. Ahora había decidido usar un atuendo un poco más juvenil. Para ello tuve que realizar un robo al clóset de Frida. Le tomé unos zapatos tenis que nunca usaba y que se había comprado en una ocasión, según ella, para hacer ejercicio; decía que iba a correr todos los días en el parque (¡ajá!). Los pobres tenis nunca vieron la luz del sol. Así que ni siquiera notaría su ausencia. Lo que no estaba tan fácil eran los jeans morados que alguna vez le regaló la tía Lola y que eran sus favoritos. Tal vez hubiera podido usar mis propios pantalones de mezclilla, pero era demasiado cómodo. Tenía que usar prendas femeninas. Sólo ropa para niñas, me había prometido, si no, no tenía ningún chiste. Me escurrí en el cuarto de Frida mientras tomaba su ducha de belleza (¿qué quieres?, así le decía ella, la muy ridícula). Tuve que apurarme, sabía que sus baños duraban menos de diez minutos. La muy tacaña decía que así ahorraba agua y gas. Claro que nos hacía tomar los mismos baños (cero placenteros) a mí y a Claudia. Lo que ella no sabía es que si estaba en casa nos tardábamos cinco minutos, pero si no, nuestros baños podían durar media hora. Y esto último era lo más frecuente. Más de una vez, la pobre Frida no pudo explicarse por qué la cuenta de gas no bajaba. Bueno, basta de divagar, el caso es que tuve que sustraer los pantalones de su cajón con rapidez, sigilo y eficacia.

Valió la pena. Eran muy lindos, aunque sufrí horrores para ponérmelos una vez que estuve en casa de Rodrigo. A pesar de que tuve que usar un truco de tipo suspensorio (que no te pienso explicar aquí, eso sí que tendrás tú que imaginarlo), para que mi aparato reproductor externo —todo él—, no quedara en evidencia, parecían hechos a mi medida. A eso le añadí una blusa muy mona que yo me había encargado de teñir de morado en alguna ocasión.

Me miré el espejo y casi —me da vergüenza escribirlo, pero es cierto— casi me beso. Un poco de maquillaje (sobre todo en mi desafortunado lunar) y la juvenil Victoria estaría en su gran momento.

Decidí usar ese tipo de vestuario, pues por el momento quería simplemente enfocarme en mi apariencia y no en mi modo de caminar, y yo sabía que los tacones me pondrían ante la seria consideración de dejar la experiencia para otro momento, por el bien de mis pobres y adoloridos pies.

Rodrigo y yo optamos por tomar un taxi y llevar nuestros aventureros cuerpecitos hasta un centro comercial en el otro extremo de la ciudad. No tenía humor de exponerme a los vapores humanos del metro y a los cavernarios modales que se respiran en un microbús. Estaba dispuesta a hacerme cargo de los gastos, así que mi amigo sería mi invitado. Cuando el taxista nos preguntó a dónde nos dirigíamos, te lo juro, Nina, que no pude resistirlo, algo en lo más profundo de la atrevida Victoria provocó que saliera un timbre desconocido para mí emitiendo un cantarino:

—Tome el Periférico, si nos hace el favor.

Estaba a punto de preguntarle a Rodrigo cómo me había salido mi voz de contralto, cuando miré su rostro, estaba más rojo que una sandía pasada, y por su gesto, parecía que hubiera oído a su abuela hablar de felaciones. Eso me hizo mirar por el espejo retrovisor la expresión de los ojos del taxista. Fue un breve instante, menos de tres segundos, menos de lo que dura un beso de piquito, menos de lo que dura decir un buen insulto, pero te juro que sentí su asco embarrarme todo el cuerpo. Nunca más cometió el error de mirar nuevamente atrás. ¿Y sabes qué? No me importó. Es más. Tu Victoria sonrió.

Me pasé molestando a Rodrigo todo el tiempo con mi recién descubierto tono femenino. No creas que se trataba de algo escandaloso y pitudo, simplemente le di a la voz una tonalidad dulce, pero no muy acaramelada, yo diría que le di un tono de manzanilla mezclada con canela, al menos así me sabía a mí.

No hicimos nada atrevido o molesto. Nada que pudiera ocasionar que nos encarcelaran por faltas a la moral o por alterar el orden público. Entramos a algunas tiendas, la mayoría de zapatos, compramos un helado, o más bien, debería decir que compré unos helados. Y después de sentir algunas miradas sorprendidas, me di cuenta de que la mayor parte de la gente en realidad se ocupa de sus propios asuntos y no suele fijarse en una chica con un vestuario tan poco provocativo como el mío. Sólo obtuve una silbatina de unos trabajadores de la limpieza que comían su *lunch* sentados en la banqueta... Solos no se hubieran atrevido, pero junta a tres o más machos y no tardarán ni un segundo en manifestar su latente homosexualidad.

Para decírtelo claramente, Nina: ABURRIIIIIDO y te lo pongo así, con mayúsculas y con un tremendo énfasis en la monótona I, para que no tengas duda de lo poco emocionante que resultó la correría. La aventura vino una hora después, justo cuando el siguiente taxista nos había dejado en la casa de Rodrigo. Esta vez resultó uno de esos viejitos que se la pasan contándote su vida y que ni una persecución policíaca sería capaz de callarlos. Yo lo perdoné porque todo el tiempo me estuvo tratando como si fuera toda una señorita, incluso llegó a asumir que Rodrigo y yo éramos pareja. Cosa que no le gustó mucho a mi amigo, a juzgar por la cara de regañado que tenía, o tal vez era que no soportaba que yo estuviera dándome vuelo con mi acento de princesa.

Cuando finalmente llegamos a su casa, Rodrigo me tomó el brazo y me dijo:

—Creo que hay problemas, porterita.

Pude ver cómo Rodrigo miraba hacia su edificio. Eran las siete de la noche y la gente que ya había arribado a sus casas tenía encendidas las luces. Eso era lo que había visto Rodrigo: una luz brillante, donde no debería haber ninguna.

—¿No decías que tus papás volverían hasta dentro de dos días?

Rodrigo lucía asustado, pero no podía verse ni la mitad de asustado de lo que yo estaba. Me pidió que me quedara en el taxi, mientras iba a verificar.

Me quedé ahí, más petrificada que una estatua de parque. Un solo pensamiento revoloteaba mi cabecita: "¿y si no puedo cambiarme en casa de Rodrigo?". Miles de opciones —todas malas— desfilaban por mi cerebro, ninguna me convenció: "¿me cambio en un Sanborns?, ¿me cambio en un callejón?, ¿me cambio en el taxi?, ¿y si mejor me lleva el taxi a la estación de autobuses y huyo?".

—Se ve preocupada, señorita.

—¿Eh?.... (Me salió sin querer la masculinidad por la boca. Tuve que rectificar)... ¿Eh?

—No se preocupe, señorita, si quiere yo los puedo llevar a un hotel.

—¿A un hotel?

Todos los colores del arcoíris desfilaron por mi cara, Nina. El metiche taxista —como suelen ser muchos taxistas— había asumido por la plática entre Rodrigo y yo que nuestro plan, al ir hasta su casa, era tener una noche de pasión, aprovechando la ausencia de sus padres.

—Conozco uno que no es caro... aquí a unas cuadras.

La sola imagen de Rodrigo y yo en un... Y haciendo... entre las sábanas... Estuve a punto de echarme a reír. La carcajada que tuve que ahogar hizo creer al taxista que estaba punto de llorar.

—No se ponga así, señorita. Es bien lindo eso de ser joven y estar enamorado... Huyyyy si yo le contara, señorita, la de cosas que teníamos que hacer mi señora y yo cuando éramos novios para poder tener nuestro momento de intimidad...

Me encantó que no dejara de llamarme "señorita", así que me sentí terriblemente tentada a seguir con la farsa, después de todo, ¿quién era yo para robarle la ilusión a un chofer genuinamente interesado en la problemática sentimental de sus pasajeros?

—Es que la verdad, hemos sufrido mucho en nuestra relación. Sus padres no me aceptan. ¿Usted, qué me aconseja?

—¡Huyyy, señorita! A buen árbol se arrima. Pero déjeme decirle esto... Cuando hay amor, no hay barrera que se pueda interponer, señorita. Yo tengo dos hijos y pues la verdad uno quiere lo mejor para ellos. Lo peor que puede hacer uno como padre es oponerse a lo que ellos escojan, señorita. Yo quiero a mis hijos felices, y estoy seguro de que los padres de su novio de usted quieren lo mismo. Va a ver cómo terminan aceptando. Usted no se preocupe, señorita, usted es muy linda.

"¡Muy linda! ¡Muy linda!" Así lo dijo, Nina. Debo confesarte que por un momento pensé que el taxista podía ser sólo una cosa: un auténtico conocedor de la belleza. "¡Muy linda!" Sólo por eso le perdoné ese horrible "su novio de usted" que había salido por su boca.

Desde que vi aproximarse a Rodrigo, supe, tanto por su pesado andar como por su gesto de funeral, que las noticias no eran buenas. Decidí bajar un momento del taxi para confirmar lo que temía. Rodrigo sólo necesitó de una palabra:

—Volvieron.

Un instante después me pasaba mi mochila con mi ropa.

Entonces lo recordé, Nina. Era día del odioso cafecito de Frida con sus amigotas. Tomé la muñeca de Rodrigo para mirar la hora en su reloj. Si me apuraba a llegar a la casa, tenía como quince minutos para adelantarme a la llegada de mi madre.

Sonaba como a una misión imposible, pero todo indicaba que eso era lo que tenía que hacer. Me parecía que era más adecuado tentar a la suerte en mi propia casa y cambiarme ahí a hacerlo en un callejón con el riesgo de acabar encarcelada o violada por un maniático oportunista tentado por mi desnuda belleza.

Le di una propina muy considerable al taxista mientras le insistía:

—Es muy importante que llegue ahí en diez minutos.

Curiosamente, el hombre manejó casi totalmente callado durante esos diez minutos. Yo creo que juraba que se había convertido en una combinación de cupido y de agente de la CIA. Mi ansiedad debió haberlo convencido de que yo iba a una cita con mi destino. Y de algún modo, así era.

—Mucha suerte, señorita. Va a ver cómo todo se va arreglar con sus padres... Al final todos tenemos que aceptar lo que no se puede cambiar.

Estas últimas palabras me parecieron mucho más trascendentales que un momento de filosofía barata de taxista y quedaron resonando en mi cabeza mientras subía las escaleras hasta el departamento y rogaba no encontrarme con nadie. Por si las dudas subí tan rápido como pude y oculté mi rostro del mundo vecinal mirando al suelo como una pecadora arrepentida.

Cuando traspasé la puerta, sentí ese cosquilleo en el estómago que acompaña los momentos de triunfo; aún los momentos más mediocres de triunfo, como cuando adivinas el color del auto que va a pasar, como cuando tu equipo favorito mete el gol del honor en el último minuto de juego, como cuando le ganas a tu neurótica madre la carrera a la casa.

Entré en el cuarto de Frida. Ni siquiera me preocupé por encender la luz. Cada segundo podía contar. Me quité la blusa en menos de siete segundos; un segundo por botón. Claro que lo que realmente me preocupaba era el pantalón. Si me había tomado tanto tiempo, sudor y lágrimas ponérmelo, no quería ni imaginar lo que me costaría quitármelo. Me divirtió pensar que los dichosos pantalones a la hora de la hora no resultaban nada sexys. Imagina a tu amante queriendo quitarlos con suavidad. Y ni hablar de un *striptease*. *No way*. Mientras enrollaba los pantalones desde los muslos hacia los pies, con un enorme esfuerzo sudoroso, tenía muy atento el oído para así poder anticipar mi salida antes de que Frida pudiera entrar en el cuarto.

Cuando por fin tuve los pantalones en mis manos y me dispuse a colocarlos en su cajón, ocurrió algo totalmente sorpresivo. La luz se encendió.

He pegado un brinco, Nina, que por poco me hace caer de espaldas.

Ahí estaba la personificación de mis más temidas pesadillas: yo sosteniendo unas prendas femeninas, desnuda, justo frente a Frida. Y tú te preguntarás, ¿cómo le hizo para entrar sin que yo me diera cuenta? Pues muy fácil, Frida nunca entró; ya estaba ahí.

Gracias a que no encendí la luz, pudo esconderse tras las sombras. Estaba acostada en su cama cuando llegué. La muy maldita había visto en la penumbra todo el show desnudista de su hija, sin decir una palabra. Imagino que había regresado temprano por algún dolor de cabeza o alguno de sus ataques neuróticos y había decidido meterse a la cama para poner fin a su ajetreado día. Yo creo que se quedó tan petrificada por la impresión que por eso tardó en anunciar su presencia; además, al verme en sus pantalones había entrado en estado de *shock* y su mandíbula tardó unos considerables treinta y cinco segundos en volver a cerrarse, para al fin decir:

—Pero ¿qué haces?

Sé que lo más lógico hubiera sido cambiarme en mi cuarto, pero qué te puedo decir, Nina, al llegar a la casa sentí que cada segundo contaba, que efectivamente Frida no estaba en el departamento y que mi cambio de ropas sería casi instantáneo… En dos palabras: me confié.

Afortunadamente, Victoria estaba ya tan instalada en mi cuerpo que no temblé ni me sonrojé y, gracias al cielo, tampoco me desmayé. Tal vez, muy en el fondo, estaba deseando que ese encuentro se diera, por eso dije con cinismo y con esa voz cantarina que cada día me salía mejor:

—Probando tu ropa, querida.

Frida con todo y su dolor de cabeza, se incorporó, sacó las piernas de las sábanas y se me acercó con la mirada encendida, y creo que las uñas afiladas y prestas a despellejarme viva.

—¿Qué dijiste?

Yo ya estaba perfectamente encarrilada, así que, a pesar de la amenazante figura que se perfilaba sobre mi pobre persona, no tuve ningún problema en decir:

—¿No te habrá contado tu amiga Liliana de su encuentro en el Metro con cierto personaje usando un vestido igualito al diseño exclusivo que te regaló?

Frida abrió los ojos tamaño búho desvelado y tardó unos instantes en darse cuenta:

—¿Eras tú?

Volvió a caer sentada en la cama, tal vez, sin dar el menor crédito a lo que su pobre cerebrito le estaba comunicando en ese momento: Tu hijo..., ahora hija, era esa despampanante mujer, de la que tu amiga ya te había contado y que estaba usando TUUUUU vestido en el Metro. Ante su obvia consternación me vi obligada a darle una ayudadita:

—Pues claro que era yo, queridita.

Un silencio más espeso que un licuado dietético inundó todo el cuarto. Entonces la expresión más sombría que yo hubiera visto en mi vida dominó el rostro de Frida, quien, mientras abandonaba la habitación, dijo esa frase que yo sabía no tenía vuelta atrás y que, de tan melodramática, por un momento amenazó con llenar el cuarto con una miel muy amarga.

—Yo ya no tengo hijos.

Día en que te cuento cómo la armonía familiar regresó a nuestras vidas

Qué crees, Nina, en cuanto le conté a Claudia lo que había pasado con Frida, cayó en el piso, dominada por un ataque de risa tamaño severo, de esos que amenazan con hacerte perder el aire y hasta provocarte un infarto estomacal.

Ahora ya éramos huérfanas. Frida desconocía que alguna vez habíamos habitado su vientre.

Por un momento no creí en sus palabras. A Claudia ya le había ocurrido varias veces, pero era la primera vez que me pasaba a mí y aún no lo podía creer. ¿Sería posible que aguantara la tentación de abrir la boca, aunque fuera para mascullar, gemir o maldecir? ¿Sería capaz de dejarse controlar por un berrinche? Pues uno nunca debe dudar del poder destructivo de un ego avinagrado como el de Frida. Todos sabemos que hay una palabra que sería incapaz de aparecer a través de sus labios: "Perdón". Tú lo sabes, Nina, ella preferiría ser secuestrada por terroristas antes que atreverse a siquiera pensar un humilde y desprotegido: "Me equivoqué".

Así que, ante mi sorpresa, la voz de Frida comienza a parecer un borroso recuerdo. Incluso cuando tiene que hablar por teléfono, lo hace desde su cuarto y encerrada. Y con el tiempo ha comenzado a convertirse en una presencia fantasmal, aunque estoy segura de que hasta el alma en pena más desventurada proyectaría una imagen más festiva que la que ahora Frida nos obsequia a mí y a Claudia cuando se deslizaba por los pasillos.

Al principio se aventuraba a desayunar conmigo y mi hermana; incapaz de pedirnos que le pasáramos la sal, que le preparáramos un pan francés o que le ayudáramos un poco con la limpieza de la cocina, masticando en silencio y evitando mirarnos aunque fuera de soslayo. Pero en cuanto se dio cuenta de que si compartía la cocina con sus dos despreciadas hijas, iba a tener que soportar una plática soez y provocadora, decidió dejarnos solas.

Fue a Claudia a la que se le ocurrió comenzar a incomodarla con vocablos altisonantes, y esto, descubrimos, tenía francamente un efecto extraordinario. Simplemente se trataba de empezar una plática inocente, casi aburrida, que de pronto se transformaba en una dialéctica de la escatología, el sexo, la perversión o la vulgaridad. La peor pesadilla de una hija consentida de la revista *Buenhogar*. Yo la primera vez no entendía lo que pretendía Claudia, pero conforme avanzaba la conversación, comprendí las intenciones de mi malvada hermana y de inmediato me le sumé, completamente deleitada.

Por ejemplo:

—¿Y cómo te fue ayer, güey?

—Bien. Nada del otro mundo.

—Yo estuve ensayando una obra de teatro bien chingona.

—¿Ah si?

—Se llama *Las amantes*.

—¿*Las amantes*?

—Sí. *Las amantes*.

—¿No querrás decir "Los" amantes?

—No. Hablo de dos mujeres. Dos amantes.

—O sea, que estás hablando de dos mujeres teniendo sexo.

—Y con furia cabrona.

—Dos lesbianas.

—Dos mujeres que a través de sus cuerpos desnudos comunican sus más impensadas y jodidas fantasías.

No necesito decirte, Nina, que en cuanto la palabra lesbiana, sexo, caca o algo parecido, surge de nuestros labios, Frida es impulsada por el resorte de la decencia y abandona la habitación.

De hecho, ya no le es posible estar con nosotras en ningún cuarto de la casa. En cuanto nos ve entrar, toma el libro que esté leyendo, su tejido o lo que sea y se retira al único sitio en el que sabe que puede estar a salvo: su cuarto, que por cierto desde el incidente en el que me sorprendió con sus queridas prendas, siempre está bajo llave. La paranoica de Frida se ha encargado de colocar una nueva cerradura a prueba de asaltabancos en la puerta de su cuarto. Como si guardara en su triste clóset diseños originales de Versace o Christian Dior. Por un momento creí que estaba enloqueciendo de verdad. Claudia y yo especulamos cuánto durará este berrinche.

—Conmigo ya duró más de cuatro meses —se jacta mi hermana.

Yo sólo pienso en que no me hace nada mal contar con este silencio durante el mayor tiempo posible.

Pero lo mejor de todo, creo, es ya no tener el menor temor de exponerme tal y como soy. Si Frida ha decidido que Victoria no puede ser su hija, pues no tiene el menor derecho de opinar no sólo de mi forma de hablar o sobre mis modales, sino sobre mi vestimenta.

El departamento se ha convertido en mi paraíso. Ya no es necesario salir al mundo para experimentar nuevos atuendos. Ahora me basta la reacción de asco o de simple desaprobación de Frida, para estar convencida de que la presencia de Victoria está progresando.

He decidido dejar mis aficiones travestidas para la seguridad y calidez del hogar. Por el momento quiero sentirme cómoda conmigo misma. Dicen que ésa es la clave de cualquier proyecto exitoso: la seguridad en una misma.

Aún estoy experimentando y añoro ese momento en el que me sienta tan bien, que hasta el mundo diga: "Miren ésta que se ve tan contenta y confiada, respétenla porque tiene su lugar bajo mi techo".

Tal vez ese momento llegue cuando yo me vea con el cuerpo completo de mujer. Tal vez sea algo que logren las hormonas o una operación.

A veces me he soñado con mis respectivos órganos femeninos, con mi dotación correcta de hormonas y una figura totalmente grácil y sensual, como si de pronto el universo hubiera decidido arreglar ese error cometido hace casi dieciocho años. Y entonces me siento como en mi casa.

Si en algún momento eso ocurre en la vida real, será como estar en el cielo, Nina. Como estar en un lugar maravilloso y desconocido.

¿Te he contado que siempre que pienso en el cielo, pienso en Mongolia?

Nunca he visto una foto de Ulan Bator. Pero cuando imagino que vuelo hacia allá y bajo del avión, veo chozas extrañas, veo hombres vistiendo gruesas pieles, veo bigotes largos, veo a Genghis Khan paseando en bicicleta.

Pero, la verdad, Nina, sé que la realidad debe ser otra. Ulan Bator debe tener grandes avenidas, autos último modelo asegurados,

taxistas ebrios, mendigos en las esquinas sin pieles que los cubran, hoteles de veinte pisos y muchos restaurantes de hamburguesas, servidas siempre con papas y refresco.

Viajar al cielo tal vez no sea ninguna sorpresa. El cielo debe estar lleno de grandes avenidas, taxistas, mendigos y hoteles de veinte pisos.

Pero aún así, ir al cielo debe ser una gran aventura, una aventura parecida a andar en bicicleta o nadar. La primera vez estás completamente temerosa, convencida de que acabarás con una severa caída o un conato de ahogamiento, pero en cuanto los dominas —tanto el vehículo como el nado de crol—, te sientes como león en carnicería.

El cambio de sexo no debe ser una promesa del paraíso, hasta las mejores opciones pueden llevarte a alguna decepción espantosa, ya me lo había dicho Alejandro.

Pero es bien sabido que las cosas que valen la pena siempre implican un riesgo. Si todo fuera tan simple como presionar un botón para obtener lo que deseas y volverlo a presionar si es que el resultado no te gustó, no estaría yo escribiendo esto, Nina.

Lo que sí me preocupa es que para dar el siguiente paso necesito algo importante: dinero.

Si en algún momento decido activar mi femineidad con hormonas o incluso opto por llevar mi aventura a la sala de operaciones, debo tener en cuenta una considerable cantidad de dinero, que, como te puedes imaginar, no tengo.

Eso es un serio problema, Nina, pues significa que tal vez tenga que buscar un trabajo de medio tiempo, al menos.

Día en que te cuento de mi encuentro con Frida. Y de cómo volvió a dirigirle la palabra a una de sus hijas

❋

Anoche me vi de pie frente a Frida y tomé aire (tanto como si estuviera a punto de atravesar una alberca nadando por abajo del agua). Ese encuentro era algo que sentía que me debía, que le debía a ella o que simplemente tenía que ocurrir.

Bloqueé la puerta, evitando que saliera de la cocina y comencé a hablar:

—Yo sé que el *shock* que recibiste fue terrible. Con todas tus ideas arcaicas sobre cómo debe ser el mundo, debes de haber creído que yo había enloquecido o algo así. Pero tienes que escucharme al menos, así que no se te ocurra levantarte e irte a esconder a tu mazmorra, porque soy capaz de derribar tu puerta o, lo que es peor, me pondré a gritar, para que todos en el edifico nos escuchen. Pues mira, la razón de que me hayas encontrado ataviada con tus vestidos... exactamente, oíste muy bien: "ataviadA" con una gran letra "A" al final de la palabra, así que no me pongas esa cara de espanto, que precisamente eso es lo que quiero contarte. Te lo diré de la manera más simple posible: soy mujer, Frida. Sí. Ya sé que tú crees que tener genitales masculinos es razón suficiente para que se me catalogue como un hombre. Sé que tu mente pequeña no da para entender que a veces la anatomía puede ser algo engañosa y que crees que uno debe de obedecer a la naturaleza. Pues aunque no lo puedas concebir, estoy obedeciendo a mi naturaleza. Una naturaleza muy diferente a la que estás acostumbrada a ver. Y ni te preocupes, que esto no tiene nada que ver con la educación —o la falta de educación— que me diste. Simplemente así soy. Ni deberías sorprenderte, pues sabes muy bien que siempre me gustó el color rosa y que odiaba los carritos de juguete que me regalaban. Sé que con tu mente medieval serías muy capaz de entregarme a la Santa Inquisición para que me ataran a un tronco y le prendieran fuego. Así que quiero advertirte que si te atreves a tocarme o a impedir que sea yo como soy, soy muy capaz de armarte un escándalo por discriminación y vejación de mis garantías individuales. Así es, soy capaz de ir hasta la misma Comisión de Derechos Humanos, por lo que te recomiendo que sigas en tu actitud silenciosa. Ah, pero si en algún momento de tu vida te dignas madurar y volverme a dirigir la palabra, vas a tener que llamarme Victoria. Sí. Victoria. Y nada de Vicky, aunque sé de antemano que tú serías incapaz de usar un diminutivo como señal de afecto.

Bueno, en realidad, no le dije nada a Frida.

Pero me hubiera gustado hacerlo. Éste es el discurso que yo tengo muy preparado para Frida, con la intención de no quedarme con la espinita de no haber intentado arreglar las cosas, pero no pude decirle nada. Creo que tan sólo lo soñé.

En fin...

Tal vez con el tiempo.

Justo cuando estaba escandalizándome (al consultar revistas y el Internet) con la barbaridad de precios que significa adueñarme de unos buenos pechos y deshacerme de mi virilidad masculina, ocurrió lo inesperado. Frida recibió una llamada.

La tía Lola está muy enferma. Después de muchos inconvenientes ocasionados por infinidad de cosas, que iban desde haber tenido un padre militar que nunca la apreció lo suficiente, el haber sido atacada por la poliomielitis cuando aún no existía la vacuna y que le dejó una pierna semiparalizada y la compañía de un bastón para toda su vida, así como el no haber tenido una relación amorosa en toda su vida (que a mi entender debe haber sido la peor de todas las torturas), finalmente un enfermo gusto por el cigarro, no sólo le ha dejado una hilera de dientes estropeados, sino un cáncer que ahora amenazaba con llevársela.

La recordé con toda su amargura y sus excentricidades. La recordé haciendo que le podara todo el pasto de su jardín y que cargara sacos de estiércol... (hasta se me enchinó la piel). La recordé encendiendo un cigarro casi al tiempo que apagaba la colilla del que acababa de terminar. Y con todo y eso debo confesar que sentí un poco de pena. Pero no tanta como para lamentar que mi hermana y yo hubiéramos dejado de ir a su casa desde hacía cuatro años, porque has de saber, Nina, que si era una pesadilla convivir con Frida, ir a casa de la tía Dolores era algo semejante a visitar tres círculos del infierno combinados (y no lo digo sólo por lo del estiércol).

Lo cierto con la tía Lola es que, por alguna extraña razón, siempre le tuvo un especial cariño a Claudia. Así como a mí me hacía trabajar, a Claudia la consentía y la ponía a tejer o le enseñaba cosas propias de una señorita. Más de una vez yo me asomé con curiosidad a ver qué hacían, ya fuera en el cuarto de costura o en la cocina. Y muchas veces lamenté que no fuera a mí a quien le enseñara los secretos de un buen pastel de tres leches, el punto de cruz o a tejer una bufanda. Siempre que me sorprendía husmeando, la tía me corría diciendo que ése no era lugar para hombres. Lo curioso es que Claudia, como era de una naturaleza poco femenina y desesperada, odiaba todo eso. Alguna vez me dijo: "Sólo hay una cosa que odio más que ir a casa de la tía Lola a hacer repostería: ir a casa de la tía Lola a tejer". Así que todo era una pequeña paradoja, mientras mi hermana era alguien que era siempre bien recibida, pero que odiaba estar ahí, yo era alguien que bien podía no existir, es más, no sé si la tía Lola realmente sabía que yo también era su pariente, y lo terrible era que yo me moría por penetrar en ese mundo femenino.

Alguna vez escuché a Frida comentar que cuando la tía Lola era adolescente, perdió a su pequeña hermana de diez años en un accidente. A mí siempre me pareció el único modo de explicar esa extraña predilección por Claudia. Claro que en cuanto llevar a rastras a Claudia se convirtió en una labor más que imposible para Frida, las visitas a la casa de la tía Lola se terminaron. Además, durante un periodo en el que Claudia fue con frecuencia a casa de la tía (obligada por Frida), hubo un pleito con la tía que hizo que mi hermana jamás se volviera a aparecer por ahí. No necesito decirte que a Frida casi le da un soponcio, mismo que manifestó con otro conocido: "Yo ya no tengo hija", y un silencio de varias semanas con Claudia. Creo que ella imaginaba que mi hermana estaba perfilándose seriamente como la heredera universal de los bienes de su tía discapacitada y no quería que echara a perder esa oportunidad.

Y a pesar del pleito entre la tía y Claudia, no había cumpleaños que la tía no le mandara a mi hermana algún vestido o suéter. En Navidad siempre le enviaba anillos o collares, y no vayas a creer que eran baratijas de fantasía o alhajas de mercado, eran joyas de considerable valor. Pero siempre que llegaba un regalo de la tía para

Claudia, ocurría lo mismo: mi hermana hacía una kilométrica cara de asco, mientras a su lado Frida, ansiosa como una escuincla, le insistía en que se apresurara a abrir el paquete. Invariablemente los regalos de la tía acababan sepultados en algún secreto lugar del clóset de Claudia. Frida siempre le pedía que agradeciera, al menos por teléfono los presentes, pero mi hermana decía todas las veces lo mismo: "No entiendo por qué insiste en darme cosas, si sabe que no la soporto". Lo cierto es que Claudia bien pudo haber convidado algunos de los obsequios a Frida, que por lo general babea cuando se topa con cualquier cosa que remotamente pretenda brillar como el oro, pero a mi hermana siempre le ha agradado hacer rabiar a su madre cuando tiene la oportunidad.

Pues resulta, Nina, que en su llamada la tía le pidió un favor muy especial a Frida: antes de morir, quiere ver a Claudia. El problema: Frida ha jurado nuevamente que no le hablará a su hija. Y ya lleva más de cuatro meses así.

No tengo que explicarte el conflicto que debió de darse en todo el interior de mi madre. Debió sentirse como un volcán a punto de expulsar lava y piedras calientes. Desde que lo recuerdo, ella ha admirado a un sólo tipo de persona: a la que tiene dinero. Por eso no es de extrañarse que siempre haya estado en contacto con la tía Lola. Estoy segura de que todos estos años ha estado gastando sus pocas neuronas en fantasear en lo que haría si su querida y acaudalada tía se dignaba a pasarle tan sólo un poco de su fortuna: cruceros al caribe, vestidos finos y, claro, joyas. Y ahora todo eso se podría perder si no se atreve a romper su promesa de silencio y hablar con Claudia.

Pero tanto tú como yo sabemos perfectamente que la ambición de Frida puede superar a la del rey Midas. Antes que dejar ir una buena cantidad de billetes verdes, amarillos o rojos (el color no importa) preferiría perder su pierna izquierda.

Así que perder su dignidad es algo con lo que puede vivir. Si la tía Lola quiere ver a Claudia, Frida se encargará de que esto suceda.

Esa misma tarde, después de tanto tiempo de silencio jurado, Frida miró directamente a Claudia, y después de un profundo respiro, abrió la boca, y de ésta salieron palabras claras y, supongo yo, bien practicadas:

—Necesito que me hagas un favor.

No tengo que decirte que el efecto conseguido en la humanidad de Claudia después de que supo en qué consistía el favor fue todo menos lo que Frida hubiera querido. No se necesitaba ser un psíquico o tener un IQ de doscientos para entender de inmediato cuáles eran las intenciones de nuestra madre.

—Tú no estás preocupada por la tía.

—Claro que estoy preocupada por ella.

—¿Ya estás harta de vender tiempos compartidos?

—Te juro que no soporto la idea de verla así.

—Eres jodidamente increíble.

—El doctor le dijo que tiene menos de seis meses.

—¿Tanto te urge?

—¿Qué cosa?

—Que te incluya en su pinche testamento.

—¿Qué estás insinuando?

—Era todo lo que te interesaba cuando me llevabas a su pinche casa.

—No es cierto.

—Por favor, al menos admite que todo esto tiene que ver con el puto dinero.

—Deja de decir groserías.

—Yo hablo como me venga mi pinche gana.

Yo creo que Frida sintió que de nada serviría intentar engañar a Claudia, que de nada le serviría intentar una representación melodramática o fingir un ataque. La conocíamos demasiado bien. Así que decidió que lo mejor en un caso como éste era el descaro completo:

—¿Sabes cuánto tiene la tía Lola? Varios millones. No estoy diciendo que podría heredártelo todo, existen otros parientes. Pero siempre hubo una sobrina favorita, lo sabes bien. ¿Sabes lo que podríamos hacer con ese dinero? Podríamos terminar de pagar el departamento. Y tú ya no tendrías que trabajar. Podrías hacer tu teatro, sin preocuparte, toda tu vida. Hasta una obra podrías producir. Lo que se te ocurra.

—Jamás podría hacerlo.

—¿Por qué? ¿Por el pleito que tuviste con ella?

Claudia se levantó. Estaba molesta (ligeramente encabronada, diría ella). Como nunca la había visto. Mi mente se volvió entonces una confusión de pensamientos. Por un lado sentía admiración y respeto por mi hermana, que no iba a ceder a sus principios. Pero por otro lado sentía que ella estaba desaprovechando una gran oportunidad. Al igual que Frida, yo creía que si mi hermana se empeñaba, bien podía sacarle una pequeña y nada despreciable herencia a la tía moribunda. Me sorprendí pensando que tal vez Frida no estaba tan equivocada, Claudia podía obtener un dinero que no sólo le permitiría comprarse unos cuantos pares de zapatos, sino casi cualquier cosa, y para ello, no tendría que hacer nada grave ni tendría que robar o asesinar a nadie, tan sólo tendría que hacer una visita, una visita que tal vez, hasta por caridad, se merecía cualquier mujer postrada en espera de la oscura muerte.

Esa noche fue bastante evidente que Frida no pudo pegar ninguno de los ojos. Desde mi cuarto podía escucharla "se cuecen las zanahorias y se aplastan. Se hace una salsa blanca espesa con la mantequilla...", mientras el rechinido de la cama retumbaba y la cabecera golpeaba la pared.

Yo tampoco estaba muy tranquila que digamos. Me sorprendí teniendo pensamientos culpables y pensando en que con el dinero que Claudia podría obtener, yo conseguiría sin problemas, no sólo mi cambio completo de sexo, podría hasta hacerme una liposucción y una cirugía estética para rematar y no en cualquier hospital, sino en el que a mí se me antojara.

Fue mientras pensaba en que tal vez no sería tan mala idea rogarle a Claudia que considerara su decisión (que tal vez yo podría prometerle uno o dos meses de esclavitud a cambio de que hiciera la visita), que me vino la idea.

Entonces sí que me fue imposible retomar el sueño.

Igual que a Frida.

Día en que te cuento cómo Frida y yo volvimos a dirigirnos la palabra

Creo que a estas alturas ya debes de haberte imaginado lo que me propongo. Y tengo que decir que aunque sí tuve mi pequeño conflicto interno, no es algo que no lograra ahogar con un buen vaso de leche *light*.

Así como los principios de Frida pueden derrumbarse con un cheque en blanco, también mis más arraigadas ideas pueden escurrirse por una coladera ante la posibilidad de ser físicamente (sin efectos especiales, maquillaje, faldas o tacones): una mujer.

Sin dudarlo me dirigí al cuarto de Frida, toqué a su puerta y carraspeando dije las palabras mágicas, unas palabras más efectivas que el "Ábrete sésamo" de Alí Babá:

—Sé cómo podemos tener la herencia de la tía Lola.

Con lagañas en los ojos, el cabello revuelto y un aliento rancio —que desafortunadamente alcanzó a tocar mi olfato—, Frida abrió la puerta.

Es tan ridículo mi plan, tan absurdo, que por eso tiene todas las posibilidades de resultar exitoso. Frida, a pesar del asco que le provoca mi apariencia femenina, a pesar de sentir una clara antipatía por Victoria, tuvo que reconocer que cualquier cosa que pudiera convertirla en un cuervo millonario, merecía ser escuchada, así que aunque su primera reacción al escucharme decir: "Yo seré Claudia" fue pelar los ojos del tamaño de un pequeño planeta, acabó por aceptar que más valía tener un plan a no tener ninguno.

Y no es tan malo el plan, Nina. Claudia y yo después de todo somos hermanas, tenemos el mismo color de cabello y ojos, una complexión parecida y sobre todo contamos con que la tía Lola, además de estar debilitada por la enfermedad, tiene algunos años de no habernos visto a mí o a mi hermana, así que no es tan descabellado pensar que, con un poco de suerte y una buena actuación, yo pueda hacerle creer a una vieja señora que no está platicando con su recién nacida sobrina Victoria, sino con su queridísima Claudia.

Frida no tuvo que decirme nada. Una leve sonrisa avarienta asomó en su rostro, cuando le dije:

—Ni siquiera tu amiga me reconoció la vez que coincidimos en el Metro.

Lo que más me atemoriza del plan, aunque no lo creas, Nina, no tiene que ver con mi dudosa capacidad histriónica para engañar a una anciana, ni con el hecho de estarme aliando con Frida para algo más que pagar el teléfono o hacer un desayuno; mi mayor temor es que Claudia se entere de lo que voy a hacer.

Me siento como cuando años atrás tomaba prestado dinero del bolso de Frida sin avisarle; no importaba que en el momento de sustraerlo yo tuviera toda la intención de reemplazarlo, sabía que en el fondo estaba haciendo algo malo. Y era así, porque en más de una ocasión no llegué a reponer esas monedas.

Si Claudia se entera de que estoy aliándome con nuestro archienemigo para quitarle su fortuna a una indefensa anciana con la que se ha peleado a muerte, jamás me volverá a hablar, así le pasara una buena tajada o —como decía Frida—, le comprara un teatro, con dramaturgo, director y coactores incluidos.

Frida y yo debemos actuar con cautela.

Tenemos que esperar a que Claudia no esté presente para poder platicar.

Fue esa misma tarde, cuando mi hermana se fue al ensayo de una obra de teatro, que Frida me reveló su plan.

Es algo simple: iré a visitar a la tía los días que Claudia tenga ensayos de la obra teatral que está preparando. Y es que ahora tendré que hacer uso de una vestimenta que no puedo encontrar en el clóset de Frida, ahora tendré que hacer una incursión en los últimos rincones del clóset de mi hermana. Si voy a visitar a la tía Lola, lo más adecuado es que lo haga usando alguna de las prendas que le obsequió a Claudia. Sólo espero que no tenga hongos o que las polillas las hayan devorado. Esto último no me parece muy posible, ya que a esos insectos normalmente sólo se les puede ver en las caricaturas, y aunque a veces me parece que mi familia es más absurda que los Picapiedra, todavía confío en que mi vida siga regida por la lógica del mundo real.

El panorama es un tanto desolador: necesitamos hacer algunos arreglos a los vestidos, las faldas, por su parte, están desteñidas y sólo se salvan tres suéteres. Tal vez será suficiente con usar éstos para engañar a la tía. ¿Quién sabe?

Día en que te cuento sobre esa primera visita

Tú conociste a la tía Lola, Nina. No era ninguna tonta.

Cuando Frida me alentó a ser cordial, amable y condescendiente con ella, incluso me puse a ensayar un tono de voz dulzón y cálido, practiqué una sonrisa abierta e investigué lo que pude acerca del cáncer de pulmón.

Ni siquiera recuerdo el camino a casa de la tía. Sólo recuerdo que para esa primera cita yo había escogido el suéter rosa tejido a mano que había recibido Claudia como regalo de su graduación de la prepa. Recuerdo haber ido al lado de Frida en el taxi. Recuerdo cómo continuaba insistiendo en que memorizara todos los gustos y aficiones de la tía, que iban desde su colección de peluches, hasta su manía por los cacahuates cubiertos de chocolate, pasando por ese absurdo vicio del cigarro. Recuerdo haber escuchado a Frida advertirme que no hablara muy rápido o muy fuerte pues a la tía eso le desesperaba, y cómo debía ayudarla a acomodar sus sábanas y sus almohadas.

Así iba, hecha un manojo de nervios, sintiéndome a punto de presentar un examen sorpresa, tal y como debía sentirse una futura princesa que va a ser presentada ante la reina del castillo.

Pero justo en el momento en que me vi caminando hacia el cuarto de la tía, por ese largo pasillo, conducida por la muchacha de la limpieza, me di cuenta del gran error que estaba cometiendo. Si quería tener éxito y convencer a alguien de que yo era Claudia, pues en realidad tenía que ser Claudia. Es decir, no podía ser una chica amable y sonriente, tenía que ser una muchacha con sueños de actriz, con un lenguaje bastante florido (por no decir vulgar), que siempre despreció los regalos y toda intención de compra de cariño.

Sin perder el paso, me quité el suéter y lo arrojé en una silla.

Tomé un respiro y me dije:

—¡Tú puedes, Victoria!

Había pensado acercarme y darle un abrazo —acompañado de un beso melodramático—, había repasado el discurso de la niña buena unas ciento treinta y tres veces y, en un segundo, tenía que cambiarlo, tenía el tiempo justo para abrir la puerta, aparecer ante la tía Lola e interpretar mi papel.

—¿Quién eres?

—Ha pasado mucho tiempo, tía.

No importa que la mujer se encuentre en la etapa terminal y que su cabeza esté cubierta por una malla. Sigue viéndose tan imponente como una tropa de asalto de guerreros zulú. Había que ser muy fuerte y hacer entender a mis temblorosas piernas qué quería decir esto.

—¿Claudia?

—Sigues viviendo en pinche peluchilandia.

La tía tiene, entre una de sus muchas terribles manías, la de coleccionar muñecos de peluche. Creo que atesora como ochocientos cuarenta y cinco muñecos. Yo estoy segura de que vivir con tanto animal de felpa no puede ser bueno para la salud, tal vez hasta es una de las muchas causas de su cáncer. Claro que no me atreví a externar mi maravillosa teoría.

—Te ves diferente.

Calma, Victoria. Es sólo una observación típica de tía.

—Han pasado algunos años. He crecido. He madurado.

Y ahora la prueba de fuego:

—¿Qué carajos quieres, tía?

Ni Claudia lo hubiera dicho con tal frialdad.

—No es cierto —dijo la tía, después de una breve tos.

Tragué saliva... (Es un decir, pero tú me entiendes...).

—¿A qué chingados te refieres?

—No es cierto que hayas cambiado... sigues siendo la misma. La misma escuincla impertinente.

Entonces sonrió. La vieja sonrió. Y pude ver que por fin había recurrido a una dentadura postiza para sustituir sus carcomidos dientes.

—Me da gusto.

—¿Te da gusto que sea impertinente?

Intentó incorporarse.

—¿Qué? ¿No me vas a ayudar?

La verdad es que había pensado en ayudarla, pero dudé si Claudia lo hubiera hecho. Me di cuenta de que no debía exagerar en mi dureza, o en vez de ser Claudia, sería evidente que yo era tan sólo alguien que estaba pretendiendo ser Claudia.

Le ayudé a colocar las almohadas en su espalda, y ella continuó:

—No me gusta la impertinencia, pero la prefiero a la adulación.

Me aparté y finalmente me atreví a sentarme en una silla. A distancia prudente de la tía, claro está. Una nunca sabe qué tipo de armas puede esconder bajo las sábanas una mujer con locura esquizoide de primer grado.

—Por un momento pensé que esa vieja arpía lisonjera te había instruido para venir a hacerme la corte.

Tardé unos segundos en entender a quién se refería. Arpía lisonjera. Nunca había pensado en ese calificativo para Frida. Me gustó.

Y luego dijo inesperadamente:

—Tu hermano... debe tener ya...

Por un momento mi dedo meñique comenzó a temblar. Pero no tuve problema en informarle:

—Cumple pronto los dieciocho.

—Caray. Cómo pasa el maldito tiempo...

Fue un ataque súbito de tos el que me permitió preguntar:

—¿Y cómo te sientes?

—¿Cómo quieres que me sienta? Como el demonio.

Y sin que me lo esperara, surgió ante mí una imagen digna, no sé si de una película de los Hermanos Marx o de Capulina: la tía sacó de entre sus sábanas... no un cuchillo, no una pistola... sino un...

—¿Sigues fumando?

—¿Te molesta?

—No, sólo que me pareció...

—Piensas que estoy loca.

Ante ese cigarrillo encendido, preferí un significativo silencio. ¿A quién se le ocurre seguir echándole fuego al fuego, Nina?

—El cáncer ya no está sólo en mis pulmones. Estoy invadida. No hay remedio. ¿Qué puede hacerme un cigarro? ¿Matarme?

La tía Lola me hizo sonreír. La vieja cabrona tenía razón.

—¿Cuánto tiempo te queda?

—No te preocupes —dijo, después de dar una fumada que expulsó con una leve tos—, aún me quedan algunos cigarrillos.

Hubo un pequeño silencio, suficientemente grande, Nina, como para que descubriera que tenía dos botones de mi blusa desabrochados. Un leve rubor me acompañó mientras corregía mi vergonzosa facha. Pero a la tía no parecían importarle las formas, después de todo, si de fachas desastrosas se trataba, la de ella hubiera ganado en ese momento un premio en el festival internacional de la pena ajena.

—Es muy sencillo. Tengo un doctor muy estricto, tanto que ha amenazado con amarrarme las manos de ser necesario. El muy imbécil. Me ha puesto una enfermera que no me permite hacer nada.

Tomó otra bocanada. Ahora la tos fue un poco más severa. Y por primera vez escuché ese sonido digno de ser comparado con el escape roto de una motocicleta, ése que te dice que el emisor de semejante escándalo no tiene precisamente bien su sistema respiratorio.

—Necesito que seas mi enfermera. Pero no te preocupes, no me vas a cuidar. Todo lo contrario. Tengo a María mi cocinera y a Lucía que hace el aseo. Ellas no se meten en mi vida. Tú sólo tendrías que ayudarme a comer, comprarme todos los días mi cajetilla de cigarros mentolados e inyectarme lo que sea necesario para detener el dolor cuando éste llegue y sobre todo no interponerte en el camino de la muerte cuando decida visitarme. —Se aproximó al buró y después de apagar su cigarro, del cajón sacó una ampolleta y concluyó—: lo que es más, tal vez te pida que le abras la puerta a la señora catrina.

Dicen que cuando uno va a morir, su vida completa pasa enfrente de los ojos, como en una película macabra tipo 3D. No se trataba de que la tía Lola o yo estuviéramos a punto de morir, pero juro que vi pasar cientos de imágenes, no sé si eran de mi vida o de la tía, tal vez simplemente me mareó el humo de la nicotina quemada. Me quedé de una pieza, como tú dirías, Nina. La bárbara desquiciada de la tía Lola me estaba insinuando que le diera un pasaporte al feliz mundo de los que ya no tienen que pagar impuestos. Creo que me mantuve tan seria y serena gracias a que todo lo que me enseñó fue un frasquito con tapa metálica, ya que si me hubiera sacado una pistola o una navaja de pandillero, yo creo que ahí mismo me desmayo.

Y no me malentiendas, no es que me impresione la posibilidad de ver muerta a la tía, la verdad es que tengo que reconocer que la idea de que semejante bicho humano ya no transite por el mundo me parece magnífica, lo que es más, creo que ha estado robándole demasiado oxígeno (y cigarros) a miles de mortales mucho más interesantes y simpáticos. Lo que ocurre es que nunca me había puesto a pensar en lo que se siente cuando alguien te pide algo así. Por un breve instante me imaginé como el ángel exterminador con un cabello rubio y volátil, unas alas diseñadas por Valentino Garavani y una espada dorada presta a terminar con la insoportable tos de una vieja fumadora. Y casi podría decir que no sólo mi lado macabro, sino hasta mi lado conservador lo gozaron.

—¿Y bien?

La voz de la tía me sacó de mis inevitables divagaciones.

—¿Necesitas pensarlo?

La verdad, la posibilidad de verme envuelta en un asesinato eutanásico no me importaba, incluso me excitaba, lo que de plano no me gustó fue la idea de ser la enfermera de la tía, no sabía si eso iba a significar realizar tareas nauseabundas como limpiar líquidos de dudosa procedencia anatómica o convertirme de plano en la esclava doméstica de la tía. Por mucho que me hubiera dicho que no iba a necesitar hacerlo, cómo podría confiar en la palabra de una mujer que haría lo que fuera por una colilla de cigarro. Después de todo, eso dicen que hacen los fumadores incurables.

Pero entonces vinieron las palabras mágicas:

—Por supuesto que esto significaría que volverías a estar incluida en mi testamento.

Otra vez vi pasar mi vida ante mis ojos, sólo que ahora era la buena vida, mi vida futura, la que prometía no sólo mi ansiada operación, sino todo un guardarropa adquirido en Milán y París con cosmetología integrada.

Justo antes de que dijera el ansiado *of course,* un pensamiento, de esos que te salvan la vida, cruzó por mi mente. "Claudia. Yo era Claudia". Y una duda me asaltó con la misma fiereza que un pandillero de Tepito: "¿No sería esa la razón del pleito entre Claudia y la tía? ¿No le habría pedido justamente lo mismo en el pasado?". A pesar de la ya segura promesa de convertirme en la rica princesa heredera, tuve que contenerme.

—Sigues siendo la misma cabrona.

—¿Qué quieres decir?

—Creyendo que todas las personas pueden ser compradas.

—Sólo es cuestión de precios.

—¿Y ahora encontraste mi pinche precio?

—Ahora no estoy pidiéndote lo que hace algunos años... y no pienso pedírtelo.

OH, MY GOD!! Así, con mayúsculas. Me tomó un segundo darme cuenta —bueno, tal vez unos tres segundos—. La tía Lola no pudo haberle pedido a Claudia que le cuidara el cáncer, se convirtiera en su traficante de alquitrán con sabor a menta y mucho menos que la sofocara con una almohada (metafóricamente hablando, claro), porque hacía cuatro años, la tía no tenía cáncer, bueno, al menos no se lo habían detectado. Así que la razón del pleito legendario entre mi hermana y la desagradable mujer que estaba postrada ante mí debía ser otra. Otra había sido la causa. ¿Cuál podía haber sido esa misteriosa razón?

—Está bien... te ayudaré.

Una sonrisa se dibujó en el rostro arrugado de la vieja y la tensión desapareció de su cuerpo, o eso me pareció, cuando la vi derrumbarse, no, no derrumbarse, eso se dice de alguien que ha sido vencido y apaleado. Corrijo: cuando la vi dejarse caer sobre sus almohadas.

Sólo tuve una petición: No iba a quedarme a dormir ahí. Ya que corría el riesgo, lo sabes, de que Claudia se diera cuenta de todo el asunto. Tenía que ser como un trabajo. Tú sabes, de entrada por salida. *Check in* y *check out*. La tía Lola no pareció estar muy convencida de ello, ya que iba a tener que conservar a su odiada enfermera nocturna, pero la posibilidad de que yo le proporcionara cigarrillos en algún momento del día, parecía ser suficiente por el momento.

Como te imaginarás no le dije a Frida todo lo que ocurrió durante mi entrevista con la tía Lola. Ella estaba ansiosa por saber el resultado, y mi lado sádico y precautorio (tal vez más sádico que precautorio) decidió ocultarle la intención de la tía de restituirnos como beneficiarios de su herencia. Le dije que la tía se tragó la sopa, *took the hook* como dicen los gringos, y que no dudó por un momento que yo fuera Claudia, le conté también del deseo de la tía de que estuviera con ella todos los días proporcionándole cigarros. Pero ni le conté lo de la herencia, ni lo de sus deseos de morir bajo la asistencia de otras manos.

—¡Qué cosa! ¿En serio quiere cigarros?

—Míralo como su última voluntad.

—¿Y te dijo de qué marca?

—Mentolados.

—¿Y tendremos que comprarlos nosotros?

—Creo que vale la pena.

—Una cajetilla diaria es mucho, ¿no?

—Podría haber pedido dos.

—En fin..., ¿y de verdad no te dijo nada de la herencia?

—Nada...

—Habrá que ser pacientes.

Esa noche en casa, recordé el día que supe que Claudia se había peleado con la tía. Ella tenía diecisiete años. Llegó a la casa furiosa, diciendo uno que otro: "chingada madre" y se encerró en su cuarto. Nunca quiso hablar conmigo del asunto, siempre creí que había sido un simple choque entre dos egos terribles. Una colisión entre dos planetas femeninos, de ésas que provocan terremotos y marejadas. Ahora por lo que había dicho la tía Lola, estaba segura de que había algo más detrás de todo eso. ¿Le había pedido algún favor a Claudia? Y pensé que tal vez lo mejor sería averiguarlo, si no, la tía sería muy capaz de descubrir que Claudia en realidad era Victoria, una sobrina que le sorprendería mucho conocer. Tanto, que podríamos perder sin remedio sus dulces ahorritos.

Así que aproveché que Claudia miraba *Los Simpson* en la televisión, para sentarme a acompañarla. ¿Te acuerdas de *Los Simpson*, Nina? Una vez te sentamos a verlos y tú, sin más, extrañada por nuestras risas, simplemente te pusiste de pie y abandonaste la habitación mientras decías: "Puras pendejadas". No tiene caso defender una de mis series favoritas. Creo que a mí y a mi hermana siempre nos ha gustado porque vemos allí a una familia tan disfuncional como la nuestra, aunque más divertida.

Te decía que mientras reíamos ante la lucha infructuosa del cerebro de Homero por hacerse escuchar por su dueño, me preguntaba en qué momento podría preguntarle a Claudia sobre aquel viejo incidente con la tía Lola. Fue entonces que ocurrió providencialmente que en el capítulo que veíamos aparecieron las tías odiosas de Bart y Lisa. Ni mandado a hacer, Nina.

—Siempre que veo a las tías de *Los Simpson* no puedo evitar pensar en la tía Lola.

—Las dos tías de Bart son un par de niñitas cantoras de iglesia comparadas con la cabrona de la tía Lola.

—¿Ya no has sabido de ella?

—Afortunadamente.

Éste era el momento. Un anuncio de suavizante (interrumpiendo la serie animada) era el marco ideal para tener toda la atención de mi hermana.

—¿Por qué fue que se pelearon?

Un breve silencio, bueno, ni tan breve, el comercial pasó a ser uno de donas glaseadas.

—Por pendejadas.

—Recuerdo que te pregunté y me dijiste que lo mejor era que no supiera.

—Así es.

Por un momento creí que la propia Claudia se apiadaría de mi curiosidad y me iba contar toda la amarga sopa, evitándome la incomodidad de tener que decir:

—¿Y ahora?

—¿Para qué chingados quieres saber? La tía Lola ya no importa... Estamos bien sin ella.

—Supongo...

Un ridículo bochornoso de Bart me arrebató a Claudia sin remedio.

Sí, Nina. Ya sé. Como investigadora doy pena. No fui capaz de lograr que mi hermana me diera la más miserable señal de nada. Habría sido más fácil abrir una lata de sopa con los dientes que abrir a la hermética de Claudia en lo que se refiere a la tía Lola. En fin, tendré que tener mucho cuidado con mi malhumorado pariente.

Día en que te cuento cómo se alteró mi pulso cardiaco como nunca antes

Así que comencé mi tarea de enfermera, cuida viejas o narcotraficante legal, lo que prefieras.

La tía Lola tiene que agradecer que esté justo en las vacaciones previas a mis exámenes, eso me ha permitido estar en su casa.

Decidí esperar cuatro días para poder contarte cómo van las cosas, Nina. Sólo así he podido sentir un poco cómo es la rutina con la tía y decidir si realmente podré soportar esta nueva etapa de mi vida.

Desde el primer día aproveché para llevar mis cuadernos y libros. La verdad es que me sentía aterrada por todos lados: primero, estaba la desagradable posibilidad de que la tía Lola me descubriera y con ello la casi absoluta seguridad de que los vientos de cambio nunca llegarán a mi vida; segundo, estaba el miedo de que se acercara el momento en que tuviera que convertirme en enfermera de la muerte y de que con ello realmente obtuviera lo que yo quería. Por el tercer lado estaba el temor en sí a la operación a la que yo ya me he propuesto someterme antes de entrar a la universidad, y que es justamente el cuarto lado de este cuadro (más bien romboide) de angustias reprimidas: ¿qué voy a estudiar? Siempre me ha atraído la medicina. Pero presiento que puedo desmayarme ante el menor derramamiento de sangre. Claro que también me gusta la idea de poder viajar por el mundo y vestir bien, ¿qué tal modelo? No sé (Como sabes, el alma de las mujeres es un océano de paradojas).

Afortunadamente entre tanta cosa, debo decirte que después de estos cuatro días de ir con la tía Lola, descubrí dos cosas maravillosas. La primera es que la tía no es tan insoportable. Se la pasa la mayor parte del tiempo dormida y lo hace profundamente acompañada de unos ronquidos que, ya te imaginarás, suenan a lavadora sobrecargada. (En más de una ocasión he llegado a pensar que no despertará o que se ahogará en su propio escándalo). Esto me permite estudiar para mis exámenes.

Ah, pero te hablaba de dos cosas maravillosas. La segunda, Nina, surgió como un espejismo, un sueño de *Las mil y una noches*. Estaba ayudándola a comer cuando tocaron a la puerta. Me levanté a abrir y ahí bastó un instante, algo menos que una décima de segundo, para que cayera enamorada por primera vez en mi vida. Todos mis antiguos supuestos enamoramientos quedaron reducidos a la categoría de retortijones estomacales. El mismo Carlos Rincón se convirtió en algo así como en la versión fea de Mortadelo al compararlo con lo que se presentó ante mis ojos.

—Te presento al doctor Cárdenas —dijo la tía.

¿Tú lo entiendes? Yo no. Una se siente como si fuera una botella de agua mineral, que de pronto es agitada y entonces todo el líquido (no sólo el gas) acaba escapando de ti, dejándote completamente vacía.

Eso sentí al verlo, Nina.

O tal vez todo fue más bien como dejar entrar un toro de lidia a tu clóset. O, tal vez, fue como ir cayendo por la montaña rusa y no

acabar de caer. Aunque también tiene un extraño sabor inesperado, como si tomaras una cucharada de helado creyendo que estás tomando sopa.

Provoca cosas impensadas, como no poder dormir (sin haber tomado una taza de café).

Y no es que sea más guapo que George Clooney, y no es que tenga una elegancia superior a la de Pierce Brosnan y un cuerpo tan impresionante como el de Joaquín Cortés. Ni tampoco que su voz al decir: "Mucho gusto" sonara más increíble que la de Luis Miguel. Nada de eso... fue algo más impresionante, que me hizo caer tan redondita que por poco ruedo, reboto y salgo avergonzada por la puerta.

Se llama Luis Cárdenas y es un médico al que si tú intentas calcularle la edad estarías rondándole los veinticinco años, pero de acuerdo a la tía Lola, tiene diez más. No tengo que decirte que me avergoncé hasta la médula de los huesos cuando me miró y me sonrió. Y por primera vez, Victoria sintió la espantosa pena de que sus facciones, la forma de sus manos y hasta el brillo de sus pupilas, revelaran la ausencia de senos y la presencia de un aparato reproductor masculino bajo las ropas.

Y aunque Luis probablemente detectó mi imposibilidad de tener hijos —de experimentar un parto, quiero decir—, se mostró de lo más amable. Nunca lo sentí incómodo o deseoso de apartarse. Se puso a examinar a la tía y yo no puede evitar temblar por dentro cuando, al pasarle una toalla, nuestras manos se rozaron.

De pronto miró inquisitoriamente a la tía, se volvió hacia a mí y dijo, ya no con una sonrisa provocadora, sino con un gesto de reproche, que me hizo temblar aún más:

—Claudia, ¿por qué me engañas?

Me pareció que de pronto mis ropas caían y ahí quedaba al descubierto, como una impostora ante la naturaleza, como alguien que se había colado a una fiesta sin invitación. Y casi sentí rabia. Pero justo cuando la aguerrida Victoria estuvo a punto de decir algo, Luis continuó:

—Ha estado fumando, ¿no?

Entendí entonces, Nina, lo que significa que alguien te desarme usando tan sólo las palabras. Creo que sentí más pena de la que hubiera sentido si hubiera evidenciado mi verdadera anatomía. No pude evitar mi respuesta:

—Fui yo quien fumó. —Y antes de que alguien se me adelantara, me apresuré a decir algo que sabía no le gustaría nada a la tía—: es que ella me pidió que lo hiciera.

No tengo que decirte la mirada cargada de balas, cuchillos y espadas que la tía Lola me lanzó a continuación. Pero yo creo que no le tomó mucho darse cuenta de que hubiera sido peor confesarle a Luis que ella había sido la fumadora empedernida, así que decidió seguirme el juego:

—Ya te dije que si voy a morir qué diferencia me puede hacer un poco de humo.

—La diferencia podría ser de unos meses...

—Meses..., ¿para qué quiero meses? ¿Para llegar a Navidad?

—¿Y por qué no, tía? —me aventuré a opinar.

—Quiero un cigarro.

—Cuento con su palabra, señorita, de que no volverá a fumar en presencia de su tía.

Luis me miró como si yo fuera una vieja amiga de la que nunca esperaría la más mínima traición. Y además me había dicho "señorita", "¡señorita!". Qué absurdo que una palabra tan ordinaria (tan sólo por venir de quien venía), sonara como uno de los mayores piropos inventados a lo largo de la historia del galanteo y la seducción.

Afortunadamente la promesa que le hice a Luis no sería nada difícil de cumplir, lo preocupante hubiera sido que me hubiera hecho prometer que no le volvería a dar cigarros a la tía, porque entonces sí que hubiera estado en un dilema. Tú sabes que los hombres pueden hacer que las mujeres hagamos las peores barbaridades, como el ir en contra de los propios intereses y metas. No importaba qué tanto me hubiera gustado Luis, yo tenía que seguir siendo cómplice de la tía. Así que una vez que me quedé sola con ella, acordamos que en adelante cada vez que quisiera fumar yo la acercaría a la terraza y que tendría que tener un poco de autocontrol los días de visita de su médico, que desafortunadamente no eran tan frecuentes como yo hubiera querido.

Hacía mucho que no sentía una emoción así por alguien, Nina. Tanto me impresionó el hombre, que tengo que confesarte (ni modo, si no para qué comencé a escribir si no voy a contártelo todo) que no he podido evitar hacer dos tonterías de chica enamorada:

Primero. La misma noche que conocí a Luis me introduje en el cuarto de Frida (otra vez aprovechando que estaba tomando uno de sus largos baños calientes de belleza), tan sólo para consultar el libro de astrología que yo sabía que guardaba bajo su cama y que leía con la religiosidad con la que un rabino revisa las sagradas escrituras. Y justo para llevarme un gran golpe en la frente, peor que el que me dio una vez Claudia cuando abrió la ventana del gabinete del comedor en el momento en que yo iba pasando. Gracias a que pude ver la credencial de Luis (en un momento en que fue al baño y yo aproveché para meter mis narizotas en su maletín), averigüé la fecha de su cumpleaños. Seis de diciembre. Siempre había escuchado a Frida hablar con sus amigas sobre la compatibilidad de los signos. "Las estrellas no se pueden equivocar", decía Frida con la misma certeza con la que debió concebir Darwin su teoría sobre la evolución. "Vivimos en el universo, ¿no? Rodeados de planetas y estrellas, así que es lógico que nos encontremos bajo su influencia. Somos materia estelar, ¿no?" Entonces alguna amiga incrédula decía, al tiempo que se proponía dar un sorbo a su café: "¿Qué tiene que ver Saturno que está a millones de kilómetros con la forma de ser de una persona?". A lo que la sabiduría doméstica de Frida respondía: "Hay cosas que la ciencia no puede entender, ¿comprendes?". Y bueno, Nina, tengo que confesarte que no es que yo crea en esas cosas, mucho menos en algo que Frida considera digno de veneración, pero me imagino que si tanta gente confía en ello, me convendría tenerlo en cuenta, aunque sea un poquito.

Pues resulta que Luis es Sagitario. Veamos. Según el libro, yo, que soy Géminis...

Géminis con Sagitario, dice: "Combinación positiva. Los dos son signos muy activos y adaptables, amantes de la libertad y el respeto", mi corazón dio un breve salto. "Claro que con una serie de consideraciones: En principio, Sagitario tendría que guardarse algunas de sus verdades dogmáticas e intentar no confundir con su lógica a Géminis, que por su lado debería evitar exagerar como lo suele hacer."

Así que las estrellas nos dan su bendición siempre y cuando yo deje a un lado mis exageraciones, que la verdad no son muchas.

Pero si el que yo me hubiera puesto a analizar nuestros signos te parece una actitud totalmente adolescente, déjame confesarte la otra cosa que hice:

Segundo. *Oh, my God!*. Escribí un poema.

Sí, ya sé que hay cosas peores, como marcar a su teléfono y colgar (que es una práctica que ya ha perdido su uso, gracias a que la

tecnología ahora permite identificar llamadas, pero siempre uno puede hacer uso de esta absurda, pero muy popular costumbre llaman-
do desde un teléfono público), sin embargo, sigue siendo terrible.

Y sólo lo compartiré contigo, porque en primer lugar no puedo
ocultarte esta conducta por muy básica y vergonzosa que sea; y en
segundo lugar, porque tengo que apuntar en un lugar decente lo que
empecé a escribir en unas servilletas de cafetería.

Sonríe.
Sonríe con la facilidad con la que la lluvia moja la
tierra.
Y no ha ocurrido algo gracioso.
Sonríe como si el aire tuviera aroma a gas hilarante.
Nadie ha contado un chiste.
Sonríe a las calles,
al taxi,
al perro del vecino,
a cualquier saludo.
Sonríe mirándote a los ojos,
y juras que tienes que ver con esa sonrisa.
Nada como una sonrisa inexplicable.
No hay misterio más agradable.
Te deja un sabor a chocolate en la boca.
Y sonríe.

No son sus ojos color madera.
Hay ojos en los que los poetas se han zambullido.
Se pescan con redes invisibles

y en sus aguas navegan perlas.

Hay ojos como cuchillos.

Cortan miradas y se alejan en silencio.

Hay ojos como relámpagos.

Incendian barcos sin dejar cenizas

y después huyen.

Pero no los suyos.

No eran sus ojos.

¿Entonces qué es?

Y sólo sonríe.

No es su cabello.

Hay cabellos como brisa traviesa.

Mueven molinos

y provocan tempestades.

Hay cabellos como olas de hojarasca.

Pintan acuarelas

y siembran lunas.

Pero no el suyo.

No es su cabello.

¿Entonces?

Sonríe.

Hay cuerpos que derraman estrellas a la distancia.

Provocan con sus sombras a los espíritus

y a los callejones.

Hay cuerpos como arrecifes de colores.

Se bañan en espumas

y naufragan en líquidos de deseo.

Pero no el suyo.

Su cuerpo no es así.

Y sólo sonríe.

Como te darás cuenta, Nina, estoy a punto de embarrar las banquetas con la miel más empalagosa del mercado.

Y no contenta con eso, tuve que confesárselo a Rodrigo, un amigo que sé que no sólo me escucharía, sino que entendería la espantosa contrariedad en la que estaba:

—¿Quién es George Clooney?

—¿No sabes quién es George Clooney?

—¿No es el que le hace de James Bond?

—No. Es el que sale en el programa de emergencias médicas.

—¿El pelón?

—No.

—¿Dónde más sale?

—El caso es que está guapísimo.

—¿Estás enamorada, porterita?

—¿Qué dices?

—¿Estás enamorada?

—Claro que no, ¿por qué?

—Pues yo opino que si te gusta deberías hacer algo y no quedarte ahí nada más mirando.

—¿Estás loco?

—A lo mejor tú también le gustas, a lo mejor es muy tímido y no se ha atrevido a dar el primer paso, pero se muere por darlo. Deberías de hacer algo. Tú eres una mujer decidida.

—No en estas cosas.

—Pues a mí me parece que tu George Money...

—Clooney.

—No va a hacer nada. Me suena como el tipo de hombre que jamás se acercaría a una chica fuerte que le guste. Debe tener toda la facha de los que creen que se lo merecen todo. ¿Estás segura de que te gustaría andar con un sangrón así?

—¿De dónde sacas que es un sangrón?

—Vaya que estás enamorada.

—De veras que estás loco.

—Como sea te envidio. Yo que tú no dejaría de cuidar mi cabello. Es lo mejor de ti. Eso, y el lunar sexy en tu mejilla (quién lo hubiera dicho, alguien pensaba que ese enemigo en mi mejilla era sexy). Si yo tuviera tu cabello, hasta la competencia te hacía.... Me da una rabia. Mi pelo por más que lo cepillo para alaciarlo, siempre se pone como de Mafalda.

Y eso que no le enseñé mi poema. Le habría dado material para burlarse de mí por el tiempo que me quedara de existencia. Sin embargo, una cosa me quedó clara: no debía ser tan cobarde ni básica y permitir que el atontamiento de su cercanía me dejara peor que una estatua de Reforma: tiesa e ignorada. Tenía que hacerle ver que de mis labios podían salir ideas inteligentes y pensamientos profundos.

Tal vez mañana me atreva. Tal vez.

Día en que te cuento cómo casi pierdo a Victoria y cómo la recuperé con una taza de té de tila

No fue algo planeado, lo juro.

Yo tenía muy claro —obviamente— que éste era el día en que Luis vendría a visitar a la tía Lola. Por eso la obligué a controlar el impulso de fumar durante la mañana. Incluso apliqué un poderoso aromatizante en la habitación, el cual provocó fuertes ataques de tos en la tía, tal vez peores que los que le hubiera ocasionado una fumada. Pero la convencí de que era lo mejor, ya que si su doctor descubría que la supuesta sobrina enfermera no tenía palabra, a ella iba a terminársele definitivamente el placer de seguirse dañando los pulmones. La ayudé a cambiarse las ropas y limpié la habitación. Ni siquiera Sherlock Holmes debía descubrir que en ese lugar había habido alguna vez un cigarro.

Respiré tranquila cuando descubrí que Luis nunca dijo nada sobre la posibilidad de que la tía hubiera caído nuevamente en las garras del vicio. Sólo se mostró un tanto molesto por el deterioro de la salud de la tía. "Pareciera que se hubiera fumado dos puros y tres pipas, señora." A la tía no le importó que su médico le tuviera tal desconfianza, de hecho a mí me parecía que en realidad ya no le importaba nada.

A lo que me refería cuando dije que no había sido algo planeado es a lo que pasó cuando me di cuenta de que Luis había dejado olvidado en la casa algo que posiblemente necesitaría. Yo estaba bastante molesta conmigo misma, de hecho, ya me había autorreprendido con suficientes insultos ("pinche cobarde", "ridícula", por mencionar los más leves), como para provocarme al menos un malestar estomacal, por no haberme atrevido a entablar la más insignificante plática con Luis (algo que fuera más allá de: "Sí, doctor". "Claro, doctor"), cuando vi el paraguas recargado junto a la puerta de entrada.

La verdad es que la tarde se veía lo suficientemente despejada como para invitar a cualquier paseante a aventurarse a salir sin siquiera una gabardina, pero yo ahí vi mi oportunidad. En el momento más inesperado podía caer el diluvio universal y si hay algo que puede disgustar a cualquiera, es el verse obligado a compartir el toldo de una tienda de abarrotes con media docena de extraños, igualmente esperanzados que tú a que el aguacero termine pronto. Yo podía salvar a Luis de semejante incomodidad si lograba alcanzarlo.

Sabía que mi querido cirujano aprovechaba la cercanía de la casa de la tía Lola con una estación del Metro, para hacer el viaje usando el subterráneo. Así que si me apresuraba, bien podría alcanzar a Luis y recibir como recompensa por mi desinteresada acción una invitación a cenar bajo la luz de las velas, como mínimo.

Yo lo sabía, Nina. Aunque la casa de la tía Lola era muy linda, la verdad es que la colonia céntrica en la que estaba situada no era de lo más confiable, sobre todo por las noches. Por eso yo siempre tomaba un taxi de sitio. Caminar dos cuadras oscuras, con certeza, no era la mejor idea que una podía tener.

Apareció como surgido de entre las paredes de un edificio.

—¿A dónde tan solita?

Evitas...

Disculpa, Nina que hasta ahora haya vuelto a esto. Los malos recuerdos son difíciles de retomar y más escribir sobre ellos.

Ha pasado una semana. Semana de exámenes finales, que no sé cómo pude presentar. Semana de reflexión, que quise dejar clara en la hoja que dejé en blanco.

Ahora, por fin, creo que puedo contártelo.

Como te decía:

Apareció como surgido de entre las paredes de un edificio.

—¿A dónde tan solita?

Evitas la pregunta y te apartas un metro, pero pronto lo tienes enfrente. Un temblor invade todas tus extremidades.

—Te estoy hablando chula.

Sólo puedes decir, sin atreverte a levantar el rostro:

—Perdón, tengo prisa.

—Pero yo no.

Un jalón te hace darte cuenta de que estás en problemas.

—Suélteme.

Todavía alcanzas a zafarte e intentas correr y cruzar la calle, pero de las sombras, otro cuerpo amenazante surge como una barrera.

—Tranquila.

Te detiene tomándote de las muñecas. El paraguas cae.

—No te va a pasar nada.

Los dos cuerpos te cercan. Quisieras pensar con claridad, pero sólo una presión nebulosa parece invadir tu cabeza.

—Déjenme ir.

Dos cuerpos que te empujan hacia la oscura entrada de un edificio. Todavía te atreves a rogar:

—Por favor... tengo que irme.

—Nada más es un ratito, linda.

—No me vayan a hacer nada.

—Si nada más queremos platicar.

Una mano comienza a explorar por entre tus ropas. Experimentas el terror frente al más hondo abismo. Sabes que pronto descubrirán que no eres lo que piensan y por un momento no sabes si preferirías tener eso que buscan. Y cuando ves por fin la mirada del que se ha atrevido a explotarte, sabes que hay algo peor que todas las angustias y preocupaciones que conocías. Y no te atreves a decir nada más. Sólo ellos hablan.

—Es un puto.

—¿Qué?

—Es un pinche puto.

—No mames.

—Es un machín.

—¡Qué pinche asco!

—¿Por qué te vistes así, cabrón?

—Te están hablando.

—¿Por qué lo haces?

—¿Te sientes muy pinche buena?

—¿Quieres que te cojan, verdad?

—Pinche puto.

—¿Esto es lo que quieres?

—Vamos a dárselo.

—¿Esto es lo que quieres?, ¿eh?

Todos los miedos se concentran en tu estómago y comienzan a ser agitados como en una licuadora, mareándote al grado mismo de la más espantosa náusea. Te imaginas atado a una alambrada, con la sangre nublándote la vista...

Y una arcada te hace vomitar.

—¡No mames!

—¡Qué pinche asco!

De pronto, ya no sientes esa opresión y caes sobre tus rodillas. En el suelo sólo alcanzas a ver cómo cae uno y luego el otro. Algo los ha apartado de ti. Y de pronto te encuentras con el paraguas a un metro de ti y la furia por primera vez surge de algún lugar de tus vísceras. Te incorporas y alcanzas a lanzar un sablazo furioso que desafortunadamente no alcanza a dar sobre tu agresor que ya corre por la calle. Trastabillas y terminas sobre el cemento mientras lanzas un grito de impotencia. Y de pronto una sombra protectora:

—¿Estás bien?

No hubiera querido contarte esto, Nina. Lo pensé mucho, pero creo que tenía que hacerlo. Lo más difícil no es confesarte el ataque, sino confesarte que por un momento extrañé a Eduardo, extrañé ese poder fingir, el poder sacar esa masculinidad que nunca existió en mí, pero que siempre pude hacer creer que tenía. Extrañé el poder sacar esa agresividad que nunca entendí y que para los hombres es tan natural.

Gracias a que Luis había decidido regresar por su paraguas, fue que pudo rescatarme. Eso y mi oportuna protesta gástrica permitieron que la experiencia no pasara de un desagradable susto.

Mientras tomaba yo un té de tila y Luis un café en la cocina de la tía Lola, la impotencia y rabia que había experimentado hacía unos minutos se habían transformado en una extraña vergüenza. Me di cuenta de que por mucho tiempo había estado abrazada a la absurda esperanza de que él me creyera toda una mujer, de que nunca se hubiera asomado más allá de mi maquillaje y mis ropas, y que hubiera sido capaz de creer en la existencia de Victoria, tal y como yo la tenía por cierta.

Apenas y me atreví a mirarlo, mientras me servía mi té caliente.

—Gracias.

—Espero que no esté muy caliente.

—Quiero decir... gracias.

Como respuesta me tomó la mano con fuerza y la apretó con ese universal gesto de solidaridad y apoyo. Y por primera vez tuve un llanto que me hizo sentir bien. Tomé un sorbo de mi bebida y no sé por qué, comencé a hablar:

—Mi madre nunca me vistió de rosas. Mi hermana nunca me maquilló... Tuve una novia en la primaria. Me encantaba estar con ella. Nunca tuve problema con tomarla de la mano. Pero cuando me pidió un beso algo extraño ocurrió. Todo lo que pude pensar es: que cosa más húmeda y asquerosa es besar a una niña... Todo fue así.

—No tienes por qué justificarte, ni conmigo ni con nadie.

—Lo siento.

—Si hay acaso un culpable en lo que te pasó hoy es la sociedad machista en la que vivimos.

Y sin poder evitarlo volví a llorar.

—Perdón, pero no puedo evitar pensar que de algún modo esto fue mi culpa.

—¿Tu culpa?

—... (No me atreví a decir más).

Entonces fue él quien, dejando su café a un lado, deshizo el silencio:

—La otra vez leí sobre un hombre extraordinario. No sólo fue oficial de lanceros para el ejército británico, también fue periodista y viajero, entrevistó y conoció a grandes personalidades, como el Che Guevara e Irving Berlin, escribió varios libros sobre sus viajes alrededor del mundo y por si esto fuera poco perteneció a la expedición que conquistó por primera vez el Everest. Se llamaba James Morris, pero cuando tenía treinta y cinco años decidió cambiar de sexo... descubrió lo que por mucho tiempo atrás ya sabía: que era mujer. Creo que el acto más valiente de este ser humano, entre todas sus hazañas, fue la de reconocer a la mujer en su interior.

No supe qué decir, tan sólo me limpié las lágrimas que ya me habían dejado un maquillaje pegajoso en el rostro.

Luis me acarició el cabello. Y aunque algo me dijo que jamás podría besar esa mano confortante, supe que al menos tenía un buen amigo que había jurado guardar mi secreto.

Día en que te cuento cómo me enteré de la cruda y telenovelesca realidad

Después de mi amargo incidente, tengo que reconocer que estuve a punto de flaquear en mis intenciones de otorgarle un cuerpo completo a Victoria, pero después de buscar y leer la biografía de Jan Morris (así se llama la aventurera de la que me habló Luis y que realizó todas esas hazañas con el cuerpo equivocado), supe que no podía ser cobarde, así que no abandoné la idea de obtener la preciosa herencia de la tía Lola. Claro que seguí sin darle grandes notificaciones a Frida, que como te imaginarás continúa pidiéndome, aunque más bien diría rogándome, cada día que no deje de complacer a la moribunda señora en lo que ella quiera.

Hoy noté a la tía un poco más débil.

No te había contado, Nina, que la tía Lola ha comenzado a perder apetito. Y si bien su muerte originalmente significaba fanfarrias y festejos, ahora debo reconocer que aunque no se me haya revelado como una gran persona, ha bastado con que la conozca, con que la oiga berrear y regañarme, para que me parezca que con su partida algo se va a perder…, todavía no sé qué, pero en cuanto sepa te lo digo.

Creo que la misma tía sabe que su final es algo que está por ocurrir, por eso arremetió con todas sus fuerzas.

Insistió en que la llevara a cierto punto de la casa. La ayudé a subir a su silla de ruedas y la conduje hasta una puerta que siempre había permanecido cerrada. Sacó una llave que tenía amarrada a una gargantilla y abrió el cuarto mientras me decía que ésa era la habitación que originalmente había hecho que prepararan para que yo me mudara. En ese momento me molesté muchísimo; por un lado, al entender que todo esto lo tenía perfectamente maquinado; y por otro, porque de algún modo no había escuchado mi rotundo *no way* de que me hiciera quedar a dormir bajo su techo.

El cuarto es grande (casi tan grande como nuestro departamento o más bien debería decir, el departamento de Frida) con unas grandes ventanas que dan a una nada despreciable vista al jardín selvático de la tía y con una cama de ésas que una sólo ve en las películas de época (de ésas en las que sale Emma Thompson), con cuatro postes y un velo que resulta más ridículo que encantador, ya que su mayor utilidad puede ser la de mosquitero para los cálidos y lluviosos veranos.

Todo me pareció arreglado a partir de un gusto cursi y pastelero (por aquello de los colores), digna residencia de una heroína de Danielle Steel, definitivamente no es el mejor lugar para que Victoria consiga sus mejores sueños. Lo que hizo que mis ojos se desorbitaran y cayera enamorada por segunda vez en mi vida, fue ver el clóset, *oh, my God!*, es más grande que mi cuarto. Y lo que hay ahí: vestidos, blusas, faldas, faldones, pantalones, jeans, mallones, abrigos, gabardinas, sacos, chamarras... y todo de mi talla. Y en los cajones: brazaletes, pulseras, anillos, medallas, gargantillas, mascadas, collares. No, Nina, me quería morir... Y después quería resucitar y morir de nuevo cuando vi dentro de un mueble que parecía como un zapatero con más de treinta pares de zapatos... y, lo más increíble...,

todos los pares de zapatos son de mi número. La muy perra de la tía dio justo en el clavo. Y todo puede ser mío si le cumplo un pequeño favor... Fue ahí donde pensé... La pelea con Claudia. Ahora lo sabré.

Esa noche tuve que hablar con Claudia. La impresión era demasiada.

Mi hermana estaba leyendo en su cuarto. Me atreví a entrar y cerrar la puerta detrás de mí. Ella me miró con la extrañeza de quien sabe que debe tolerar una intrusión semejante y no decir una palabra, sino esperar que alguien diga (en este caso, yo) algo como:

—¿No tienes nada que decirme?

Nadie dijo en ningún momento algo sobre la tía Lola, nadie habló de aquel añejo pleito, pero Claudia no tuvo ningún problema en reconocer, tal vez en mi voz, a qué me estaba refiriendo.

—¿Viste a la tía Lola?

Me quedé en silencio.

Esa tarde, Nina, la impresión que tenía de la tía Lola cambió, bueno en realidad se intensificó; de parecerme una vieja cabrona, me pareció una vieja astuta y cabrona.

Me dijo sin el menor reparo:

—Quiero que conozcas a mi hijo.

—¿Perdón?

—Si quieres seguir siendo mi heredero, tendrás que ganártelo.

... (Me quedé, así, en puntos suspensivos... ¿Había dicho "heredero" con esa "o" masculina al final?).

—¿Crees que soy tonta? Supe desde el primer día que tú eras Eduardo.

Me invadió una ligera rabia, no porque me hubiera descubierto, sino por escuchar ese nombre nuevamente.

—Mi nombre es Victoria.

—La verdad por mí te puedes llamar María Guadalupe Reina de Dublín. No importa.

—¿Por qué no dijiste nada?

—Después de pensarlo, me di cuenta de que tal vez Claudia nunca iba a ceder, así que decidí que si tú me haces el favor, pues me doy por bien servida.

—¿Saludar a tu hijo? ¿Sólo eso?

—Si lo haces, volverás a estar en mi testamento... y si logras que Claudia te acompañe... todo este cuarto será tuyo.

Juro que mi corazón se detuvo un segundo... después del cual, la tía continuó:

—Te doy hasta mañana para que me des una respuesta.

—¿Respuesta de qué?

—Habla con tu hermana.

Claudia me lo contó todo.

Agárrate, Nina. Juro que lo que te voy a contar no es un invento mío. Juro que no pertenece a la mente de un novelista desesperado, ni a una telenovela colombiana que se introdujo en mi inconsciente.

La tía Lola no es nuestra tía...

¿Sabes lo que es una casa chica? Esa fue la pregunta que me hizo Claudia cuando la increpé sobre la tía Lola. Claro, le dije. Nosotros, me contestó, nosotros éramos algo parecido a una casa chica.

Ésta es la triste historia de hadas:

Hubo un apuesto hombre que conoció a una pobre mujer campesina y quedó profundamente enamorado de ella (a pesar de que la campesina tenía muy mal humor y piernas bastante delgadas) y le pidió que vivieran juntos, apenas a los dos meses de noviazgo. Sin embargo, nunca se casaron, lo que hicieron fue vivir juntos, lejos del mundo, bajo las reglas de algo que muchos en los años sesenta llamaban "unión libre".

A pesar de la insistencia de la campesina de que contrajeran matrimonio, el hombre siempre le daba largas. Tan sólo existía la promesa de que algún día se casarían. El hombre se ausentaba por largos periodos, pero la campesina no se atrevía a cuestionarlo. Su madre siempre le dijo: "La mujer a la sombra del hombre".

El hombre insistía en que pronto se casarían. Pero ese pronto se convirtió en un periodo que abarcó dos partos y que los niños resultantes de esos embarazos llegaran a tener ocho y cinco años. De pronto, y sin que la pobre campesina se lo esperara, el hombre la abandonó. La mujer despechada no tardó en averiguar que su pareja se había casado. Averiguó que su hombre era un rico príncipe heredero que ahora tenía una esposa legítima. Había sido obligado por su madre, la reina, a cumplir un matrimonio arreglado.

La campesina no tardó en buscar justicia, llamó al príncipe con cualquier cantidad de improperios (el más leve y pronunciable en un cuento de hadas como éste era: "cobarde"), pero la reina le pidió que no hiciera escándalo. En compensación, recibiría una buena pensión y un departamento en el centro de la ciudad. Pero eso no fue todo, además, la reina exigió que sus nietos la visitaran y la llamaran tía.

Aunque molesta, la campesina, decidió que la dignidad no pagaba las colegiaturas y se dio cuenta de que ceder a las exigencias de la reina era lo mejor que podía hacer por sus hijos.

Todo parecía bien. Salvo porque los hijos de la pobre campesina abandonada creyeron siempre que su padre había huido al no soportar más a su mujer (sus piernas demasiado delgadas y su mal humor, ahora perfectamente explicable), nunca imaginaron que su progenitor era en realidad un príncipe cobarde, que tenía un heredero y una casa en las montañas.

Pero entonces, unos años después, ocurrió que, en un accidente en una carroza deportiva, murieron la esposa del príncipe y su pequeño hijo. El príncipe cobarde se había salvado milagrosamente. Se decía que la experiencia le había hecho cambiar por completo y que ahora arrepentido quería volver a ver a sus olvidados hijos. Fue entonces que la reina quiso ayudarle a recuperar a aquellos niños campesinos. Tal vez podría comprarlos... Tal vez la pequeña campesina, que pronto cumpliría dieciocho años, aceptaría la riqueza y el abrazo de su padre.

Sí, Nina. Tú lo debes saber. La campesina es Frida; el príncipe, nuestro padre; y la reina malvada, la tía Lola.

La tía Lola es nuestra abuela. Nuestra abuela paterna (Ya decía yo que tanto mal humor y tantas arrugas sólo encajaban en una mujer que anduviera rondando el siglo de vida).

Cuando Claudia cumplió diecisiete años, la abuela intentó recuperarla. La intentó comprar.

Fracasó.

Ahora iba por mí.

Si yo reconozco a nuestro padre, tendremos la herencia de la tía... digo, la abuela Lola.

Y si yo convenzo a Claudia de ir conmigo... tendré ese clóset de ensueño.... Para volverse loca, Nina.

Día en que, después de muchos años, recuerdo al ser culpable de mi genética

Apenas recuerdo a mi padre. Mirando el futbol, fumando esa pipa negra y llenándolo todo del olor a maple.

Apenas tenía unos cuatro años cuando se lo dije.

Lo sorprendí mirándose al espejo, se estaba alistando para ir a una fiesta o una boda. Estaba todo de negro, vistiendo un impecable smoking. Yo sabía que ésa era la vestimenta de los novios y la pequeña niña Victoria, que ya latía en mi interior, no pudo evitar decir:

—Cuando yo me case quiero hacerlo con alguien como tú.

Recuerdo la mirada de mi padre y un extraño gesto acompañado por una leve sonrisa. Y desde entonces no he sabido interpretar esa expresión en su rostro. Estoy segura de que era un gesto de sorpresa. Lo que no sé es si esa sorpresa le causó incomodidad o diversión.

Y no contenta con lo que acababa de decir, ahí voy para rematar. (Ya me conoces, Nina, a mí a veces debían ponerme un zíper en la boca y cerrarlo bien):

—Cuando sea mujer así será.

Cuando tenía cinco años creía que no había hombres y mujeres, sino que todos éramos iguales y que intermitentemente pasábamos de un sexo al otro. Tú sabes: un año de mujer y al siguiente como hombre. Claro que en ese extraño mundo, todos seríamos bisexuales ya que nuestra pareja sería a veces del mismo sexo que el nuestro y a veces del sexo contrario. Los embarazos tendrías que tenerlos muy bien programados y tu guardarropa femenino tendría que esperar todo un año para volver a ser usado. *No way.*

Quién iba a decir que esa frase dicha con esa inocencia imaginativa, me iba a marcar.

Tengo que confesarlo, Nina. Fue una de las últimas veces que vi a mi padre.

Desde entonces tuve enterrada en lo más profundo de mi tranquilidad, como una espina de rosa de castilla (de esas que te dejan tremendos arañazos en las manos), esa mirada enigmática y esa sonrisa indescifrable.

Siempre había pensado muy en el fondo que él nos había abandonado por eso. Sí. Ya sé que estoy loca, pero tengo que reconocer que mi agitada cabecita últimamente ha hecho gala del más barato psicoanálisis, y ha llegado a concluir que la pequeña Victoria siempre le ha echado la culpa a Frida de la partida de su padre, pero como un mecanismo de defensa, y que en el fondo siempre ha temido ponerse un buen par de lentes para ver la terrible posibilidad de que la razón de que su padre huyera, fuera el temor de verse convertido en progenitor de un niño predestinado a los tacones o una niña con cascarón de escuincle.

Ahora lo sé. No fui yo. No fue Claudia... Ni siquiera había sido Frida la culpable.

Sólo había un culpable.

Y ahora tendría que visitarlo si es que quería sacarle algo a nuestra abuela. Aunque fuera un poco de dinero.

Ahora entendía la ambición de Frida. No estaba motivada por una vulgar codicia, sino por un simple deseo de sacarle algo a la mujer que se había encargado de dejarla sin un esposo.

Visitarlo. Ésa había sido la terrible petición que la abuela le había hecho a Claudia cuatro años atrás y que había ocasionado una típica pelea de silencio entre Frida y mi hermana. Ése era el secreto que no se había atrevido a confesarme. Y ahora lo sé.

¡Qué impresión, Nina! Nuestra familia siempre fue un terrible "había una vez", eso por no decir que éramos una barata radionovela con horario vespertino (de ésas que nadie oye, para que me entiendas).

Y ahora soy yo el que tiene el dilema instalado en las venas, como un veneno que circula por todo mi cuerpo. Si visito a mi padre, podré tener mi anhelada operación, pero me convertiré en algo peor que las hermanastras de Cenicienta (las dos juntas). Ahora que, si no lo visito, la abuela Lola me privará del placer de poseer el cuerpo que Victoria se merece, y lo que es más, si no llevo a Claudia, me perderé de un clóset con tanta ropa como la que tienen Paris Hilton y su hermana (las dos juntas). ¿Qué hacer?

Tengo que reconocerlo, Nina... No será fácil llegar a la respuesta, pero lo lograré...

Día en que decido reencontrarme con el príncipe cobarde

Dos días después de su oferta, es decir, ayer, llamé a la abuela Lola y le dije que lo haría. Visitaría a mi padre.

Claro que como ya habrás supuesto —y con toda certeza— la abuela pretende que haga una visita no sólo de cortesía, sino de reconciliación, una visita en la que —lágrimas en los ojos incluidas—, me arroje a sus brazos diciendo un melcochoso: "¡Papá, nos abandonaste, pero yo te perdono! ¡Y no sólo te perdono, querido y extraviado padre, también te ruego que tú a tu vez me perdones por todas las barbaridades que pude haber pensado de ti!", y, claro, para rematar, con un: "Enjuga esas lágrimas, querido y mortificado padre, vamos a nuestra casa y vivamos nuevamente como una familia! ¡Recuperemos esos años que nos hiciste perder, digo, que perdimos sin que ninguna de las partes se lo propusiera, en lamentos y congojas!". "¡Crucemos el puente del perdón y lleguemos unidos al país de la concordia y la felicidad!"

¡Jamás de los jamases! Ridiculeces, no gracias.

He decidido que si mi padre quiere retomar una relación, si quiere tener una hija, a pesar de haber abandonado a su familia por otra mujer, bien puedo perdonarlo. Si el hombre está acongojado por una

175

terrible culpa y sólo quiere un poco de perdón para poder morir en paz, bien puedo complacerlo. ¿Qué tan terrible puede ser? ¿Dos visitas a la semana? ¿Una comida los sábados en el mejor restaurante de la ciudad? ¿Tener que decir "papi" a un extraño? Todo por una operación que cambiará mi vida. ¿Vale la pena? *Of course.*

El problema es Claudia. Sí. Si quiero llevarme ese guardarropa de premio, tendré que llevar a mi hermana. La ambiciosa de la tía Lola, no sólo desea mi perdón, sino también el de Claudia. Ya sé que está mal que una codiciosa critique a otra, pero creo que hay de codicias a codicias. Y la de la tía es imperdonable. Yo creo que se puede ser codiciosa con los autos, las joyas y hasta con los edredones. De hecho, tener una sola cosa de algo, a veces no sólo es malo, sino hasta miserable. Pero hay cosas con las que no se puede andar de acaparadora. ¿Para qué quiere la tía dos perdones? ¿No le bastaba con el mío?

Sí, Nina. Si aspiro al paquete completo tendré que llevar a Claudia conmigo. Tú sabes que entre Frida y yo la llevaríamos vestida de Heidi y amarrada a un camello si sólo de eso se tratara. El problema es que ella tiene que ir por su propia voluntad.

Pero ¿tú crees que a estas alturas me voy a rendir, que voy a permitir que mi hermana se interponga en mi camino a la felicidad transexual y travestida?

Claro que no. Y si crees que me voy a poner de rodillas implorando su ayuda, estás muy equivocada (aunque lo haría si eso sirviera de algo). No. Yo tengo mi propio plan.

Pero no será una visita ordinaria en un Vips de la colonia Roma.

Al llamar a la abuela Lola para decirle que, tanto Claudia como yo iremos a ver a nuestro padre, me enteré de que, después del accidente, nuestro querido progenitor sufrió un severo daño y desde entonces vive en un hospital. Así que, la gran escena donde nuestro padre implorará por nuestro perdón será en horario de visitas, entre gritos de dolor y batas con la retaguardia descubierta. Yo no sé exactamente qué tiene mi padre, pero para vivir rodeado de cuidados y doctores, la cosa no debe de ser nada linda. Victoria y su mente melodramática no pudieron sino pensar en varias posibilidades: una contusión en la cabeza que lo ha mantenido un buen rato en una irremediable amnesia, una parálisis de la cintura para abajo o un coma del que acaba de despertar. Pero Victoria no irá sola. Rodrigo será su cómplice.

No fue tan difícil convencerlo. El día establecido para la visita, coincidió con la foto de mi grupo de prepa, que estaba a punto de graduarse. Y ni Rodrigo ni yo teníamos ninguna intención de aparecer como pruebas de que alguna vez circulamos por el desagradable mundo de la educación media superior.

Cuando llegamos al cuarto 306, tuve que sostenerme por un momento del brazo de mi amigo, quien a pesar de su voluminosa humanidad, no se veía nada sólido, es decir, parecía que él mismo se derrumbaría en cualquier instante:

—Mejor me voy a la sesión de foto.

—Tú me dijiste que me ayudarías.

—Es ridículo. Tu padre se va a dar cuenta inmediatamente.

—Jamás se dará cuenta...

—¿Por qué?

—Porque tiene un tumor cerebral... (mentí, sin saber si realmente estaba mintiendo).

No estaba segura si mi padre notaría que Rodrigo no era su hijo querido y que Victoria no era precisamente Claudia, pero sabía que tenía la oportunidad de engañarlo. A fin de cuentas, habían pasado más de diez años y si nos descubría, yo ya había cumplido con mi parte, así que la herencia ya la tenía ganada y por lo que estaba apostando todo era por kilos y kilos de ropa de primera calidad.

A quien, con toda seguridad, no habría engañado habría sido a la abuela Lola. Afortunadamente ella estaba postrada en su cama y le era imposible ser testigo de la reunión padre-hijos. Tendría que confiar en mi palabra y la de su hijo.

En el momento de cruzar la puerta, ahí estábamos: Eduardo y Claudia, es decir, Rodrigo y Victoria. Dispuestos a escuchar una disculpa con lágrimas en los ojos, rodillas al suelo y varios besos en los pies de parte de aquel hombre que los había abandonado hacía más de una década. Si quería volver a ser padre, tenía que humillarse. Y tenía que pedir el perdón de sus dos hijas, aunque una de ellas estuviera representada por un voluminoso defensa central. Si lo lográbamos, mi futuro brillaría con más intensidad que el camino amarillo del Mago de Oz.

Otra vez mis piernas temblaron al entrar en la habitación... no lo pude evitar.

Apenas lo reconocí. Debía tener menos de cincuenta años, por las cuentas que ya había hecho, pero me pareció como alguien de setenta. Su piel tenía un leve tono verde (lo juro) y su cuerpo estaba sumergido en una silla de ruedas. La enfermera que lo atendía lo dejó, nos pidió disculpas y abandonó la habitación.

El silencio fue tan espeso como un chicloso de chapopote. Él sonreía levemente. Por un momento estuve segura de que no se tragaría el cuento. Estuve segura de que se daría cuenta inmediatamente de que yo no era Claudia y que ese ropero humano a mi lado, no era yo. Pero para mi asombro, dijo:

—Vaya que han cambiado.

—Igual tú —dije casi sonriendo.

—Siéntense, por favor.

Rodrigo y yo tomamos asiento en un sillón de dos plazas, tan juntos entre nosotros como pudimos.

Me parecía que mi amigo se desmayaría, no sé si por el olor a desinfectantes y medicinas combinados o por la posibilidad de que mi padre le pidiera un abrazo.

Decidí entonces que lo que procedía era escuchar y esperar. Esperar su humillación. Esa sería la señal de que Victoria lograría todos sus sueños.

—Me da gusto verlos.

Y de pronto no encontré palabras para responder a ese comentario. No creí correcto decir: "A mí también me da gusto verte". Sólo pude carraspear. Un leve gruñido era todo lo que ese hombre en silla de ruedas se merecía por el momento.

—¿Y cómo estás? —salió la voz de Rodrigo de algún lugar de su más recóndita valentía.

—De la chingada. Pero así es esto, ya lo saben.

Mi mente se quedó en pausa. No entendí qué pasó. ¿Dónde estaba ese hombre arrepentido? ¿No había buscado vernos para pedir nuestro perdón? Ya habían pasado cinco minutos, que a mí me habían parecido como cinco horas atada de los tobillos y colgada de cabeza, y aún no escuchaba la palabra mágica: "perdón", ni siquiera el más leve gesto que buscara una disculpa por haber ido a comprar cigarros a Tailandia y haber olvidado el camino de regreso (espero que hayas entendido mi ironía, Nina).

Ni siquiera se había atrevido a mirarnos para reconocer en nuestros rostros a sus hijos adorados.

Entonces dijo, aún con una expresión fría y una mirada distante:

—Ya no soporto una diálisis más... Desde el mismo día del accidente sabía que mi único riñón acabaría por fallarme del todo, desde entonces no perdí la esperanza de encontrar un donador... pero la lista de espera ha sido interminable. No les haré perder mucho tiempo. En un momento regresará la enfermera para el análisis de sangre.

Y de pronto. Sin que yo misma lo esperara. Algo pasó en mi interior.

Todos los volcanes del mundo no podían llegar a igualar la erupción que estaba por suceder dentro de mi sorprendido cuerpo. ¿Había escuchado bien, Nina?

—¿Nos estás pidiendo un riñón? —No pude sino sentir que el destino emitía una fuerte carcajada contra mí.

—A eso vinieron, ¿no?

—¿Cómo?

—¿La abuela no les dijo?

Imagino que mi rostro adquirió la dureza y color de un carbón encendido, pues inmediatamente después, el hombre que se decía mi padre, dio un golpe con su puño en la codera de la silla:

—¡Carajo!

Se llevó una mano al rostro y después de maldecir unas cuantas veces más, respiró hondo y continuó:

—Bueno, no importa. El caso es que ya están aquí y de que hay bastante probabilidad de que su tipo de sangre sea compatible con el mío.

Mi padre no sólo tenía problemas para orinar, también parecía que el cerebro le había fallado por completo. Tal vez toda aquella porquería que no podía salir de su cuerpo se le estaba yendo directo a la cabeza.

Apenas si pude ver a Rodrigo. Estaba más impresionado de lo que Claudia hubiera estado si hubiera venido en su lugar.

Sólo hasta ese momento nos miró directamente a los ojos.

—No me miren así. Les pagaré una fuerte cantidad. Ella debió decírselos...

En sólo dos segundos cruzaron por mi mente trescientos veintisiete insultos, que estuvieron a punto de inundar el hospital y llegar a ser oídos hasta en la misma sala de urgencias. Pero entonces, Victoria supo qué era lo que tenía que hacer.

—¿A dónde van?

Tuve que jalar a Rodrigo, que había adoptado la personalidad de una estatua, para que reaccionara y saliera conmigo de ahí.

Todavía el hombre de la silla de ruedas alcanzó a gritar algo, pero yo estaba tan furiosa que mis oídos estaban bloqueados, seguramente no era nada que tuviera que ver con "gracias por la visita" o con la esperada disculpa, debía ser algo más parecido a un grito desesperado ante la perspectiva alentadora de vivir muchos años más orinando con la única ayuda de una máquina.

Lo confieso, Nina. Yo fui por el dinero. Estuve a punto de perder por completo mi dignidad. Y sólo por un par de pechos de tamaño regular.

Pero en el momento en que escuché su inesperada petición, me di cuenta de que más me hubiera valido ir por un mero deseo de vengarme, que más me hubiera valido acercarme por el morbo de ver de nuevo al padre que alguna vez había considerado el novio perfecto o que más me hubiera valido ir en busca de la liberación de un peso invisible y desconocido... Pero no era así.

Yo me había acercado por el dinero. Y eso era terrible. En la búsqueda del cuerpo de Victoria, me estaba transformando en algo que no era Victoria. Estaba permitiendo que, por dinero, una anciana con cáncer y su hijo me hicieran comportarme como algo que yo no era.

Mi padre me había intentado comprar para obtener una operación, pero yo me estaba vendiendo para obtener otra.

Estaba perdiendo a Victoria, a la verdaderamente importante, a la que vive bajo mi piel... Si quiero recuperarla sólo hay un modo de hacerlo. Sólo hay una manera de salvarme y de no ser igual a ellos.

Y esa manera no tiene que ver con salir furiosa de una sala de hospital.

Cuando le conté a Claudia (justo después de mi visita al hospital), el asunto de nuestro padre, no lo pudo creer. A ella nunca le llegaron a decir la razón por la cual él quería verla. La abuela Lola nunca se atrevió a externar la verdadera razón de su petición. Mi hermana ni siquiera llegó a ver a nuestro progenitor y siempre creyó en una intención real de reconciliación.

Entonces nos dimos cuenta de hasta dónde podía llegar la perversidad de la abuela Lola. Había buscado a sus dos nietos ilegítimos, tan sólo para comprarlos. Únicamente para conseguir el órgano que podría salvar la vida de su hijo. Y sabía que ese regalo sólo podría obtenerlo de ellos cuando tuvieran los dieciocho años. Por eso intentó reconciliar a Claudia con nuestro padre cuando estaba por alcanzar la edad para votar.

—Pero, ahora que la tía Lola pidió verme. ¿Cómo pudo saber que tú acudirías y te harías pasar por mí?

—No creo que lo haya sabido. Lo que sí creo es que en cuanto me vio ahí ante su cama, decidió que yo era tan buena opción como tú, para ser donante.

—Tal vez me hubiera gustado darme el gusto de rechazarlo yo personalmente.

—Se puede decir que así lo hiciste.

Y era cierto. Ese día en el hospital yo fui Claudia. No pude reprimir una leve sonrisa. Nuestro padre absurdamente creyó que habían sido sus dos hijos los que lo habían rechazado. El maldito viejo estaba tan desesperado por obtener ese órgano que ni siquiera tuvo la decencia de averiguar a quiénes tenía enfrente. Bien hubiéramos podido ser Rodrigo y yo, un enano de circo y un luchador de sumo, y él de cualquier modo les hubiera pedido sus riñones. Qué ironía, Nina, el hombre del aparato urinario atrofiado, el que había contribuido con su genética para que yo tuviera genitales masculinos, había sido una de las pocas personas a las que pude hacer creer que mi cuerpo era el de una mujer.

Día en que decido no reencontrarme con el príncipe cobarde

❋

Dos días después de su oferta, es decir, ayer, llamé a la abuela Lola y le dije que no lo haría. No visitaría a mi padre.

Tengo que confesarlo, Nina. Todo el asunto que te conté antes, acerca del hospital y del riñón, fue un invento mío... Un ejercicio mental surgido de mi más pura vena melodramática, copia directa de una telenovela colombiana y una que otra mexicana en horario estelar.

Es cierto que la abuela quería que Claudia y yo nos reuniéramos con nuestro padre y es cierto que lo estuvo planeando por mucho tiempo. También es cierto que me ofreció integrarme en su testamento y regalarme aquella cueva de Alí Babá si conseguía que mi hermana formara parte de esta reunión familiar.

Pero sobre todo es cierto que si yo me hubiera acercado a mi padre, habría sido tan sólo por el dinero... por eso tuve que imaginarlo en una situación deplorable y vil, para saber hasta dónde podía yo llegar... pero bastó que imaginara todo el asunto para darme cuenta de que tenía que hacer lo mismo que Claudia había hecho años atrás.

Mi padre no necesita ser una rata en busca de un riñón, como para que yo lo considere alguien indigno de mi cariño... Él nos abandonó, eso ya es en sí mismo un acto despreciable (y eso lo había entendido Claudia). Y como si eso fuera poco, además, ha demostrado su incapacidad para portar bien un par de pantalones, al no atreverse a buscarnos él, sino usar a una anciana con cáncer de pulmón como intercesora. Eso lo convierte en algo peor que un pobre gusano cobarde...

Y si lo mejor que puedo hacer con mi padre es despreciarlo con mi apabullante indiferencia, he decidido que debo hacer algo parecido con mi abuela: no volver a hablarle. Si quiero ser la Victoria correcta, tengo que olvidarme de ese dinerito, de la pronta cirugía y de, ¡aaaaay! (me da un dolor en el alma de sólo decirlo), de esa colección de zapatos Jimmy Choo.

Así que llevé a cabo una última acción que la inmiscuía: hablé por teléfono con Luis y le dije la verdad sobre su consumo ininterrumpido de cigarrillos. Sí, ya sé, Nina. Si la abuela sigue fumando, se irá más pronto de este mundo, pero yo no puedo dejar que se salga con la suya... y tampoco puedo quedarme yo sin una pequeña sonrisa, marca venganza, dibujada en el rostro.

Creo que para acabar con este asunto, mañana intentaré congraciarme con Frida.

Ahora la entiendo.

Claro que supongo que ella también lamentará haber perdido la herencia de la tía, digo, la abuela Lola, ahora que le cuente todo. Y casi lamento que el asunto del sistema urinario disminuido de mi padre sea un simple producto de mi imaginación ya que de no ser así, Frida hubiera podido sentirse agradecida por algo: el nunca haberse casado con un bicho de riñones atrofiados como mi padre y, gracias a ello, haberse librado de esa peculiar cláusula del contrato que dice: "...en la salud y en la enfermedad...".

Me sorprende darme cuenta de que no me he atrevido a llorar por todo este asunto de mi padre y mi abuela. Lo que es más, me he prometido que nunca más pensaré en ellos. Después de todo, la experiencia me confirmó que la gente no cambia. Así como yo nací siendo Victoria (y afortunadamente sigo siendo Victoria), él nació siendo un cobarde egoísta y nunca ha dejado de serlo.

Lo que sí puedo decir es que ayer que decidí darle la espalda a mi padre... En ese momento lo supe con certeza, Nina. Victoria es un hecho. Voy a operarme, y nadie me detendrá.

Aunque tenga que trabajar para ello... (*Oh, my God!*).

Día de la víspera. Día en que te cuento cómo finalmente diré adiós a mi envoltura masculina

Sé que dejé de escribir por unos meses, Nina. Y me disculpo. Pero he tenido mucho trabajo.

Primero las noticias obvias: ¡Ya tengo dieciocho años y me gradué!

Ahora las importantes:

¿Recuerdas mi temor al psicoanálisis? Pues creo que lo he superado.

Hace unos meses comencé a ir a terapia con una muy buena psiquiatra: la doctora Torres, una doctora que me recomendó Luis y que ha estado desde el principio convencida de que mi sexualidad real sí es la de una chica.

Sus métodos son un poco extraños para mí, pero creo que han resultado ser efectivos. Sólo te comento que una de sus ideas (que me pareció genial) fue que escribiera un diario. No tengo que decirte que le comenté sobre ti y que me pidió que la dejara leerte. Con un poco de pena te presté, y ella, lejos de burlarse, me felicitó por el ejercicio. Después me pidió que, en adelante, todos mis pensamientos también los compartiera con ella de viva voz. Y no resultó nada mal, nunca hubo intentos de apoderarse de mi fortuna alegando mi locura o de aprovecharse sexualmente de mí.

Creo que ella fue quien me puso realmente en el camino hacia el cambio completo de sexo.

Otra de las cosas que me gustó de mi psiquiatra fue que casi después de empezar con las sesiones, me recetó hormonas.

Y la verdad fue una maravilla cuando sentí el ligero cambio de mi voz y el aumento de los senos. Desde entonces tengo sueños en los que Penélope y Nicole se pelean (Luana e Irene, aquellas imitadoras de mi primera fiesta travesti) y no por el compartido hombre, sino por mí. Yo intento detenerlas diciéndoles que no soy lesbiana, pero ellas insisten en que yo soy la mujer de la que están enamoradas. Y yo me despierto sudando y preguntándome por qué no son Tom Cruise y Antonio Banderas los que luchan por mis encantos.

Nunca quise contarle mis fantasías a la doctora Torres, son algo privado, además, no quiero ni pensar lo que me hubiera dicho. Tal vez habría asumido que lo que mi inconsciente quería era detener mi sueño de convertirme en una linda ginecóloga. Sí, Nina, ya he decidido que en cuanto pase mi tiempo de ajuste me inscribiré en la escuela de Medicina, para convertirme en la doctora Victoria (casi como de telenovela gringa).

Una cosa que no puedo dejar de contarte es que después de trabajar durante meses en una zapatería como una pobre esclava (para poder pagar mi operación, mis medicinas y mi psiquiatra), llegó a mí una enorme sorpresa: el apoyo incondicional de Frida con respecto a la operación Victoria, y cuando digo incondicional, me refiero a que ella misma ha decidido apoyarme con algo más que el soporte espiritual: ha puesto sus ahorros (obtenidos en años de ventas de tiempos compartidos) a mi disposición. Sus palabras se van a quedar grabadas en mi mente con letras de platino: "Estaba pensando en hacerme crecer los senos, pero Manolo (Manolo es el Número

Trece y ha resultado un buen tipo para Frida) dice que no soporta a las mujeres de grandes pechos".

La verdad no supe si creerle o no, tal vez simplemente le dio miedo enfrentarse a la mesa de operaciones y al bisturí, pero yo no iba a desaprovechar semejante regalo. Un presente que tiene un especial significado, considerando que nunca nos ha sobrado el dinero y que, a final de cuentas, habíamos fracasado en el intento de obtener el dinero de la tía Lola. Por cierto, hablando de ella, cuando nos enteramos de su fallecimiento, unos días después, casi casi lamenté no haberle echado la mano (como ella originalmente me había pedido) y que hubiera sido un ataque cardiaco (cortesía del cigarro) el que se hubiera encargado de ella. Después de todo, una abuela capaz de inventar semejante teatro con tal de obtener un perdón para su hijito, merecía una alta dosis de desprecio.

Ahora, el presente:

Te cuento que mi madre y Claudia por fin se hablan (esta vez duraron cinco meses sin hacerlo. El récord no cayó). El mes pasado, Frida incluso fue a un examen de actuación de mi hermana. He llegado a pensar que algún día, Claudia y yo, casi sin darnos cuenta, le llamaremos mamá...

Aunque pensándolo bien, no lo creo...

Mañana a estas horas estaré esperando a Rodrigo para que me lleve al hospital a ver a la doctora Torres y al doctor Millán (el cirujano que hará mi operación), y sólo una cosa me falta por contarte: Anoche soñé con la ya clásica pelea entre las ex del señor Cruise.

Sólo que ahora entraba a escena Alejandro, vestido de blanco y con unas alas en la espalda, cantando con toda la voz de Cerati, *Persiana Americana* y conforme avanzaba la canción, las dos peleoneras se iban esfumando.

Mientras la frase: "Sé que te excita pensar hasta dónde llegaré" rondaba una y otra vez por mi cabeza, la imagen de Alejandro se conjugaba con la de Luis, que en una bata blanca, con alas también en la espalda y un bisturí dorado, me mostraba con una gran sonrisa una puerta, la puerta de entrada a una sala de operaciones, que en el marco exhibía un letrero que decía: "Bienvenida a Ulan Bator".

No sé, la verdad, qué siginifica ese giro en mi sueño, pero me gusta pensar que todo lo que te he contado a lo largo de este cuaderno (que estoy a punto de terminar), no ha sido sino una lucha por encontrarme y alcanzarme.

Recuerdo esos primeros miedos que casi me hacen desistir en mi intento de poder ver al espejo a Victoria y no puedo evitar pensar en la frase que te oí decir por teléfono, hace muchos años, a tu amiga mientras le dabas palabras de aliento: "Ánimo, comadre, acuérdese de que la esperanza es la buena".

Ahora que despierte Victoria, prometo que seguiré en otro cuaderno contándote todo lo que me pase y que volveré a pedirte consejo. Quién sabe qué otras cosas se me vayan a ocurrir y espero en cada momento escuchar tu voz diciéndome: "Ánimo, hija, que la esperanza, con un poco de lucha, es la buena...".

Noviembre 2005

PARA NINA
Un diario sobre la identidad sexual

se imprimió en el mes de junio de 2009, en los talleres
de Tipográfica, S. A. de C. V., Cerrada de Imagen núm. 26,
Col. Lomas de San Ángel Inn, C. P. 01790, México, D. F. •
Se utilizó la familia ITC Leawood • Se imprimieron 2 000 ejemplares
en papel cultural de 90 gramos y con encuadernación rústica •
El cuidado de la impresión estuvo a cargo de Ediciones El Naranjo.